BOOKS BY PATRICIA GIBNEY

The Missing Ones
The Stolen Girls
The Lost Child
No Safe Place
Tell Nobody

FINAL
BETRAYAL

PATRICIA GIBNEY

bookouture

Published by Bookouture in 2019

An imprint of StoryFire Ltd.

Carmelite House
50 Victoria Embankment
London EC4Y 0DZ

www.bookouture.com

ISBN: 978-1-78681-849-2
eBook ISBN: 978-1-78681-848-5

Daisy, Shay, Caitlyn and Lola
My grandchildren, bringing new life into mine.

PROLOGUE

Ten years earlier

The body was heavier than he'd thought it would be. How could one so young and thin weigh so much?

He dragged her to the opening and shoved her down into the depths with the sole of his boot. Unwrapping the tools he needed from the hessian cloth, he deposited them in the rucksack and hauled it onto his back, then lowered himself down after her.

Hauling her along the ground until he reached the area he wanted, he positioned her upright so that her dead eyes could see him work. It took some time, but when he was finished, he didn't get the feeling of accomplishment he'd thought he'd have. But no one would ever see her. Not down here.

Walking backwards, he made his way like a hunchback, sweeping away all indications that anyone had been here with a small brush he'd had in the bag. Squeaks and swishes accompanied his movement. Down here it was like another world. He felt safe and free. He didn't want to leave. At this moment he felt he could go back there and lie down on the earth, close his eyes and join her in her final resting place. A black hole for a bitch who had rejected him.

He slogged on, untangling his jacket as it snagged on a jutting rock. The climb upwards was more difficult than his descent had been. He clutched the protrusions on the wall and heaved himself up and out. Sliding the covering back over the hole, he made sure there were no visible clues left behind. A quick glance around told him no one had seen him.

Back at the car, he threw the rucksack into the boot. The temperature had dropped in recent days and winter was biting on the horizon like a ravenous dog. He didn't like winter. Or the cold. No, he much preferred the long summer nights when he could wander around for hours; when the moon appeared in a sky full of stars and he could howl like a wolf in heat if he had a mind to.

He felt the first drops of rain and jumped into the car before the black clouds burst. He had done the job. All would be well now. He was safe.

It wasn't until the next day that he discovered his nightmare had only just begun.

CHAPTER 1

Conor Dowling stood outside the gates of Mountjoy Prison and breathed in the city air. It was the same air he had breathed inside the walls for the last ten years, but somehow it seemed fresher out here. Free. He blew out a long breath, shouldered the bag that held his meagre possessions and took his second step to freedom. Alone.

There was no one waiting to pick him up. No reporters even. But he hadn't expected any. Once he'd been found guilty and consigned to spend the best part of his life, his twenties, behind the grey walls of the prison, his story had gone so cold it had merged with the snow of time.

He listened to the city sounds as he walked away, one foot in front of the other, without a backward glance.

Back in Ragmullin, Conor stared from across the road at the terraced house. It hadn't changed at all in the last ten years. It appeared the grass hadn't even been cut. It was still early morning as he crossed the road and opened the creaking gate hanging on one hinge. He didn't have a key, so he raised his hand to knock on the door. It was his own home, and here he was, like a stranger. Lowering his hand, he moved to the front window. The reflection of a stranger stared back at him.

At thirty-five, he was tall and skinny, with a head of uneven stubble. Gone was the shoulder-length hair his mother had called high-maintenance. When he was fourteen, she'd gifted him a second-hand battery-powered razor, which he'd become fascinated with, and along with shaving his head, he had taken to shaving his body hair. That was what he wanted to do again now. His fingers itched to find a razor and feel the sharpness run down his chest and legs. To free his skin of fuzz.

He moved back to the front door. Tried the latch. It opened. He put one foot on the worn laminate floor inside, and then the other. The familiar smell was the first thing to bring back memories.

The pungent odour of bacon and cabbage, along with stale grease, wrapped around him. How could that be? Conor knew his mother had been the recipient of Meals on Wheels for at least the last four years. His friend Tony Keegan had told him that. Some friend, Conor thought. At least he visited him in prison every couple of months. But Conor had the feeling he only did that to check that he was still safely inside. His mother had never visited him.

He opened the door to the living room, expecting it to be empty. Gulping down a deep breath of the fetid air, he saw his mother sitting in a faded, well-worn armchair. She looked taller than he remembered, but then he noticed that the legs of the chair were propped up on slats of timber.

Vera Dowling was only sixty-five years old, but she was eaten up with rheumatoid arthritis, which gave her the appearance of a woman at least twenty years older. Standing behind her, he noticed her lumpy hands crooked around the arms of the chair. Slowly she turned.

'Today's the day, is it?'

Her voice had once been sharp and strong. It was still sharp, Conor conceded, but no longer strong.

'Yeah, Mam. I'm home.'

'I hope you weren't expecting a party with balloons and flags. Not my scene at all.'

'I wasn't expecting anything.'

Still he stood behind her chair. He'd faced up to the most danger-ous criminals in jail, and here he was like a schoolboy frightened of the class bully.

'Come round here where I can see you, lad.'

He didn't want to face her, but eventually he shunted the message from his brain to his feet and moved to stand in front of her.

'Did they not feed you in that place?' She raised a swollen hand; scrabbled around the side of the chair and found her walking stick. Holding it like a sword, she pointed it at him, jabbing his chest. 'Bones, that's all you are. Now that you're back, you can start cooking for me and for yourself. You can cancel that plastic food, too.'

Taking a step backwards, out of range of the stick, he said, 'Plastic food?'

'Whatever about the wheels, I wouldn't call them meals. Only old Mrs Tone going around with her arms full of plastic tubs, and by the time she gets to me, it's cold. How do they expect these knobbly fingers to turn the dial on the microwave?'

Conor was about to say she could have got a new digital model, but he stopped himself. His mother was displaying all the signs of the bully he remembered from his childhood; there was no way he would win this or any other argument. It was as if the last ten years had just folded into themselves and absolutely nothing in this house had changed. But *he* had.

Rubbing his hand over his head, he felt the beginning of bristles sprouting and itched to get upstairs to his razor, if it was still there. He guessed it probably was; the living room looked as though his mother had slept downstairs for years. Then a thought struck him. They only had an upstairs bathroom and toilet. How did she …? His eye was drawn to the bag of urine nestled between her veined legs.

'I'm glad you're home, son,' she said, stretching out her hand. He stuffed his own resolutely into his jeans pockets. 'You can cook for me. Did they teach you new recipes in … in there?'

Shrugging his shoulders, Conor walked to the window and stared out through the dirt and grime. He rubbed a hand on the glass and it stuck to the grease lining the inside of the pane. Where the hell did she think he'd been? Cookery school?

'I'm going to have a wash,' he said, and turned to leave. She shot out a hand and grabbed his arm. Goose bumps erupted on his flesh as he tried to shuffle away. Still she held firm.

'I know what you did, Conor. I know. So you'd better treat me right.'

As the knobbly hand fell away, Conor rushed from the room, almost tripping over the holdall he'd dropped in the hall. In the kitchen, he glanced briefly at the mess, at the commode she'd once used, standing in the corner beside an overflowing rubbish bin. The odours infested his nostrils, and old memories threatened to drown him, like a biblical flood.

To distract himself, he stared out through the small window. And there it was. Still standing. His shed, his place of escape, his refuge from reality, rising like a castle in the midst of reedy grass and discarded furniture.

But what was that? He leaned over the sink, full of plastic food containers, and tried to see more clearly. No use. He opened the back door and stepped out into the garden, where the flattened grass made a pathway to the shed door. No, he hadn't been mistaken. The lock on the door was hanging open.

'Mam! Who the hell has been in my shed?'

Conor stood amongst the chaos of the shed that had once been his haven. His tools looked okay, though they were not in the correct order. Not on the right shelves. Not laid out the way he had left them. He shook himself. It was so long ago, maybe he was imagining it. But he wasn't imagining the padlock in his hand. Someone had been in here.

He'd begun by making little wooden dolls for craft fairs. He felt a flush creep up his pale cheeks as he remembered how he'd started that, aged thirteen, not long after his father had left. Went to work one morning without a goodbye. Only when he didn't return home did they discover he'd taken a small case with his few possessions. A lifetime ago, but Conor recalled it like it was yesterday. Abandoned by his father and left to his mother's wrath.

The prospect of spending the rest of his life with his mother was decidedly more chilling than the memory of the years he had spent in jail. He reminded himself miserably that she was only sixty-five, so the odds of her croaking any time soon were remote. Not of her own accord, in any case.

Running a finger over the woodturner, he stepped back in shock. There was something missing. One of his tools. The one he'd moved on to when he'd got fed up with working with wood. There was only one other person who knew how to use his tools. And it wasn't his mother.

CHAPTER 2

Lottie Parker was excited at having a home of her own after living in her mother's cramped house since mid February. Being a detective inspector in the town of Ragmullin brought its fair share of dangers. During one recent case, her house had been burned down. Though it had been ruled accidental, she still wasn't convinced.

'You could at least smile,' Mark Boyd said as he struggled with an IKEA flat-pack box wider and taller than the door space. 'And get Sean to give me a hand.'

'He's gone for a ride. And that's your fault. Buying him a new racing bike.'

'At least it gets him out of his room. That's a good thing, isn't it?'

'Sure, but we could do with an extra pair of hands right now.'

She gripped one end of the box and began to shimmy it in through the front door with Boyd huffing and puffing on the outside. Sean, her fifteen-year-old son, was becoming more of an enigma with each passing day. He had succumbed to another bout of depression a few months ago, and only when Boyd arrived with the sparkling new bicycle had his eyes shed their deep darkness.

Boyd stopped moving the carton.

'What?' she said. He was looking at her over the angles of the now crunched cardboard.

'This is the right thing to do, Lottie. You know that. But you have to accept that everything you had in your old house is gone.

This is an opportunity to start over. Leave the ghosts of the past blowing in the ashes.'

She shook her head, surprised to find that tears were gathering. She sniffed them away. Boyd was her detective sergeant and a good friend. 'This isn't going to work.'

'Of course it will. Just give yourself time to get settled.'

'I mean this goddam carton. We'll have to open it up outside and bring the stuff in bit by bit.'

'What's in it anyway?'

'I have absolutely no idea.'

Boyd let out a loud laugh, and Lottie couldn't help it. She had to laugh too.

As it turned out, it was a bookcase that had been in the box. Now Boyd was sitting cross-legged in the middle of the sitting room, instructions in one hand and a handful of screws in the other, and slats of timber everywhere.

Lottie switched on her new red kettle and got two mugs from the cupboard. Maybe Boyd was right, she thought. She had to admit that he knew her better than she knew herself sometimes. They had been going through a good patch over the last few months. He was a loyal friend. More than a friend at times, if she wanted to be totally honest with herself.

Her hand stalled on a jar of coffee as she realised the truth. Boyd was her *only* friend. What kept him around? He'd got his divorce from his wife, Jackie. He seemed content. But she knew he wanted more of a commitment from her. Of that she was certain. She couldn't give him any more, though. Not now. Not yet. She'd lost her husband Adam to cancer five years ago, and ever since she had struggled with grief, widowhood and raising her children.

The house was going to be full of life soon. Her twenty-one-year-old daughter Katie with her baby son Louis, seventeen-year-old Chloe and Sean were due to move in tomorrow. They'd already snapped up the bedrooms they wanted, without any major rows, and most of their clothes were now hanging in newly painted wardrobes. She wondered how Rose, her mother, would cope with an empty house. She smiled. Rose would probably be delighted to have her own space back, after the long months of them all living there like transient gypsies.

'I think there's a screw missing,' Boyd shouted from the other room.

'I knew that about you a long time ago.' Lottie smiled and started to make the coffee. Maybe it was time to leave Adam's ghost resting among the ashes of her burned-out house. Maybe.

CHAPTER 3

Tony Keegan opened the door and felt his jaw drop as he tilted his head to one side.

His one-time best friend, Conor Dowling, was standing on the doorstep. Shit. He gathered his wits quickly and arranged his face into a forced smile.

'Hello, bud. Didn't know you were out.'

'You'd have tidied up a bit better and locked the door if you'd realised, is that it?'

'What are you on about?' But Tony knew all too well what Conor was referring to. 'Thought you had another year to serve.'

'See what thought did to that numbskull brain of yours.'

Tony felt himself being slapped back against the hall wall as Conor pushed past him.

'Home alone?' Conor asked.

Closing the front door, Tony followed the tall, skinny figure into the kitchen. A lot had happened in the last ten years that Conor didn't know about. And Tony wasn't at all sure he should tell him.

Conor had opened the fridge and was bent over, hands inside, pulling out packets of cheese and ham.

'Got any bread? I'm starving.' He slammed the fridge shut with his booted foot and stacked the food on the table.

Before Tony could move an inch, Conor had found the bread and taken a knife from the drawer. He flicked the lid off a tub of

Flora and began spreading, slamming cheese on the thick buttered slices. When he seemed happy with his work, he kicked out a chair, sat down and began to eat.

Tony didn't know what to do, so he sat down too. 'Good behaviour, was it?' he said.

'No. I sliced the governor's throat and escaped.' Conor laughed, his mouth wide open, cheese and bread stuck to his teeth.

'Don't be messing with me.' Tony noticed that his friend's eyes were not laughing, so he picked up a crust from the table and began to chew. When he could no longer hold Conor's cold stare, he dropped his gaze to his buttery fingers.

'Messing?' Still Conor wasn't laughing. 'Thought you knew me better than that.'

Tony glanced up cautiously and almost recoiled at the hardness of Conor's eyes boring into him. He knew instantly that his friend had changed. Prison would do that to you, he supposed. Not that he'd ever been inside himself. He'd cleaned up his act after Conor had been convicted. Now that he was out, he'd have to be wary once again, and watch his back.

'You're my friend, Conor. Course I know you.' He put down the half-eaten crust. 'What are you going to do with yourself?'

He held his breath as Conor wiped his hands on the white lace tablecloth. For God's sake! It was the good one. The cloth his gran had brought home for his mother from Spain, like a million years ago. And now Mam, Dad and Gran were all pushing up daisies. So it shouldn't matter. But it did.

Sniffing loudly, Conor said, 'I have plans. But first you have to tell me why you were putting your mucky paws all over my workshop.'

'What workshop?'

'My shed. In my garden.'

'It's your mother's garden.'

The hand grabbed the collar of Tony's T-shirt before he could defend himself. He was dragged across the table, clutching at the Spanish heirloom as butter, bread and knife hit the floor.

'Tony, don't act like a dimwit with me. What were you doing in my workshop?'

'I ... I ...'

'What?'

'C-can't b-breathe.'

As Conor let go and pushed him away, Tony tried to come up with a decent excuse, but nothing was anywhere near as good as the truth, and he definitely couldn't tell him that.

Swallowing loudly, he ran his hand over his throbbing throat and coughed. 'I was bored, so I asked your mother if I could do some work in your shed ... your workshop. She said she didn't mind. Just asked me to put something in the microwave for her and take out the bins and stuff.'

'What work?'

'You know, trying to make things, the way you used to do. But I'm useless at it. I was only fiddling around.'

'Well there are some tools missing.'

'I took nothing.'

'You didn't lock the place.'

Digging his greasy hand into his jeans, Tony said, 'Sorry. I must have left in a hurry.'

'Nothing in this world could make *you* hurry.'

He felt his flabby cheeks flush, and put a self-conscious hand on his protruding belly, trying unsuccessfully to hold it in. Smiling weakly, he changed the subject in an attempt to mollify his friend. 'I'm glad you're back, Conor.'

Conor was already out in the hallway. 'I'm not one bit glad to be back.'

'See you later then? Maybe?'

But Tony was talking to the slammed door.

You know when someone wrongs you and you feel like an arrow has speared through your very soul? Let me tell you, that feeling is a lot worse when the wrong comes from a person you loved. What gives them the right to break you up into little pieces and feed your flesh and blood to rabid dogs?

That's what happened to me. I was deeply wronged. I don't think the person who hurt me actually realised the enormity of their crime, their deception, but I knew it. Because I am one of those people who makes a list of the wrongs committed against me. I then file that list away until the opportunity arises to present it and seek my price. When the time is right.

And the time is right now.

CHAPTER 4

The Parker family sat around their new table, in their new kitchen, in their new house. Lottie was determined that this was to be a fresh start to family life. She promised herself that she was going to be a better mother. Fingers crossed. But sitting down with her children was proving to be strained and uncomfortable. Maybe she had let things get out of hand. Or maybe they had all just become too used to living with their gran. She wasn't sure what to do.

Sean was sitting with a sullen look pasted on his face. Chloe pushed her food around the plate with her fork, while Katie shovelled mashed potatoes into one-year-old Louis' mouth. This should be a happy time, Lottie thought, but there was still something missing. She glanced up at the wall, devoid of paintings and photographs. The framed wedding photo, faded to sepia, that had always hung in the kitchen had perished in the fire, along with most of the other physical reminders of her dead husband. Boyd was right. She had to move on. But how was she to fill the void in her heart? Boyd had tried, but invariably she'd spurned him. Was that why there was still a corner of emptiness lodged there?

'Mam? I asked you a question.' Chloe pushed her plate to the centre of the table.

'Sorry. I was miles away.' Lottie shook her reminiscences out of her head and concentrated on her daughter.

'As usual.' Chloe kicked back her chair and stood.

'What did you say?'

'Oh, whatever.'

'Chloe! I'm listening now.'

'Can you babysit Louis for Katie at the weekend. We want to go to out.'

'Where is out?'

'Jomo's. Please.'

'The nightclub?'

'Yeah.' Chloe rolled her eyes as if her mother were a dinosaur.

'You're not old enough.' Lottie wasn't in the mood for a row. This was their first night in their new home. They should be happy. Shouldn't they? But she knew that while the four walls surrounding them might be different, inside they all remained the same.

Chloe stood in the doorway, her fingers turning white. 'Why do you continue to treat me like I'm twelve? I'll be eighteen next month. Life is too short to worry about what age you have to be to get into a nightclub. Come on. Let me live.'

'You have school. Exams. Study. You're too young.'

'You didn't answer the question though,' Katie piped up.

Damn, she'd forgotten the question. 'What was it again?'

'Can you babysit?'

Lottie glanced over at Louis and winked at him. Immediately the baby opened his mouth in a smile full of mashed potatoes. She sighed. 'Let me see how work is set and I'll let you know.'

'They get to go everywhere,' Sean said sulkily. 'And I'm stuck here with you and a baby. Such a gross life.'

'Sean?' Lottie was speaking to air as her son left the kitchen.

'Don't mind him,' Chloe said. 'Teenage problems.'

'And what are you? You're still a teenager too.'

'But I'm mature.' Chloe straightened her back and followed her brother.

Katie dabbed at Louis' mouth with a wet wipe and handed him over to Lottie. 'Can you change him, Mam? I'll go and talk to Sean.'

Alone with her grandson, Lottie eyed the mess on the table and the counter full of saucepans and dishes. She suddenly missed living at her mother's. She'd never thought she'd feel that emotion. Not after everything that had happened in the last year.

'What are we going to do with the lot of them?' she asked Louis. She was rewarded with a burp and a dirty nappy.

CHAPTER 5

At twenty-five years old, Louise Gill felt she had been through her life twice. At times, she even felt like she was two people living in alternate states of mind. Her mother worried that she might be schizophrenic, but Louise had refused all medication. She didn't want to live in a fugue state. She had to study, and she wanted to be normal.

She checked the notifications on her phone for possibly the tenth time since she'd woken up. Nothing of interest on Instagram and no new Snapchats. She hadn't many friends, so that was normal. Putting the phone to one side, she pulled her laptop onto her knee.

The coffee shop she was sitting in had recently opened in an old bank building, and she loved the anteroom situated in what had once been a fireproof vault. The door was six inches thick, but these days it was perpetually open, having been cemented at an angle to the floor. Louise didn't experience claustrophobia like some of her friends, who refused to join her in the dimly lit cavern. In here, she felt safe. Away from the world.

Her thesis was tough and she had to submit it in mid December. Criminal psychology was her favourite subject, and writing about miscarriages of justice had awakened memories deep within her psyche.

She had been right, hadn't she? About seeing him running frantically that night. What age had she been? Fourteen. She was confident in the testimony she had given. Wasn't she?

Catching sight of her reflection on the screen, she realised her laptop had slipped into sleep mode. Just like her brain. Her eyes were hollow and dark-rimmed. The nightmares had returned. He had been released from jail. He was back in her town. Walking among people on the street. He could be in here now for all she knew. Her eyes flared wide. She couldn't see their colour in the reflective screen, but they were dark brown, like her long hair, which she had never dyed. Her skin was sallow, with a sprinkling of freckles on her nose.

She had to concentrate. No point in going back to that disturbing time. Or was there? Recently the nightmares waking her at three in the morning had left her wrapped in soaking sheets with a raging fever. Her subconscious was telling her she had made a mistake all those years ago. Her conscious self told her she hadn't. Which was correct?

A shadow dimmed the light in the doorway and she looked up. Her mouth formed a perfect O and pearls of perspiration dribbled down her spine. He was there, accusation flaring in his eyes as he stared at her. Then in an instant he was gone, and she shook her head. Had she imagined it? Had it been a vision from her subconscious mind? Her hands clutched the laptop tightly. She couldn't move. Couldn't breathe. Couldn't talk.

She realised she'd been holding her breath. As she exhaled, her eyes filled and tears began to leak down her cheeks.

Louise Gill didn't know what was real any more. She had to talk to Cristina.

Unwrapping herself from her lover's arms, Louise went to search the refrigerator for something to drink. She felt safer with Cristina than anywhere else. The fact that her best friend was now her partner, was her secret. The two of them had debated long into the summer nights, often resulting in heated arguments, about 'coming out' to her parents. Louise was no longer the fourteen-year-old who had idolised the only man in her life. The man who had let her down so badly that she'd talked herself into believing that that was why she was attracted to a woman. Or maybe it was just that she loved Cristina more than anyone since she'd been fourteen years old. In any case, whatever the reason, she didn't want to tell her father.

'Why are you so on edge?' Cristina's voice followed her into the kitchen.

'I don't want to talk about it.' A can of Coke would have to do. Too early to drink the white wine that nestled in the door, condensation running down the bottle.

'It's him, isn't it?'

Louise turned to see Cristina leaning naked against the door frame, smoke curling from the cigarette in her long-fingered hand. She looked like an exotic actress who had stepped from a 1930s movie set. Her black hair lay like a snake over one shoulder and her eyes were dark and inviting, displaying her Asian heritage. At four foot eleven, she was six inches smaller than Louise, but today she appeared taller.

'I don't know who you mean,' Louise said, biting the inside of her lip.

A smile lit up Cristina's face. 'See. I was right. You are thinking of him.'

'I don't want to talk about Conor Dowling.'

Cristina's hand caressed Louise's arm. 'Whether you do or not, I think you have to. Otherwise, sweetheart, it is going to eat you up inside.'

'Leave it for now, okay?' Louise took a drink of the Coke. 'Maybe later.'

Cristina moved away, back into the bedroom. But her voice carried loud and clear to Louise's ears. 'You can't keep everything for later. First of all you have to face up to Dowling, and then you need to tell your father about us. That arsehole needs to know the truth.'

CHAPTER 6

Wind feathered up along Amy Whyte's bare legs as she pulled hard on her cigarette before dropping it to the floor and grinding it out with the heel of her silver-glittered sandal. A drift of cold air swirled around her shoulders and she felt the first smattering of rain. Oh no! Her false tan would run down her legs. She wanted to go home. Now.

Looking around for Penny, she saw her laughing with a group of lads under the Perspex roof of the smoking shelter. How was she going to get her to leave? It was gone one o'clock and the nightclub was in full swing, but Amy was tired. Getting too old, she thought as she scanned the crowd of teenagers. It was supposed to be strictly over twenty-ones, but that rule was never adhered to.

She approached her friend. 'Penny, are you coming?'

'No, it's just the way she's standing,' one of the men joked.

Typical of Ducky Reilly. He always had to be the smart one. Amy's lips trembled with the cold and she couldn't find a suitable reply in her vodka-soaked brain. Maybe she shouldn't have had that last drink. Too late now, she told herself, and wished she had a warmer jacket.

'Let's have one more,' Penny Brogan said, smiling coyly at Ducky while wrapping her blonde hair around her hand, her little finger sticking up in what looked to Amy like a sexual gesture. Penny should know better, even if she was drunk.

'Yeah, one for the road, as my auld fella says. Or a little blow?'

Amy wasn't sure who had said this, but she wasn't hanging around to find out. She shook her head and balled her hands in frustration. 'I've to work tomorrow, so I'm heading off.' Working on Sunday was a bitch.

'Don't be a spoilsport.'

She felt her arm being clutched by someone who dragged her into the middle of the crowd lounging under the canopy. Cigarette smoke clogged the air. She was sure the last vodka had yet to reach her stomach, and it was likely to rise up her gullet if she didn't get out quickly.

Arms snaked around her shoulders, huddling her into a group, as a phone appeared and someone took a photo. Shit, now she'd feature in a Snapchat or Instagram story. Bad enough trying to hide a hangover without the world seeing the evidence of how she'd come by it.

Wriggling out from the centipede of limbs, she squeezed through the pulsing bodies and headed back towards the club. 'Text me when you get home.'

'Yes, Mammy,' Penny laughed, and the crowd around her shouted, 'Night night, Mammy!'

Immature imbeciles, Amy thought as she barrelled through sweating torsos towards the chair where she'd been sitting earlier. Her jacket was nowhere. Now she'd have to walk home in the rain bare-shouldered, and would probably catch a cold. Hoisting her sparkly red top up as far as it would go, she dragged her skirt down to her knees. It was the best she could do.

Outside the nightclub, she looked up and down the narrow lane hoping to see a taxi. The taxi rank was on Main Street and she estimated she'd be drowned by the time she reached it, and anyway, she didn't want to waste a tenner. No, she'd walk. Get some air in her lungs before she reached home. Might keep the hangover at bay.

Deciding to take the shortcut down by the railway, she turned left. At twenty-five, she was long past phoning her father to collect her, and past fearing being attacked. There were plenty of drunk and high teenagers who stumbled through the town nightly, and not one of them had been harmed. Not that she'd heard about anyway. She straightened her shoulders in her resolve and continued to walk. Quickly.

The street narrowed into an alley between a row of apartment buildings, and Amy saw a moth shimmering under a lamp outside a door. She stopped and stared as the large-winged, furry-bodied insect flapped against the light, trapped by its inability to see a way out. She felt a trickle of fear nestle in the nape of her neck, and a shiver skittered down her spine.

Turning around, she picked up speed and headed towards Petit Lane car park. It was even quicker to scoot down that way, under the railway bridge. The thump of music from the club permeated the night, and she wondered how anyone in the apartments she'd just passed could sleep at night. Then again, maybe they were used to it.

She heard the windshield wipers, swishing away the rain that was now becoming more persistent, before she heard the car. Standing to one side, she paused and waited for it to pass her. Instead, it stopped and someone got out. She moved to skirt around the back of the vehicle, but a hand caught her arm and pulled her backwards.

'Hey, let go!' she yelled.

'Just a minute.' The voice was low and hoarse. Like someone with a sore throat trying not to strain it. 'I want a word with you.'

'I'll scream if you don't take your hand off me.'

Amy thought her own voice sounded like that of someone else. Someone who was not terrified like she was. The car park light was behind the person and she couldn't make out the features beneath their hooded coat. She felt like the moth she'd just seen flapping against the brightness. Sirens screeched in the distance; the music continued to boom from Jomo's and she felt the night darkening with each passing second.

The grip tightened on her arm and she wriggled, trying to free herself. She fell off the high heel of one sandal, and with the strap caught around her ankle, she stumbled. An arm shot around her waist, and as she opened her mouth to scream, a hand clamped tightly over it. She thought she felt something prick the skin behind her ear.

The hoarse voice was behind her. 'If you keep still for a moment, I will explain.'

Amy tried to scream, but the hand was stifling her cries. She was trapped. Her words were lost and her ankle pulsed with pain. As she was pulled tighter, she felt her assailant's body against her spine. The smell of fresh mint mingled with the rain, and lips brushed close to her ear. She struggled to hear what was being said as the sirens blared louder and the music thumped relentlessly through the rain.

At last the noise faded and the only sound Amy heard was the thudding of her own heart. Her hair was plastered to her scalp but the hand held firm. She scanned the car park, the deserted spaces slipping in and out of focus, but it offered her no safety. She felt the head lower to her face again. And this time she heard the words.

If she could have screamed, she would have, but Amy could do nothing but slump against her captor as all the power disappeared from her body.

*

Katie Parker hadn't been out on the town in almost two years. This was supposed to be the start of the new Katie, but now her ass of a sister was ruining it for her.

'I told you not to drink shots, Chloe. You're too young, plus you haven't the constitution to withstand so much alcohol.' Katie held her sister's arm, trying to keep her upright.

'You sound just like Mother. Dictators, that's what the two of you are.' Chloe folded into a hoop with a bout of hiccups. 'And I'm nearly eighteen. So there.'

'Yeah, well you're a fool and you've ruined my evening.' Katie guided her away from the gathering crowd and into the ladies' toilets.

The cubicles were all empty. Chloe dropped the toilet lid and plonked herself down. Katie watched her in the mirror as she ran a finger around her smudged mascara. She turned on the tap and brown water spluttered into the sink.

'What the hell is that?'

'Water?' Chloe offered.

'No, the sink. It's all gooey.' Katie touched a finger to the bowl and knew instantly what it was. She moved to one of the cubicles and noticed the same substance on the cisterns. Vaseline. Dotted with white powder.

'Coke, is it?' Chloe slurred.

'In my day, a few joints was all we could afford.' Katie recalled with a wry smile her illicit smokes with Jason, her boyfriend and the father of her son. Jason had been murdered, and it seemed like a whole lifetime ago. She suddenly felt a lot older than her twenty-one years. Maybe she was getting too like her mother. 'What am I going to do with you?'

'What do you mean?' Chloe said.

'You can't go home drunk as a skunk. Mam will kill you.'

'Don't want to go home.'

With a sigh, Katie hauled her sister up off the toilet, stretched her arm around her and hugged her tightly.

'You and me, we have to make life work for us. And getting blotto on a Saturday night isn't doing either of us any favours.'

'I think you're drunker than me,' Chloe said.

'I'm being pragmatic.'

'Ooh. Big words now.'

'Yeah, and you're a big girl, so quit the melodramatics and act your age.'

'Yes, Mam.'

Katie held her at arm's length. 'I'm serious. We've been through some bad times. Both of us. And Mam has always been there for us. I think it's time we cut her some slack and helped her out.'

'What has that got to do with me enjoying a rare night out?'

'Everything.'

'You're talking like a jigsaw puzzle, and I'm sick as a dog.'

Katie stepped out of the way just in time as Chloe puked all over the toilet seat. She realised the lid was coated in Vaseline too. She coiled Chloe's hair around her fingers and waited until her sister raised her head.

'Can we go home now?' Katie said.

'Yeah. I think that's a very good idea. But …'

'But what?'

'Don't tell Mam.'

Katie laughed at the childish plea. 'I won't tell her if you promise not to throw up all over our new bathroom.'

'Pinky promise.' Then Chloe turned and vomited once again.

One down. And I'm not finished yet. I pull off the Teflon apron and gloves and roll them up with the paper hat.

I have to have two of them. That was the plan all along. To cause as much confusion as possible. But I knew it would be hard to deal with two together, so I have to go back for another. I thought I wouldn't have the stomach for it, but now that I've dispensed with the first one, I feel thirsty for more. That feeling. It was like an electrical surge through my body. A torrent of life infused me while she spluttered out of existence.

I dump the clothing in the boot of my car and take out a fresh sealed pack, then sit and watch. I have an eagle-eyed view of the club. I look on as two girls come out the door, one holding the other upright. Easy prey. Easy pickings. But should I deviate from my plan? Or keep them for later? The urge to take them now, to make their mother pay for her wrongdoing, is all-encompassing. Will I ever have another opportunity to get them both together? Possibly. If I'm clever enough.

With it all settled in my mind, I let the seat back and wait.

CHAPTER 7

Baby Louis was snoring lightly but Lottie was wide awake.

She couldn't sleep until her girls were home safe. She usually wasn't this pent up, but some unknown and possibly unrealistic feeling of foreboding was crawling through her blood tonight. She had to do something, because they were not answering their phones. Maybe she'd have a soothing warm bath. Throwing back the duvet, she padded across the newly carpeted floor, relishing the warmth between her toes, and stepped into the bathroom.

'Oh Holy Mother of God,' she said. The white ceramic-tiled floor and walls were smeared with fake tan. It was like a troupe of actors had used the small space to get ready for a stage performance. She traced the edge of the integrated shower tiles above the bath with a finger. It came away smudged brown.

'I'll kill them. Both of them,' she whispered. Picking up discarded items of clothing, she dumped them into the wash basket and with all thoughts of a relaxing soak in the bath scuppered went downstairs to heat a mug of milk. One of her mother's remedies for sleeplessness.

The milk didn't work. She paced the hallway, phone in hand. It was now past two o'clock. Their curfew was one a.m. For sure she was going to kill the pair of them. Why had she allowed Chloe to go out? She argued with herself in the silence. But she knew she had to trust her girls, even though they had a habit of finding trouble. Or did trouble find them?

Her bare feet slapped against the hall floor. She couldn't go out to look for them. She had the baby to watch. Unless she roused Sean. She tried Katie's phone again. Dead. She tapped Chloe's number. Same thing. Why didn't they charge their phones? She toyed with the idea of calling Boyd to see if he'd go out to look for them. No, she dismissed that thought. He'd tell her she was being overprotective and to let them live a little. Her new resolution of being a better mother was quickly evaporating, and still she couldn't shift the quiver of unease fluttering at the base of her neck.

Where the hell were her daughters?

*

Penny Brogan knew she had a wide smile on her face and that her cheeks were flushed. She felt slightly giddy, and it wasn't just from the last two shots Ducky Reilly had dared her to drink. She ran her tongue slowly over her lips, trying to feel the memory of his. Ducky was a friend. Just a friend. But after the last Jägerbomb, she'd kissed him. Leaning against the scratchy wall behind the seats in the smoking garden. And oh my God, she'd never have guessed in a million years how good it would feel. She was glad she'd worn her lace knickers and not a thong, because she could still feel his hands moving beneath the elastic waistband of her shimmery dress and his fingers toying with the knickers. She shivered with delight. His hands on her bum. Searching and probing. A soft squeal escaped her lips now as she stood outside the nightclub wondering where the hell Amy had gone. Stupid bitch. Should have waited the five minutes.

She glanced at the screen of her phone and realised it was half an hour since she'd last seen her friend. Why hadn't Amy waited? But Penny wasn't going to allow that inconvenience to dim the glow that was warming her body. She couldn't even feel the rain.

Making her mind up, she set off in the direction of her apartment. She wasn't that drunk; she knew how to get there. She might even take off her shoes and dance in the puddles the whole way home. She giggled out loud. She should have more sense at her age, she thought, then laughed.

As she turned the corner at the end of the street, a figure loomed up in front of her. Her hand flew to her mouth, cutting off her scream. A head bent in towards her ear and she had no option but to listen.

'Amy? Is she okay?' she said, hearing her friend's name.

'She's in a bad way. You need to come.'

Penny stalled under the street light. The person was still in the shadows. The light caught their eyes and she took a step backwards. 'Maybe I should call her dad. Or the guards. Maybe I—'

'Maybe you should hurry up. She might have been raped. She sent me to get you. Said not to tell anyone. She's in a right state. Are you coming, or are you going to stand there with your mouth open catching moths all night?'

A hand rested on Penny's shoulder and she was sure she felt something prick the side of her neck. Damn moths. She didn't know what to do. The memory of Ducky's fingers on her skin dimmed and was replaced by a sick feeling of unease. But she had to make sure Amy was all right. Then she'd call her dad. Or the guards.

'Okay, I'm coming.'

She slipped her high-heeled shoes off and set off through the puddles, slipping and sliding on the greasy footpath in her efforts to keep up. Her mind was whirling with insane thoughts and she was finding it hard to focus.

As they hurried down Petit Lane towards the bridge under the railway tracks, Penny wasn't at all sure she was doing the right thing.

CHAPTER 8

Lottie was sitting on the bottom step when the flash of lights lit up the hall through the glass at the side of the door.

Opening it, she saw her daughters falling out of a taxi and exhaled a sigh of relief. They were home. They were safe. That was all that mattered.

'Mam, do you have the loan of a fiver?' Katie called out.

Lottie rummaged in her jacket pocket hanging on the banister beside her and found enough coins. She was barefoot, so she held the money out to Katie and noticed that she was walking upright and in a straight line. As one daughter went back to pay the taxi driver, the other wobbled up the path.

'Hi, Mother.' Chloe always called her that as she knew it rattled her. It was what Adam had called her in front of the children. It had been endearing to her at the time; now it spelled out the loss she felt without him.

She shook her head. One minute Chloe had been standing in front of her. The next she was nowhere to be seen.

'Chloe?'

Katie came up the path, bent down to the right of the door and hoisted up her sister, who'd fallen into a patch of shrubs.

'Come inside before you wake the neighbours.' Lottie got hold of Chloe's other arm and helped Katie to drag the inebriated girl inside. She shut the door and leaned against it, relief mingled with anger. 'And don't wake Louis, or I'll kill you.'

A cry bellowed from upstairs.

'Now see what you've done.' Katie bundled past Lottie and raced up the stairs to her son.

Shaking her head, Lottie followed Chloe into the kitchen, where she found the girl puking into the sink.

'This is the last time, Chloe. Don't even think about asking to go out again.'

'Do you have to shout?' Chloe washed out the sink, then stuck her mouth under the tap. 'My head is killing me.'

'It's nothing to the ache it will have in the morning by the time I finish with you. Get up to bed and bring a basin.'

'Righto so, Miss Trunchbull.' Chloe attempted a salute but stuck her finger in her eye instead.

Lottie shook her head once again. She would have some serious talking to do tomorrow.

*

Rose Fitzpatrick closed her eyes as she sat alone in her kitchen. The peace and stillness washed over her and she welcomed them. At last.

She loved her family unconditionally, but she had spent so long living alone that it had almost worn her to the bone having them all around her.

She had to admit she missed the sounds, though. Of running water in the shower. Constantly. Of baby Louis' laughs and cries. Of her daughter Lottie talking to her again. Really talking. Despite the awful revelations she had uncovered a year ago about her true heritage. Rose thought their relationship had been damaged irreparably at that time, but although it felt awful to admit it, the fire at Lottie's house had saved them. Brought them together again.

She tried to get comfortable in her chair. She would love a snooze, but now the silence was beginning to intimidate her. She felt a lump beneath her cushion and pulled out a soft toy belonging to Louis. Maybe she could call over in the morning to bring the toy to him. Don't be silly, she admonished herself. Let them lead their own lives again. She'd only get in the way. But the silence was like a physical being all around her, whispering in her ear, shrouding her shoulders in unease. Maybe she should go to bed.

Rose Fitzpatrick realised she didn't like the silence at all.

And that was when the doorbell rang.

CHAPTER 9

Lottie awoke on Monday to the sound of leaves blowing off the trees. She twisted in the bed and squinted out through the slit in the curtains, which refused to close in the middle. Her mother had told her she needed to buy size 90x90 curtains, but they weren't on special offer so Lottie had plumped for the 65x90. As usual, her mother had been right.

The narrow slit acted as her alarm clock. An orange glow lit up the backdrop to the trees at the end of the garden. Two wood pigeons nestled on a branch and Lottie shot upright. Had they followed her from her old house? The new place was in a quiet, secluded area. It had a low-maintenance garden and the trees on the lane behind it made it feel like home. It *was* home now, Lottie thought, though for how long, she had no idea, because she was still waiting for the insurance payout following the fire.

She listened to see if Louis was awake. No sound. Katie had had a short relationship with Louis' dad, Jason Rickard, before he'd been murdered, and Jason's father, a local developer now living in New York, had provided them with the house at a minimum rent. Lottie had wanted nothing to do with Tom Rickard, but as Rose was apt to say, beggars can't be choosers.

Once Lottie had showered and dressed in her usual outfit of jeans and long-sleeved white T-shirt, she pulled on a pair of flat black leather boots, At five foot eight, she didn't need the addition of heels. She headed down the stairs to the kitchen, where she pulled up the blinds and filled the kettle. Chloe had bought a coffee machine with money she'd made from her part-time job, but Lottie didn't have the patience to follow the instructions. As she took out a mug and fetched the milk from the refrigerator, she was almost afraid to admit that for the first time in a very long time, she actually felt almost happy.

But she didn't want to jinx her happiness by over-thinking. She made her coffee and sat at the table debating with herself on the need to have a proper breakfast. She opened a box of cereal bars and munched one in the silence, admiring the kitchen's stark white walls. This place was such a contrast to the well-worn house she had lived in with Adam. She didn't think of him as often as she used to. His memories were housed in the ash of their old home. But she kept him locked tightly in her heart, and that alone kept others out. Except Boyd. At last she was beginning to let him in, just a little bit. And it filled her with a warm feeling. Or maybe that was just the coffee.

She drained her mug, grabbed her jacket and keys, and went to see why Sean and Chloe were not yet up and ready for school. Some things would never change.

*

Leo Belfield had arrived at the Joyce Hotel early that morning, and now he sat on one of the single beds and stared at her. His sister. His twin sister. After so many years of searching within himself for the reasons why he felt only half a man, now he knew why.

He was a captain in the New York Police Department, and his blood flowed with curiosity. It had taken a multitude of emails and a slew of corrupt officials to get his sister released into his care. He had made it his mission, especially after the woman he believed to be his half-sister, Lottie Parker, had refused to answer any of his questions. But at least she had sent him in the right direction. The Central Mental Hospital.

A slight smile curled at the corner of Bernie Kelly's cracked lips.

'Well, brother dear.' Her voice had the rasp of someone who had not spoken for a long time. 'You succeeded.'

Leo wasn't at all sure that he would describe what he had done as a success. It had been hard work, but in the end, he had secured a day of freedom for his sister. He hoped that would be long enough to find out the truth.

As she pulled herself upright, he noticed the thinness of her legs encased in jeans a couple of sizes too big; the strip of flesh sagging at her chin; and her eyes … the way she looked at him. The stare was cold and bitter. But it wasn't his fault she had endured such deprivation while he had lived a happy life in New York. She had been committed to the mental facility following a series of murders. He couldn't bring himself to believe that she'd actually committed the horrors he'd read about. But now he had the opportunity to find out the truth.

'How did I succeed?' he said.

'Getting me out of that hellhole. I swear to God, I thought I was going to rot away in there.'

'Bernie, you realise you are only out on day release, don't you?'

She laughed then. Long and harsh. And he, a cop of twenty-five years, having served in the toughest districts the NYPD could throw at him, felt a shiver crease his chest in two.

'That's what you told them. But I know you're not going to let me go back inside. I can tell you the family secrets, but only if you guarantee I will never have to live behind bars again.'

She lay back on the bed and drummed a long finger against her temple. And Leo Belfield wondered just what the hell he had done.

CHAPTER 10

Lottie looked up when Boyd walked into her office.

'Good morning,' she said. 'Anything up?'

'Nope, but now that I see you …'

'Boyd!' She laughed. 'All quiet so?'

'So far.'

As he retreated, she clicked through her morning emails, thinking of the couple of hours they'd shared last night in his apartment. Suddenly the door burst open once more. She looked up expecting Boyd again, but it was Acting Superintendent David McMahon who stood there, black hair glistening and his eyes sparkling with something she couldn't decipher. He'd probably balanced a spreadsheet, she thought unkindly.

'Good morning, sir,' she said, though adding 'sir' galled her. She should be acting superintendent while Superintendent Corrigan was on extended sick leave, but no, the powers-that-be had drafted McMahon in from Dublin. A right kick up the backside for her.

'Nothing good about it,' he said, and flopped onto the chair in front of her desk.

'Go on.' She leaned towards him, interested.

'Amy Whyte, twenty-five years old, didn't come home after a night out on Saturday, and she didn't turn up for work yesterday or this morning. Her father is downstairs to lodge a missing persons report.'

'When did he last see his daughter?' Lottie asked.

'Saturday evening, before she headed out for Jomo's nightclub.'

Lottie felt a moment of discomfort, thinking of her girls. 'She's sleeping off a bellyful of booze somewhere.'

'You and I both know that is entirely possible, but try telling her father that. Will you do a little investigating? Just to demonstrate that we are doing something.'

'You know him then? This Mr Whyte?'

McMahon leaned back in the chair, stretched his arms to the ceiling and yawned. He was usually jumping around like a toy on long-life batteries on Monday mornings. Not just Mondays. Every morning, come to think of it.

'Not really,' he said. 'As you know, I've spent most of my working life in Dublin, but Whyte is a county councillor, so do me this one favour. You never know when we might need one in return.'

'I know what I need. More staff. I can't just go off on a wild goose chase when there's so much to do. Court cases, budgets, KPIs to be met.' She smiled inwardly. Key performance indicators were McMahon's babies, and if he uttered the phrase once a day, he said it a dozen times. She felt a glow of pleasure in spouting it back at him.

'You really know which buttons to push. For now, I just want you to talk to the man. See what you can find out. He'll be pacified if he thinks an inspector is investigating.'

'I need more staff.' She folded her arms. 'I've told you often enough. Since Gilly …' Her words caught in her throat. The loss of the young garda had decimated morale in the station. Most affected was Detective Larry Kirby, who had been Gilly's boyfriend. 'And Detective Lynch is on maternity leave. We need new blood in here.'

'I'm trying my best to get someone assigned from another station.' McMahon stood up and moved to the door. 'Now go and talk to Richard Whyte. That's an order.'

Lottie shook her head as he marched out the door and into the general office. She rolled the name around in her mind. Amy

Whyte? Could it be the same Amy Whyte? She would find out soon enough.

The man sitting in the room off reception seemed to fill the space with his bulk. And when he stood, Lottie remembered exactly who he was. Ten years ago, his daughter, then just a teenager, had been a key witness in a trial.

'Good morning, Councillor Whyte. Take a seat.' She squeezed in past him and sat down, and Boyd squashed in beside her behind the small desk. She silently warned herself to watch her Ps and Qs, because it would all travel back upstairs to McMahon.

'I want to report my daughter missing.'

'What's her name and age?'

'Amy Whyte. Twenty-five.'

'When did you last see her?'

A whistle of air escaped his lips. 'Saturday evening. Around seven.'

'Okay,' Lottie said as Boyd wrote in his notebook. 'Today is Monday. You weren't expecting her home Saturday night, or even yesterday, then?'

'She went out with her friend Penny Brogan on Saturday, like she does every weekend.'

'Has she a boyfriend?'

'No one regular as far as I know.'

'You weren't worried when she didn't come home Saturday night?'

'No, I wasn't. Sometimes she stays over at Penny's … or, you know … a friend's.'

'What has you worried now?'

'Amy works in my pharmacy. She didn't turn up for work yesterday morning or today. She always opens the shop on Mondays.

I got a call from one of the assistants at eight thirty to say the staff had no way of getting in.'

'And that was unusual?'

'Of course it was. Amy rarely misses work, and if she were ill, I'd know. It's very unlike her.'

'What did you do?'

'I opened up the shop and let the staff in. Turned on the lights. Set up the tills. All the stuff that Amy usually does.'

'And did you try to find out where she might be?'

'I was busy with the shop, and customers started coming in. The day got away from me. I was sure she'd be at home when I got there. But she wasn't.'

'What did you do then?'

'I just assumed she had met a fella on Saturday night and was still with him.'

'Has she done that before?'

'A few times. But she's twenty-five, not a child, Inspector Parker.'

Lottie didn't like the rebuke in his tone. She straightened her back and tugged up the sleeves of her T-shirt. As usual, Boyd remained silent. Letting her dig herself into a big black hole.

'Did you contact her friends?'

'Of course.'

'And?'

He fidgeted in the chair. 'Well, I don't know all of them …'

'Can you give me the details of those you did contact?'

'I can. But they're no help. No one knows where she is.'

'They might be able to tell us when they last saw Amy.'

'At the nightclub, Jomo's. That's the last time anyone saw her.'

'Anyone you've contacted, that is.'

'Correct.'

'I need the names and numbers.'

'Sure.'

He took a page from his breast pocket and handed it over. Lottie glanced at the handwritten list. It was short. Very short. Three names.

'I'm sure there are more,' he said quickly, 'but they're all I had in my phone.'

'Some of these might be able to provide me with further names and numbers,' Lottie said. 'And what about the people she works with?'

'They told me they hadn't see her since Friday evening, when she locked up. She was off on Saturday.'

'Are you in the shop every day?'

'Only when Amy is off. I trust her to run it for me.'

'I need a list of all the employees.'

'I'll email it to you.'

'Thanks.' Lottie considered the burly man in front of her. He seemed genuinely worried. 'Are things okay at home, Mr Whyte?'

'At home?' He ran a stubby finger along his cheek. 'Everything's fine.'

'Your wife?'

'She's dead.'

Lottie thought that perhaps she should have done a quick Google on Mr Whyte before she met with him. 'I'm sorry.'

'No need to apologise.' He waved a hand in dismissal. 'She died six years ago.'

'Are things okay between you and your daughter? Any recent arguments or fallings-out that we should know about?'

'We acknowledge each other's space. Lead our own lives. We're both adults.'

Reading between the lines, Lottie gathered that Mr Whyte allowed Amy to do just about anything she liked.

'Why are you reporting her as missing?'

'I can't find any trace of her. Usually she'd send a text if she was staying with someone, and she rarely misses work. Like I said, it's totally out of character.'

Lottie knew she'd have to dig a bit deeper, but at the same time she hoped Amy would waltz home this evening, contrite and full of explanations, false or otherwise.

'Have you a photograph of her?'

He extracted a creased photo from his wallet. It showed the two of them sitting at a bar drinking cocktails. 'Barcelona. Last year. I have a holiday home there.'

'Did you check that her passport is still at home?' Lottie said.

'No. But she wouldn't … not without telling me. I know my girl.'

Not well enough, Lottie thought. 'Can I hold on to this?'

'Mind it for me, please.'

'I will.' Lottie smiled involuntarily as she studied the happy face of the dark-haired girl in the picture. Her glass was gripped by a hand with long red nails sporting little diamond studs in the tips, and her ears were adorned with similar heart-shaped studs. 'She's very pretty.'

'And very happy. She has no reason to disappear or run away. Wherever she is, she's not gone voluntarily.' Richard Whyte dropped his head.

'I'll find her for you,' Lottie said, and immediately felt Boyd's foot strike her ankle. She knew she shouldn't be making promises she wasn't sure she could keep. But something in Whyte's demeanour made her feel sorry for him. A thought occurred to her. 'Your work with the council. Could someone you've been dealing with have anything to do with Amy going missing?'

He looked up, his face a mask of incredulity. 'No way. Amy has nothing to do with my council work.'

'Any elections coming up? Maybe projects you've been involved in that might result in someone making threats against you or your daughter?'

'You're completely off track there, Inspector. Amy has no interest in that side of things. It's very dry and dusty for a girl of her age.'

'I'll have a chat with her colleagues in the pharmacy, but if she contacts you in the meantime, let me know immediately.' Lottie tidied up her papers and Boyd stood. Whyte remained seated. 'Was there anything else, Mr Whyte?'

'Amy's friend. Penny Brogan. I can't get hold of her. I spoke with her father an hour ago. He hasn't heard from her either. It seems she might also be missing.'

CHAPTER 11

Lottie walked back up the stairs with Boyd.

'If Amy's friend hasn't been seen since Saturday night either, why has no one reported her missing?' she said.

'That's according to Whyte. We'd better check it out.'

'Give her parents a ring, and I'll get Kirby to head down to Whyte's Pharmacy to see if Amy's colleagues can give us a head start. And we need to find out where Penny works also.'

Boyd nodded and moved over to his desk.

Lottie made for her office at the end of the general one. Kirby was still sitting in the same position as when she'd left. She was going to have to do something about him before McMahon started complaining that he was dragging down performance targets.

'How are things, Kirby? What are you working on?'

'What? Oh, sorry, boss. I was miles away.' Kirby raised his head. Black rings circled his eyes, and his nose was redder than usual. Lottie caught a waft of stale alcohol. Yes, she thought, he's in a bad way.

'I'm not being unkind here,' she said. 'I understand your situation because I've been through the whole grief thing. But Kirby, listen to me. You need help. Professional help. If you don't access it soon, the super is going to go apeshit. He has no loyalty to the people in this station, only to whatever can get him quickly up the career ladder, and at the moment, you are dragging him down. I understand what you're going through, but that's the way he sees it.'

Repeating myself, she thought. What the hell did she really need to say to her colleague? Knuckle down and buck up? No. That had been said to her too often, and it just made her veer in the opposite direction. She settled for 'What can I do to help you?'

Kirby looked at her with pleading in his eyes. 'Bring Gilly back?'

'Come on, be realistic.' Wrong thing to say. Kirby suddenly shoved back his chair and stood up. She put a hand on his arm and gently tugged his sleeve. 'I'm sorry.'

He ran his hands through his bushy hair, his fingers snagging in the mop.

'Boss, I don't know what to do with myself. I'm sick of paperwork. It's driving me demented. I need something to get stuck into. Something to get me out on the streets, talking to people. The four walls in here are suffocating me.'

'I like the passion in your voice. So here goes. Councillor Whyte's daughter, Amy, seems to have disappeared. He hasn't done much legwork in finding her, so I want you to make it your priority. Okay?'

'Sure. That's great. I'd like that.'

Lottie sighed with relief. 'She works at Whyte's Pharmacy. Go and talk to her colleagues face to face. You might be able to find out something from them that they didn't want Amy's father to know about when he spoke to them.'

'Whyte's Pharmacy. At the end of Main Street?'

'Yes.'

Kirby grabbed his coat from the back of his chair and was out the door before Lottie could move.

'You are a true motivator,' Boyd said.

'Doesn't work with you, though.' She slapped him playfully on the shoulder as she passed, her hand tingling from the touch. Boyd was having a good effect on her recently. 'Have you located Penny Brogan yet?'

'Working on it. I rang her father, but like Whyte said, he hasn't seen her.'

'Okay. Let's start with this list of friends.'

'All three of them,' Boyd said, holding up his fingers.

'Better than none.'

'Ducky Reilly. I'd like to start with him.'

'Right. Where does he work?'

'As a security guard for the construction company working on the courthouse renovation.'

'Let's go.'

The renovation of Ragmullin's courthouse had been ongoing for over a year. The building dated from 1829 and had been falling into disrepair for the last twenty years. It was costing forty million euros to restore it, and Boyd told Lottie he'd heard that it might go way over budget.

Rain fell in sheets as they left the car and approached the guard hut at the entrance to the site. Lottie held up her ID and the guard slid back the window.

'What can I do for you?' he said.

'We'd like to have a word with Ducky Reilly. Is he at work today?'

The young man's face paled. He closed the window and opened the door. He was about five foot five and had short curly brown hair peeking out from the edges of his beanie hat.

'What's this about? I didn't do anything, no matter what anyone says.' His voice was high and petulant.

'And who would be saying anything about you?' Boyd muscled in.

'No one. Nothing. Shit, you guys are making me nervous.' He pulled off his hat, then, as the rain poured down, quickly clamped it back on his head. Water dripped off his yellow work jacket and sprinkled a grey sheen onto the mucky ground.

Lottie shifted her feet, trying not to get her boots too soiled. A losing battle. 'We're here about Amy Whyte.'

'Who?'

'Come on now.' Lottie could tell that he knew exactly who she was talking about. 'When did you last see her?'

'Amy? Let me think ...'

'Jesus, answer the question.' Boyd was losing patience.

Lottie tried to be nice. 'Ducky, what's your full name?'

'Dermot Reilly.'

'Which do you prefer us to call you?'

'Everyone calls me Ducky.' He shifted from foot to foot, splashing mud onto the leg of Lottie's jeans.

'Ducky it is so,' she said, and Boyd sniggered. She threw him a dagger stare and turned back to the young man. 'Can we talk inside?' She indicated the hut.

'It's too small. Just my chair and the security cameras.'

'Oh, I think we can squeeze in. Boyd, you wait in the car.'

As she followed Ducky into the warm confines of his miniature workplace, she had to agree with him. It wasn't made for two people. She leaned against the door and he sat on the chair with a couple of screens behind him. Nothing hi-tech. She could see Boyd outside, trying to light a cigarette in the spilling rain.

'So, tell me about Amy.'

'Her dad rang me this morning asking about her too.'

'When did you see her last?

'Saturday night. We were all in Jomo's. That's the nightclub round near Petit Lane car park. You know, at the back of Main Street, past the chipper.'

'Yes, I know it.' Lottie squirmed as she recalled her daughters falling out of the taxi on Saturday night. Sunday morning if she wanted to be pedantic about it. 'Who is the "all" you're referring to?'

'Myself and a few of the lads. And Penny, of course. She and Amy hang out together.'

'Penny Brogan?'

'Yeah. Amy and Penny are joined at the hip. So my mother says.'

'Your mother's met them?'

'We're friends. Since school. Amy is a bit up her own hole because her father's a councillor. But Penny's fun. Always up to something.'

'You like Penny better, then?'

He blushed. 'Suppose so.'

'What happened at the nightclub? Anything out of the ordinary?'

'Nothing happened.'

'Did you leave with the girls?'

'No.'

'Come on, Ducky.'

'What's this about anyway?'

'I'll tell you after you answer my questions.'

He sighed and picked up a pen from the narrow ledge that Lottie supposed was his desk.

'There were about a hundred and fifty other people at the club on Saturday night. It was packed.' He twisted the pen around his fingers.

'Did Amy and Penny leave together, or were they with you?'

'I'm not going out with either of them,' he said quickly. She could tell by his face that he wished he was.

'Which of them do you like the most?'

'Penny.'

'You don't like Amy?'

'I didn't say that. For feck's sake. That's what you lot do, isn't it? Twist everything. I'm saying nothing else.'

'Sounds to me like you have something to hide.'

'I haven't. So there.' He dropped the pen and folded his arms.

'Did the girls leave together?' Lottie asked again.

'I don't know. No, wait a minute. Amy left first. Me and Penny, we had another shot … and a snog.'

Lottie smiled to herself. A shot and a snog. 'So you remained there with Penny after Amy had left?'

'Amy wouldn't wait. We were out in the beer garden. It was drizzling rain. Don't think she even had a jacket.'

'What was her rush?'

'I have no idea.'

'Did she take a phone call or anything?'

'I told you, I don't know.'

'Where was she going?'

'Home, I presume.'

Lottie decided not to give him time to think. 'Did you leave with Penny?'

'No. She left maybe twenty minutes later. Could have been longer, I don't know. I'd had a lot to drink.'

'And the girls, did they drink much?'

'A few shots maybe. I wasn't keeping count.'

'Any drugs?'

'Now you're definitely pushing it.' Ducky looked up at her and his eyes narrowed. 'All these questions. Has something happened to them?'

Lottie decided to give him a little information. 'Amy's dad says she never came home Saturday night. She didn't turn up for work yesterday or today.'

'That's a bit weird all right. What does Penny say?'

'We have yet to talk to her.' Yet to find her, Lottie thought.

'But you came to me first. Why?'

'Your name was on the list of contacts that we got from Amy's dad.'

'Amy's very popular. Must be a long list.'

'Actually, it's short. Can you give me the names of anyone else who might know where she could be?'

'Not really. Ask Penny.'

'I will. When I find her.' Lottie considered the young man. He wasn't displaying any signs of concern for the girls. He just seemed nervous. Because she was from the guards, or was it something else? Did he know where they were, or was he usually this calm? 'Where does Penny work?'

He shrugged. 'She worked for a while with Amy in the chemist. But I think she got fired or something. The last I heard she was on the dole.'

'Where does she live?'

'She has a flat on Columb Street. Don't know the number. She never invited me. I only visited her at her parents' house. Try there.' He gave Lottie the address, and she turned to leave.

'Thanks for your help. If either of the girls contacts you, this is my number. Call me straight away.'

She handed over her card and escaped out the door. Ducky Reilly seemed to know a whole lot of nothing.

As she made her way towards the car, in which Boyd was now sitting, Lottie heard the rumble of an engine behind her. She stood to one side and a black Mercedes SUV pulled up beside her. The driver's window whizzed down.

She recognised the man behind the wheel immediately. Cyril Gill was well known in the town. A shyster, her mother had once said. He was a developer and builder.

'Mr Gill,' she said, appraising him. He was dressed for an office meeting, not a site visit. Pristine blue shirt with a white collar, and a red silk tie. His face was clean-shaven and his black hair had a hint of grey above his ears. She thought his blue eyes looked jaded, but his face was clear of wrinkles.

He took her card and glanced at it.

'Detective Inspector Lottie Parker.' The soft, silken voice immediately put her on her guard. 'What are you doing here?'

'Having a look around, though it seems I'm not authorised to go on site.' She wasn't going to let Ducky sink, not yet.

'Anything I can help you with?' His eyes were shifty, and Lottie thought he hadn't the slightest intention of helping her with anything. Not that she needed help from him.

'No, it's fine.' She drew away from him and headed to her car.

'Access is strictly by appointment,' he said, and the window whizzed back up.

She raised her hand in a wave. Back at the car, she sat in beside Boyd.

'Was that Cyril Gill?' he said.

'One and the same. And trouble is never too far behind him.'

'He was involved in some planning scandal years ago.'

'So the story goes.' Lottie waited for Boyd to start the car. 'Nothing was ever proved, if I remember correctly. As usual in this country.'

'Never liked him. Who can look so fresh at seventy?'

'I don't think he's seventy. More like fifty-one or two.'

'Whatever.'

'That's Chloe's favourite word.'

'Whatever.' He grinned. 'Where to next, then?'

'Penny Brogan's family. And let's hope Amy Whyte is there with her.'

*

Cyril Gill parked in his private space, the only place without sludge running over it. He got out of the car and stared at the sky. Black and purple clouds chased each other across a grey blanket, and the rain continued to slap against his face.

'Three months behind, and now this,' he muttered as he headed to the Portakabins. The job was proving more difficult than he'd imagined at the tender process. Because the courthouse was a listed building, the exterior had to be maintained in its original form. And that hindered the total renovation required to modernise the place into a functioning twenty-first-century courthouse.

A blast of heat thrust its way outside as he entered.

'What did the guards want?' he called over to the foreman, Bob Cleary. 'And why are you in here and not out there cracking the whip on the arses of those lazy fuckers?'

'Came in for a cuppa. It's my break. I am entitled, you know.' Bob put the mug to his lips and slowly sipped the steaming liquid.

Cyril poured himself a coffee from the dispenser and wiped crumbs off his chair before sitting down.

'What guards?' Bob said.

'They were at the gate as I drove in.'

'Didn't see them. Ducky must have stopped them.'

Cyril lifted the phone. 'Ducky, what did the guards want?'

'Nothing to do with work. Just enquiring about some girl I know.'

Hanging up, Cyril stared at Bob. 'Three months behind? Is that right?'

'More like five or six if this weather doesn't improve. There's a storm warning for the weekend.'

'Oh for Christ's sake.' Gill slapped the desk and a file slid to the floor.

Bob picked it up and handed it back. 'I'll get back to work.'

'Do. And I don't want to hear anything about five or six months. Ever. You need to catch up on lost time.'

'It's the tunnels, Mr Gill. They need shoring up. The crane wobbled last week.'

'Cranes don't wobble. And those tunnels have been there for five hundred years, so they're not going to shift any time soon.'

'But once the lift shaft—'

'I thought you were getting back to work?'

Once he was alone, Cyril pulled off his jacket and rolled up his shirtsleeves. The fumes from the gas heater were giving him a headache, but he had work to do. He opened the daily work schedule spreadsheet and tried to figure out where he could make up the lost time. Otherwise, he would be in worse trouble than he had been last time. And Cyril Gill did not want to revisit that *annus horribilis* ever again.

CHAPTER 12

Whyte's Pharmacy was one of the few old-fashioned family-owned enterprises to survive in Ragmullin. When he arrived at the shop, Kirby was brought into a back room, where he sat himself down on the chair offered by the pharmacist, who introduced herself as Megan Price. The room was small and shelved from floor to ceiling, packed with medicines and drugs. Kirby kept his hands firmly clasped on his lap and was glad the boss wasn't here. He knew about Lottie's struggle with prescription medication, though he thought she was now over that addiction.

'Ms Price,' he said. 'I'm making enquiries on behalf of Amy Whyte's father. Do you have any notion of where Amy might be?'

'No. Not a clue. Richard, Mr Whyte, arrived this morning all concerned.' The pharmacist appeared to be in her mid thirties, with deep furrows grooved into her forehead. She rubbed a hand along her chin and eyed Kirby. 'That's not entirely true. He was more angry than concerned. Couldn't believe she hadn't turned up yesterday either.'

'You hadn't informed Mr Whyte that Amy was absent yesterday?'

'I didn't see the need to land the girl in any trouble.'

'What kind of trouble?' Kirby fumbled with one hand in his pocket for his notebook. Damn, he'd left it at the office, along with his phone. He'd have to remember the salient points of the conversation.

'I shouldn't have said that.' The pharmacist was furiously back-pedalling. 'I just don't like telling stories out of school, if you catch my drift.'

'And what stories might those be?'

A loud sigh was followed by a strained cough before Price spoke again. 'Amy's a good girl. She has her heart in the right place. Her father thinks she's a saint.'

'But you know different?'

'You could say that. More often than not, she doesn't appear on Sundays. Likes to party with that friend of hers who used to work here. Penny something … Let me think. Brogan. That's it. Used to work here too. Richard had to let her go.'

'When was that?'

'About a month ago.'

'Why did he let her go?'

'She was lazy. Wouldn't lift a hand to do a good turn for anyone. And in this type of job, you have to be prepared to help out. Some of our customers are ill, or caring for someone who's ill, so they need to be treated with care and attention.'

'And Penny wasn't like that?'

'No. Quite the opposite. I'd often find her trying out the lipsticks, testing nail polish or spraying expensive perfumes. Not good for business.'

'Amy recommended her for the job, did she?' Kirby wasn't sure this had any relevance to where Amy might be, but just as well to let the pharmacist have her say.

'She did. But I think Penny's behaviour got too much even for her.'

'Did they fall out?'

Price paused and rubbed her chin nervously. 'Not that I know of. I think they're still friends. They go clubbing together after all.'

'Can you think of anyone else Amy was friendly with?'

'She has a lot of friends. Not that I could name any of them. Amy's a vivacious girl. Always smiling. She has a good word for everyone.'

'Boyfriend?'

'Never heard her speak of one. That's not to say she doesn't have one.' Megan Price twisted one hand around the other.

'Can I have a word with the other staff? They might know of someone she was close to.'

'You don't know where she is then?'

'We're looking for her.'

Price said, 'Richard's a very influential man. He has a lot of friends in high places. I'd pull out all the stops if I were you.'

Kirby scratched his head, reminding himself to have a quick shower this evening, and wondered if the pharmacist was laying on a threat or a warning.

'Usually people like that have a lot of enemies,' he said.

'You read my mind perfectly.'

*

'I told you on the phone,' Jordan Brogan said. 'I haven't seen her.'

'We just want to ask a few questions.'

'Are you deaf? Penny doesn't live here any more. Kicked her out, so I did.' Brogan was a small man with a big voice. Lottie had to stop herself putting her hands over her ears as she and Boyd followed him inside his rather cramped house.

'When was that?'

'What?'

She noticed then that he was wearing a hearing aid. 'Can you switch on your hearing aid, Mr Brogan?'

'I keep forgetting. Sorry.' He fiddled with the small peanut-shaped device and put it back in his ear. 'Ah, that's better. Damaged my hearing while I was in the army. Dragged the bastards through the courts, and what did I get? I'll tell you what. Six grand. Sure these yokes cost me four grand. Disgrace, that's what it is.' He sat at the table and indicated for Lottie and Boyd to join him. 'Why are you asking about Penny?'

'It's really Amy Whyte we're trying to locate, but we thought maybe your daughter might know where she is.'

'That smart-arse madam got Penny fired, so she did.'

'Where exactly is Penny living now?' Lottie felt that if she didn't stick to what she wanted to know, Jordan Brogan would give out about everything and anything all day long.

'She has a flat. Number seven Columb Street. Don't know how she's paying for it. Must be that rent assistance shite from the social. Or maybe it's from the council. I don't know, because I haven't seen her in like a month. She's breaking her mother's heart, so she is.'

'And your wife, can we have a word with her?' Lottie thought maybe Penny was in contact with her mother.

'Breda's at work. Works in motor tax at the council.'

Lottie stood. 'I'll call in and see if she's seen your daughter. Does she work anywhere now?'

'I told you. Motor tax.'

'No, sorry, I mean Penny.'

'I haven't a clue. Whyte's was the last place I heard. But sure I don't hear that much,' he tapped his hearing aid, 'and no one tells me anything around here.'

Lottie headed for the door. 'Thanks for your time, Mr Brogan.'

He followed her out. 'Do you think my Penny is missing?'

'We just need to talk to her in relation to our inquiries.' Lottie smiled, hoping she sounded reassuring, but her stomach was tightening into a knot of disquiet. Where were Amy and Penny? Then again, they were both adults and they were entitled to their privacy. But something was niggling away in her gut. A warning of sorts, telling her to take note of everything she heard.

Jordan Brogan was shouting now. 'That Amy is bad news. Ever since she got that lad sent down for armed robbery.'

Lottie's heart stopped. 'What do you mean?'

'Oh, it must be ten years ago now. You remember Conor Dowling. Amy Whyte and another lassie said they saw him running from Bill Thompson's house. Poor Bill used to own the pub on Friars Street. He's dead now. Stroke, I heard. Maybe not more than a year after the assault. He got a right beating that night. All his cash was taken too.'

'Amy must have been fourteen or fifteen at the time.'

'That'd be about right.'

'Thanks, Mr Brogan. Let me know if Penny contacts you.'

As she opened the car door she said, 'Gosh, Boyd, I hope those girls are not in any trouble.'

'As you said earlier, they're probably sleeping off a massive hangover somewhere.'

'I hope to God that's all that's wrong.'

CHAPTER 13

Katie Parker pushed the stroller along the footpath, walking briskly into town. Louis was asleep with a see-through plastic cover over him, though she had no idea how long that would last. She allowed the rain to spritz against her skin and dampen her long hair. She'd recently taken to dying it a stark black, and had toyed with the idea of returning to using a kohl pencil around her eyes, goth-like. But that was from another lifetime. A time she'd shared with Jason before he'd been taken so cruelly away from her.

She turned into the shopping centre and headed for her favourite boutique, Jinx. They had advertised their autumn collection on Facebook, and she just had to have the leopard-print jeans.

The door was a tight squeeze with the stroller, but she was not going to leave her son outside. The second she entered, Louis opened his eyes and let out a squeal, then stretched out his hand and grabbed a white silk blouse from a hanger.

'Ah Louis, can you not give me two minutes to myself?'

'Is he a handful?' asked June, the sales girl.

'Sometimes. But most of the time he's good.' Katie knew June from their school days, and she welcomed speaking to someone her own age now and again.

'I thought you were going back to college?'

'I put it on hold again. It's so expensive, and then there's the childcare costs and the train fares. I don't know how I'd manage it.

I really need to get a job, but I'd still have childcare to pay for.' She laughed. 'Vicious circle.'

'He is so beautiful.' June tickled Louis under his chin.

'I know. I'm blessed really. That's what my gran says. She tells me that I should be grateful to have him when so many women can't have kids. And I am. Grateful, I mean. But sometimes … you know … it just gets too much for me.'

'Get a part-time job maybe. Here. Try this on,' June said, hanging the silk blouse on the door of the changing room. 'I'll keep an eye on the little lad. What's his name?'

'Louis.' Katie bit her lip. 'I'm not sure I want to try that. Do you still have the leopard-print jeans?'

June whisked them from a rack and hung them in the changing room with the blouse.

'Any special occasion?'

'My sister's eighteen next month and I was going to plan a surprise party for her. Haven't told my mam yet.'

June took Louis out of the stroller and shoved Katie towards the changing room. 'Try them on. They'd look great together.'

The cost didn't worry Katie too much. Louis' grandad sent her a monthly allowance for the baby's upkeep. Lottie didn't know about that because Tom Rickard had insisted Katie not tell her. Maybe she could ask him to pay for childcare. Now there was an idea.

June said, 'I'll leave the door open a little so you can see Louis.'

As she stepped into the cupboard-sized enclosure, Katie had a sudden feeling that someone was watching her. She looked towards the large plate-glass window of the shop but could only see people rushing around outside.

'June, I think someone out there is watching me,' she said.

'What? God give me strength.' June came and stood in front of the saloon-type fitting room door. 'Some people have no life.'

*

Bernie Kelly looked at the person who was watching Lottie Parker's daughter through the shop window. She ducked into the newsagent's doorway and smirked. Maybe she could get someone else to do her dirty work. That would be fun.

A shriek of excitement must have escaped her lips, because a young child who was walking along with his mother squealed. Bernie stuck out her tongue and laughed silently as the mother gripped her son's hand tighter and almost ran from the shopping centre. Maybe she needed to quieten down a little. It wasn't a good idea to draw attention to herself. But after twelve months locked up in a hospital for the criminally insane, there was something liberating about being out in the real world. And she had a mission.

Leaving the other person to their voyeurism, she pulled her hood up over her head and decided it was time to eat. She had no fear of being recognised. Well, maybe Lottie Parker would recognise her, but that didn't worry her at all. Not one iota. Because Lottie Parker was the endgame.

As she walked out of the shopping centre, she gave a quick glance up and down the pavement, just to be sure. Then she made her way slowly around the corner and into Fallon's pub. A hot whiskey would go down a treat.

CHAPTER 14

Boyd sat on the edge of Lottie's desk. 'So, we know Amy Whyte was involved in a case ten years ago. I don't think it's relevant.'

'Sit on the chair, Boyd.'

'Sorry.'

Lottie couldn't help the snarkiness in her voice. It stemmed from the twisting of her gut instinct. 'Something's wrong. I'm worried about both Amy and Penny. No one has seen either of them since Saturday night. Their phones are off. And there's no answer at Penny's apartment.'

'Her mother wasn't much help either,' Boyd said.

Lottie thought of the navy-suited woman they'd met at the council offices. Breda Brogan was efficient and to the point. She hadn't seen her daughter in over a week. Penny had her own place now. Did her own thing.

'We'll need to check out her apartment again.' Lottie looked out to the general office. 'Where's Kirby?'

'Talking to the Whyte's Pharmacy employees.'

'Jesus, it doesn't take a whole morning to talk to a couple of shop assistants. I hope he's not in the pub.'

'I'm here.' Kirby shoved his bushy-haired head around the door. 'Nothing to report, I'm afraid. But it was good to get talking to real people again.'

'And what are we?' Boyd said. 'Rhetorical question.'

Lottie asked, 'None of them know anything about where Amy might be?'

'No, boss.'

'Any arguments or rows?'

'All hunky-dory as far as I could gather, until about a month ago. The pharmacist mentioned there was a bit of trouble with Penny Brogan, and one of the assistants told me that Amy got her dad to fire Penny.'

'What did she do?'

'Pilfering.'

'Pilfering? That's an odd choice of word.'

'Stealing, then. Hiding stuff in her handbag. Cosmetics. Lipsticks and nail polish. Not drugs. Not as far as they knew, anyway.'

'And none of the staff know where Amy might be? A boyfriend that her dad doesn't know about? Come on, Kirby.'

'Sorry, boss. They appear to know nothing about her private life. Just that it was very unusual for her to miss work unless it was a Sunday. Everyone said she was dedicated.'

'Right so. Thanks.' Lottie leaned back in her chair and resisted the urge to slam her feet up on the desk. 'It's not yet forty-eight hours since the girls were last seen or heard from; once that deadline has passed, we need to publicise their disappearance.'

'I'll do that tomorrow, then,' Kirby said.

Once the detective had left with a visible bounce in his step, Lottie smiled over at Boyd. 'One man's misery is another man's joy.'

'What?'

'Nothing.'

Her mobile phone rang. She saw 'Mother' on the screen and handed the phone to Boyd.

'Tell her I'm not here. I went out and left my phone on the desk. Anything.'

Boyd answered it. Lottie straightened up in her chair as she saw the colour fade from his face.

'What? What is it, Boyd?'

She leaned across and took the phone from him.

'Oh no.'

*

The tunnel beneath Ragmullin courthouse reminded Conor Dowling of his time in prison, though at least there he had been warm and comfortable. Maybe it was his imagination, or he'd watched too many prisoner movies, but he sensed this was what a real jail should feel like.

He wasn't supposed to be down here. But he'd felt drawn to the darkness.

He inched back into the light and looked at the hollow shell of the old courthouse.

He felt lucky, in a way, that Tony Keegan had got him the labouring job, although he made sure to stay well out of Cyril Gill's way. Tony had told him that Gill knew who he was, and had still given him the job. That bothered Conor. Gill's daughter Louise was one of the reasons he'd been convicted ten years ago, so it was a mystery why her father had agreed to employ him. He wasn't going to ask questions, but it worried him nonetheless.

'What did you say?' Tony was lounging against the wall, trying to light a cigarette in the rain.

Conor hadn't realised he'd spoken aloud. 'Got one for me?'

'You don't smoke,' Tony said, the lighter clicking with no effect.

'Just shows how much you know about me.' Conor took a cigarette from Tony's pack and secreted it in his pocket. 'I'll keep this for Mother. She likes a smoke now and again.'

Tony succeeded in getting a light going on the plastic Bic, but before he could put the flame to the cigarette, Conor took his chance.

He snatched the cigarette, ground it under the heel of his boot and at the same time caught Tony by the throat.

'My mother might have allowed you to roam around our house while I was in prison, but that stops now. Do you hear me? I'm home, and things are different. *I'm* different. Being locked up for ten years did that to me. We might've had good times long ago, but not any more. So stay out of my face.'

A gurgle sounded in Tony's throat, but no words came out.

Conor let his hand fall away. 'Just don't mess me around.'

'Sure thing.' Tony clutched his reddening neck. 'We'd better get back to work. I'm not losing my job over you.' He tugged his beanie down over his ears and slapped his hard hat on top of it as he trudged through the muck away from Conor. 'And you can piss off, Dowling,' he muttered when he was sure he was out of earshot.

Conor took the cigarette out of his pocket and debated calling Tony back for a light. But then he caught sight of the guy standing outside the security hut, staring straight over at him.

'What are you looking at, shitface?'

Shoving his hand back into his pockets, Conor took off after Tony. He really didn't need to be drawing attention to himself. Not now that he was free. But was he really free?

With a backward glance at the entrance to the tunnel, he wondered about that conundrum. Freedom. What the hell was it, when you boiled it down? When your heart was tainted with the undying urge for revenge. It was something he had thought about for ten long years, and he had still to come up with a good answer.

*

Rose Fitzpatrick was sitting on a chair by the unlit stove. The kitchen was cold. Lottie flicked on a Dyson heater, a leaving present she'd bought for her mother, and pushed it in beside her.

'Why didn't you tell me straight away?' She dragged a chair from the table, pulled off her jacket and sat.

'I didn't know what to do. That man, Leo Belfield, he dredges up such painful memories, I just wanted him gone. But today I went over and over it in my head and I thought, I can't keep this to myself. What if he does something to you? What if he actually gets that wretched woman out of the asylum? What then, Lottie?'

'He can't do that.' Lottie hoped he couldn't. Having Bernie Kelly outside bars, or walls for that matter, was an option she had never considered. It was just over a year since her half-sister had been committed to the Central Mental Hospital on the grounds of insanity, rather than standing trial for multiple murders. Lottie still found it hard to believe that someone with her biological mother's blood flowing in her veins had succeeded in wiping out a family plus two drug dealers in such a horrific manner. She didn't want to have to dwell on the evil that had shrouded Ragmullin due to Bernie's actions. And though she had never admitted it, she recognised that the woman *was* evil, not insane.

'But Leo Belfield is a New York police captain. He told me so himself. He said he was taking her out on day release or something like that.' Rose rubbed her hands together so vigorously that Lottie thought she was going to draw blood any minute.

'Calm down.' Lottie wasn't used to seeing her mother like this. In a state. 'Did he leave a contact number?' She began scrolling through her phone. 'I think I have it somewhere.' Leo had hounded her last July, but they'd just lost Gilly and she'd only talked with him briefly. 'I thought he'd gone back to New York.'

'He said he's just arrived back in Ragmullin. Got the release organised from his own office. God knows who he's in cahoots with.'

'Must be someone high up the ranks to pull a stunt like this.' Lottie stopped scrolling. 'I can't find his number.'

'He left a card with his contact details. It's up on the shelf beside the coffee.'

Lottie fetched the card. NYPD logo on one side, with a host of numbers. She turned it over. A handwritten mobile number in blue ink.

'Are you going to call him?' Rose asked.

'You bet I am.' Lottie switched on the kettle. 'I'll make you tea first. You're as white as a ghost.'

Rose stood and walked to the counter. She put her hand over Lottie's. 'No need to be fussing over me. I'm just glad you know now. I haven't slept a wink the last few nights, worrying about what was the right thing to do.'

The leathery touch of her mother's skin on hers made Lottie pause. She looked into the older woman's eyes. She had wondered at one time why they were so different from her own. She'd found out the reason after the bloody encounter with Bernie Kelly in a dungeon under her maternal grandmother's house. Lottie had been fathered by Peter Fitzpatrick all right, but not with Rose. No, her biological mother was a poor demented young woman called Carrie King, who was also mother to three others. Two of whom were twins. Leo Belfield and Bernie Kelly. Carrie had died in St Declan's Asylum, and now Bernie was awaiting a similar fate. That was until Leo Belfield had started snooping about, trying to unravel his family history.

'You were right to tell me. I just need to put the lid back on this can of worms before something terrible happens.'

'Good girl, Lottie. But be careful. You still carry the physical wounds that woman inflicted on you.'

Lottie hadn't the heart to remind Rose that the emotional scars ran much deeper.

She made the tea, gave a mug to Rose and sipped her own before throwing it down the sink. The world that had been so bright and hopeful this morning had suddenly turned dark and menacing.

*

Louise Gill pulled off her clothes and slipped into fleecy pyjamas.
The legs had shrunk a bit in the wash, so she rooted in a drawer and
found a pair of multicoloured fluffy socks.

Suitably comfortable, she lay down on her bed and flicked
through Instagram on her phone. A message appeared.

'Go away, Cristina,' she mumbled, and swiped the message up
and off the screen. She didn't want another argument. There was
no way she was telling her father about them. Not if she wanted to
remain under the comfort of his luxurious roof.

She didn't know whether to love or hate her father. He put on
the public persona of an upstanding citizen. Parading to Mass on
Sunday; donating to the right charities; smiling for the camera. But
at home he was the boss of Louise and her mother. What he said
was gospel, and none of it was in any Bible Louise had ever read.
He had set about moulding her since she was fourteen years old,
and she was certain he had something far more damning to hide
than she had now.

With nothing catching her interest on Instagram, she got out her
laptop. Maybe doing a little work would help her relax. Getting into
the minds of killers was sobering.

CHAPTER 15

Lottie tried calling Leo Belfield every fifteen minutes. No answer. Wherever he was, he wasn't answering his phone. The rest of the day was filled with budget reports she had to prepare. By the time she left for home, there was still no word of the missing girls.

She'd invited Boyd round for dinner, and when he'd cleared the dishes away, he poured her a sparkling water and sat on the couch beside her. The house was gloriously quiet. Katie had gone to bed when Louis fell asleep after being out in the fresh air most of the day. Sean and Chloe were doing homework in their rooms. At least she hoped they were.

'Everything was going too well, Boyd,' she said. 'I just knew it. When I woke up this morning, I was content with life, even though a slight feeling of foreboding was settling on my shoulders.'

'Don't be so melodramatic. Now I know where your kids get it from.' Boyd casually placed his feet on the coffee table before Lottie patted his leg.

'Take them down. That's a new table.'

'I know. I put it together.' He drained his glass. 'I'd better get home. I want to do a half-hour on my turbo bike before bed.'

She turned towards him. 'Is my company that bad?'

'Not at all. But I think you need to put that phone away and stop worrying about Leo Belfield and his sister.'

'They're *my* brother and sister too.'

'Only in name. You don't *know* them. You've hardly met them.'

'I've been close enough to Bernie to feel the stab of steel in my flesh.'

'That was a year ago and she's been locked up. Stop fretting.' Boyd stood, and Lottie could see irritation written in the hard line of his jaw.

She shoved the phone between two cushions. 'I'll walk you to the door.'

She followed him out and waited as he shuffled into his jacket.

'I'm sorry, Lottie. I didn't mean to be ratty. Thanks for dinner, by the way. My turn next time.'

She smiled wryly. 'So there will be a next time then?'

'Of course. Go to bed. Shut off the phone. Stop worrying.'

She felt the soft caress of his lips on her cheek and a warmth filled her abdomen. She wanted to reach out, to pull him to her and then drag him back to the couch. But instead she opened the door and waved him to his car. 'Another time, Boyd,' she whispered to the rainy night.

Closing the door, she rushed back to the sofa and grabbed her phone. Still no reply from Leo. She'd try his number once more, and then she was doing as Boyd had instructed her. Hopefully she'd get some sleep.

Just as she turned out the light and headed for the stairs, she heard Louis screech in wakefulness.

Then again, maybe sleep was a little way off yet.

*

Freddie Nealon turned round to find his friend Brian McGrath pissing on the overgrown grass. He was so out of it, he couldn't say anything. They'd spent hours sitting on the canal bank drinking beer and smoking weed, and were both drenched and cold. There were six houses on Petit Lane, five of which were derelict. Freddie staggered up to the middle one and pushed open the door.

'This doesn't look like your house, Freddie.' Brian followed him inside. Maybe he wasn't as far gone as Freddie had thought. At least he could get the words around his tongue and out of his mouth.

A flicker of light cast a shadow along the torn wallpaper.

Freddie jumped. 'Fucksakeyou … you … fuckyou …' He saw Brian looking down at the lighter in his hand, and at the scorched black glove in his other. 'Shit, fuck, shit.'

Darkness returned.

'Where the fuck are we?' Brian pushed back his hood and attempted to flick on the lighter again. No luck. He threw it on the ground. 'Wait, man. Wait up.' He put a hand to his ear in dramatic fashion and pulled Freddie backwards. 'Listen up. Shit, did you hear that?'

'Wha'?' Freddie said.

'A noise. Upstairs.'

'Can't hear nothing with you mouthing. Give us a can and a light.'

Brian bent down to find the lighter, but it was too dark to see anything. He rooted around in the plastic bag trying to extract a can to placate his spaced-out friend. He stopped. 'You hear it that time?'

'Hear what?' Freddie said. 'I just want a light and a piss.'

'Shh. It's like footsteps. Come on, Freddie, I'm getting out of here.'

As Freddie turned around, a constellation of stars burst behind his eyes. In the same moment, he saw Brian already in a heap at his feet. That was when he realised that someone had thumped him on the back of his head. As he sank to the floor, a second blow came, and blackness descended.

*

The light bulb flickered, once, twice, then went out. Megan Price dropped her bag on the hall floor and cursed loudly.

'For pity's sake. Not tonight, please.'

She kicked the bag under the hall table and picked up her post. In the living room, she switched on the lamp. At least that worked. She slumped into her armchair, pressed the recliner and lay back, staring around at the empty space. Her arsehole of a husband – no, scratch that, her *ex*-husband – had taken almost everything. Said he'd paid for it, he was entitled to it. Well, no shit, Sherlock, she'd told him. Wrong move, Megan. He'd filed papers with his solicitor to get her to sell the house. He wanted money. She was fighting him like her life depended on it, mainly because he was just a greedy creep. And now he'd sent her another solicitor's letter. Crumpling it up, she stuffed it down the side of the chair.

Closing her eyes, she let the events of the day wash over her. Penny Brogan had been fired because she was stealing from the shop. But why was Amy Whyte still friends with her? They were a world apart in class. Not that Megan was a snob. But all the same, it rankled with her. Maybe it was because her ex-husband was a step below *her* in class. Make that a complete ladder, she thought.

He was going to pay for making her life one big shit bowl. Then she thought of the nice detective she'd spoken with today. He was kind of cute in a sad sort of way. Maybe things wouldn't be so bad after all.

CHAPTER 16

It was still dark outside when Conor Dowling rolled off his bed and got dressed on Tuesday morning. He bundled up yesterday's work clothes to put in the washing machine, then brushed his teeth and splashed cold water on his face. Running a hand over his shaved pate, he knew there was nothing he could do to remove the extra years ingrained around his eyes.

There was no sound from the living room, which his mother still used as her sleeping space. She was welcome to it, he thought, as he loaded the washing machine and went to scoop some powder out of the box. A few wayward grains settled in the bottom of the scoop.

Oh God! He'd have to buy washing powder. With nothing else for it, he switched on the machine without any detergent.

'Conor, is that you?'

'Who else did you think would be in this dump at this hour of the morning?'

'What did you say?'

Conor shook his head. He was speaking his thoughts out loud all the time now. Was he going demented? Maybe it was in his genes after all.

'I'm putting on toast. Do you want some?' he shouted back.

'Toast? I want a bowl of porridge. Make it with milk. Don't like that stuff you pour water on top of.'

He knew they had no milk. He boiled the kettle. Tipped a tub of ready-made porridge into a bowl. She'd never know the difference, he thought. Even if she did, he didn't care.

As the kettle settled into a slow whine, he stared out at his shed, and wondered again why Tony had needed to invade his workspace.

*

Chloe Parker hated going to school, even though it was her final year. She would much rather continue working at the pub. She'd enjoyed her summer job at Fallon's, but because she had a dictator for a mother, she'd had to give it up to don her hideous school uniform and head back through the gates of hell. She was so looking forward to the mid-term break.

She kicked an empty Coke can ahead of her, grumbling beneath her breath.

'What did you say?' Sean switched his heavy rucksack of school books from one shoulder to the other.

Chloe looked at her brother. He was a good head taller than her, and his blonde hair and blue eyes broke her heart every time she looked at him. He was the image of their dead dad.

'I was just thinking that Katie has all the luck,' she said.

'I don't think that's fair,' Sean said.

'Why not, dope?' She connected with the can once again and sent it skidding from the footpath out onto the road under a car.

'Well, for one, her boyfriend was murdered. For two, he left her pregnant. Three, she had to give up college to care for Louis, and now he's getting to be a handful.'

Chloe had to agree that Louis was a bundle of beautiful trouble, but she wasn't giving in that easily. 'Remember what Granny always says. "Every cloud has a silver lining."'

'I don't follow you.' Sean sighed and yawned.

Chloe felt anger growing in her chest. He wasn't even listening to her. No one listened to her any more. Properly listened, like.

'Katie uses Louis as her excuse for everything. Twisting every situation to suit herself. She has Mam and Gran fawning over her with sympathy.'

'You're just jealous.' Sean swallowed a snort.

'Feck off, Sean Parker.' Chloe kicked up wet leaves and walked on ahead of him.

He said, 'You have to make a drama out of everything.'

As they reached Chloe's school gates, Sean went to carry on towards his own. Grabbing his arm, pulling him to a halt, she said, 'Wait a minute.'

He stopped, looking nervously around at the swarms of girls strolling through the gates.

Chloe said, 'She gets to skive off college.'

'Who?'

'Katie, you moron.' Chloe rolled her eyes. Shit, her PMS was brutal this month. She didn't want to start bawling in front of her brother. He was two years younger than her and probably the most sensible of them all, when he wasn't depressed. They really were an odd family.

'Look, Chloe, I think she really wants to go back to college. It's just that with Mam working and Gran getting on, she has no one to take care of Louis. Think of it from Katie's point of view. She's twenty-one years old and stuck at home with a baby.'

'That's just because she doesn't push herself outside of her comfort zone. She could get Louis' grandad to pay for childcare. He's rolling in dollars. No, she's a lazy bitch.'

Sean took a step back. 'You *are* jealous. You need to wake up. And I need to get to school. See you later.'

Standing at the corner of the lane that led up by the canal, a shortcut to Sean's school, Chloe blew out a breath of frustration. As she turned to enter the school gates, she felt uneasy. It was as if someone was breathing down her neck, causing the tiny hairs to stand to attention.

She swirled around on her heel, scanning over the heads of the girls rushing to make it inside before the bell, staring after Sean's loping figure disappearing into the distance. Then, shaking her shoulders, she slipped her rucksack of school books down to her hand and, biting the inside of her lip, walked slowly through the gates. She was late, but she didn't care about that.

For the rest of the day, she couldn't shake off the feeling. And by the time school was over, she had her skin scratched red raw.

*

At the reception desk in Ragmullin garda station, Garda Tom Thornton flicked through last night's call-out list. He was old enough to remember a time on the force when you could read the local newspaper, eat a sandwich, drink a mug of coffee and even smoke a cigarette at your desk.

He'd often been paired with Gilly O'Donoghue, and he missed the young guard's smile and the way she looked at Detective Kirby over her freckled nose. She'd been a breath of fresh air in an otherwise stale station. At least her murderer had been apprehended.

Looking up as the station door opened, he realised that things had been too quiet. Ragmullin didn't do quiet, he thought. He caught a whiff of Old Spice and was surprised to see a tiny woman tapping the counter.

Putting on his sweetest smile, the one his wife of thirty years could see through straight away, Thornton said, 'What can I help you with this fine morning, Mrs Loughlin?'

'Have you been outside yet, young man? It's pissing out of the heavens.'

Garda Thornton was a bit taken aback by the eighty-year-old's language, but he kept the smile in place. 'So it is,' he said, peering over her shoulder through the reinforced-glass door.

'Now, young man, I want you to come with me. There's been a lot of disturbances at Petit Lane lately. Druggies and junkies, or whatever the PC term is nowadays. All hours. Making a racket. Banging on walls. Shouting and singing. You'll need your coat. Come on, now.'

Thornton watched as the old lady turned and headed for the door. 'Mrs Loughlin? I can't go with you. I'm on desk duty.'

'I'm sure the desk can mind itself.' Her brows knitted into a scowl. 'And if not, get someone else to take care of it. I'm not leaving this another minute. You have to do something.'

'Did you try the council?'

A loud laugh filled the reception area and Mrs Loughlin hammered her long umbrella against the floor. 'The council? Are you making a joke of me? That shower wouldn't listen to Jesus himself if he came down off the cross and walked into their fancy new offices looking for a glass of water and a pair of trousers.'

*

Lottie felt refreshed after her morning shower, despite a night of disturbed sleep. Louis was coming down with a cold, and her fingers still smelled of Vicks VapoRub. She searched her bag for a pack of tissues and came up with baby wipes.

As her computer screen blinked to life, she eyed her detectives out in the main office. Kirby looked like he'd slept in his suit, but then he always looked like that, didn't he? She'd have to keep a close eye on him. Boyd was at the filing cabinet, taking files from a box on the floor and sorting them into the drawer. She felt a slow smile creep in at the corner of her lips. She liked the feeling he was giving her. Then she thought of Leo Belfield, and the smile slipped quickly from her face. She had to get to the bottom of what he was up to. Why wasn't he answering his phone? For a few weeks during the summer he had plagued her with calls. But now he was uncontactable. A cold shiver of warning slithered down her spine. Something wasn't right. Her gut was telling her, and her gut was never wrong. Or almost never. Then she remembered Amy Whyte and Penny Brogan.

'Kirby?' she called through the open door. 'Any word on the two girls?' His eyes were bloodshot and his hair was badly in need of a cut, or a wash at least.

'Nothing new on the system. Will I put it out on social media now?'

Lottie sighed. She stuffed the baby wipes back into her bag and went to his desk. The screen quickly flicked to black as his index finger clicked the mouse.

'Are you with us, Kirby?'

'Of course. Just a little slow this morning. Didn't get much sleep last night.'

'You and me both,' Lottie said.

'Why not?' Boyd turned round, sleeves rolled up, files in both hands.

'Louis has a cold.'

Her phone vibrated in her jeans pocket. 'That could be Katie. I told her to let me know if she has to bring Louis to the doctor.'

Back in her office, she checked the phone.

A message. But not from Katie. From Leo Belfield. *Meet at one o'clock. Joyce Hotel.*

*

Garda Tom Thornton had realised Mrs Loughlin was not going to listen to any excuses. He managed to bribe someone to cover the desk, then pulled on his heavy hi-vis jacket. By the time they reached

Petit Lane, he was soused in sweat. For an old lady, she sure could walk quickly, he thought.

'This is where I live.' Mrs Loughlin pointed out the first house in the boarded-up terrace. 'The others sold up like rats, and now look at the place. The economic crash put paid to the building plans.'

Thornton looked. He walked by here most days on his way to and from work, and knew the history of the developer pulling out and leaving the council with egg on their faces, but he'd never given the terrace a second thought.

He pushed open the gate of the house next door to Mrs Loughlin's, and noticed she was standing out on the pavement scowling.

'Not that one, the next one down,' she said.

'This one?' Thornton moved to the third house in the row. It appeared even more derelict than the one beside the old lady's.

'I heard a noise last night,' she said. 'Not that I don't hear it most nights. It's just lads, and I know they mean no harm. Probably sheltering from the rain. I saw two of them, with hoodies up over their heads, arms full of plastic bags. Beer, I'd say. They were falling through the gate, dragging each other up to the door. One even had a wee in the garden.'

'Why didn't you ring it in?'

'I'm blue in the face ringing these things in to you lot. I'm beginning to think you're as bad as the council.'

'So why call in this morning?'

'The thing is, I saw two people go in, but only one came out. Unusual, wouldn't you say?'

'Right so.' Thornton pushed his peaked cap back on his head and knocked on the door.

'It's open. How else do the junkies get in?' Mrs Loughlin's voice was laced with derision. 'Go on. In you go.'

'Did you enter the premises?'

'Do you think I'm stupid? I don't want to be leaving my DNA in there. What if there was a murder or something? You'd be knocking on my door mighty quick then, wouldn't you?'

Thornton's head was beginning to thump. He made sure his gloves were firmly in place and pushed open the door.

The smell wasn't as bad as he'd been expecting, but there was a distinct fustiness emanating from the walls. The hallway was dim, lit only from the outside via the open door behind him. He chanced a look over his shoulder and noticed that Mrs Loughlin had retreated to the rusty gate. Taking another step inside, he felt his boots sticking to something. Oil? Or something more human? He shuddered and moved forward.

That was when he saw two figures lying at the foot of the stairs. He leaned over the first one. As he put a gloved finger to the throat, the eyes flashed open. Thornton jumped back against the wall.

'Jesus Christ. I thought you were dead. What happened? Are you okay?'

He got a groan in reply. Moving to the second figure, he heard the moan before his fingers were in place. He was ready for the eyes to open, but they didn't. At least both lads were alive. He'd have to check for injuries.

Then the smell reached him.

CHAPTER 17

The sirens wailed as the ambulances carried the two lads off to hospital.

'Told you something funny was going on,' Mrs Loughlin said, folding her arms and leaning on the wet wall.

'So you did.' Garda Thornton couldn't get the sickly smell out of his nostrils. He itched to get back to the station and maybe find time to grab a quick shower.

'Fancy a cuppa?' she said.

'That'd be grand, but I have to get back to the desk.'

'The desk isn't going to run away, is it?'

'No, it won't, but I have a job to do.' Thornton looked up at the house and was struck by a recollection. 'Mrs Loughlin, you said you saw two people go in and only one come out.'

'I did,' she said. Then she opened her mouth in a perfect O. 'Someone else must have been in there. Someone who attacked those two poor boys before running off.'

'Go put that kettle on,' Thornton said. 'I'm going to have another quick look inside.'

'Here, take my umbrella.'

He laughed. 'I'll be grand.'

As the old lady headed towards her home, Thornton moved up the footpath to the door of the derelict house. Was this more than two lads falling out over a bag of weed or a can of beer?

Up the stairs he went, and as he climbed, the odour became more pungent and fetid.

He knew it was not just dry rot he could smell. It was something rotting all right, but also metallic. Blood, he thought, though not the blood from downstairs. It was up here, and he wasn't at all sure he wanted to find the source. But he had to see for himself.

When he did, he plucked his radio from his uniform and, with a trembling voice, called the station.

*

Lottie zipped up her protective suit and fastened the ties of the mouth mask behind her ears. Then she followed Boyd's long, lean figure under the crime-scene tape.

'Why can't people discover murder victims on a fine day?' he said. She didn't bother answering him, knowing it was a rhetorical question. As she passed him, he added, 'And they could pick warmer and drier places to be found.'

'Boyd, will you shut up?'

Lottie dipped her head under the lintel, careful not to brush up against the door, which was hanging precariously from a single hinge. The weather-beaten wood bore evidence that there had once been a lock and a handle, but they were no longer there.

'What were those lads doing in here anyway?' Boyd continued, his voice like a sharp breeze on the back of her neck. She'd pinned her hair up this morning, disguising the fact that it was overdue a cut and colour. She pulled up the white hood. He was still talking. 'This is no place for youngsters. What age do you think they are?'

'Who?'

'The two lads that Thornton found.'

'How would I know that?'

She sighed loudly and trudged up the wooden stairs, her protective booties snagging on the worn timber. In the time since Garda Thornton had called in the incident, uniforms had trampled all over the scene, one even vomiting in a corner of the landing, before they had realised the area needed to be preserved and the scene-of-crime officers called in. She would deal with the aftermath of their ineptitude in due course, but first she had to assess everything for herself.

The house was one of a terrace of six. She knew this area had been earmarked for urban development years ago, with plans for retail units and a paved pedestrian area linking to new council offices. The offices, which looked like a giant aquarium, were the only thing that had been built. The terraced houses were slap bang in the centre of the plans, but something had happened to stall the project, and Mrs Loughlin had stubbornly refused to uproot herself.

Lottie paused at the top of the wooden stairs and noticed the activity in the room to her left. She took a step towards it. In front of her was a bathroom with all its fittings plundered and removed, pipes standing forlornly from raised floorboards and the window boarded up. Two SOCOs were hunched over what she presumed was the body, lying where once a bath had stood. The stench of vomit at the doorway rose to her nostrils and she found that perversely it drowned out the smell of putrid flesh. Crime-scene tape hung across the doorway of another room to her right. She squeezed into the bathroom, leaving Boyd outside.

'Hello, Detective Inspector Parker.' Jim McGlynn, SOCO team leader, turned his head for a fraction of a second, and in that moment she witnessed the victim. Immediately she sympathised with the uniformed officer who had deposited his breakfast on the landing.

'Jim,' she said, barely daring to look at the carnage. 'Tell me what we have here?'

'Female. Deceased at least two days. Possibly longer. Good job the weather's been so miserable, or there'd be more than one officer chucking up his guts.'

'No need to be so crass,' she said.

'Just telling it how it is. And he should be reprimanded. He could have destroyed evidence.'

'How did she die?' Despite herself, Lottie couldn't keep her eyes off the body lying face down on the floor. A dark hand curled around her spine and clawed into her chest to clamp her heart.

'Stab wound to the throat,' McGlynn said.

The words sent a shiver through Lottie. Just last July, young Gilly O'Donoghue had been viciously stabbed in a similar way.

McGlynn continued. 'A lot of blood. I reckon the killer must have been saturated in it. Unless he came prepared.'

Lottie focused on the victim. Blinked once and allowed herself to print the image on her brain. She struggled to get the words out of her mouth, needing to say them out loud so that it all made sense.

'Dressed for a nightclub. Jomo's is just around the corner,' she said. 'Maybe she was coming from there and some psycho picked her up.' A diamond heart stud earring was hanging loose from the victim's ear, and Lottie had to stop herself from reaching out to twist it back in place. She knew who the victim was. 'Sexual assault?'

'Not evident externally. Underwear is intact, but the post-mortem will tell you conclusively.'

Her hands trembled. Recently she'd become more and more affected by the work carried out by the state pathologist, Doctor Jane Dore, in the morgue. It must be my age, she thought.

The victim's toenails were painted with crimson nail polish and her legs were smeared with fake tan. Lottie could see, beneath the hardened blood, that the girl's hair was dark brown.

'Turn her over,' she instructed McGlynn.

'We should wait for the state pathologist.'

'I said turn her over.' She hadn't meant to sound angry, but she needed to be one hundred per cent sure.

As McGlynn and his assistant carefully turned the body, Lottie felt a gasp lodge in the back of her throat.

Even though the face had begun to bloat, stark eyeshadow and black eyebrow pencil accentuated the victim's features in death. Averting her eyes, she scanned the immediate area, looking for the weapon. As she did so, she caught sight of something shiny beneath the girl's right hand.

'Stop!' she said. 'Don't move.'

'What?' McGlynn held both hands in the air.

'Tweezers?'

He handed her a pair. She squeezed in beside him and nodded for his assistant to take photos as she lifted the victim's hand in her own gloved one. On the ground lay a silver coin. Once the photographer had finished, she picked it up with the tweezers and held it to the light.

'What do you think it is?' she asked McGlynn.

He shook his head. 'No idea. It's not currency.'

'Just plain silver, no engraving,' she added. 'About the size of a one-euro coin.'

She dropped the coin into a clear plastic evidence bag held out for her by McGlynn. With a Sharpie marker, he scribbled a code and details on the bag and handed it over to his assistant.

'Looks like it was dropped after the girl was killed. No blood on top of it.'

'Any sign of a phone or handbag?' Lottie looked around the small room. The space seemed to close in on her as the fetid air clogged her throat.

'No handbag,' McGlynn said, lifting the girl's hand once again to inspect her balled fist. 'That's a phone in there. But I daren't remove it yet.'

'Why not?' Lottie asked.

'Got in trouble before, with you know who.' He laid the hand back on the ground.

Lottie knew he was talking about Jane Dore. As a result of decentralisation by the government, she was based about forty kilometres away, at Tullamore Hospital, where she conducted post-mortems.

'Is she on her way?'

'Later today, hopefully. She's attending the High Court in Dublin this morning. Giving evidence in a case.'

So much for decentralisation, Lottie thought. 'The minute you find any evidence, let me know. And give me a call once Jane arrives. I want that phone from the victim's hand.'

'Right, and I've yet to examine the second body,' he said.

Lottie stared at the back of McGlynn's hooded head. She had been so consumed with the discovery of Amy Whyte that she'd forgotten about the second victim.

'In the other room,' he said, and kept on working, measuring, lifting and probing.

Lottie edged out backwards and stood with Boyd on the cramped landing. After a moment, she moved towards the crime-scene tape at the entrance to the other room. She looked in and couldn't stop her hand flying to her mouth to stifle the groan.

This female body was also lying face down. At first glance, Lottie could see that the feet had no shoes or sandals, and were filthy. The legs were streaked with fake tan and the black dress was short and rumpled around the buttocks. She couldn't see any blood on the legs, but as she scanned the outstretched arms and the hands with their long acrylic nails, she noticed the pool of blood beneath the head of matted brown hair. A mobile phone lay beside the body, redundant with a cracked screen.

'Have you been in here?' she shouted back at McGlynn.

'Just did a quick exam. Don't go in,' he warned.

'I need to see her.'

'And I'm saying wait until the state pathologist gets here.'

Lottie looked helplessly at Boyd. He shrugged and turned back to McGlynn. 'Jim, give us two minutes. Come on, we need to see her.'

McGlynn grunted and put down his tools, then changed his gloves and moved out to the landing. He was shaking his head as he undid the tape and entered the room.

'This young woman is around the same age as the other, and was killed in a similar manner. Stab wound to the neck.' He pointed to the walls. 'Plenty of arterial spray, so she was standing when he struck. I'd say he was behind her, holding her, and drew a sharp object, possibly a knife, across her throat. One cut. That's all it took. She died quickly.'

'And how long has she been dead?'

'Same as the other girl. Two, maybe three days. But we'll know more once the post-mortem is conducted.'

'Can I move her?'

'No.'

'But you did,' Lottie said, crouching down beside the SOCO.

'I had to determine that she was dead.'

'Just for a second. I want to see if there's anything under the body.'

'There isn't.'

'Humour me.'

He sighed and carefully turned the body to one side. Lottie flinched. The girl was not much older than Katie, and that thought sent a shiver down her spine. Her open eyes were brown, but the whites were speckled with bloodied dots and the lips were frozen in a scream.

'I don't see any coins,' Boyd said from the doorway.

Lottie scanned the floor around the girl's body. Ripped-up floorboards. Broken bottles and dead woodlice. 'You got a flashlight?'

McGlynn fetched one from his case and shone the beam around the area where the body was lying.

'There!' Lottie kneeled down beside him, the boards sharp against her knees, and pointed to a spot directly below where the girl's hand had been. 'Two coins.'

'Tweezers!' McGlynn yelled, and his assistant rushed in with them. After photographs had been taken, he picked up the coins and held each one aloft for examination before dropping them into individual bags and marking the area with evidence numbers.

'Same as the coin with the other victim,' Lottie said. 'Too much of a coincidence to think they were here prior to the attack on the girls. The killer left them here.'

'That's a huge assumption,' McGlynn said.

'Look at them,' she said, pointing to the bags. 'They're spotless. No rust or discoloration.'

'No engravings or markings, though. Some sort of talisman, perhaps?'

'Maybe the girls had them with them,' Boyd offered.

'Possible,' Lottie said, but she didn't believe that. 'I think they're the killer's calling card.'

McGlynn interjected. 'I've work to do before the state pathologist arrives. If you don't mind, I'd like to get on with it.'

'And no handbags or identification for either victim.' Lottie ran a gloved finger over her forehead. 'That seems calculated. Boyd, organise a contingent to do a fingertip search of the surrounding area, gardens, bins and the car park.'

'Those handbags are long gone,' Boyd said, folding his arms.

'Just get it done.'

Lottie gave the victim one last look, then pushed out past Boyd and stood on the landing trying to get some air into her lungs. But they just filled up with the damp, musty air, like a mixture of mushrooms and death.

'We need to interview those two lads Thornton found earlier,' Boyd said.

'I doubt they had anything to do with this, but once they get medical clearance, we'll see what they have to say for themselves. First off, the victims have to be formally identified.' She looked around the small space. 'But you and I both know that those two girls are Amy Whyte and Penny Brogan.'

'We have to inform the families,' Boyd said with a groan.

Lottie pictured Councillor Richard Whyte and shivered. It was going to be nasty.

She paused, thinking. 'This has the air of planning about it. The killer knew about this place. He probably staked it out, so every inch of it has to be examined minutely.'

As she walked slowly down the stairs, she was still trying to catch her breath.

'You okay?' Boyd said behind her.

Shaking her head, she jumped down the last two steps and stepped out through the front door. Outside, she pulled down the hood of her suit and gasped in a lungful of fresh air. The rain had eased to a misty drizzle.

A crowd had gathered beyond the front wall; among them she glimpsed Cynthia Rhodes, a crime reporter with national television.

'She's all I need,' she croaked.

'Want me to have a word with her?' Boyd asked.

'It's okay. I'll give her a no comment.'

'Perhaps you should be polite and make an appeal for witnesses?'

Lottie ignored him. Beyond the inner cordon, she pulled off her protective clothing, bundling it into a brown paper bag held out by a SOCO, and marched over to the wall. The feeling of unease that Cynthia always generated in her knotted her shoulders together. The reporter had a way of causing her to spout the wrong words, so she silently warned herself to form her sentences fully in her head before she spoke.

'Detective Inspector Parker,' Cynthia shouted, pushing a damp microphone under her nose. 'Can you tell us what's going on here this morning?'

Seeing the camera being swung in her direction, Lottie squared her shoulders. She had to make herself look in control of the situation while her mind was whirring in a myriad of directions.

'Thank you for coming out in this terrible weather. Two bodies have been found in suspicious circumstances in the house behind me. I'd like to ask the public if they have any information in relation to this crime to contact our helpline or phone Ragmullin garda station. All information will be treated with the utmost confidentiality.'

Even as she spoke, Lottie didn't believe her own words. It was impossible to keep anything confidential in Ragmullin.

'Can you tell us anything about the victims? Who are they?' Cynthia persisted.

'As I said, I welcome the public's help in this matter. If anyone is aware of any inappropriate activity in the area over the last week or two, they should contact us.'

'Do you think one of them could be Councillor Whyte's daughter? She's been reported missing. I read an alert before I arrived here.' Cynthia's black curls clung damply to her forehead and her dark-rimmed spectacles were misted.

Lottie fought an urge to thump the reporter. Cynthia was always one step ahead of her. Perhaps it was her own fault for allowing

Kirby to go ahead with the social media appeal for information on the missing girls.

'This is no time for speculation, Ms Rhodes.' She forced steadiness into her words. 'Think of the families who have yet to be informed. Thank you.'

She caught up with Boyd at the car. 'Let's get out of here before I slap the puss off her.'

'She's only doing her job.' The tyres skidded on the greasy road as he drove up to Main Street.

'You have a soft spot for her, don't you?' Lottie sniped.

'I'm not even going to grace that comment with a response.'

She looked out of the rain-smeared window at the shops. Boyd sped up the street and in two minutes had parked at the rear of the station. She was out of the car before him and rushed inside.

Kirby was slouched over his keyboard.

'You could have held off on the social media appeal.' Shit, why had she said that?

Kirby looked crestfallen. 'What? You ordered me to go ahead. How was I to know they were already dead?'

'Sorry. It's just an awkward situation. I didn't mean to take it out on you.'

Once she was in her own office, she hung up her damp jacket and sat at her desk musing over the problem of Kirby. She had to get him involved in this case but she needed him focused. With Maria Lynch on maternity leave and no one to replace her, Lottie's resources were limited. And now she had two murders to investigate.

She glanced up as Boyd divested himself of his own jacket before sitting at his desk. There was a history of infrequent liaisons between them and he had once asked her for a commitment she couldn't give. Her mother thought she should. But then Rose was old-fashioned and didn't see how Lottie could sleep with Boyd now and again without any formal arrangement. Ah well, Rose would have a long wait if she thought she was going to be walking her daughter up the aisle any time soon. And anyway, Lottie wasn't even her biological daughter! That made her think of Leo Belfield. There was no way she could leave now to follow up on a matter that was strictly private.

Her computer pinged with an email containing photos from the crime scene. Something to start on. Kicking herself into action, she jumped up. 'Incident room. Let's get this investigation up and running.'

And then she remembered they had yet to tell the parents.

CHAPTER 18

Tony was ignoring Conor, giving him a wide berth. Conor didn't want to care, but he did.

'What's the sour face for?' he said.

Tony stopped and turned. 'You. That's why. It's because I put in a good word for you that you got this job, and you repay me by almost choking the life out of me.' He rubbed his dirty gloved hand around his neck, leaving muddy streaks behind.

'I was just having a laugh, that's all. Don't be such a dickhead. I've enough of that shite at home without having no one to talk to here. Come on. Pint after work? What do you say?' Conor wrapped his arm around Tony's shoulder, but was shrugged away.

He watched the changing expressions on Tony's face as he struggled within himself to stand his ground, to say no. But Conor knew Tony well; he would give in. Hopefully he could squeeze him to pay for the pints too.

'Okay. First round's on you,' Tony said.

He'd have to come up with a plan. At least Tony was talking. That was something.

'Where are we scheduled to work next? Not the tunnel, I hope. That place reminds me of prison.'

Tony laughed and Conor followed him as they made their way to the foreman to get their orders for the day. Phase one of his plan had worked.

*

The incident room smelled of body odour and fried takeout food. Lottie sniffed the air; despite the smell, it was much fresher than the abandoned house at Petit Lane where two young women had met their deaths. She walked to the first board and pinned up prints of the photographs that had been emailed to her.

'Shouldn't we notify next of kin?' Boyd said. 'We need positive IDs.'

'Let's just go through all this quickly first.' She knew she was putting off the inevitable, but she didn't want to face either parent just yet. Perhaps McMahon would do the job, seeing that he was so well in with the councillor.

'I believe the victims to be Amy Whyte and Penny Brogan. Only Amy was officially reported missing, but nobody's seen Penny for a few days. I've seen photos of both young women and I'm confident they are the two deceased. So far, we know they were last seen on Saturday night at Jomo's nightclub. Going by the attire their bodies are still dressed in, it's likely they were abducted shortly after they left the club. We need the security footage from Jomo's, Kirby, and try to get a list of those who attended.'

'I've been there on the odd occasion,' Kirby said. Lottie noticed him blush. 'With Gilly.' He swallowed down a gulp.

'Go on,' Lottie said, encouraging him. 'Do you remember anything that might help us?'

'It was over six months ago. If memory serves me correctly, most of the clientele were years younger than me. Anything from sixteen upwards. Loud music and plenty of booze, and I'm sure a plethora of drugs. But nothing stood out as particularly sinister.'

Garda Tom Thornton put up his hand. 'Friday and Saturday nights are our busiest here in town. The usual rows at two or three in the morning as the clubs begin to empty and the crowds spill out.

Drunk and disorderly, mainly. With so many people around, I can't see how the girls could have been abducted without being seen.'

'I spoke to one of their friends, Ducky Reilly,' Lottie said. 'He says that Amy left first and Penny about a half-hour after her. Before the club finished up.' With a shudder she remembered that her daughters had been there Saturday night also. 'But both victims ended up murdered in the same place. Kirby, canvass the streets around the club and see what security tapes you can pick up.'

Boyd said, 'We have no evidence they were taken Saturday night, though.'

'True. But we have to start somewhere.'

'If you're making your assumption based on their clothing, it's possible they may have gone on to a party somewhere.'

'They may have done a lot of things, but my gut tells me that Saturday night/Sunday morning is our best bet, and I—'

A sharp grunt at the back of the room caused her words to stall in her mouth. Shit, she hadn't seen McMahon enter.

'Your gut isn't always right, is it?' The acting superintendent strode towards her, buttoning up his jacket over his neatly ironed white shirt. He swiped his fringe away from his eyes and turned to face the room.

Lottie felt her skin bristle, and clenched her fists so tightly, her nails cut into the palms of her hands.

'Sir?' she said. 'I'm the senior investigating officer on this case and I can fill you in once this briefing is over.'

He didn't turn around to face her, but she sensed his dismissal of her as his shoulders broadened and his back straightened.

'Councillor Richard Whyte is a very important member of this community,' he began, his strong Dublin accent cutting through the room. 'I want every hour you can possibly give to finding out who killed his daughter. The poor man is devastated and—'

'What?' Lottie tugged his sleeve, forcing him to turn to her. 'You've informed him already?' Secretly she was glad she wouldn't have to do that job.

'You need to make haste, Detective Inspector Parker. Amy Whyte was probably killed late Saturday night or early Sunday morning. You're losing valuable time. The killer could be in Spain by now.'

'That's not my fault. Her father only reported her missing yesterday.'

'Give us time to have a piss first.'

A voice from the gathered troops caused Lottie to roll her eyes. Annoyed as she was by McMahon's intrusion, she had to humour him. Her job depended on it.

'Who said that?' McMahon slapped a hand onto a desk. He turned to Lottie again. 'Keep your team in order. I won't stand for insubordination.'

'You and me both,' Lottie said. 'I realise the significance of Mr Whyte's importance in the community, but we can't forget another young woman also lost her life. We need to look at all angles, means, motive and opportunity, in order to catch the killer.'

McMahon grunted. 'It stinks of a random crackhead to me. I want this investigation up and running in the next ten minutes, and I want the crime solved by this evening.' He turned to look at the photos on the board. 'There's a houseful of evidence right there. Find the bastard who did this.'

With that, he turned on his shiny pointy-toed leather shoes and left the room.

'Prick,' Boyd said.

'Dick,' Kirby said.

'Bollocks,' Lottie said.

Kirby stood. 'I'll get to work on the door-to-doors and collect whatever security footage I can. I'll check our own traffic cams as well.'

'I'll interview Mrs Loughlin again,' Garda Thornton said, picking up his cap from the desk and slapping it on his head.

Lottie held up a hand. 'Wait a minute. I need to talk through the crime. If we rush head first into this, we might miss something that could save us a lot of time.'

Kirby sat back down and Thornton took off his cap. Boyd lined up the pages in the thin folder on his knee.

'Okay. We have an abandoned house in the middle of a terrace of six at Petit Lane. All derelict except for Mrs Loughlin's. When we have the nightclub footage, we should be able to find the exact time the girls left the establishment.'

'They may have walked through the car park to take the shortcut via the underpass,' Boyd said. 'We need to contact the council to see if they have anything on their security systems.'

'Good point,' Lottie said. 'Once we establish their last movements, we might get lucky and see the killer on camera.'

'Do we know if either of the victims had a car?' Thornton piped up.

'Check that out. If they drove to the club, then maybe the car is still in the car park.'

'Penny had a flat nearby, so that needs to be searched too,' Boyd said.

'Must have been hard to overpower two women at the same time,' Kirby mused.

'As far as we know, they didn't leave together.' Pulling at the frayed hem of a sleeve, Lottie added, 'It's possible he took one, subdued or killed her, and then went back for the second.'

'Or the second girl was just an opportunistic killing,' Boyd said.

'Or she saw him and he needed to negate that threat.'

'But why?' Kirby said, his eyes sagging with unshed grief. 'It's all so pointless.'

'If we establish a motive, we'll know why. There might be a clue on their phones.'

'Any sign of those?' Kirby asked.

'Both phones were in the vicinity of the bodies. McGlynn won't release them to me until Jane has carried out her prelim of the scene and bodies.' She sighed, hoping the state pathologist wasn't delayed at the High Court. 'But there are no handbags or personal belongings other than the phones, so it's imperative that gardens and bins are checked.'

'There are three large recycling banks in the car park,' Boyd said. 'I'll get them checked too.'

'And then there are these,' Lottie said, pinning up a zoomed-in photo of the coins.

'What are those?' Kirby stood and walked up to the board. 'Not cash, anyway.'

'No. But they're similar to a one-euro coin, though thinner. No embellishments or engravings. We need to find out what they are and if they're of any relevance.'

'They might have fallen out of one of the victim's bags,' Kirby said. 'In a struggle, maybe?'

'What about the weapon?' Thornton asked.

'Not at the scene,' Lottie said. 'If it was discarded by the killer in the vicinity, I want it found.'

'We're very short-staffed on the detective side of things,' Boyd said.

'I'll talk to the super. I want an extensive background check on everyone associated with the victims. Relatives, friends, colleagues … anyone who so much as sneezed on them. And check out the girls' online histories. We're not going to balls this up like previous investigations by leaving some stone unturned. Got it?'

'Got it.' The reply came in unison.

She debated internally for a moment, then said, 'This may have nothing to do with the murders, but it's worth keeping in the back of your minds. Amy Whyte was one of two key witnesses in an aggravated burglary over ten years ago. A house belonging to a local publican, Bill Thompson, was broken into, the pub takings stolen and the man himself severely battered. A local man, Conor Dowling, got ten years for robbery and grievous bodily harm. He is now out of prison. Mr Thompson has since died. I'm just putting that out there so you can keep it in the back of your minds. Okay?'

'Okay, but what about—'

'Concentrate on these two murders, Boyd. The media rabble are already drumming up a shit storm, and I for one don't want to have to wade through it for too long.'

'Right so,' Boyd said.

Lottie thought he looked a little dubious, but she hadn't time to indulge him. She said, 'Anything else before I let you all out into the wild?'

'Who's going to talk to Penny Brogan's parents?' Boyd again.

Sitting into the nearest chair, Lottie closed her eyes and rubbed her temples with her thumbs. 'I suppose that will be you and me.'

Her phone vibrated with a message.

Leo Belfield. Again.

Shit.

CHAPTER 19

After delivering the stark news to Penny Brogan's father, who greeted it in stunned silence, and arranging for his wife to be brought home from work by a family liaison officer, Lottie organised for the couple to attend the formal identification whenever Penny's body was ready to be viewed. She then returned with Boyd to the crime scene at Petit Lane.

'I think we should have a chat with Mrs Loughlin, the woman who alerted us. She's the only one living nearby,' Lottie said. 'Perhaps we can jog her memory.'

In the car park, Boyd switched off the engine. A third crime-scene cordon had been erected, ensuring the reporters were a further ten metres away from the sad little row of houses.

About to get out of the car, Lottie felt Boyd's hand on her arm. 'What?'

'Are you okay?'

'Of course I'm okay.' Though she wasn't. Not really. Seeing the two bodies had rattled her, and what annoyed her most was that she couldn't pinpoint exactly why that was. Perhaps it was because her daughters had been in the same nightclub on Saturday night. And then there was Leo Belfield. She was itching to get to talk to him.

'You don't look okay. Lottie, I know you better than you know yourself sometimes. If there's something wrong, please tell me.' He raised his hand palm outward in submission. 'And don't go saying I'm worse than your mother.'

'She probably put you up to it.'

'No, she did not. I'm concerned. I want you to talk to me when and if you feel you need to. Okay?'

She shrugged away the tears that were beginning to bubble at the corners of her eyes. Must be the menopause, she thought.

'Could be,' he said.

She laughed. 'Did I actually say that out loud?'

'You did.' He gripped her hand tightly. 'You need to unwind a bit. You never left the phone out of your hand last evening when I was at yours. How about dinner out tonight? Indian? You like that place. My treat.'

Lottie felt her stomach flip. The thought of food made her grimace. 'Boyd, we still have two young women lying in there. Food is the last thing on my mind.'

He drew back and took the keys out of the ignition. 'You're slipping into frosty, Lottie. I thought for a few weeks there that you were thawing. But I was wrong. I can't do this any longer. Honestly, you need to grow up a bit and move on.'

'What the hell do you mean?' She tried to cover her hurt with indignation.

'I thought the new house might have released some of your sadness and grief. Take it from me, as a friend: you need to ditch Adam's ghost and find your own life.'

He opened the door and got out of the car.

'Whatever,' she said, and followed him to Mrs Loughlin's door.

It opened immediately.

The smile on the woman's face slid downward and a crease folded into the lines on her forehead. 'Oh, I thought it was that nice guard. The young Thornton lad.'

'Can we come in, please?' Lottie showed her ID and smiled. Tom Thornton must be at least ten years her senior.

'Come along. Don't mind the smell. Rising damp, you know. But I still won't sell to that smug-faced developer, no matter how many offers he shoves through my letter box.'

'Who would that be?' Boyd asked, pulling out a chair and sitting down.

'You can sit if you like,' Mrs Loughlin said, turning up her lip.

Boyd had the grace to blush.

'Thank you.' Lottie smiled. The kitchen was small and warm, but there was the same damp smell that had been in the crime-scene house.

Mrs Loughlin opened the door of the small range and threw in two briquettes, then put a kettle on the hot plate.

'That shiny-suited Gill man. I've got his letters here somewhere.' She pulled a bundle of mail from the centre of the table.

'No, it's okay,' Lottie said, trying to hide a smirk. 'I know who you mean. We need to talk about what happened at number three.'

Mrs Loughlin sat at the table and flicked crumbs from the green and white oilcloth. 'Awful business. Those poor lassies. I don't know what this town is coming to.'

'I want to ask you a few questions.'

'Go ahead.' She stood and opened the cupboard.

'We don't need tea, thank you.' When the woman was seated again, Lottie began. 'I've read Garda Thornton's report of your visit to the station this morning. I'm wondering if you can remember any further details.'

'Do you think those two lads had something to do with the murders?'

Lottie sighed. 'The cause of death won't be released until the state pathologist carries out her post-mortem, so I'd prefer it if we just referred to them as suspicious deaths for the moment.'

'Two girls are dead, no matter what fancy words you try to dress it up in, young lady.'

Lottie felt a flush creep up her cheeks. Mrs Loughlin had a way of making her feel she was back in school and getting blamed for something she didn't do.

'I understand that, but we are up against the clock to find out what happened. You told Garda Thornton that you heard a lot of noise coming from that house. Can you be more specific?'

'Why don't you ask those two junkies he found knocked out in the hallway? Are they okay, by the way?'

'They're under observation at the hospital. As soon as we get the go-ahead, they'll be interviewed.'

'Drugs. The bane of young people's lives nowadays. Conscription is the only thing that'll iron the creases out of their young lives. I hold their parents responsible.'

Cringing, Lottie recalled how Katie had once got caught up in smoking weed and she herself had done nothing about it. Turned a blind eye. She could not argue with Mrs Loughlin on that score.

'Anyway,' the old lady said, folding her arms, 'I've a habit of going off track, so reel me in any time you find me doing that.'

'I will.' Lottie felt sorry for Mrs Loughlin, living out her days alone in a damp-ridden house, but she admired her tenacity in standing up to Cyril Gill.

'It's always gone on. The noise, the drugs. Especially at weekends. Youngsters fall out of that nightclub and come down to the underpass to make out or shoot up. Is that what you call it?'

'Something like that,' Boyd said, tapping his notebook with his pen.

Lottie nudged his ankle under the table. She was beginning to think she was interviewing her own mother. Mrs Loughlin spoke the same language.

'Last night I heard an awful carry-on altogether. About two thirty, or maybe it was three o'clock, I'm not sure. Monday night. Who'd have thought it? I looked out the window and saw two lads staggering up the footpath to number three. They just walked in bold and brazen as you like. I was going to get up and go in after them, but it was raining. I was raging. They'd woken me up. Don't know when I last got a full night's sleep.'

'And did you notice anyone else around?'

'No, just them two with hoods up over their heads. I came down to make a cup of hot milk to try and get myself back to sleep. I sat in the armchair in the living room and looked out the corner of the curtain, and that's when I saw one of them leaving. But now I know it had to be someone else.'

'Can you give me a description of that person?'

'Whoever they were, they were taller and broader than the two lads, now that I think of it. Didn't look like a teenager. Not that I saw the face, but at my age, I notice these things.'

Lottie wondered about that, seeing as Mrs Loughlin had called her a young lady and Garda Thornton a young man.

'To make this easier for you, we'll assume it was a man. What else do you remember?'

'He'd pulled the jacket collar up around his face, and he had a hat on. One of those … what do you call it? Pea hat?'

'A beanie?' Boyd offered.

'Yeah. Down over his face it was. I couldn't make him out, but he was walking quickly and ran off through the car park.'

'Great, that's excellent, Mrs Loughlin. We'll be able to get CCTV footage of that,' Lottie said.

'I doubt it.'

'Why do you say that?'

'Most of the cameras are smashed. I've a path worn to the council to try and get them fixed, but I might as well be talking to that wall over there.' She pointed to a spot over Lottie's shoulder and shook her head wearily. 'Anyway, he ran down to the right, towards the recycling banks. Maybe he had a car parked there, I don't know, but that's the last I saw of him.'

'Did you see two young women enter number three on Saturday night?'

'I would have told you if I had.'

'Anyone else acting suspiciously at the weekend?'

'I heard the usual carry-on from the nightclub, but nothing that I don't hear every weekend.'

The air was pierced with a whistle and Mrs Loughlin got up to move the kettle off the stove. 'Sure you don't want tea?'

'No thanks.' Lottie stood and handed over her card. 'Contact me if you remember anything about last night, or about any other night, particularly last weekend.'

'Do you think someone was staking the place out?'

'It's possible.'

'Am I in danger?' Mrs Loughlin's eyes were sharp.

'No, not at all,' Lottie hurriedly assured her. 'Uniformed officers will be guarding the area for the next few days, or at least until we finish our examination and searches.' The dampness was catching at the back of her throat, and she wondered how the woman survived in such an environment.

'I'll see you out.'

'Thank you for all your help,' Boyd said, and shook Mrs Loughlin's hand.

'You're a nice boy. Very mannerly.'

Lottie caught Boyd's wink as he walked past her.

They got nothing out of Freddie Nealon or Brian McGrath at the hospital. The lads' last memory was of hearing a sound upstairs in the old house, and then they'd been knocked out.

Lottie sat at her desk with Boyd opposite. He began tidying up her workspace. She shot out her hand towards him.

'Stop.'

'What?' he said.

She stood up and paced the small enclosure. 'If the girls were killed on Saturday night, who was it in the house last night?'

'The two boys.'

'Yeah, I know that. But according to Jim McGlynn, the girls were killed where their bodies were found and had been dead for at least two days. So they were already dead when Freddie and Brian stumbled into the house last night. The lads were attacked by someone who came from upstairs. So who was it?'

'The killer? Maybe he came back for something he'd dropped.'

'Or to leave something. The coins?'

'We have to get an exact time of death and then try to map out a timeline.'

'First we need those nightclub tapes and any other footage we can lay our hands on.' She stood with her hands on her hips. 'I seem to be repeating myself an awful lot and not getting anywhere.'

'I'll check with Kirby to see what he's found.'

When Boyd left the office, Lottie slumped into her chair. If Freddie and Brian hadn't meandered into the derelict house, how long would the bodies have lain undiscovered? And who was the mysterious person the two young men had disturbed?

CHAPTER 20

Lottie found it a pain in the butt having to drive all the way to Tullamore for post-mortems, but she knew it was handier than navigating her way into Dublin city centre.

She took off her damp jacket, robed up in protective clothing and followed the pathologist into the morgue.

'I haven't started properly yet,' Jane said, as she assembled various pieces of equipment so that she could cut and slice and record. Her assistant was busily lining up instruments on a steel tray.

'I figured that. But I need something to guide my investigation.' Lottie dabbed VapoRub beneath her nose and pulled the face mask loops around her ears.

'Well, let's see if I can help, though I can't tell you anything officially until I've completed my work.'

The bodies of the young women were laid out side by side on two tables. Jane walked around them. 'You know who they are?'

'This is Amy Whyte.' Lottie pointed to the first table. 'And that's Penny Brogan.'

'Ages?'

Lottie exhaled loudly. The two girls reminded her so much of her own daughters. 'Twenty-five.'

Jane turned towards the first body. 'Both look normal and healthy for their age. Amy here seems to have suffered the deeper wound. Once I have fully examined her, all will be clearer. I can estimate unofficially that she was held from behind and a knife was stabbed into her throat.'

Lottie knew the pathologist was being cautious. It wasn't in her nature to offer unsubstantiated information. 'That confirms what I was thinking. It didn't look like a slice to me.'

'It's a deep stab wound. Her airway would have been immediately cut off. A few superficial cuts around it suggest she tried to struggle. If she had consumed a lot of alcohol, it might have hindered her responses.' She turned to Lottie. 'The amount of blood at the scene suggests the artery was severed, resulting in death within seconds.'

Lottie thought that was small comfort. 'Can you determine the type of weapon used?'

'Not at the moment, but it was something with a sharp edge. If the weapon was thrust in deep enough to leave a patterned abrasion, then maybe …' Jane feathered a gloved finger over the wound. 'I can't determine that from a visual examination, but I'm hopeful it's possible.'

'Were they sexually assaulted?'

Jane leaned her head to one side and opened her eyes wide, as if to say, how would I know at this stage? 'Their underwear doesn't appear to have been disturbed and there's no visible evidence to suggest they were sexually assaulted. I still need to take samples and perform the autopsies.'

'Jane, I need something. Anything. A clue to guide me.'

The pathologist's eyes flared above her mask. 'You're pushing too hard. I need time to do my job properly. Give me a few hours. I'll do everything in my power to get a preliminary report to you today.'

Lottie bit her lip, struggling with the consequences of lost time and how the murderer had a few days' head start on her. 'Can you process the bodies for DNA and fingerprints first? Then check if they'd been drugged. That might help.'

Jane shook her head. 'I will do my job. I strongly advise that you do yours.'

Feck it. Now she'd alienated the one ally who might help her. She had gained nothing by this trip; only succeeded in losing time and sowing the seeds of hostility with the state pathologist. And she still had to catch up with Leo Belfield. Her day was deteriorating fast.

*

Louise Gill kept her phone switched off and made good headway with her coursework. She'd try to talk with Amy later. It was a few months since they'd been in contact, even though they both lived in Ragmullin. They'd once been best friends. A long time ago. Back before Conor Dowling went to prison.

In the kitchen, she poured a glass of water and leaned against the antique sink. Her father walked in and Louise put her phone away. She rinsed her glass under the flowing water from the tap, then made to edge by him towards the door. He grabbed her elbow.

'Where are you off to?'

'Dad, I have work to do.' She put one foot over the threshold, but he held firm.

'You know he's back in Ragmullin,' he said.

She stalled. Yes, she knew. He was the reason that fear now stalked every footstep she took. He was the reason she needed to speak with Amy. He was the reason for her life being total shit.

'I know.'

'I put him on my payroll where I can keep an eye on him. But that's not twenty-four seven. You need to be careful.'

'Why?' She felt a little braver when his hand dropped from her arm. 'I'd have thought you were the one who needed to be careful.'

'You told the lies.'

She couldn't believe the streak of darkness that flitted across her father's indigo eyes. 'I wasn't even fifteen. Young and impressionable. So, as the saying goes, the buck stops with you.'

He raised his hand so swiftly that she almost didn't duck in time. He'd never struck her; not once in her life had he even come close. She loved her father with all her heart, but sometimes she hated him just as much.

As if he realised what he'd been about to do, he let his hand fall away and took a backward step. 'I'm sorry, sweetheart. I don't know what came over me.'

Louise rushed out into the marbled hallway, almost colliding with the replica statue of Michelangelo's *David*, and was halfway up the winding marble staircase when she shouted back at him, 'I hate you.'

Shutting her bedroom door, she heard her mother come out of the study, and the pad of her bare feet on the plush cream carpet as she went into her own room and softly shut the door.

'That's right, Mummy dearest.' Louise leaned her head against the robe hanging on the back of the door. 'Bury your beautiful Botoxed face in a bottle, like you always do.'

*

The velvet red curtains seemed to be oozing blood, and the walls were crawling with thorns. Leo Belfield lifted his head from the pillow and immediately dropped it back again. He squinted through one eye. The room was spinning. Round and round.

Reaching out for the bottle of water he had left beside the bed, his fingers swiped clean through the air. No bottle. Suddenly he remembered.

He lurched upright and fell to the floor, his legs caught up in a swirl of white cotton sheets. Where was she? What had she done to him?

Stumbling around the room, he searched the closet, the bathroom, looked out into the corridor. Back inside, he leaned against the door.

Bernie Kelly had disappeared.

He checked his wallet. Cards okay. Cash gone.

He grabbed his phone and rang Lottie Parker.

CHAPTER 21

The drive back to Ragmullin relaxed Lottie's brain a little. The rain cleared and a pink sky lit up the horizon as she sped along the motorway. Her phone buzzed and she was tempted to ignore it. The number came up as unknown, but she knew it off by heart now. She tapped the screen to answer and was glad she'd put it on hands-free mode.

'Lottie? Is that you?'

'Who do you think it is, Leo? I'm sorry I missed meeting you today, but work got a little hectic.' She indicated and took the slip road off the motorway. 'I'll be back in the office in ten minutes if you want to give me a call then.'

'No, no. Don't hang up. This is serious.'

His voice was frantic, and Lottie clutched the steering wheel, her knuckles turning white. 'What's happened?'

'She's gone. Bernie. She's disappeared.'

'What the hell? Leo, what have you done?'

'Listen up. There's no point in taking this out on me. What I did, I did for the benefit of us both. But now she's gone.'

'Where are you? You sound drunk.'

'I think she drugged me. My head is in bits. The room's spinning around me …'

'Where are you?'

'The Joyce.'

'Don't move. I'll be there as soon as I can.'

She hung up.

Called Boyd.

And pressed the accelerator to the floor.

*

'I can do without this shit right now. What a mess.' Lottie stormed through the lobby of the Joyce Hotel.

'Calm down,' Boyd said. 'You can't do anything if you get yourself into a state. Let's see what the man has to say for himself before you explode.'

Belfield was sitting at the bar, a tumbler of what looked like whiskey in front of him. He turned as Lottie strode towards him. The urge to slap him was greater than the fear of what Bernie Kelly might be up to.

'How could you?' she said. 'Why on earth would you want to take her out of a secure facility?'

'I'm sorry. I wanted to know the truth.'

'And you thought you'd get that from a lying, conniving, murderous bitch, did you?'

'Whatever I thought, I know now that I was wrong.'

Lottie stuffed her hands into her jacket pockets. Safer there. God, she needed a Valium, or a Xanax. A crutch on which to lean all her worries. But she'd ditched her habit. New home, new life, new Lottie. She felt Boyd's hand on her elbow, steering her towards the stool beside her half-brother.

'Tell us exactly the sequence of events,' Boyd said.

As she sat up on the stool, she noticed that Leo had aged since she'd last seen him. He was no longer the fresh-faced NYPD cop. He looked like an old man staring back at her, troubled, with something like physical pain etched on his face.

He gulped a mouthful of whiskey and spoke into the glass. 'I got her released yesterday. She's due back this evening. No need to go into the technicalities of how I managed it; safe to say I made a mess of things. She was so endearing and persuasive that I was taken in. I reserved a twin room here. I'm not that much of a fool as to let her have her own space. And then … I woke up and she was gone.'

'But you texted me this morning. Arranged a meeting for one o'clock today,' Lottie said, incredulous.

'I didn't do that. She must have used my phone.' He pointed to the device on the bar counter.

'Check if she sent any other texts or made any calls.' Lottie felt the shift of urgency in her chest, like a sharp pain. This was serious shit. A woman incarcerated by reason of insanity with the blood of God knew how many on her hands, and now she was free. Double shit.

Leo shook his head. 'Just the one to you.'

'Did you check with the manager? The reception staff? Did anyone see her leave?'

'I did, and they didn't.'

'Boyd, get them to go over their security footage.' Lottie's voice quivered with panic.

'But we have no idea when she left,' Leo said.

'He's right,' Boyd said. 'She could be anywhere now. What good is an image of her back as she runs out the door?'

'They have cameras on the street. Check those. For the last twelve hours,' Lottie said.

'I have no idea how long I've been out,' Leo said.

'This is going to cause a shit storm.' Lottie slammed her fist on the bar, shaking the glass. 'I have two young women lying dead in the morgue and a full-scale investigation to conduct. I don't need this.'

She caught Boyd's eye. He was shaking his head, silently telling her to shut up. He was right. There was nothing to be gained by losing her temper. But she had no idea how to handle this.

'What will we do?' she said.

'What will *she* do is a better question,' Leo said.

'Oh shut up,' Lottie said. 'We need to find her. Scratch that. *You* need to find her!'

*

The fact that the evil bitch was out and free to roam through her town settled like a black shroud of death on Lottie's shoulders. She'd sent Leo to search and told him to check in every hour on the hour. They'd made a decision – rightly or wrongly, she wasn't sure – to keep word of Bernie's escape between them. For now. As soon as she got her head together, she would think about it. She rang Katie and instructed her to keep the doors locked, and told Rose the same. She hoped Chloe and Sean were safe at school and put a reminder in her phone to pick them up at four.

'Kirby, please tell me you have good news for me.' She dropped into a chair in the incident room and stared intently at the detective.

'We got their computer devices from their parents and McGlynn dropped off both girls' phones. Tech guys are going through them now. So far there's nothing to suggest they were targeted online.'

'And?'

'And what?'

'Give me something, Kirby. It's been a shit day.'

'Is that my fault as well?'

She jumped up and paced the room, coming to a stop in front of the boards. Someone had pinned up photos of the girls beside their victim photos. She traced a finger over the outline of first Amy's face, and then Penny's.

'Two young women with their lives ahead of them, cut down like meat in an abattoir. Why?'

She leaned her head against the board, thinking. Trying to dispel the image of her evil half-sister on the loose. Hopefully she was somewhere they could find her easily. Maybe she should send out a search team? But this was Leo's mess. Let him deal with it. Until it went tits-up. She pressed her fingers into the palms of her hands and squeezed her eyes shut. She'd made a mistake, she was sure of it, but she had two murders to solve. They took priority. She just hoped she could keep her family safe.

'The coins are home-made, according to McGlynn. Edges appear smooth but are rough to touch. There's no engraving so it's impossible to trace them,' Kirby said.

'Who's organising interviews?' Lottie sat down again, facing him.

'We need more staff, boss.'

'I'm working on it.' She made a mental note to follow up with McMahon.

'I drew up a list. Penny was unemployed, but she did manicures and gel nails, whatever that is, based at her apartment. SOCOs are there now. She might have a customer list.'

'I doubt her killer has gel nails,' Lottie said, 'but I'll head there and have a look around. What else?'

'Amy's colleagues have to be interviewed again. I'll do that myself.' Kirby ticked an item on his list.

'Good. Check your notes and cover anything you missed at the pharmacy last time.'

'Will do.'

She caught a glance from the detective. 'What?'

'Were the victims sexually assaulted?'

'No evidence to suggest it.'

'That's one small mercy in this brutal world we live in.'

She stood and squeezed his shoulder. 'Keep at it, Kirby. Keep busy. It helps.'

Leaving him scouring a list of people who had to be interviewed, she went to find where Boyd had disappeared to. Anything to keep her mind off Leo Belfield and what he'd done.

CHAPTER 22

Penny Brogan's apartment was situated in a three-storey block on Columb Street, just down from the car dismantler's yard and across from a coal depot. The road was black from the tyre tracks of trucks pulling in and out of the fuel yard. Lottie gazed over at the mounds of coal and briquettes, shielded beneath a struggling Perspex roof.

'First floor,' Boyd said.

'I'm coming.' She followed him into the small courtyard.

The garda technical van was positioned in front of the terrace of apartments. She entered through the open door. Two SOCOs were dusting and searching. She could do with ten minutes on her own in here, but they had their work to do too.

Boyd said, 'It's like a shoebox.'

'You can talk. Yours isn't much bigger.'

'I suppose she was happy to have her own place, though I'd say it was tough trying to pay the rent in today's economy, especially as she had no job.'

Lottie spied a small table in the corner of the room and made her way around a settee that she guessed doubled as a bed. On the table sat all the equipment needed to run a little black-market business in nail care. A wooden shelf held baskets filled with bottles of varnish, polish and cleansing products.

'Penny must have worked on Amy's nails.' Lottie picked up a see-through container no bigger than a matchbox and shook it. The rhinestones glittered as they slid around.

She opened a drawer in the small bedside-type cabinet pushed beneath the table and drew out a black plastic-covered appointment book.

'This might help us,' she said.

'It'll give us a bigger headache,' Boyd said, 'leading to a ton of interviews and no doubt nothing of interest to our investigation.'

'Ever the optimist,' Lottie mumbled as she flicked through the pages with her gloved fingers. Nothing jumped out at her, so she bagged the book and glanced around.

A kitchenette was separated from the main room by a three-foot-long breakfast bar with two high stools. Upturned mugs and plates sat on the draining board. The sink was empty. She moved through a door to her right. A small bathroom; the walls and shower door were smeared with false tan.

'Just like mine,' she said.

Boyd stuck his head over her shoulder. 'Yours is a little cleaner.'

She shoved out past him. 'Where does she keep her clothes?'

'There's a cupboard over there.' Boyd pointed to a set of double doors to the left of a gas fire.

Lottie opened them up and found hangers with clothes pressed tightly together. Beneath them was a line of shoes and two pairs of ankle boots. She searched through every item of clothing with pockets but came up empty-handed.

'There's nothing here,' she said. 'We need to look in Amy Whyte's house.'

'I wish you luck getting past the councillor,' Boyd said as he searched through a basket of nail polish.

'Didn't you know my middle name is luck?'

'Luckless, more like. What's this when it's at home?' He held up a small bottle with white liquid inside.

'Let me see.' Lottie took the bottle and shook it. 'Doesn't look like a nail product.' She opened the lid and sniffed.

'Jesus Christ,' Boyd said. 'It's like ammonia.'

'Nail polish remover then.'

Boyd took the bottle, screwed back the lid and replaced it in the basket. 'SOCOs can analyse it.'

As she was leaving, Lottie noticed a jacket hanging on the back of the door. She searched the pockets. 'Bingo.' She held up her find.

'What the …?' Boyd stared.

'Must be a couple of hundred euros here.' Lottie flicked through the roll of notes.

'Would she make that much from nails?'

'Depends on who her customers were.'

Boyd patted the appointment book. 'This might be more of a help than a hindrance after all.'

'We're trying to catch a murderer, Boyd. Not nail a tax-dodger. Pardon the pun.'

'You're so funny. Not.'

As he left, she turned around to look at the two SOCOs. They were not going to find anything here, unless the killer was into nail fetish. Then again …

She sighed and followed Boyd to the car.

*

Bernie Kelly curved her back into the wall of Grove's Coal Suppliers. She didn't care that a black slick of oil would leave a mark on her jacket. She only had eyes for the tall, hooded figure of Lottie Parker getting into the car with her sergeant. She needed to feel that freckle-skinned neck beneath her fingers as she crushed and squeezed the life out of the woman who had halted her personal crusade of retribution against the family that had never acknowledged her. She knew she had to get a knife. She would plunge it deep into Lottie's body. Deeper than the last time. And this time it would be fatal.

A drop of water nestled into the nape of her neck. She flicked it away. The blue lights on the car grille flashed before the car turned right and headed away. She moved out from her secluded corner and began to walk in its wake.

Lottie Parker could wait.

It was time to have some fun with her family.

CHAPTER 23

Sitting on a bench outside the courthouse, Conor Dowling smoked the cigarette he'd swiped from Tony. From his vantage point he could see the activity in the car park beyond the council buildings.

Guards. Plenty of them.

'What are you looking at?'

He jumped up at the sound of the voice. Cyril Gill was towering over him. Conor's reply died in his throat. All the words and sentences he'd concocted during his prison time evaporated into the misty air as just a jumble of letters; nothing connecting; nothing forming even a word, let alone a full sentence. He dropped the cigarette and made to move around his boss.

Gill grabbed his arm and pulled him to his chest.

'If you so much as look crooked at my daughter, I'll personally flay you alive. Got it?'

Conor gulped and dropped his chin to his chest. He'd thought Gill wouldn't remember him. Stupid. Of course the man knew absolutely everything about him. Maybe he'd hired him on purpose. To keep him in his sights. That sounded about right.

When he looked up, he found himself alone. Gill's car was speeding up Gaol Street. How long had he been standing like an idiot, staring at his mucky boots? Too long. He glanced down at the half-smoked cigarette drowned in a puddle. Shouldn't have started, he thought, because now he'd have to go buy a pack.

With a backward glance at the guards searching around the recycling banks, he took a deep breath and headed to the newsagent's. Maybe he'd buy two packs.

*

Richard Whyte made no objection to a search of Amy's room. He was dry-eyed and talking on the phone to an undertaker.

'When will my daughter's body be released?'

'As soon as the state pathologist says so,' Lottie said. 'Which room is it?'

'Up the stairs. Third on the right.' He returned to his phone call.

The Whytes lived on a private estate close to the ring road. The hum of traffic permeated the triple glazing and the house seemed to tremble. The hallway was spacious and the staircase winding, but the decor was soft and soothing. Amy or her late mother must have had some input, Lottie thought, because she found it hard to believe Richard Whyte had a soft bone in his body.

Her feet sank in the plush cream carpet and she wondered if she should have removed her boots. Too late now.

Upstairs she was met with a wide corridor and a line of white doors with brass handles. She tried the first one.

'He said the third door,' Boyd offered.

'I want a quick look at how the other half lives.' Lottie stepped into a bathroom. 'This is the size of Penny's flat. And not a streak of fake tan anywhere.' She ran her gloved fingers over the white ceramic.

'Genuine Armitage Shanks.' Richard stood in the doorway, shoulder to shoulder with Boyd.

'Oh, sorry, Mr Whyte.' Lottie stumbled over her words and her feet in her haste to exit the bathroom.

'That's okay. I have a housekeeper three days a week. But you should see it after Amy has got herself ready for a night out. I'd say there's cleaner dressing rooms on Broadway.'

Lottie smiled thinly and edged by him. In Amy's room she was stunned by the contrast to the bathroom.

'She doesn't allow the housekeeper in here. The only room that remains like a pigsty. But it's Amy's space, and she loves her privacy. It's the least I can give her after all she went through.'

He was still speaking about his daughter in the present tense, Lottie noted, but she didn't have the heart to correct him.

'What did she go through?'

Richard rubbed his jowly cheeks. 'That business at Bill Thompson's. Then the loss of her poor mother to cancer. And now … and now my Amy's gone too.' He slumped in a heap of hand-tailored suit and fell against Boyd.

Lottie indicated for Boyd to take him downstairs and began her search. She hated trawling through victims' possessions, but she knew that the dead spoke to her through the evidence left on their bodies and in their habitat. This was one of the last places Amy had been. Tell me about her, she pleaded silently.

The king-size bed was made up with plain white cotton covers and sheets. Here and there Lottie saw little scratches of tan that had failed to disappear in the wash. She had to pick her way through discarded clothing on the floor until she reached the dressing table under the large window. Venetian blinds helped cast an eerie pattern of lines along the wall as she slipped a finger between two slats and looked outside. Trees guarded the end of the garden, but beyond that she could see the dual carriageway, with traffic travelling along in both directions at speed.

She sat on the small white stool and opened the drawers. Finding nothing of interest to her investigation, she hurriedly closed them again. This part of the job made her feel like a grave robber, but someone had to do it.

She admired the expensive row of perfume bottles on the surface of the dressing table, and thought how her girls would love to possess even one of them. The make-up was all Mac, but the brushes were clogged and well worn. Lights surrounded the mirror, with a photograph stuck under each bulb. She squinted at the images, thinking that most people didn't get photos developed any more. They were all saved in phones and in clouds, available at the swipe of a fingertip. She detached a photo of a woman in her forties. Amy's mother, she assumed, then noticed that all the photos were of the same person. Definitely the mother.

As she flicked up each photo, she noticed that one of them had a small envelope taped to its back. She extracted both the picture and the envelope and laid them on the table. Carefully she peeled back the tape and stared at the envelope. Just the name AMY scrawled on the front. No address, no postmark. She lifted the flap and extracted the white page. It was cheap paper, and as she opened it up, she stared open-mouthed.

Four words were typed on the page.

I am watching you.

She tipped the envelope on its side, and a single silver coin slid out.

Richard Whyte claimed he knew nothing about the note or the coin. Had no idea when Amy had received it. He'd shrugged his shoulders and Lottie believed him. For the moment. They'd rushed back to Penny's flat, but there was no envelope, note or coin to be found.

At the office, Lottie photocopied the note through the plastic evidence bag and pinned the copy up on the incident board.

'It's a blatant threat,' Boyd said.

'Someone targeted her,' Lottie said. 'Was it because of the old court case? The one where she gave evidence against Conor Dowling? We need to bring him in. I want to interview him. Preferably before he gets his hands on a solicitor. Do we know where he is?'

'I'll find out from the probation service.'

'Do it now.'

'Was it just the one note?' Kirby asked, joining Lottie at the board.

'I pulled the bedroom apart. It's the only one.'

'And she didn't tell her father?'

'He claims he knew nothing about it. But I'll grill him again.' Her phone pinged. A reminder. 'I almost forgot. I have to go collect Chloe and Sean from school.'

'Why? Aren't they big and bold enough to walk home?'

'Don't ask, Kirby. Just don't ask.'

She flew out of the office and down the stairs while texting her two children to stay at the school gates until she arrived.

*

Rose strained the pot of potatoes and fetched the masher. She would put on a fried egg later and that would do for her dinner. She missed having her grandchildren around. Rushing in from school and grabbing plates and cutlery, sometimes eating at the table, but more times in their rooms. She'd never allowed that kind of behaviour when Lottie was young, but now life seemed too short for nonsense rules. She put the pot to the rear of the stove and went to get the frying pan from the shelf.

The doorbell rang.

Lottie had told her not to open the door, but she could see through the glass that it was just a woman in a rain jacket standing on her step.

When she was bundled backwards into her own hallway, she knew she'd made a mistake.

Lottie would kill her.

If Bernie Kelly didn't do it first.

CHAPTER 24

In Whyte's Pharmacy, Kirby was glad of the mug of coffee offered to him by Megan Price. She was seated opposite him, her dark hair feathered with strands of grey held back in a ponytail and her black dress with brass buttons down the front adding an air of regality to her appearance. She had hung up her white work coat when he'd arrived. He inhaled the antiseptic smell of medicines emanating from the stacks on the shelves around them, and when she stared at him, he dropped his eyes and drank a mouthful of coffee.

'I can't believe it,' Megan said. 'Two lovely young women in the prime of their lives. Who would want to do such a thing?'

'It's a brutal old world we live in,' Kirby said. 'I need you to think over everything you know about each of them. People they may have spoken about. Anyone who came into the shop that they reacted to in any way that you can remember as being … let's say unusual.'

'You'll have to let me think about it.'

Kirby put the mug on the floor between his feet and noted how scruffy his shoes looked. The toes were scuffed, and when he lifted his foot, he could see where the sole was coming away. Gilly would have had something to say. He gulped loudly.

'Is anything wrong?' Megan Price said. He felt her hand brush his knee.

'No, no, it's fine. I'm fine.'

'You look tired, and if I may so, there's a deep-rooted sadness in your eyes. I know that look.'

'And what look might that be?' Kirby tried a wry smile. He didn't want to talk about Gilly. How was it that she invaded his thoughts at the most inopportune moments?

'Sorrow. Unrelenting, unforgiving sorrow. Did you know her well?'

'Who?'

'The young guard who was murdered during the summer.'

He couldn't stop the tears that dripped one by one down his cheeks. He wiped them away with the back of his hand.

'Let's get back to Amy and Penny.' He straightened himself on the small stool. 'When did you last see either of them?'

'Death leaves a big fat hole in your life,' Megan said softly, leaving his question unanswered. 'That's the worst part. Trying to find something to fit into it and knowing in your heart that it will always be there. What was her name?'

Kirby gazed into the pharmacist's dark brown eyes. They were kind and sympathetic.

'Her name was Gilly. She was a lot younger than me, so she made me feel young. And she had the craziest smile you'd ever see. Not crazy like crazy, if you know what I mean.'

She laughed nervously. 'Is infectious the word you're looking for?'

'That's it. I'll never hear her voice again. Do you know how terrifying that is? To know you will never hear someone's voice again.'

'I know it well. It's tough, Detective Kirby. With time, the pain will ease. It never goes away, but you learn to live with it.'

'Are you speaking from experience?' He patted his pockets. He could do with escaping outside for a quick smoke.

She stood. The cluttered space seemed to fill, though she was as thin as a rake. 'Enough about personal trauma. I'll rack my brains and let you know if I remember anything out of the ordinary about Amy and Penny.'

'I'd appreciate that.' Kirby edged by her.

He noticed the downturned heads of the two assistants, who'd made themselves busy when he and Megan returned to the main shop. He welcomed the multitude of scents vying with each other for supremacy.

'Did Amy have a locker? Somewhere to store personal stuff?'

Megan blushed. 'She used a small cupboard in my office, but I checked it this morning when I heard the news. There was nothing in it.'

Kirby addressed one of the shop assistants; Trisha, according to her name badge. 'Did you like working with Amy?'

Trisha's face drained of all colour and she began to sob. 'She was fantastic. We all loved her. Didn't we?'

He noticed she'd directed her question to Megan and not the other assistant. Megan nodded and steered Kirby to the door. 'I have your card. I'll have a chat with the girls too and contact you if we think of anything.'

Out on the street, Kirby couldn't help feeling that he'd missed something. He scratched his head. For the life of him he couldn't work out what it was. One thing he knew for sure, he was totally embarrassed. When he'd been in the claustrophobic storeroom, he'd realised he needed a shower. Badly.

*

The recording equipment was running, and names and details had been outlined. Lottie had picked up Chloe and Sean and dropped them home, where she was surprised to see that Katie had prepared dinner. She'd declined the offer to eat and rushed back to work, where she found Conor Dowling had been brought to the interview room. Boyd did the introductions for the recording before she began.

'So, Conor, you're working for Cyril Gill, is that right?'

'You know I am because that's where you had me picked up from. Don't be asking stupid questions. I know the drill. Been here before, haven't I?'

'Yes, you have. When did you get out of prison?'

'You know that too.'

'Two months ago. And you started working for Cyril Gill two weeks ago.'

He clamped his mouth shut, arms folded, legs stretched out under the table. A lip curled upwards. His nails were crusted with mud and the backs of his hands laced with dirt. He'd dropped his work coat on the floor and rolled up his sleeves. His arms were inked with a myriad of tattoos.

'Odd choice of employer,' Lottie said.

Dowling said nothing.

'I mean, Cyril Gill is the father of one of the two young women who gave evidence against you ten years ago. Why would you want to work for him?'

He sniffed and eventually said, 'Keep your friends close and your enemies closer. That's my motto.'

'Do you see Mr Gill as your enemy?'

'What do you think?'

'He did nothing to you.'

'That scum bitch of a daughter of his did.'

'Have you been in contact with Louise Gill recently?'

She thought she noticed a slight blush, but he quickly rubbed his hands over his cheeks and up onto his bald head.

'No,' he said.

'And Amy Whyte. What do you know about her?'

'She lied too.'

'Lied about what?'

He scanned his surroundings with narrowing eyes, which landed on her. 'Why have you got me here? I'm entitled to my solicitor and a phone call.'

Lottie felt Boyd kick her ankle. It hadn't taken long for the 'entitled to my solicitor' line to raise its head.

'You're not under arrest,' she said.

'I can go so?' He unfolded his arms and made to stand up.

Slamming her hand on the table, Lottie felt Boyd jump at the same time as Dowling.

'Sit down!'

'I am sitting.'

'Listen to me. I want the answers to a few questions first, then you can leave. Okay?'

'Suppose so.'

He was either stupid or pretending to be stupid. She intended to fire right ahead and find out.

'When did you last see Amy Whyte?'

He half closed his eyes and watched her through the slits. 'Might have been 2006. My memory's not the best from all the beatings I got in jail. Where you and that pair of liars landed me.'

'You've been free for two months. Did you make contact with Amy in that time?' Chancing her arm, watching his expression, waiting for the break. But he remained calm.

'I don't want to clap eyes on that bitch ever again.'

'Not likely, is it, seeing as she's dead.' Lottie let the sentence hang in the silence and watched his face for a reaction. But he simply stared right back at her.

'When was the last time you saw Amy?'

'What do you mean?' At last. Realisation dawned on his face. He sat forward. 'Look here. This is a joke. You pinned one crime on me, and sure as there's a fire in hell you're not going to do it again. You can piss off, you skinny bitch.'

'I'll take that as a compliment,' Lottie said. Boyd nudged her again. She glared at him. She wanted Dowling riled. He might inadvertently say something he didn't mean to say. Hopefully.

'Take it any way you like,' he snarled. 'I'd say you'd like it up the arse!'

'That's abusive language.'

'What are you going to do about it?'

Ignoring his anger, Lottie said, 'Where were you on Saturday night from eleven p.m. onwards?' She kept her tone even, her voice clear and strong. No way was this bald shithead going to get under her skin.

'At home.'

'And all day Sunday?'

'At home.'

'Can anyone verify that?'

'None of your business.'

'It is my business.'

He let out a strangled sigh. 'My mother is there all the time. She's disabled. Chronic arthritis, if you want to know.'

'She can vouch that you were at home all weekend?'

'Yes.'

'You never went out anywhere?'

'I went to the shop for milk and bread.'

'What shop?'

'Tesco.'

'I'm sure their security cameras will confirm that, if you provide me with the times.'

'I don't know what time it was. I'm not Superman with a super-brain.'

'No, you're most definitely not.'

'Are you being smart with me?'

'No. But you're being smart with me. So give me the truth.'

'I'm saying nothing until I get a solicitor.'

Lottie wasn't giving up so easily. She rolled up the sleeves of her T-shirt and extracted a laminated sheet from the buff folder in front of her.

'What's that?' Dowling said.

'Read it,' she said. 'You can read, can't you?'

He turned the sheet around and scanned it. 'So? What's it got to do with me?'

'We found it in Amy Whyte's bedroom. Did you write this note and send it to Amy?'

'You didn't ask if I can write.'

'Come on, Conor. Playtime is over. This is serious,' Lottie said, trying hard to keep it professional.

'Answer the question,' Boyd said.

'What question might that be?' Conor sighed loudly. 'Yes, I can write, and I can read too. Happy?'

'No, I'm not.' Lottie took the page and slipped it back into the folder. 'And your smart mouth is not endearing you to me at all.'

'Tough shit.'

'This is a photocopy of a coin found in the envelope with the note.' She showed him an image of the round piece of metal. She held back on talking about the coins found with the bodies. No point in showing her hand too early.

'Never saw it before.'

'I think you did. You refused to talk last time, but you can tell the truth about this crime.'

'Would you ever fuck off?' His face flared red, and his knuckles, crunched into fists, were white. He stood up. 'I'm leaving. And don't think you can frame me for whatever this is about. I won't stand for it a second time.'

The door swung closed behind him.

Lottie said, 'Interesting young man, don't you think?'

Boyd said, 'Did you notice he never once asked how she died.'

'Maybe he already knew.'

'Like he'd heard about it?'

'No, like he did it.'

*

The cathedral bells rang out the hour as Conor walked past the wrought-iron gates. He didn't even bother to check how many chimes. Time was his enemy. Time had betrayed him and continued to do so. He'd learned that in a cell with the shouts and roars of the other inmates for company. A plump black crow perched on a railing ahead of him. He picked up a drink can from the path and toyed with the idea of hurling it at the bird. As he came closer, he noticed that the crow's beak was thick and hard. The eyes black. He paused and stared. The bird did not move. Which of us has the darker soul? he wondered. Then he laughed. Birds had no souls.

He dropped the can and kicked it down the footpath in front of him. He kept on kicking it until it ended up in a muddy drain. Then he thumped his fist into a car door. His probation officer would be pissed off to learn he'd been questioned by the guards. Well, tough shit.

He needed a pint. Hadn't he promised Tony he'd buy him a drink after work? He didn't fancy going into Cafferty's. All the guards drank there. He took out his phone and found his hands were shaking. Goddam you, Parker.

He texted Tony. Told him he'd meet him in Fallon's pub.

No reply.

He'd have one pint anyway, then go home to see what his mother had got up to during the day. And then he remembered he'd put on a wash that morning. The clothes had probably been in the machine all day. They'd be rank. He'd have to wash them again. After he'd had his pint.

CHAPTER 25

'Rosie, Rosie, you were always the sly one. You and that husband of yours. Shot himself, I heard. Got fed up with the lies, did he? Or had he had enough of your frosty face?'

Rose was seated at the table, clutching her hands together. Her skin felt like a thousand spiders had taken over and were spinning a multitude of webs. She unclenched her hands and flattened the palms on her knees.

The woman in front of her had eyes steeped in the depths of evil. Rose was no psychiatrist, but she knew that look. From true-life dramas on television. Interviews with serial killers. That look. That deep black nothingness.

'Answer me.'

Bernie was lounging against the kitchen wall, her dirty coat flung across the back of a chair. Her legs were thin, clad in dark jeans, and her black sweater was stained. Her skin was pale, but her nose and cheeks were flushed, and tufts of wild red hair sprouted around her ears. She looked like a circus clown who had run away before the make-up artist had completed the job.

'What do you want?' Rose thought her voice sounded like someone else's. Was that what stark fear did to you? she wondered.

'I wanted to see you. To see what type of person steals another woman's baby.'

'I did not steal anyone.'

'Your parasite of a husband did.'

'Don't you dare talk about Peter like that.'

'Peeeter!' Bernie's voice was mocking. 'He raped a defenceless young woman. Impregnated her and then stole her child. Does your precious Lottie know she's the spawn of hate and rape?'

A force of energy swelled through Rose and she had to fight the urge to lunge for the knife rack. She had to keep calm. God only knew what weapon Bernie was carrying, though it was hard to see how she could conceal anything on her person.

'Don't you go near my Lottie.'

'My Lottie?' Bernie laughed. 'She's my half-sister. Her biological mother's blood runs through my veins. We are blood sisters and you are nothing!'

'And she is nothing like you. Stay away from her.' Rose tried to make her voice threatening, but all that emitted from her lips was a timid cry.

'I will get what I came for.'

'And what is that?'

'Revenge. Lottie Parker betrayed me in front of my own daughter. She stole my freedom. We could have been a family together. But no. That woman put her job before her blood sister. And I won't rest until I extract every last drop of that blood from her body.'

'You're insane.' Rose cowered as Bernie lunged from the wall and landed on her knees in front of her chair.

'You know it's very dangerous to say that to an *insane* person.'

The eyes were now wide spheres of hollowness. Rose could almost see through them, as if she was staring down the shaft of an old well. She wondered if Bernie Kelly's very core was a tightly bound ball of hatred, wound so that one snag on the thread and all her family would disintegrate in the ensuing horror. She could not let that happen. But what could she do?

At last she said, 'I'm sorry.'

'That's a start.' Bernie hauled herself up and sat onto the side of the table. Swung her legs like she was a five-year-old. 'This is what I want you to do.'

*

On her way home, Lottie pulled into a garage and bought the last lonely sausage rolls in the display cabinet. They looked stale and unappetising, but she was starving.

In the car, she switched on the engine, turned the heat up high and sat with the rain beating against the windows as she munched the soggy pastry. She concluded that the trade descriptions people would have a good case here. More pastry than sausage. She crumbled the remainder of the first roll into her mouth and glanced at the time. She was too late to wish Louis goodnight. She loved the little fellow with all her heart, more so since the dangerous episode in Rose's house a few months before. All her family were at risk because of her job, she knew that better than anyone, though sometimes the threat was hard to quantify. It was little more than a feeling. But the last few days that feeling was growing between her shoulder blades like an unreachable itch.

She balled up the paper bag and scrunched it under the seat. Time to go home. As she drove out of the forecourt, she was looking forward to a peaceful evening, but at the same time she knew she could never erase the loneliness that stalked her bones. Maybe Boyd was the one for her. Maybe not. She had no idea.

She indicated to turn left, then remembered she no longer lived down by the greyhound stadium. At the last minute she drew the car back into the correct lane. It was then that she noticed the car behind her. She knew exactly who it was.

*

She pulled up outside the Indian restaurant. When she stepped out of the car, the aroma of spices swirled around her. She waited as the car that had been following her came to a halt on double yellow lines. She could write him a ticket, if she had a mind to.

'Leo, I hope you have good news for me, because I've had one bitch of a day.'

'I've searched the whole town and I have no idea where she is.'

'Have you reported to the hospital that you've lost her?'

'No. But she's due back there at nine, so I'm sure, as you say, the shit will hit the fan.'

'Maybe you should get out of Ragmullin. Head to the airport. Get a flight back home and never darken my doorstep with your troubles again.' She leaned against her car, feeling the dampness seep into her jeans.

'There's no need to be like that. We're in this together.'

'Like hell we are.' Lottie moved away from her car and stood in his space. The smell of sweat coming from his body was so pungent, she could almost taste it. Belfield was terrified. 'You took Bernie Kelly out of a secure mental facility. You brought her to Ragmullin. You lost her. You broke the rules. None of that has anything to do with me.'

He stared at her. An exact replica of her own eyes fixed on her face. It was eerily unsettling.

'Lottie, we have to work on this together.'

She didn't like the pleading tone in his voice. 'There is no together. You find her. I have two dead girls to worry about. I don't need to be looking over my shoulder for the rest of my life. I've work to do. Real work. Find her and then go home. There's nothing in Ragmullin for you.'

'There is, Lottie. I have to find out the truth.'

'Talk to your mother. Alexis is the one who betrayed you and Bernie. She's the only one who knows the truth, and when she feels like it, she will tell you.'

'Alexis died.'

That stopped Lottie in her tracks. 'When? I didn't know. I'm sorry.' She wasn't, but it was the right thing to say. Alexis was her biological mother's sister, and she had separated the twins as toddlers, taking Leo to New York with her and leaving Bernie to live half her life in an institution.

'A few weeks ago. That's why I came back. It's eating me up. I have to know, and I thought Bernie could fill in the gaps.'

The door of the Indian restaurant opened and a man walked out with two bags of takeaway food. Lottie felt her stomach rumble. The sausage rolls had done nothing to fill the hollow.

'You have phone calls to make. I wish you luck. Don't come near me again unless it's to tell me she's locked up. Okay?'

As Leo returned to his rental car, Lottie felt a little bit of her heart break away. She'd lost one brother at the hands of a madman; was she about to lose another? She cared about Leo but didn't want to show him. She had enough shit to worry about.

CHAPTER 26

'I was better off in jail,' Conor muttered to himself as he stuffed his mother's soiled clothing into the washing machine. At least inside there'd been a full laundry service. He put the morning's wash into the dryer and hoped it worked properly or he'd have nothing to wear to work tomorrow.

'What did you say?' came the voice from the living room.

Nothing wrong with her ears. Not a thing. Even though she played the martyr and liked him to think she was losing her hearing as well as her marbles.

He didn't answer. Let her think he hadn't heard. It had been a long, miserable day and he wanted to crawl into his own bed without having to make up hers. But she was putting a roof over his head, as she'd told him a million times since his release, and he was expected to do bits and pieces around the house. He set the machine to a quick wash and opened the refrigerator. She had to have warm milk every night.

'Oh no,' he said to the bare door of the appliance.

'What's that?'

'I've to go out to get milk. We've none left.' He shut the door and grabbed his jacket from the back of a chair before going to the living room door. 'Have you got any change?'

'Why didn't you make sure we had enough? It's your responsibility now that I'm giving you a place to stay. You need to pull your weight. I …'

He tuned her out. Saw her purse on the mantelpiece. Took out a five-euro note.

'I want that back when you get paid,' she said.

'Sure.' He buttoned his jacket. 'I won't be long.'

'It's raining out. I can hear the wind …'

She was still talking when he pulled the front door shut behind him. He had no idea how much longer he could stick this life. It had been better in jail. And that had been total shit.

*

Katie whispered a kiss on Louis' head and turned on the dim night light. He sucked hungrily on his bottle and she smiled. He was such a good baby really. Not a baby any more, she thought, as she recalled his first steps two days after he turned one.

She wondered what her life would have been like if Jason hadn't been murdered. These days she found it hard to remember Louis' dad. The only photos she had of him had been lost when she'd upgraded her phone. But she told Louis all about him. Made most of it up, if she wanted to be totally honest. She'd only been with Jason a few short months when he'd been killed. He hadn't even known she was pregnant. But she'd kept the baby and never regretted her decision.

She thumbed the curtains apart and looked out. The dark evenings gave her goose bumps, and she hoped Louis was warm enough in his sleeping-bag and fleece blanket his grandad had sent from New York. The wind was rising and leaves whistled down to the ground from increasingly bare branches. She liked the new estate. It was quiet. Maybe too quiet. If it wasn't for the wind, she'd describe it as deathly silent. Rain began to spill in diagonal sheets, sweeping the leaves down the road. Shadows danced in the rain and she turned away.

The sucking ceased, so Katie took the bottle from her now sleeping son. A finger of fear traced a line down the nape of her neck. She rushed back to the window and looked out. Was that a shadow she'd seen behind the wall across the road? Someone crouching at the entrance to the laneway that led to the rear of St Catherine's retirement home? But there was no one there now. Why had she felt fear? As she turned back to watch her son, she remembered that she'd sensed the same feeling yesterday in the shop. Should she tell her mother? Good God, no. Lottie would go into detective mode and put a clamp on her freedom, even if she was only imagining things.

Pulling up the old chair she'd brought from her granny's house, Katie sat down, drew her legs beneath her and snuggled under a blanket. She suspected that tonight she wouldn't be able to sleep in her bed. She had to keep watch over her son. Because she was convinced that someone else had been keeping watch over her. And not in a good way.

*

Sipping a pint at the bar in the Parkland Hotel lounge, Tony Keegan was trying to ignore the wedding crowd singing loudly on the opposite side of the room. Stilettos and bling usually excited the hell out of him. Girls with caked-on make-up, mascara so thick it looked like ink, and fake-tanned legs hovered around encroaching on his thoughts. Despite trying to be oblivious, he couldn't help the hard-on giving him an ache in his groin. His hair was still damp from the rain. It was a curse of a night to be out. He should feel pity for the anonymous bride who had to brave the downpour on her wedding day, but fuck her and her fairy-tale ideas. This was real life, where there were no happy endings. Not that he'd seen so far.

The pint tasted bitter. Probably dredged from the end of the barrel. He should send it back, but the girl behind the bar was already struggling with the crowd. She had good legs, natural. No fake tan for her. He found himself wondering if she had been to Spain on her holidays. That would be a nice escape. If he had the money. Which he hadn't. And now Conor was back.

He took a gulp of the putrid beer and let out a loud belch. Awful. He raised a hand to summon the girl, but she either didn't see it or just plain ignored him. She knew who the good tippers were. Not him. Clever girl. Didn't change the fact that he still had to drink a pint of slop.

He drained his glass and stood. Despite the rain outside, he knew he would feel better out there.

Gathering his change into his pocket, he heaved on his coat and trudged a lonely trek through the merry crowd. He couldn't escape quickly enough.

*

Cyril Gill poured a double whiskey from the decanter and stood looking out the window of his million-euro dream house. Just when business was going so well, despite the delay with his current project, that thorn in his side was back in Ragmullin. Along with him, the only other person who could make trouble for Cyril was his own daughter Louise.

He swallowed his drink and poured another. He was used to getting his own way, but when it came to family, his hands were tied. Leaning his head against the cool glass of the window, he tried to think of a way out. One thing he knew for sure, he had to do something, and quickly.

He felt his phone vibrate in his pocket.

'I thought we agreed we would not be in contact. It's too easy to track our—'

'It's Amy. She's dead. Some bastard murdered her. What are you going to do about that? Tell me! What the hell are you going to do about it?'

'Jesus, back up there. Amy? Dead? What the—'

Richard Whyte hung up.

Cyril dropped the phone and the glass and raced up the stairs. 'Louise! Louise! We have to talk. Now!'

*

Louise thought it safer to be away from the house at the moment. Huddled in her silver-coloured parka jacket, she rushed down the shingle driveway and out onto the road. It was dark. Of course it was. Her father had built this house in the middle of nowhere.

She hated living outside the town, and never having mastered the skill of driving, her red Mazda sports car continued to rust away in one of the four garages at the back of the house. More extravagance on her father's part. Compensating? For what? She wondered about that as she made her way along the narrow path that edged the side of the road.

It was all her father's fault again. Shouting and roaring up the stairs about Amy being dead. That couldn't be true. She'd rushed past him, out into the night, without her phone or bag. She had to find out for herself. As the lights of approaching cars illuminated her route and then plunged her into darkness again, she had no fear for her safety. She'd lived in Ragmullin all her life. She knew the town inside out.

It couldn't be true about Amy. Their relationship had suffered badly. Teenage friendships rarely survived into adulthood, Louise knew, but she also knew the two of them were intrinsically linked by their past.

The road once again became silvery grey with yet another car behind her. Head down, she continued to walk. But this car didn't pass her. The light snaked alongside her and stopped. She kept walking. Almost there. Three minutes and the Parkland Hotel would be in view and lights would pave the way towards Amy's house. Perhaps she should nip into the hotel. A hot whiskey with cloves stuck in a lemon would warm her up. She was beginning to feel the cold through the feathered layers of her jacket. And something else, too. A tinge of fear. That car hadn't moved.

Quickening her steps, Louise was jogging when a hand gripped her arm and swung her round. She opened her mouth to scream, but only a groan accompanied the spatter of rain on the road.

'Louise? I thought it was you. How are you doing?'

'Oh God!' She shuddered. 'You terrified me. Don't you know you shouldn't creep up on a defenceless woman on a dark road.' The words tumbled out of her mouth as she tried to disguise the terror thumping double beats in her heart.

'Fancy a drink?'

He was insistent without sounding it. It was his body language. Head twisting and turning. Trying to see if anyone had noticed them? A tic at the edge of his mouth, and continuously sniffing. She needed to appear calm.

'No thanks. I wanted some fresh air. Had to get out of the house. I'm fine. I love the rain.'

She extracted her arm and began to walk again. He kept pace.

'Leave me alone.' Brave words, but she was shaking all over now.

'Ah, come on. A drink will warm you up.'

She stopped and swirled around. Drew back her hand and hit him. She surprised herself almost as much as she shocked him. His jaw slackened and his mouth hung open.

'That was a silly thing to do, wasn't it?'

Seizing the opportunity while he was apparently stunned by her action, Louise turned and ran. Further into the darkness, where the road was empty.

The one thing she had feared had happened.

Her past had caught up with her.

All she could do was try to outrun it.

*

Megan Price took the last of the china ornaments out of the box she kept under the bed. He hadn't found that when he'd ransacked the house for things he could sell. She took them out every night and cleaned them. Because these little figurines were precious. They were all she had left of long ago.

Lining them up on the mantelpiece she shifted them around until they were in the exact positions they should be in. The way he used to arrange them.

She caught her reflection in the mirror above the fireplace and rubbed a smudge from her brow with the yellow duster. Her father would have said she looked like death warmed up. And he'd have been right. If he was still alive.

As she brought her hand downwards, it clipped the corner of the porcelain shoe decorated with gold filigree, and before she could react, it had smashed on the bare floorboards.

She dropped to her knees and frantically tried to gather the pieces back into shape. Superglue might do it. But you'd still be able see the cracks. She crunched up the pieces into the palms of her hands. Felt the sharp edges cut her skin and let them fall away.

She needed air. She had to get out of the suffocating walls pulsing with memories, before her entire world fell apart.

*

He had stopped following her. She no longer heard the slap of feet on the path. Pausing to catch her breath, she chanced a look over her shoulder.

Darkness. Nothing. No one.

Louise exhaled and slowed to a brisk walk. Where had he come from? She wished she had her phone to call her dad to come pick her up. That had been an impetuous act, running out of the house. Like a petulant teenager. The one she used to be. The one she thought she had left behind ten years ago. The impressionable one. Yeah, she thought. She and Amy had a lot to answer for. Amy could not be dead.

Amy's house was on a gated estate built by Louise's father's firm in an area where no one had ever envisaged houses being situated. It probably helped that Mr Whyte was on the council. She keyed in the entry code from a long-held memory, and as the gates swung open, she saw the convoy of cars parked on the road up near Amy's house. Louise was rooted to the spot. Something was wrong. Very wrong. Her dad was right. Amy was dead.

She forced her feet to move and set off towards the house. No. She did not want to go in there. She wanted to go to someone who would comfort her. She turned back, edging between the closing gates before they banged shut.

Reaching the apartment block, she ran up the steps and pounded on the door. When it opened, she fell into the other girl's arms.

'Oh, Cristina,' she sobbed.

'What's wrong, hon? You're soaking wet. Come in. Come in.'

Louise allowed herself to be engulfed in a hug before stepping into the warmth of the apartment. As she did so, the door crashed open behind her and Cristina was thrown to the floor.

'Hello, girls,' a voice said.

Standing with her mouth wide open, her body convulsed with shivers, Louise only had eyes for the knife glinting in the gloved hand.

'Aren't you going to invite me in?' The knife moved to the other hand.

Louise felt the prick of something sharp on the side of her neck. She tried to remain standing, but her entire body felt paralysed. Her legs gave way and she slumped against the wall. As her eyelids drooped, she heard Cristina scream.

CHAPTER 27

Before heading up to bed, Lottie checked that all the doors and windows were locked. At the front door she thought she saw a shadow move behind the glass. Boyd?

She unhooked the chain, turned the key in the mortise lock and opened the door. There was no one there. The day had been exhausting and she felt her knees creak with tiredness. Seeing things now, she told herself. The image of the two murdered women lying on slabs in the morgue wouldn't dissipate. Must be that, she thought.

About to close the door, she decided: no, best to have a proper look. She walked down the narrow path and onto the road. No cars. No cats or dogs. The rain had eased. Silence and serenity despite the whisper of a slow drizzle.

She went back up the path and paused as light spilled out from her hallway onto the step. What was that? Bending down, she studied a scattering of small seeds spread across the concrete. Had they been there when she went out a moment ago? She swung around. No one there.

And then she knew. She knew who had left them. Were they a warning, or an invitation to battle?

A bolt of fear slashed through her body. It was like someone had cut her veins and her lifeblood was slipping away. There was only one person she knew who had an unhealthy obsession with seeds and herbs. She had discovered this fact during her investigations which led to the arrest of her half-sister.

Bernie Kelly had been outside her house.

*

The woman curled away from the bush across the road as the door slammed shut. She was smiling to herself.

Lottie had got the message.

Shoving her hands deep into her pockets, she hummed a tuneless song deep within her throat. She wasn't stupid enough to sing out loud. She couldn't sing anyway.

Turning the corner, she moved out onto the main road, keeping close to the hedges. After a year cooped up, hands cuffed to her bed more often than not, it was good to be out in the fresh air. She didn't care how long that freedom lasted, as long as she completed the task she had set out to do.

Now it was up to Rose Fitzpatrick to play her part and deliver the second piece of the message.

And then the serious business could begin.

*

He'd forgotten to get the milk. But she was already asleep when he returned home, so he went straight to his room. He needed a shower, but the exertions of the last few hours had drained his energy. He stripped naked and lay on the hard mattress.

He hadn't bothered to draw the curtains. The lights from the road shone in on the walls, and he stared at a myriad of cobwebs clinging to the light bulb in the ceiling. Just like him, clinging on to reality.

Her deep green eyes were everywhere. Her sharp nose and inquisitive lips. And the eyes. They were what he remembered most clearly. How she'd peered at him from the witness box while she stood there telling her lies. She knew they were lies, because he knew the truth.

His fingers cramped from the cold and his toes were freezing. The Raynaud syndrome was back. It was too cold to get back out of bed to fetch socks. Pulling the thin blanket up to his neck, he thought of her again. Lottie Parker. And her coven of witches who had conspired against him.

Lying awake, he tried to think up new ways to make them pay for the ten years of his life that were lost for ever.

*

The shower was too hot, but Tony stood under it, scrubbing and scrubbing until his skin was almost raw. When he was sure he was clean, he stepped out and wrapped a towel around his waist, letting the air cool his throbbing flesh.

He missed her. On nights like this, he craved the sheen of her flesh against his. The aroma of their lovemaking. The taste of her body. The loving look in her eyes. No. Stop. She never had a loving look in her eyes. Derision and disgust. That was all he ever witnessed in the blackness. And now it made him shiver and his skin shrivel.

Eventually he dried himself, switched off the shower and the light, and padded flat-footed and naked to bed.

*

Bernie had left hours ago, but Rose still sat in the same position.

What was she going to do? She had to tell Lottie. But how?

She bit down on her already shredded nails and shook her head. In all her seventy-odd years, with everything that had happened to her, she had never experienced the anguish and terror that she now felt.

She could not tell Lottie what Bernie had said. But at the same time, she had to protect her daughter and her grandchildren.

She sat and pulled at her nails until the sky slowly began to light up the kitchen once again.

CHAPTER 28

The sky on Wednesday morning was more beautiful than Lottie had seen it all week. Though it was dawn, a few golden rays broke through the trees where birds perched. Tiny flies flitted in the half-light. But she could not shed the unease sitting between her shoulder blades.

She picked up the bag holding the seeds she'd gathered from her doorstep last night. Must be about fifty of them, she thought. Did the number mean something? Or was it an indiscriminate figure, meant only to confuse her as she tried to decipher the significance? It was enough to know that her half-sister had been that close to her home, to her children and grandson. She'd left her calling card.

The warmth and comfort of her new home was suddenly distilled into darkness as a shudder of trepidation crawled up her vertebrae. Stop. No way was she letting that woman ruin her new-found happiness. Ghosts had plagued her life for long enough. She was not returning to that monstrous dungeon of despair and uncertainty.

'Damn you, Bernie,' she said.

'What?'

Lottie swung around. 'Katie! Oh my God, you scared the life out of me.'

'Sorry, Mam.' Katie opened the cupboard and extracted a box of cereal.

'What has you up this early? I didn't hear Louis wake.'

Katie sat at the table and shoved a handful of cornflakes into her mouth. 'It's not Louis.'

'Don't talk with your mouth full, and what's wrong with getting a bowl and spoon?'

Pushing the cereal box across the table, Katie clenched her hands and lowered her chin to her chest without reply.

Dragging out a chair, Lottie sat in front of her eldest child and wrapped her hands around Katie's. 'What is it? You can tell me.'

'It's okay. It's nothing.'

'You're not pregnant, are you?' The possibility caused Lottie's heart to lurch in her chest. No way could she handle that scenario.

Katie looked up from beneath long lashes and smiled. 'Unless it's the immaculate conception, I don't think so.'

Lottie let out a shadow of a sigh. 'What has you worried then?'

'It's nothing. Honestly. Just my mind playing silly games.' Katie looked away.

Lottie gently turned her daughter's head and looked into her eyes. 'It's something, otherwise you'd still be asleep and not up raiding cornflakes at this hour.'

'You'll think I'm crazy.'

'No, sweetheart, I'm the crazy one in this family.'

'It's just this feeling I have. A weird sensation that someone is watching me. Following me.'

Lottie dropped her hand and shifted uneasily on the chair. 'When? Where?'

'Don't rush into detective mode, Mam.'

'Tell me.' Lottie spied Louis' wool jacket on the back of the chair. She picked it up and began to fold it. She needed to be doing something.

'In town, the other day,' Katie said. 'I thought someone was watching as I tried on clothes in Jinx. And then last night, I had this awful feeling that someone was looking in the window. Which is ridiculous seeing as my room is upstairs. It's probably all my imagination. Hormones or something.'

Or something, Lottie thought. She was going to find Bernie Kelly and string her up from the tallest tree she could find in Ragmullin. This was too much.

'Don't worry about it,' she said, lacing her voice with as much nonchalance as she could muster. She didn't want to frighten her daughter, but at the same time she needed her to be wary. 'It could be hormones, or just the time of year. Halloween coming up and all that. But be careful all the same. Keep a close eye on Louis. And Chloe and Sean.'

She ran her fingers over the soft knitted ribs of the little tan jacket. Maybe she should tell Katie. Warn her. But what good would that do? Terrifying her children wasn't going to keep Bernie away. After all, she was sure she was after her, not her children. But just in case, she would organise a taxi to ferry Chloe and Sean to and from school every day.

'Perhaps you should stay in today. Louis has a touch of a cold and it might be best to keep him in an even temperature.' She placed the jacket on the table.

'There's something you're not telling me, Mam.'

'Just be watchful. That's all. I'm investigating two brutal murders of young women not much older than you, so you never know.' She had already spoken to her daughters about the murders, but they had no recollection of seeing anything untoward on Saturday night at the club.

'Thanks for the reassurance,' Katie said.

'Is that a cynical reply?'

'No, Mam. Only *you* do the cynical stuff, along with the crazy stuff.' Katie stood, and Lottie felt the warmth of her daughter's arms circle her shoulders in a hug. She smelled Louis on her, and it was calming.

'Now, get a bowl, spoon and milk. I've to go to work.'

Lottie picked up Louis' jacket to hand it to Katie. As she did so, she heard the tinkle of something hitting the floor. She looked down at the dizzying white tiles. What was it? A small disc, glinting in the half-light shining through the window. Her breath caught in her throat. She recognised the coin. An exact replica of the ones found at the murder scene and in Amy Whyte's room.

'What is it, Mam?'

Lottie dropped to her knees to inspect the coin. 'Katie … where were you yesterday? Who were you with?'

'You're scaring me now. What's that? Did it fall out of Louis' pocket?'

'I think so. How did he get it?'

'I don't know.'

'Where did you go with him while he was wearing this jacket?'

Katie shrugged. 'Town. To Granny's house for a few minutes and the chemist for lemon syrup for Louis. I stopped at Fallon's for a bowl of soup. Then I came home. That's all.'

'And you had Louis in your sight at all times?'

'Of course I did. What's this about, Mam?'

'Are you absolutely sure?'

Lottie saw the colour that had risen in Katie's cheeks slip slowly away. Her daughter's eyes were darkening, and not just from the effect of smudged mascara.

'When?' she said. 'When do you think you might not have had your eyes on him?'

'I don't know. Maybe when I was trying on clothes on Monday, in Jinx. But the shop assistant, June, she watched him for me. Mam!

You're scaring the shit out of me. What is it? What's going on?' Katie dropped to her knees beside Lottie.

She had to defuse this immediately.

'I think it's just a cheap home-made disc of some sort. Maybe someone thought it was a euro and put it in his pocket trying to be kind.' Lottie didn't believe a word she'd just said. She added, 'Now get your cereal and let me deal with this.'

'Is it evidence of some sort?' Katie got up and fetched a bowl and filled it with cornflakes and milk.

Lottie shook her head slowly. 'I doubt it. Leave it to me.'

When Katie had left the kitchen, Lottie ran to the counter and unwrapped a pair of plastic gloves from a box in a drawer. Pulling on the gloves, she found a small freezer bag and placed the coin inside. She took it to the window where she had left the bag of seeds and wondered just what the hell was going on.

CHAPTER 29

The construction team had hit a brick wall. Literally.

The foreman, Bob Cleary, scratched his head with a thick calloused finger, knocking his hard hat backwards so that its lamp pointed towards the roof, plunging the wall directly in front of him into darkness.

'What the hell?' He took out his flashlight and pulled the architect's drawings from his pocket. Flattening the paper against the damp wall, he shone the light on it. The drawings were wrong. There was no wall in them. But he was standing facing it. Bloody unbelievable.

He scrunched up the pages and shoved them back into his pocket. Placing his hard hat securely back on his head, he scanned the surrounding area. He'd known there were tunnels deep beneath the old courthouse and they had been clearly marked out. But this obstruction, or construction, whichever it was, was not documented on anything he'd seen.

'This damn job gets harder by the day,' he muttered. Already three months behind schedule, and this was another unforeseen obstacle.

He hammered his fist against the wall, as if this action could make it disappear. Mortar crumbled against his fingers. With the nail of his index finger he scratched around the edge of the bricks. The cement wasn't new, just damp from underground condensation. Bob had no idea how long the wall had been here, but he had to get rid of it, and quickly.

His phone had no signal, so he began the trek back through the tunnel. There would be a lot of phone calls to make. And this cock-up was on the head of the architect. No way was Bob Cleary taking the blame for this one.

'No way.' His voice echoed back at him as he reached the top of the steps.

Cyril Gill was going to chew his arse over this. Fuck and double fuck.

*

Lottie popped into McDonald's for a coffee on her way into work. She was still convinced they did the best coffee in town, though Boyd was currently pontificating about Ragmullin's newest coffee shop, The Bank. But she couldn't be arsed looking for parking. Familiarity was the handier option. A television was streaming a twenty-four-hour news channel with the sound muted. Subtitles scrolled across the bottom of the screen.

She had a dilemma to solve. Her family needed protection, but how was she going to convince McMahon to allocate resources when they were already stretched? If she relayed the reason why, she'd have to mention Bernie, and she didn't want to do that if at all possible.

As she waited for her coffee, her eye was drawn to the television screen. She felt her jaw slacken. Cynthia Rhodes was standing outside Ragmullin garda station. Lottie quickly followed the script scrolling beneath the reporter's camel coat.

Bernie Kelly, the serial killer who stalked Ragmullin a year ago, is reported to have escaped from the Central Mental Hospital. It is not known when she absconded. Authorities are warning the public to be on the lookout and not to approach her, but to contact the helpline.

'Can you turn it up?' Lottie frantically knocked on the steel counter, trying to get the barista's attention.

'Sorry. It's controlled from the office.'

'Just give me my coffee.' She threw down two euros and grabbed the drink.

As she turned away, she caught the last scrolling words before the bulletin moved to its next story.

I can exclusively report new information that has come my way. Bernie Kelly is a sister of the detective who put her away. Detective Inspector Lottie Parker.

'Fucking shit.' Lottie ran out.

She parked her car in the yard and was debating entering through the back door when she saw the melee of cameras and reporters turning the corner and heading for the gate. Nothing for it but to brave the storm.

Of course Cynthia Rhodes was at the head of the pack, microphone in hand, camera held aloft by someone behind her. And a sea of smartphones raised high. Bollocks.

Squaring her shoulders, Lottie headed straight towards her nemesis, intent on elbowing her in the gut as she passed.

Cynthia smiled. 'Detective Inspector Parker, can you tell me if it's true that you were instrumental in gaining a day release for Bernie Kelly? The same woman you helped put behind bars?'

'No comment.' She was going to kill Leo. As soon as she found him. And then Bernie. As soon as she found her too.

'Is it true that Bernie Kelly is your half-sister?'

Lottie stopped, her blood rapidly reaching boiling point. 'Oh, it's half-sister now, is it? Ten minutes ago she was a fully fledged sibling.' Her skin prickled.

'My sources inform me that—'

'What sources?' Wrong to engage her, but she wanted to know.

'My sources are confidential. Can you tell me—'

'No comment.'

'Is she linked to the deaths of the two young women discovered yesterday?'

Dipping her head, Lottie shouldered her way through the crowd, ignoring questions and almost tripping up the front steps when she reached them.

'Where is she, Inspector?' Cynthia's voice carried over the pack.

'I wish I knew.' Lottie let the door slowly close on the reporter.

Inside, she found Cyril Gill ranting and raving at the desk sergeant.

'Mr Gill, can I help you?' She dropped her keys into her bag and eased the man away from the desk and into the small interview room to her right. 'What's the matter?'

The suave business persona she'd witnessed on Monday had been replaced by a wet and dishevelled-looking man. Lines of worry were etched into his jaw, and his eyes drooped, circled with black rings. He ran one hand furiously through his hair while trailing the other up and down his suit jacket, as if he was searching for something. The hem of his shirt was sticking out untidily over his belt.

'My daughter, Louise. She didn't come home last night. I've no idea where she is.'

'Sit down, please,' Lottie said as she took off her jacket. A sense of worry wormed its way through her veins. 'Do you want me to make out a missing persons report?'

'I want her found, that's what I want.'

'Please sit.' Experience had taught her that distraught people needed to be taken in hand. Maybe she should take a leaf out of that bible herself. She was surprised when Gill complied.

'When did you last see her?'

'About eight o'clock last night. We had an argument.' He seemed to think better of this and added, 'It wasn't really an argument. I was trying to tell her that Amy Whyte, her old friend, had been found murdered. But she wouldn't believe me. Ran out of the house with no phone or anything. And I haven't seen her since.'

'How old is Louise?' But Lottie knew the girl's age. Louise Gill had been with Amy Whyte ten years ago when they'd witnessed the aftermath of a crime and ID'd the culprit, Conor Dowling. Lottie couldn't shake the feeling that Louise being missing and Amy being dead were connected.

'Twenty-five,' Gill said. 'But she's still my baby girl.'

'Tell me more.'

He sighed and clenched his hands into fists on the table. 'What's to tell. I don't know where she is and I'm worried.'

'Was she still friends with Amy Whyte?'

'I'm not sure. I don't think so.' He seemed evasive, shifty somehow. 'A few years after the Dowling court case, they drifted apart. College and stuff.'

'Why was she so upset when you told her about Amy's murder?' Lottie was intrigued, and worried.

'I don't know. Honestly.'

'Maybe she went to Amy's house. Did you check?'

'I went round there first thing this morning. She hadn't been there. Richard's in a state.'

'Did you ring her?'

'I told you already, she left without her phone. Inspector, my Louise is a quiet girl. Reclusive even. She spends every waking hour studying and writing up her thesis. I have no idea why she hasn't come home.'

'Has she any other friends?'

He shrugged slowly, like his shoulders were struggling to hold up his head. 'Not that I know of.'

'Boyfriend?'

'Why are you asking these questions?' A light flared in his eyes. Anger? Or desperation? Lottie wasn't sure, but she was certain he was holding something back.

'Because it's possible Louise is with a friend.'

'I don't think so.' He fidgeted on the chair. A lie, she thought.

'Do you have her phone?'

He slipped it out of his pocket, unlocked it and placed it on the table.

'Have you checked her contact list?'

'I rang everyone on it. It's not a huge list, as you can see.'

Scrolling through the contacts, Lottie was surprised to find that a twenty-five-year-old girl could have so few people listed. Then a thought struck her. 'Has she a second phone?'

'A second phone? What would she want with another one. This is the latest model.'

He obviously didn't know how young people operated. Lottie tapped on Louise's social media apps. There were no recent updates.

'There must be someone she confides in.'

He was shuffling his feet. Biting the inside of his mouth. Scratching away at an invisible speck on the desk. 'There's this girl, Cristina. Louise doesn't know that I'm aware of their … friendship. But I rang her and there's no answer.'

'What's her full name and where does she live?' Lottie's intuition told her Cyril Gill was uncomfortable with Louise's relationship with the girl.

He gave her the name and address. Cristina Lee. A name she thought she'd heard somewhere recently. She wrote down both. 'And is this Cristina a good friend?'

'I don't know what she is, but I want my Louise home.'

'I understand your concern and I'll see what I can do.' With Conor Dowling out of prison and two murder victims lying in the morgue, Lottie was more than concerned for Louise's well-being, but she couldn't convey that to Cyril Gill. 'Strictly speaking, we have to wait forty-eight hours before classing this as a missing person case, so in the meantime, I'd advise you to do your best to find your daughter yourself.'

'You're a waste of space. I'm going straight out to talk to those reporters outside. Then we'll see who puts resources into finding my daughter.'

'Mr Gill …'

But he was gone.

Lottie hoped Louise was safe, but instinctively she knew something was drastically wrong. She stood up slowly and wondered what other shit was going to blow up a storm today.

CHAPTER 30

There was no sign of Cyril Gill, and he wasn't answering his phone. Bob Cleary felt the perspiration of desperation pooling between his shoulder blades, soaking his shirt. He tore off his work jacket and paced the enclosed confines of the Portakabin. The walls dripped with condensation, and he felt every one of those drops like a hammer pounding against his skin. Gill was going to crucify him. What the hell was he to do? Deal with it. That's what the boss would say. Yeah, that's what he had to do.

He stuck his head outside and searched for a few lads he could trust. When he had three of them, he loaded up a jackhammer and tools on a trolley and directed them to follow him.

With four sets of lights beaming the way forward, he made it to the obstructing wall quicker than he had exited. He barked out orders and the men set to work. Bob watched them drilling. He was certain that the wall was not part of the original tunnel. Maybe that was why it hadn't shown up on any drawings or plans. So what was it for? Why was it here?

As they made the opening larger, he put up his hand to halt the excavation. He shoved his head into the narrow aperture, which was illuminated dimly by the light on his helmet.

'What the holy fuckin' hell?'

'What's up, boss?'

One of the men shoved Bob sideways and he almost collapsed against the drenched tunnel wall.

'Jesus. Oh my God. It's bones,' the man shouted.

Bob regained his balance and control of the situation. That was why he was the foreman, after all. 'Hand me a proper torch,' he said.

'Should we drill away a bit more so you can get in?'

'Give me a minute, for God's sake.' He shone the torch around the now exposed cell. Because that was what it looked like. It appeared to be man-made, and there was an opening on the far side. He drew his eyes back to the bones. They were clothed in no more than rags, but it was enough to make him realise he was staring at the remains of a human being. Male or female? He had no idea. Now he had a dilemma. Should he call the guards, or try to make contact with Mr Gill?

'Boss, I think that's a body.'

'You don't say, Einstein.' Bob made a face at Tony Keegan. The man was a right dope. 'Let me have a closer look. Oh yeah, you're right. It is a body. How could I have missed that? Lucky you were here.'

He felt Tony step back, and a cloud of fetid air seemed to fill the void.

'Been down here a while,' another brainbox said.

'When I want an opinion, I'll ask for it, okay?'

'Okay, boss. But I still think—'

'Shut up.' Bob was sorry he hadn't done the job himself. Without an audience. This would be around town before lunchtime. He had to act fast.

'Right, you might not agree with this course of action, but I don't want a word of this outside of us four. Got it?' Some hope of that happening, he thought.

'Got it,' came the chorus of replies.

'We're going to forget about it until I decide what to do.' He picked up the drill and directed the men back up the tunnel. This was going to be messy, and not just removing the bones. The consequences for the job. The aftermath.

*

The morning was so hectic, Lottie almost forgot about the seeds she'd picked up from her doorstep and the coin that had fallen from Louis' jacket. She was sure the seeds had something to do with Bernie, but for the moment she was more concerned about Louise Gill and the coin. It was a definite link to the two murders, so why had it been placed in her grandson's pocket? Forensics needed to examine it. She had to log it and do it by the book.

Perhaps the coin would help her convince Superintendent McMahon to provide a squad car to keep watch over her family. If he didn't agree, she was going to organise it herself and feck the consequences. Her family were more important than her job.

*

Conor followed Tony around the side of the courthouse and took a cigarette from his friend's shaking hands.

'What are you on about?' he said, and lit both cigarettes

'I swear to God, it's a real live dead body.'

'You're talking pure shite. Calm down.' Conor took a drag and curled up in a fit of coughing. He should never have gone back on them. Tony's fault. Again. 'Where?'

'Down there.' Tony pointed to the entrance of the tunnel. Bob Cleary was walking around in circles, his phone clamped to his ear.

Conor took another drag. What had they found? 'Long dead, then?'

'It's just bones. Some clothes falling off it in ribbons. Who the hell could it be?'

'Someone dead, I presume.' Conor tried to be flippant, but Tony's words had sent a dagger of unease plunging through his chest. He threw down the cigarette and ground it out with his muddy boot. 'What's Cleary going to do about it? This could jeopardise our jobs, you know.'

Tony rounded on him. 'Is that all you have to say? Some poor eejit got locked down in that tunnel and probably starved to death, and you're worried about the job? You're worse than Cleary.' He made to walk away, but Conor caught the sleeve of his jacket and pulled him back.

'If the guards come snooping around, they're going to look no further than me. They've already brought me in for questioning about those two women found dead at Petit Lane. They'll try to pin this on me too.'

'Don't be such a dick. You've been in prison for ten years. This has nothing to do with you.'

'I know, but try telling that to my probation officer. It won't look good. They want to pin every fecking death that happens in this town on me.'

'You're always thinking of yourself. Why don't you get out of Ragmullin then? Go somewhere else.'

'And what about my mother?'

'She managed for the last ten years without you, didn't she?'

Conor watched Tony move away from him, then stop and look back before continuing on.

His eye was drawn to Bob Cleary. He had to find out what was in the tunnel.

CHAPTER 31

Lottie completed the paperwork on the coin she'd found at her home and dispatched it for analysis. Then she glanced at the boards in the incident room. Nothing new had been added by the night crew. She hoped Louise Gill's disappearance wasn't linked to Amy's death. But the odds were stacked that way.

Kirby was eating a sandwich out of a plastic wrapper. He lifted a slice of bread to peer in at the soggy cheese, and she noticed there was no butter on it. Her heart almost broke for him.

Drawing Boyd to one side, she said, 'Cyril Gill was down in reception when I arrived.'

'Oh, and what's all that fuss with the reporters outside?' Boyd leaned against the wall, settling in for a chat.

She sipped her coffee, made a face and put the cup down on a desk, then steered him out through the door. Spying McMahon turning the corner, she pulled Boyd by the hand and escaped down the stairs.

'Parker!' McMahon's voice reverberated off the walls like an echo.

'Lottie.' Boyd stalled. 'You'd better talk to him.'

'No. There's a friend of Amy Whyte's missing. Cyril Gill's daughter, Louise. Those two girls were the key witnesses in Conor Dowling's trial. Come on. We can't waste time.' She threw the car keys to him. 'You drive.'

Outside, he stood at the car, leaning over the roof. 'I'm going nowhere until you explain.'

A window opened two floors above them. McMahon shoved his head out. 'Parker. Come back here this instant.'

'Please, Boyd,' she said through gritted teeth. 'I think Louise could be in real danger.'

Boyd unlocked the door.

With one leg inside, Lottie glanced up at her red-faced superior shaking his fist out the window. She'd have to say something.

'Be back in five,' she called up. 'Emergency.' She slid in and slammed the door. 'Lights and siren, Boyd.'

'What for?'

'Impression.'

She told Boyd to switch off the siren when they turned onto Main Street, having successfully negotiated the swelling crowd of satellite news vans parked at the front of the station. She sank into the seat, her feet snagging on empty cans and smelly food wrappers.

'Your car is a dump,' he said.

'Tell me something I don't know.'

'You're in big trouble for running out on McMahon.'

'Boyd! Something I don't know.'

'Who killed Amy and Penny?'

She bit down on her thumbnail. 'Besides Conor Dowling being out of prison, no clues so far.' The nail broke. Shit.

'If he wanted revenge on Amy for giving evidence against him, where does Penny come into it?'

She bit the side of her thumb, thinking. 'That's what doesn't make sense.'

'Are you going to tell me where we're going?'

'Park Lane. It's where Cristina Lee lives.'

'Who?'

'A friend of Louise Gill. Can't you drive faster?'

'In this crock of shit? No.'

He flicked the indicator and swung left, pulling up at the foot of the concrete steps leading to Cristina Lee's first-floor apartment.

'You think Louise could be here?' he said.

'According to her father, she left home with no phone after hearing about Amy's death. So I reckon she's gone to see her girlfriend.'

'They're a couple?'

'Possibly.'

Lottie waited while Boyd locked the car, though she thought it was a waste of time. No one was going to steal it, the state it was in.

At the top of the steps, she paused to catch her breath. Her lungs were tight. Stress. She had to check that Katie and Louis were okay. She'd organised a taxi for Sean and Chloe, so she was secure in the knowledge that they were safely in school. She sent a quick text to Rose asking her to drop in on Katie.

'It's open,' Boyd said, rousing her from her strained musings.

She immediately pulled a pair of gloves from her pocket and slipped them on. She knocked on the door, then pushed at it.

'Something's wrong,' she said. As Boyd opened his mouth to reply, she added, 'Gloves.'

While he struggled to get them over his fingers, she put one foot into the dark hallway. A narrow table stood askew; keys and coats on the floor.

'Hello? Anyone home?' She listened and waited. 'What's that smell, Boyd?'

He sniffed the air as he joined her inside. 'Incense. Cinnamon or some sort of spice.'

Instinctively she knew she should have put on protective booties, but she had to investigate why the door was open and the hall in disarray. She made her way carefully into the room in front of her. It was dark. The incense scent was stronger here, and she could smell something else. Something cold and metallic.

Sliding her hand up the wall, she found the switch and flicked it on. The scene before her caused her to step back onto Boyd's toes.

'What the hell?' he said.

'Call it in,' she ordered. 'Quickly.'

As Boyd made the calls, Lottie stared without moving. She could not contaminate the crime scene. There was no need to check for signs of life. The two young women were dead. Throats slashed. Blood spatter up along one wall, and though the carpet, either Indian or Turkish, was woven in red thread, she could make out the darkness soaking into it.

One woman was distinctly of Asian origin. Hair matt black and skin slicked with blood. She was in a state of undress. Underwear, but no outer clothing save for a blue silk kimono. Lottie tried to visualise what had occurred. Cristina had risen from her bed to let Louise in. Then what? She gazed sadly at Cyril Gill's only daughter. Her long brown hair matted and snarled around her face, her throat with a single deep cut. Her clothing dishevelled and disturbed.

'I need SOCOs here as soon as possible. This place needs a forensic sweep and I want to see if any coins have been left with the bodies.'

'You think this is the work of a serial killer?' Boyd made to step into the room, but Lottie caught his arm.

'We can't disturb the evidence.'

'Never stopped you before.'

'I know, but … this seems different. McGlynn's methodical work is necessary before we contaminate anything.' She leaned into Boyd, comforted by his proximity.

'What is it, Lottie? What's holding you back?'

'I'm thinking about something that is particularly scary right now.'

'And what is that? Nothing fazes Lottie Parker.'

'This is the work of someone who has killed before.'

'The person who killed Amy and Penny?'

'Even before them.'

Boyd's face showed dawning realisation. 'Bernie Kelly? No, that doesn't make sense. As far as we know, she only killed people she believed to be family or people she was involved with illegally, and there's no way she could know these girls. She only escaped yesterday morning.'

'What if she hired someone to kill Amy and Penny and then she herself killed Cristina and Louise in a similar manner?' She looked at him intently. 'What do you think?'

'I think you're losing it. Come outside and get some air.'

'No.' She tapped the camera icon on her phone and quickly photographed the scene. 'Let's have a look in the other rooms.'

She turned and edged past him. Opening the door to her right, she walked into a compact living room. Two armchairs, a gas heater and a small window. She lifted the blinds and looked across at the gated enclave where Amy Whyte had lived. Sirens wailed in the distance. A squad car pulled up outside the block of flats, followed immediately by Jim McGlynn's station wagon and the technical van.

She watched as McGlynn robed up and took his equipment from the boot. He was soon joined by members of his team, and Lottie wondered how they were all going to fit into the tiny apartment.

Moving away from the window, she was struck by the subtle decor in the small room. Wall hangings depicted large images of the Buddha, while others portrayed Japanese gardens with trailing greenery and pink flowers in open bloom. A single shelf in one corner held crystals and a clear orb that reflected the light from the window onto the wall. She lifted it up and watched the light sprinkle a rainbow of colour all around her. As she was putting it back, the corner of a white card caught her eye. She slid it outwards with her gloved finger. It was a business card. And the name on it made her gasp aloud.

'Boyd!' she yelled.

'What are you doing in my crime scene?' Jim McGlynn said.

Lottie imagined his angry spittle spraying the inside of his mouth mask.

'The crime scene is in the next room.'

When he made his way out, she slipped the card into a small plastic bag and pocketed it.

At the entrance to the kitchen, she found herself backed up behind the SOCOs. She needed to know about the coins before she left. There was no sign of Boyd. Probably out having a smoke.

By the time she elbowed her way in, McGlynn was directing a team member with a video camera.

'Any coins?' she asked.

'Will you give me a minute?'

'Just look, will you? I didn't set foot in there. I could have, but I waited for you.'

He slowly clapped his hands. 'It's only taken you twenty years to figure that out, Inspector.'

'I can do without the sarcasm today.'

'I wasn't being sarcastic.'

She forced away another retort and watched eagerly as he hunkered down beside the body nearest to him. Louise Gill. Her skin bristled with panic. She'd have to deliver the news to Cyril Gill and his wife.

'One,' McGlynn said, holding up a silver disc. He dropped it into an evidence bag, sealed it and wrote the details with a marker.

'Any more?' Lottie scrunched up her hands, nails piercing her skin. They now had four bodies. This was the work of a serial killer. But what did the coins mean?

'You have no patience whatsoever.' But he continued with his work and produced a second coin, and then a third.

'Fuck!' Lottie exclaimed. 'What is this all about?'

'That's your job to figure out.'

'How long have they been dead?'

McGlynn paused, hands in the air, one holding a pair of tweezers, the other with an evidence bag. 'Can't you go do something else and come back in an hour. If you keep talking, I won't get anywhere.'

'A ballpark time, then?'

He shook his head but put down his tools and carefully examined Louise Gill's body. When he took out a thermometer, Lottie turned away and waited.

'Rigor, and body temp … so no longer than twelve hours.'

'Okay, thanks. Let me know if you find any more coins, and send in their phones if they're here too. And anything else—'

'I know. I know. Now can you feck off and let me work?'

CHAPTER 32

The tunnel was dark and damp. Conor had been down in some of the other tunnels over the last two weeks as they dug the supports for the lift shaft in the new section of the courthouse, but he hadn't been in this one. He walked with trepidation in each step. When Cleary had disappeared into the office he'd made his move, not sure why he was even doing it. But he had to see for himself.

The lamp on his hard hat cast eerie shadows ahead of him, and a few times he felt as though he wasn't alone. Shrugging off shivers, he sped up. He had to be quick before Gill arrived.

He stopped abruptly when the hole in the wall appeared before him. His heart plummeted right down into the soles of his boots. Shit.

Taking off his hat, he angled it into the hole and stuck his head in after it. His gaze landed on the body. He tried to keep the light from jigging around, but his hand was shaking so badly he almost dropped the hat. His breath caught in the back of his throat and he thought his heart was going to break out through his chest. The palpitations thumped so loudly in his ears, he felt he might go deaf.

Once he'd seen all he needed to see, he extracted his arm, slapped his hat back on his head and leaned against the damp wall, trying to think. But his thoughts were a jumble of letters he was unable to fuse into words.

Slowly he made his way back along the tunnel, his mind in free fall.

This discovery might just jeopardise everything.

*

Lottie found Boyd outside the apartment, organising door-to-door inquiries with a team of uniforms.

'We need to talk to Richard Whyte,' she said, striding across the road to the gated enclosure.

'But Cyril Gill and his wife have to be informed,' he protested. She kept walking. 'Lottie! Wait up.'

She slowed her march until he was in step with her, then sped up again. The gate was code-locked, with an intercom. She began pressing buttons.

'You'll have them calling the station.' He pulled her hand away. 'Look there. Read the names. That's Whyte's intercom.' He pressed the button, but the gate was already sliding to one side.

'I can't remember which house it is,' Lottie said, looking around the immaculately manicured estate.

'The door with the black wreath might give you a clue.'

'Smart-arse.'

Lottie rang the bell. The door opened almost immediately and Richard Whyte stood there in a creased white shirt, beige chinos and loafers.

'Come in,' he said, leading the way into the enormous living room. 'Have you news about Amy's death? And what's going on over at the apartments?'

'Mr Whyte, I'm sorry, I've no update on our investigation into Amy's murder, but I would like to ask you a few questions about Cristina Lee.'

'Cristina? Why? What did she do?' He sat in an oversized armchair.

Lottie glared at Boyd when he sat down too. She remained standing. Whyte had breadcrumbs stuck to his unshaved chin. She resisted the urge to reach down and brush them away.

'You told me you had a housekeeper. I found a card in Ms Lee's apartment that says she provides cleaning services. Does she clean for you?'

'She does a few days a week. What's this about?'

'There's been an incident at Park Lane. We are currently investigating it. Ms Lee lives over there, is that correct?'

'Cristina? Yes, she does.'

'Did she know Amy?'

'Sure she did. But I've already told you, Amy wouldn't allow her into her room. Cristina's a good worker. She told me she'll help out at the wake … you know … when Amy's allowed home so I that can bury her. When will that be?'

'As soon as the state pathologist allows.' Lottie sat, feeling that there was no reason for her to be intimidating a grieving father. 'Richard, this is very important. Look at me.' When he raised his head, she looked into his eyes. 'Had Amy been in contact with Louise Gill recently?'

'Louise? No. I don't think so. Why?' He paused, wringing his hands into a knot. 'Conor Dowling is out of prison. When I heard about Amy's murder, he was the first one I thought of, but then I thought, no, the case was too long ago. But if that scumbag killed my girl, I won't be responsible for what I do to him.'

Feeling the need to get on top of things before Richard took matters into his own hands, Lottie said, 'We have no evidence to support that idea. We're exploring all avenues. Nothing can be left to chance.'

Whyte eyed Boyd, then turned his attention back to Lottie.

'Are you sure you're the best officer to be leading this investigation?'

'Of course I am. Why would you say that?'

His eyes flicked to the blank television screen hanging on the wall above their heads.

Shit, Lottie thought. Cynthia Rhodes and her damn reports. 'I give you my word, I will do everything in my power to bring to justice the perpetrator of these heinous crimes.'

'You see that you do or I'll personally ring the garda commissioner to have you removed.'

She knew he meant every word, and he had the clout to make it happen. She had to watch her step, and her back.

'Richard, did you know that Cristina was friends with Louise Gill?'

An unreadable expression flitted across his face. 'No, I did not. What are you driving at?'

'Were Cristina and Amy close?'

'They hardly knew each other. I'm not sure they even bumped into each other here more than a couple of times. Amy worked in town. I don't know where else Cristina worked. Maybe they met socially, I have no idea.'

'How long has Cristina been in your employment?'

He blushed, and she knew Cristina wasn't on the books. Something to hold over him, if things went belly-up at any stage.

'About a year,' he said.

'How did you find her?'

'After my wife died, I couldn't cope with the house as well as the shop and the council. Amy was working too. I saw a card on the noticeboard in the pharmacy. I called the number on it and Cristina started working for me. Cleaning in the pharmacy and also here. She brought sunshine and polish into this house. I don't think I'd ever seen it sparkle so much.'

'How could she afford her apartment if she was just a cleaner? I imagine the prices are sky high over there,' Lottie said.

He shot up out of the armchair and leaned over her. 'If you're insinuating what I think you are, you have some cheek. Cristina is a beautiful person. She has an aura about her. I had no relationship with her other than to compliment her on her work and hand over her wages. So you can squash that idea.'

A sting of discomfort shot through Lottie. She hadn't even thought that Whyte could have been in a relationship with Cristina, just that he might have paid for her apartment. But now that he'd planted the seed of that idea, she couldn't uproot it.

'Does she keep any personal items here?' Boyd said, and Lottie silently thanked him for defusing the situation before she said something she would regret.

'Just the cleaning stuff. It's in a cupboard in the utility room. Has something happened to Cristina?' A streak of unease skittered across Whyte's face.

'Can we take a look?' Boyd said. 'If you don't mind.'

Whyte led the way out the door, through the kitchen and into the utility room, which was as big as Lottie's entire kitchen.

They found nothing of interest in the baskets of cleaning products, all neatly stored away. As Lottie shoved a basket back in, it snagged on something. Getting down on her knees, she ran her hand over the shelf and dragged out a small old-fashioned mobile phone.

Holding it up, and dropping all familiarity, she said, 'Is this yours, Mr Whyte?'

CHAPTER 33

Kirby was still hungry. He missed having Maria Lynch around to have lunch with. He should call and see how she was getting on with the new baby. But not now, not yet. He had no idea how to make small talk about stuff like that. He'd spent all morning collating information from house-to-house inquiries in relation to the Whyte and Brogan murders. Nothing unusual had jumped out at him. As usual with this town, no one knew anything.

As he moved to the photocopier, he felt the little box shift in his trouser pocket and his chest tightened. He gripped it tightly, feeling the soft velvet beneath his fingers, and his heart broke all over again. The surprise he'd planned for Gilly. The ring he'd ordered but never got to give her. Just yesterday, the jeweller's had called to say it was ready for collection. He could have said it was too late; he didn't need it any longer. But he didn't. Instead he'd gone in, paid the balance and taken the little blue box home with him. He couldn't find the willpower to open it up, to stare at the cluster of diamonds on the white-gold band.

She was gone. She'd never known of his intentions. Never got to answer his unasked question. Would never slip the ring on her freckled finger. He gulped back a sob, glad that everyone was out of the office. Working. Unlike him. He needed to do something or he was going to go stark raving mad.

He took his hand away from the box of shattered dreams, found his coat and trudged out of the office and out of the station.

He had to eat.

*

As Boyd drove back to the station, Lottie leaned her head against the window. When they reached the Dublin bridge, she sat up straight and looked down into the valley of her town. The cathedral's twin spires, the Protestant church's single one, and what Sean called the hangman's crane over the courthouse. They all stood as if holding up the businesses and homes that nestled in their shadows. In a few years, she thought, there might be a little more life in Ragmullin.

'You didn't have to be so cynical,' Boyd said, interrupting her musings.

'What do you expect? When you have a grieving father lying through his teeth.'

'Richard Whyte wasn't lying.'

'Oh come on, Boyd. He tried to pretend he knew nothing about that phone. But he did. I was studying his expression. He didn't think we'd find it. And then he got all flustered, saying it must have been Cristina's. Do you know what I think?'

'No, but you're going to tell me.'

'I think it's Amy's secret phone. And now I have it.'

'And do you think it will lead you to her killer?'

She didn't answer, just leaned her head against the glass again. The traffic lights turned green and Boyd put his foot to the floor.

'Lottie, it was in the cupboard with the cleaning products, so chances are it belongs to Cristina.'

'We'll have to wait until our technical guys have a look at it.'

'Right.'

'What's eating you now?' she said.

'Nothing, and you still have to tell me why you're avoiding McMahon.'

'It's about Bernie Kelly. The media broadcast about her escape. I was accosted by Cynthia this morning. Needless to say, shit from the fan is swirling around McMahon at the moment.'

'Are you sure you want to go back to the station?' He was already turning up the street.

'We now have four murders to investigate, so yes, I have to go back.'

They entered the station through the back door, and negotiated the stacks of box files that lined the narrow corridor.

'Make sure that door is shut,' Lottie told Boyd. 'Don't want little Miss Nosy Rhodes getting in.'

The media scrum outside the front door had swelled in the couple of hours since they'd left. Avoiding McMahon was going to be impossible.

'I think you're better off talking to him now instead of spending the remainder of the day in hiding.'

Boyd was right, she knew that, but the prospect of McMahon's anger was enough to make her want to avoid him at all costs. It was taken out of her hands when she entered the incident room. McMahon was seated at one of the desks, going over a stack of reports. She noticed a stranger sitting at another desk.

The acting superintendent raised his head. 'My office.'

By the time he had pushed out past her, she still hadn't formed her reply.

'You'd better get it over with,' Boyd said.

'Everything might be over by the time he finishes with me.'

'What are you going to say?' Boyd said.

'I'll think of something.'

She dropped her jacket and bag on a chair and followed her superior.

*

He'd moved the furniture around in his office again. Where did he get the time? Lottie searched for a chair to sit on, but couldn't see one. Was this a KGB-type ploy to make her faint at his feet and spill her secrets? Feck you, McMahon. She leaned up against the wall inside the door and waited while he settled himself behind his desk.

'Explain yourself,' he said at last.

'Sir?'

'Don't play the innocent with me. I know your type.'

'What type might that be?' As an afterthought, she added, 'Sir.' Best not to irritate him, though she suspected he was about to explode at any minute.

'The type who protests their innocence knowing they're guilty as hell.'

Unable to trust the words that might flow from her mouth, she remained silent.

'I'm going to ask you a couple of questions and I want straight answers.' He shifted a solitary pen from one side of his desk to the other. Then he leaned across and glared. 'Are you related to Bernie Kelly?'

'Sir, let me explain—'

'Answer the question!'

'Yes, I think so.' Feck him, she thought, he was going to screw her.

'Did you know that fact at the time of the investigations you were conducting last October into the murders of Tessa Ball and Marian Russell?'

'No, sir, I did not.' Lottie squirmed against the wall. She'd discovered back then that Marian Russell too was her half-sister.

'When did you become aware of your relationship to Bernie Kelly?'

'After the case closed.'

'The truth.'

'That is the truth. I uncovered a little information during the course of the investigation, but when I was recovering from my stab wound, I confronted my mother and she told me what she believed to be the facts.' Lottie felt like sliding down the wall and sitting with her hands around her knees like a child. But she remained standing, her head held high.

'That's a crock of shit.'

'It's the truth. Ask my mother.'

'If I'm to believe Cynthia Rhodes, your mother died in a lunatic asylum.'

A gasp caught in her throat. He was nothing other than a grade-A shithead. 'She might not be related by blood, but Rose Fitzpatrick is the only mother I've ever known.'

McMahon moved the pen to the other side of the desk again. 'I'll park that for the moment. When did you become aware that Kelly had escaped custody?'

Time for fudging the truth. She crossed her fingers. 'When Cynthia doorstepped me this morning.'

He snorted. 'You're in serious trouble over this.'

Lottie copped the hint of a smirk curling his lips. Don't say the wrong thing, she warned herself. That was what he wanted.

'So what are you going to do about it?' she said, lobbing the responsibility back into his court. She wasn't going to make this easy for him.

'You've compromised a historic murder case. You've put this whole district under the spotlight. I can't have you pissing all over another investigation, especially with your half-sister on the loose.' He still hadn't said what he was going to do, but she read between the lines.

'You can't take me off the current cases. I'm senior investigating officer. I have suspects, and clues to follow up. Two more murders discovered this morning, and I—'

'You need to shut up. I know I can't take you off the case immediately. I have assigned a detective from Athlone to your team. Sam McKeown. Be nice to him.' He paused, and Lottie held her breath. She knew what was coming. 'This is a formal warning. One step, one bloody step out of line, and you'll be suspended.' He held up a hand to stop her saying anything else. 'You're not off the hook. When you find this Bernie Kelly – and you will find her – I will know the whole truth of the matter.'

'You think she'll tell you the truth? You're delusional, if you don't mind me saying so.' She couldn't stop herself talking. She pushed away from the wall, leaned both hands on his desk and stared down at him. 'Bernie Kelly was bred on lies. She lives in a world of her own making. She doesn't know right from wrong. She couldn't stand trial for the murders of Marian Russell or Tessa Ball or any of the others, on grounds of insanity. And you're going to believe her over me? Come on! She's threatened me already. My family and I need protection, not suspension or suspicion.'

'Are you finished?' he said.

She was breathless, so she nodded and took a step back as he stood. All the resolutions she'd made since moving into her new home – to be a good mother, to be the best at her job, to stop being dependent on pills and alcohol – suddenly seemed to dissolve into this single moment, and she felt totally lost. All she could see through the haze was one fact. She could not lose her job.

'Threatened you? How?'

She could tell him about the seeds on her front step, but he wouldn't get it. She should tell him about the coin, but she didn't want to. She was in a bind. Before she could open her mouth, he continued talking.

'You bring me the killer or killers of these young women without alienating Richard Whyte and Cyril Gill, two upstanding gentlemen of this town, and I will have a think about what I'll do with you. Dismissed.'

Bollocks, she thought as she closed the door.

CHAPTER 34

Conor straightened his shoulders as he marched over to Bob Cleary. Tony had got over himself and agreed to give him support.

'Mr Cleary,' he said, 'can I have a word?'

'I told him about the tunnel,' Tony added. 'You know … what we found down there.'

Cleary rounded on him. 'Can you not take a direct order? Didn't I tell you to say nothing?'

'Yes, you did, but Conor is … well, he's my friend and I had to tell someone. He won't say anything.'

Watching the exchange, Conor decided he had to say something before Cleary took a swipe at Tony. Only God himself knew what would happen if he did that.

'Mr Cleary, sir. I'm part of the team here. I need this job. Is it true, what Tony said? About there being an old body in the tunnel?' He didn't want to let them know he'd already been down there.

Cleary sighed, tipped back his hard hat and ran a muddy gloved hand through his straw-like hair. 'I don't know how old it is. But it's been there a while, by the state of it. There'll be guards and archaeologists and every Tom, Dick and Harry down there before long. So I have to tell Mr Gill about it now.'

'Why?' Conor shoved his hands into his pockets and leaned his head to one side. Trying to look intelligent.

'Why what?'

'Why do you have to tell him? Can't you just ignore the fact that you found the body, do the job that has to be done in the tunnel and close it up again? That's what I'd do.'

Cleary scratched his head vigorously but said nothing.

Conor decided to go for it. 'If you report it, the job will be shut down. It could be months before we're allowed back on site. The boss won't like that. It's already behind schedule, isn't it?'

'Yes, it is,' Cleary conceded.

'The tunnel hasn't caved in in the last two hundred years and who's to say there aren't more bodies down there. Reporting your find will affect the job.'

'The weight of the new lift shaft that has to be constructed might cause subsidence. The whole thing needs to be supported. That tunnel is make or break on this job.' Cleary looked around wildly. 'Oh, I don't know what to think.'

'Can I go down and have a look, and then we can decide?'

'Since when did you become the decision-maker around here?' Cleary said.

'Since no one else can make a decision.' Conor held his breath, waiting for the onslaught, but it didn't come.

'Okay. We'll have another look.' Cleary walked off towards the tunnel.

Conor looked at Tony, who shrugged his shoulders, and they both followed the foreman.

*

Kirby opened the door for Megan Price and followed her into Cafferty's. It was quiet. And very dark. They ordered sandwiches at the counter and sat down in a corner of the lounge.

'It's never too busy at this time of day,' he said.

'I'm delighted you asked me to have lunch with you, even though it's way past lunchtime. You need someone to talk your grief through with.'

'I was just hungry,' Kirby said, 'and didn't feel like eating alone.'

'You're full of charm.' Her big eyes drank him in.

'It's been said before.'

He tried to relax, but every nerve in his body was sprung tightly. This was a mistake. What had he been thinking? Megan wasn't Gilly. She wasn't even his friend. Before Gilly, impulsive behaviour had been one of his traits. She had been so good for him. And now she was gone. He shook his head.

'What is it?'

'Look, Megan. I don't think this is a good idea.' He would take his sandwich and eat it back at his desk. Like he'd been doing for the last two months.

He felt her hand on his and squirmed. This was wrong. But she was only trying to be friendly. He had to calm down.

'You need to eat,' she said. 'I need to eat. Let's just wait for our food. You don't have to talk if you don't want to.'

She had hung her coat on the back of her chair, and he noticed that the top button of her dress was undone. Had it been like that earlier, when he'd called into the pharmacy? He couldn't remember. Surely she didn't think he fancied her? God, no, he thought.

'Okay so,' he said, pulling his hand out from beneath hers. He consciously tried to unwind his body before the springs shot out of it, causing him to run out the door.

'Tell me about Gilly,' she said.

Ah, no. Not Gilly. He couldn't talk about her.

'How about you tell me about yourself?' he said.

'Not a lot to tell,' she said, leaning into the chair's upholstery. 'You wouldn't be interested.'

The change was instantaneous. He knew the signs off by heart. Because he did the same thing every single day. Withdrawal. He tried again.

'How long have you worked in the pharmacy?'

'A while.'

'What's Whyte like to work for?'

'Richard? He's fine. He's not in too often. But now that Amy … now that she isn't around any more, he'll have to either employ someone else or take on the mantle himself. Poor man.'

'Talking of Amy …' Kirby said, but at that moment the food arrived.

With cups, saucers, teapot and plates, the little round table threatened to topple over. Though Kirby had lost weight in the weeks after Gilly's death, recently a combination of takeaway food and too much alcohol had restored his considerable bulk. For the first time in a long time, he felt conscious of his size. Was it the way Megan winced when he took a large bite out of his sandwich? Or was it when she put out her hand to stop the table wobbling when his belly nudged it? Whatever it was, it sparked a serious bout of self-consciousness, and Kirby put down the food.

'Sorry, my appetite has disappeared.'

'A big man like you has to eat.' She delicately teased open her own sandwich with a fork.

Was that an insult or genuine concern? He noticed that she had extracted all the red pepper from her sandwich and lined it up neatly on the edge of the plate.

'Since Gilly … you know … I haven't been following any regular pattern. In anything, not just food. I just try to do my best in my job, though sometimes it's way below par.'

'Did you take compassionate leave?'

'A week. I nearly drove myself mad. I'm better off at work.'

'I was like that when my husband left. Can't stand my own company any more. Me and the four walls don't get along too well.'

'How long ago was that?' If he could keep her talking about herself, then she wouldn't ask him questions.

'Oh, a while ago now. I'm over him. He was a prick.'

'Where is he? Local?'

'I don't want to talk about him.' She took a tiny bite of her food and chewed it delicately.

End of that conversation, Kirby thought, and shoved a giant mouthful of chicken, peppers and chilli into his mouth.

She was eyeing him again.

'What?' he said, with his mouth full.

'Nothing.' She poured two cups of tea. 'Milk?'

'I'll add my own, thanks.' This was the most awkward he'd ever felt.

'My husband was and is a bum. I should never have married him. He tried to fleece me for every penny I had, but I stood up to him. I'm happier without him.'

Kirby nodded, not trusting that he'd say the right thing. He wanted to get her on to safer ground.

'Tell me about Amy. What was she like? You know, to work with.'

'Mmm. The detective has an ulterior motive in asking me out to lunch.'

He felt his cheeks flush, but she laughed. 'It's fine. Most people want me for what they can get from me. I've grown used to it.'

'I'm sorry. I didn't mean …'

'Don't worry.' She sipped some tea and put her cup down. 'Amy was a challenge. To her father at home and to me at work. She was one of those girls who grew up with privilege. She latched on to Penny Brogan. Different backgrounds. Different upbringing and education. Amy lorded it over Penny. In a way, Penny brought it on herself.'

'How do you mean?'

'She never tried to better herself. I mean, come on. Stealing from her employer. That was a bit of a cheek. Especially since Amy had got her the job.'

'But despite their differences, they still got on well?'

'I suppose they did. Opposites attract, so they say.'

Kirby was sure she'd fluttered her eyelashes at him, but her face was unmoving. He must have imagined it. He pushed his plate away and finished his tea. 'What did Mr Whyte think of his daughter being friends with the likes of Penny Brogan?'

'I couldn't comment on that.'

'Why not?'

'You'd have to ask Richard. I don't want to gossip.'

Reading between the lines, Kirby guessed there was some animosity over Penny. He would have to see if that had any bearing on the murders. But no matter which way he looked at it, he couldn't imagine the councillor murdering his own daughter.

'Right, so,' he said. 'I better get back to work.'

He paid the bill, ignoring Megan's pleas to let her go halves.

'It's only a few euros,' he said as he helped her slip her arms into the sleeves of her coat. He could have sworn she let her hand linger on his. No, he didn't want that. It was too soon.

He couldn't wait to get back to work.

CHAPTER 35

There was no answer when Lottie and Boyd called to Cyril Gill's home, so they headed to the building site at the courthouse.

He had just pulled onto the site before them. Boyd parked on the footpath outside the hoarding and Lottie jumped out of the car.

'Mr Gill? Can I have a word?'

He dismissed the man he was talking to and turned to her.

'Have you come with news about Louise?'

'Can we talk inside?' Lottie said.

She watched as the high colour that had flamed his cheeks slipped down his face.

'No,' he groaned. 'Please. Not bad news.'

Lottie took him by the elbow and steered him past the open-mouthed man at the office door.

'Sit down,' she said.

He obeyed, and she wheeled a chair across and sat in front of him. Boyd entered and closed the door. The air immediately warmed up and the stench of mud and damp caught at the back of Lottie's throat. There was no easy way to do this. In fact, she thought, each time became distinctly harder. She hoped she was never on the receiving end of such news about any of her children.

'Mr Gill, I'm afraid to tell you that we do indeed have very bad news. It—'

She didn't get any further before he crumbled, hands clutching at the roots of his hair.

'No. No. Don't do this to me. Not my Louise. She's all I have left.' Then, as if he'd just remembered he had a wife, 'This will kill her mother.'

'I'm sorry—' Lottie began again.

'Sorry?' He raised his head, anger flashing in his eyes. 'Don't tell me you're sorry. I don't want to hear it. But I do want to know what happened to my princess.'

'It's the early stages of our investigation ...'

'Don't fudge the issue. Tell me straight.'

If that was what he wanted, that was what she would give him.

'We found Louise's body in an apartment on the outskirts of town.' Should she tell him about Cristina? Maybe not yet. 'She was the victim of a vicious assault.'

'What do you mean? What kind of assault?'

'A post-mortem will have to be held, but we are treating your daughter's death as suspicious.'

'Some bastard murdered her?'

'As I said—'

'I heard you.' He tore at his hair, then wrenched his knuckles into his eye sockets, but still the tears escaped.

'I'm sorry, Mr Gill,' Lottie added helplessly.

He raised his head, eyes streaming. 'She's only twenty-five, you know. Her whole life ahead of her. And some bastard does this. Why?'

Lottie went to speak, but he raised his hand.

'I don't want your apologies, I want you to find whoever did this. Today. And I want to throw the first punch. What did he do to her?'

'I think it best to wait until the post-mortem is completed.'

'Is Louise's murder linked to Amy's?'

'I can't speculate at the moment.' But Lottie knew she was dealing with the same killer. 'Can I phone anyone for you? Do you want us to accompany you home? To tell your wife?'

'No. I'll do that.' He found a handkerchief in his pocket, wiped his eyes and blew his nose.

'Do you know of anyone who would want to harm Louise?' Boyd said.

'She was just a girl. Not much of a social life, but she was dedicated to her studies …' He paused.

'What?' Lottie asked, feeling he had been about to say something else.

'She was studying criminal behaviour, or something like that. She even talked to jailbirds, or whatever the PC term is nowadays. Maybe one of them …'

He jumped up. Ran for the door. Boyd stopped him. 'What is it, Mr Gill?'

'Conor Dowling. He's out on my site. I took him on so I could keep an eye on him. The slimy bastard. Wait till I get my hands on him.'

'Sit down,' Lottie said forcefully. 'Leave Mr Dowling to us.' The grieving father's shoulders slumped and he returned to the desk, where he picked up a sheet of paper and began shredding it into long, thin strips. She continued, 'This is my card. If you think of anything, call me. And we will need to have a look through Louise's things.'

He waved a handful of paper. 'Yeah. But let me talk to Belinda, my wife, first. She gets hysterical at times.'

'Okay. Go home, Mr Gill. And stay away from Conor Dowling, you hear?'

'I hear. Doesn't mean I won't throttle the good-for-nothing with my bare hands.'

'Let justice take its course. We don't know that he's done anything wrong.' Yet, she thought.

'I bet every cent I've ploughed into my business that he's involved.'

'Don't go near him,' Lottie warned again, and made for the door as Boyd opened it.

'One other thing,' Gill said. 'You said you found Louise in an apartment.'

'That's right.'

'Whose?'

'Cristina Lee's.'

'Cristina? That's the girl I suspected Louise might be in a relationship with. I could never bring myself to talk to her about it.' He shook his head wearily. 'Now it seems so inconsequential. My girl is gone. Was Cristina there? Was she harmed? Is she okay?'

The questions came fast, and Lottie knew she had to tell him.

'I'm afraid not, Mr Gill. Cristina's body was found with your daughter's.'

When they exited the office, Lottie walked over to the man she'd seen at the door earlier.

'Is Conor Dowling around?'

'He was here a minute ago. We were working in the tunnel. Do you want me to look for him?'

'What's your name?' she said.

'Bob Cleary. I'm the site foreman.'

'Can I have a look around?'

'No can do. Health and Safety.'

'I need to speak with Mr Dowling. Urgently.'

'What's he done?'

'Nothing, as far as I know.' She handed over her card. 'Call me the minute you find him.'

She looked around. Boyd was talking to the Ducky lad at the security cabin. To her right, a group of builders were huddled together near a gaping hole at the edge of the old courthouse wall. Conor Dowling was with them, talking to an overweight man of around his own age; she thought she knew him from somewhere but couldn't remember where. She took a step forward. Cleary stood in front of her.

'Inspector, we're on a tight schedule,' he said.

'Oh, come on. I'm investigating a series of murders.' She shouldered her way past him and approached the men. 'Conor Dowling, I'd like you to come with me.'

'Seriously?'

'Yeah, seriously.' She watched as he folded his arms defiantly. Fuck this for a game of shite, she thought, and walked into his space. 'Now isn't the time to play the smart-arse with me. I have four murdered women. You're just out of prison and you have connections to two of them, so I need to talk to you.'

'This is victimisation.'

'Get in the fucking car!' Grabbing him by the elbow, she steered him across the site towards Boyd.

Once Dowling was safely in the back seat, she exhaled loudly. She'd thought he would fight or run. She hadn't expected him to acquiesce to her demands. He had acted like an innocent man.

CHAPTER 36

With Conor sitting in the interview room, Lottie went to find someone who could fetch them all coffee.

'You've nothing to hold him on.' Boyd marched up and down the corridor.

'Keep your voice down. McMahon will hear you. Jesus, the whole town will hear you.'

'So what? It's true. You've singled him out just because he's been released from prison and has a decade-old connection to the dead women. This is ludicrous. You need something more.'

'Right then, I'll interview him alone and you can pussyfoot around for the rest of the day.' She walked away, then stopped. 'And get the damn coffee.'

'Get it yourself,' he said, and stomped in the other direction.

'Boyd!'

But he had disappeared around the corner. Shit. She needed him on her side. With no sign of McMahon's new recruit, she'd have to look for Kirby to sit in. Then again, maybe she could let Dowling stew for an hour. She checked the time. No. It would have to be now.

Once they were seated and Kirby had made the introductions for the recording, Lottie began.

'So, Conor, nice to have you back with us.'

'Don't you have to read me my rights or something?' He sniffed away a bubble of sweat that had gathered at the end of his nose.

'Would you like to take off your coat? It's warm in here.' It galled her to be nice to this piece of scum who had robbed an old man and beaten him up so badly in his own home that he'd died not twelve months later. It was ten years ago, but as her mother would say, a leopard rarely changed its spots.

'I'm fine, thanks.'

'Nice to see you've found your manners.'

'Fuck you.'

'Ah, normal service.'

Lottie leaned back in her chair and tapped the buff folder on the desk with the tip of her pen, as if there was startling evidence between the covers. There was nothing. But he didn't know that.

'Tell me where you were last night.'

'Why?'

'Because I asked nicely?'

'None of your business.'

'You're not going to start that again, are you? I can detain you for six hours initially. And if we charge you, what will your poor disabled mother do without you to care for her?'

'She did fine all the time you had me locked up. And I won't be here one hour, let alone six, because I've done nothing wrong.'

'Louise Gill was found murdered this morning. You know who I'm talking about. Louise Gill who along with Amy Whyte gave witness against you in that trial.'

She watched his face carefully. Checked for signs of guilt. But all she saw was his skin pale beneath his ginger freckles and his lips begin to quiver.

'This is some kind of sick joke. You're perverted, that's what you are.' He straightened himself in the chair.

'No, I'm not. Louise is dead. Brutally murdered along with another young woman. So that's four bodies in a few days. And two of them link back to you.'

'You're trying to stitch me up.' He turned his attention to Kirby.

Lottie thought the detective might have fallen asleep. His eyes drooped and his arms were folded, his chest moving rhythmically up and down. She nudged him with her elbow and he turned to look at her.

'What?'

'Are you listening?' she whispered.

'Course I am.'

'This is a joke,' Conor said.

Lottie slapped the table. Kirby jumped. Conor remained still as a statue. 'Look, smart-arse. Tell me where you were last night.'

'At home.'

'When did you last see Louise Gill?'

He hesitated. 'Ten years ago.'

'You don't seem so sure.'

'I'm sure.' His eyes bored through her. 'Either charge me or let me go. You don't have jack shit on me.'

She had to admit he was right on that score. But she wasn't letting him off that lightly.

'I want a DNA sample. I want your fingerprints and I want a list of everywhere you've been and everyone you met since last Saturday.'

'And I want my solicitor.'

She had to leave Dowling in a holding cell while the solicitor was being contacted, so she cornered Boyd and drove to the Gill residence.

The Gills lived in a modern mansion situated on a hill overlooking the town. Belinda Gill led them into what she called the reception room. The ceiling was high and white. The walls, decorated in deep red paint, looked as though someone had emptied a truck of blood down them and walked away. Expensive-looking paintings were dotted here and there, but it was the furniture that caught Lottie's attention. She threw a look at Boyd, who turned up his nose.

'Junk?' he whispered.

'It's all antique,' Belinda said, catching sight of Lottie's interest. Lottie hoped she hadn't heard Boyd's comment. 'The rest of the house is modern and bright, but Cyril allowed me to indulge in my love of auctions. In my opinion, the contents of this room are worth more than the house itself.'

Lottie wondered if Belinda had been informed of Louise's murder. The woman wasn't displaying any signs of grief, though her eyes were glazed and her voice was slightly slurred. She was wearing stained jeans, and her shirt was buttoned up incorrectly. Her short hair appeared unwashed, her skin pale. She might have been pretty once, but now she looked lined and haggard despite the fact that she couldn't be more than fifty years old.

'You're here about Louise, I gather.'

'Yes,' Lottie said. 'You heard the news?'

'I did.'

'I'm so sorry for your loss. Is your husband home? Would you like him to be present while we talk?'

Belinda's laugh cut through the air and rebounded off the ceiling. 'I don't need Cyril for anything. Do you know, I was out shopping when he phoned me to tell me our daughter was dead? That slimeball is afraid of his own shadow.'

'He phoned you?' Lottie didn't know what to say. What type of a man did that to his wife? Not a very nice one, she surmised.

'Would you like a drink?'

Before Lottie or Boyd could answer, Belinda had crossed to the distressed-looking cabinet beside the enormous wrought-iron fireplace. She poured herself a large gin, no mixer.

'Nothing for us,' Lottie said. 'We're on duty.'

Belinda returned and sat down. 'I drink. There. Got that out of the way. I'm an embarrassment to Cyril. Says I damage his reputation in the business world. He drinks too, but there's not a word about that. He makes up the rules as he goes along.'

She tipped her glass towards Boyd and downed it in one go. 'Be a good man and get me a refill.'

Lottie caught Boyd's bewildered glance and nodded for him to go ahead.

'Mrs Gill … May I call you Belinda?'

'Of course you can. I've been called everything from bitch to whore in this house. Be nice to be called by my name for once.'

'Belinda,' Lottie said softly, 'is Cyril here?'

'No. He's at work. Where else do you think he'd be? That project means more to him than his own flesh and blood. What happened to Louise?'

Lottie couldn't believe the detachment in the woman's voice. It was like it hadn't registered with her that her daughter was dead.

'I'm afraid we suspect she was murdered, though it has yet to be confirmed by the state pathologist. Can you tell me how she was behaving recently? Did you notice anything unusual or concerning?'

'Do you think she killed herself?' The glass was pointed at Lottie in an accusatory fashion, clear liquid spilling down the side.

'I'm trying to build up a profile of your daughter that might lead us to who did this and why.'

'How did she die?'

Lottie looked at Boyd for support.

He said, 'We can't divulge details yet, but we really need to learn all we can about Louise.'

'I don't know a whole lot, to be honest. Suppose you want to see her room?'

'Yes please. But can you answer our questions first?' Boyd said soothingly.

Belinda sipped her drink and seemed to consider. 'Louise was a troubled girl. Ever since that business over Mr Thompson's case. I was sure she was depressed, but her father wouldn't believe me. I secretly arranged counselling for her, but she didn't buy into it. She only ever listened to her father.' She paused. 'Why do you think I drink? I can't stand the man.'

'You could leave him,' Lottie said.

'It's complicated.'

She decided to abandon that conversation. Her main concern was to discover what she could about Louise. 'What was Louise's relationship with Cristina Lee like?'

'Cristina Lee? I've never heard that name mentioned. But I don't know much about Louise's friends. She didn't really talk to me.'

'Did she get any unusual letters or notes recently?' Lottie was thinking of the threatening note she'd discovered in Amy Whyte's bedroom.

Belinda sipped and shrugged. 'I don't know.'

'Can I search her room?'

'I'll take you up.'

Lottie made for the door. She couldn't wait to get away from the woman. Something in her demeanour clanged warning bells in her head. She thought it might be because Belinda reminded her of when she herself had been snared by the talons of alcohol after Adam died. Or was it something else entirely? She didn't know.

Boyd rolled his eyes as they waited for Belinda to refill her glass before she led the way up the winding staircase. She stopped outside one of the doors on the wide landing.

'That's her room. I think I'll lie down for an hour. If you have to take anything away, please bring it back in one piece.' She disappeared behind a door at the end of the landing.

'What the hell was that all about?' Boyd said.

'Your guess is as good as mine.'

Stepping into the young murdered woman's personal domain, Lottie was immediately gripped with a sense of loss for Louise. A sense of loss that her mother had not displayed. She was standing in the preserve of a twenty-five-year-old girl who was never going to lie on her bed again, or flick through her phone, or complete her university course.

The room was tidy. In the wardrobe, clothes hung in neat lines. The dressing table had everything lined up perfectly. The bed covers were rumpled, with a T-shirt and jogging bottoms draped across them. Possibly used as nightwear. On the window seat Lottie spied a laptop, notebooks and a ring binder.

'This must be her coursework,' Boyd said, picking up a folder in his gloved hands.

'Must be, Sherlock.'

Lottie glanced out through the window. A trio of magpies sat on the bare branches of a tree. She tried to remember the rhyme, but it escaped her. Instead, she concerned herself with the laptop. It was charged and switched on, and password-protected. 'Shit. We need the password.'

'Her mother might know.'

'I doubt it very much. The technical crew can have a look at it.'

'Or you could ask her father.'

'Perhaps.' Lottie wasn't sure she wanted to talk to Cyril Gill any time soon.

'Do we need anything else?' Boyd asked.

She couldn't help but feel the distance his tone was placing between them. She was wrong to have yelled at him at the station, but the day had been stressful. McMahon was gunning for her. Cynthia Rhodes knew stuff she shouldn't. Bernie Kelly was prowling around on the loose. And to cap all that, they had two more bodies.

'Her phone.' Lottie found the jewel-encrusted iPhone lying on the pillow. She tapped the home key. Like the laptop, it required a passcode.

She bagged the phone. Boyd did likewise with the laptop. Then, while he flicked through the pages of the notebooks, she took a quick look around the en suite bathroom. She opened the mirrored cabinet above the washbasin without looking at her appearance. Toothpaste, electric toothbrush, hair serum, small bottles of shower gel. No medicines of any sort. No contraceptive pills either. She shut the cabinet.

Returning to the dressing table, she inspected each bottle of expensive perfume and nail polish. The drawers held an assortment of jewellery still in the boxes they'd been bought in. The remainder were filled with underwear. All luxurious, though there was nothing flimsy or erotic.

'No sign of a coin. No note,' she said.

'Her death may not be connected to Amy and Penny,' Boyd said.

'It has to be. There were coins left with the bodies. It is the same killer.'

As Boyd lifted a black leather-bound Moleskine notebook, Lottie heard something fall to the floor.

'What was that? Don't move. Stay where you are,' she instructed him as the hairs on her arms tingled.

'Not going anywhere.'

She got down on her knees and searched around his feet. 'Something fell out of the notebook. I heard it.'

'You're imagining things.'

She scrabbled around under the bed. Nothing. Eased her hand beneath the bedside cabinet. Feeling something through the latex of her gloves, she dragged it out and lifted it up to the light.

'A coin,' she said triumphantly.

CHAPTER 37

His mother's voice carried out to the hall door before he'd hardly had a chance to step inside.

'What are you doing home at this hour of the day?'

'We were let off early,' he lied, and put one foot on the stairs. He'd been lucky. This time. His solicitor had got him released immediately. The guards had had no evidence to hold him on.

'Come here!'

He sighed and went into the sitting room. His senses were now accustomed to the stench and dirt but his eyes could not deny the vision of degradation. He really should get his mother into a care home. How had she managed while he'd been away? He wasn't sure he wanted to know.

'What?' He remained standing behind her.

'Come over here where I can see you.' She tapped her walking stick on the floor beside her.

'Give me a minute.'

Back in the hall, he draped his jacket on the banister and went to the kitchen. He needed a drink. The fridge only held a carton of milk. Instead he poured a glass of water from the sink tap, drained it, then went back to his mother.

'Okay. I'm here. What's all the rush for?'

'I need a wash.'

For the first time since he'd left prison, he noticed the balding patches on the top of her head. Pink scalp peeked out in odd spots, and the strands of hair that remained were oily and plastered to her head. Suddenly he realised that in the two months since he'd been home, she hadn't had a proper wash or shower. No wonder the room smelled putrid.

He straightened his shoulders, preparing himself for a battle he could do without after the day he'd just had. 'Mam, I think you need a proper carer. I can't work and look after you.'

She said nothing. He took that as a good sign.

He hunkered down, stared into her watery eyes. 'Would you consider a care home? I can make enquiries and—'

The first smack of the walking stick caught him above the ear and knocked him backwards. The second smashed across his knees and he fell on top of the commode, turning it over. Urine spilled across the floor and seeped into his jeans. He wondered why she wasn't using her catheter.

'Wh-what did you do th-that for?' he stammered, and rubbed a hand over his head trying to find the wound he knew must surely be there.

'You will not put me in any home. Do you hear me? This is my house. If anyone has to go, it will be you. Good-for-nothing jailbird. Thief. Murderer.'

'I didn't murder anyone, you crazy bitch.' He tried to stand, wanting to exude the impression of bravery. But she was the one person in the world who could reduce him to a snivelling wreck.

'Is that the type of respect you learned in prison? Who do you think you are, calling your only living flesh and blood crazy?'

She was standing now. Leaning heavily on the stick she had wielded so strongly a moment ago, and Conor wondered if it was all an act. He'd hardly seen her on her feet in the last two months. But as she stood, her knees wobbled and she fell back into the rancid armchair.

'You break my heart, Conor. Crushing your poor mother's spirit with talk like that.'

He was saved from offering an insincere apology by a knock on the door. As he moved, she raised her stick again.

'Send them away. I want that wash. Now.'

He eased out of the room and opened the front door. Tony bundled in past him.

'Put the kettle on and tell me all about that long-legged detective.'

Conor groaned, but for once he was glad of Tony's presence.

*

Lottie stemmed her anger at Dowling's release and stared at the photographs of the four victims on the incident board. On the second board someone had pinned photos of Richard Whyte and Cyril Gill.

'Who put those up there?'

The detectives in the room all muttered and shrugged their shoulders. The new guy put up his hand. 'I did, Inspector.'

'What's your name again?'

'Sam McKeown.'

'Where's Kirby?'

Her new detective shrugged. She thought he looked handsome, in a rugged sort of way. Square jaw, neatly shaved head, eyes as green as her own. His shirt was creased, sleeves rolled up to his elbows. She hoped that was a sign he was a hard worker. Time would tell.

She was about to unpin the two fathers' photographs, then thought better of it. Leave them there. She opened a file and took out Conor Dowling's photo, pinning it alongside the others.

He was their only real suspect.

'I want to know every single thing about Conor Dowling. What he got up to in prison and what he's been up to since he was released.'

'Yes, boss,' McKeown said.

She went back to her office. Boyd had dropped a bag of notebooks and folders belonging to Louise Gill on her desk. Hopefully she would find something. Through the open door she saw him sitting at his desk fiddling with Louise's laptop.

'Thought you were going to send that to technical.'

'I'm having a go first.'

'You haven't the first clue how to unlock it.'

'At least I can remember my password without having to write it on a Post-it,' he said without raising his head.

She grimaced at his dig. She couldn't even think of a retort. She opened the plastic bag and took out one of Louise's notebooks. 'Where's Kirby?'

'Maybe he went out for something to eat.' He looked up at her. 'I'm kind of peckish myself. Fancy anything?' Then he grinned.

'Perhaps later.' She smiled back at him. Maybe the day would improve. Maybe not.

*

'How are you doing, Mrs D?' Tony said, sticking his head into the sitting room and just as quickly extracting it. 'What's that whiff?' he said to Conor.

'Shh. She's in a foul mood.' Conor switched on the kettle and shook the milk carton to make sure it wasn't sour.

'Foul smell, if you ask me.'

'I didn't ask, so shut up.' He placed two mugs on the table. 'What happened after I left?'

'What are you whispering for?' Tony said. 'Oh-oh. You haven't said anything to Mommy dearest?'

'No, I haven't, and she won't have to know if you keep your gob shut.' Conor eased the door closed with his boot.

'I'll have a cup of whatever you're making.' His mother's voice was still audible from the sitting room. Conor ignored her and sat at the table.

Tony eyed him expectantly. 'Go on. What did the detective want? Nice set of legs on her. I like them skinny. How about you?'

'Shut up, Tony. She's a pig. And she's the one who got me put away.'

'Thought it was the witnesses who did that.'

'Those two little bitches.' If he was still in prison, Conor would have spat on the floor, but he thought better of it and kept his mouth closed.

'Two little bitches who are now dead.' Tony attempted to fold his arms over his girth, but gave up and placed his hands in his lap.

'Yeah, well, your skinny-legged detective thinks I might have had something to do with it.'

'Really?' Tony dropped his eyes, and Conor noticed the colour rise up his cheeks.

'Afraid to be friends with me now that I could be a serial killer?'

'No. Not at all. Jesus, man. This is all … too weird.'

Seeing Tony at a loss for words, Conor realised how serious the situation could get. If Inspector Parker was out to pin these murders on him, how was he going to stop her? He'd need Tony on his side.

'For your information, I didn't kill them.'

'Where's me tea?' His mother's voice had risen to a screech.

'Coming.' Conor threw a tea bag into a mug. 'Here, you bring it in to her,' he told Tony.

'Ah man. I'll puke my ring up. Can you not smell it?'

'Oh, fuck off then.'

Taking a biscuit from an opened packet, he brought it with the tea to his mother.

'What about a plate?'

Biting down a retort, he went back for one, then returned to sit with Tony.

'She's doing my head in,' he complained, grabbing a biscuit from the pack before Tony ate them all. 'What about the body in the tunnel?' he said, anxious to change the subject.

'What about it?' Tony said, crumbs sticking to his stubble.

'Is Cleary going to report it? What happened after I left?'

'Not a lot. The boss was in a state. Shouting and roaring about his daughter. He was looking for you. Screaming that he was going to string you up.'

'Me? Just because I've served time, everyone has me tagged as a mass murderer.' When Tony remained silent, Conor added, 'Cleary said nothing to him about the body in the tunnel?'

'He didn't have a chance to get a word in edgeways.'

'I think he should forget it's there and continue with the job. We all need the work. If that body's reported, the site will have to close.'

'I think the boss is more concerned about the murder of his daughter than some old bones that've probably been down there for a hundred years.' Tony slurped his tea, then dunked the remainder of his biscuit into the liquid.

Conor was about to say that the rags of clothing on the bones didn't look like they were a hundred years old, but he decided to say nothing. He'd have a word with the foreman. He couldn't lose this job. Then again, maybe Gill would sack him anyway. He heard his mother calling him.

'Conor? Take this cup away before I let it fall. My poor hands are in bits.'

'Tony. Be a best friend and get it for me.'

'Piss off.'

'Please? And I'll forget that you messed up my workshop.'

'I didn't mess it up, you wanker. Some friend you are.' Tony grabbed his jacket and was out the front door before Conor got another word out.

'Is Tony leaving already?' Vera shouted as the cup shattered on the floor.

Conor clenched his hands into tight fists.

CHAPTER 38

Bernie Kelly waited and watched.

Leo Belfield was going round in circles, looking for her in all the wrong places. She kept tabs on him. Cat-and-mouse stuff, but she was so much cleverer than him. She should pity him, but she carried not a shred of sympathy in her heart. He had thought he was bribing her for information when she was stringing him up and down like a puppet.

Once she saw him re-entering the Joyce Hotel, she was free to roam. She had plans for him, but not just yet. Her half-sister Lottie Parker was going to pay dearly for incarcerating her with the lunatics who had pled insanity. Bernie wasn't insane. She was just a very clever woman. She laughed, then realised that people were starting to look at her and tugged the cord on her hood, tightening it around her face. It was a dark evening and that suited her just fine.

She headed in the direction of Lottie's house.

*

Rose knew that Katie was fed up with her hovering around, but she had to stay until Lottie got home. Sean and Chloe had been safely delivered from school in a taxi. None of her grandchildren had any idea why their mother had arranged it. But Rose was relieved.

'Granny, why don't you go on home? We're fine,' Katie said.

Glancing at a basket of laundry, Rose got out the iron and ironing board. 'I'll do this before I go.'

'Mam doesn't iron. The wrinkles fall out of most of our stuff once we put it on.'

'In my day you wouldn't go outside the door without a crease pressed into your trousers.' She slid the iron up and down the arm of one of Sean's school shirts.

'That was like a million years ago,' Katie laughed.

'Less of your cheek, madam. I'm not that old.' But I am, Rose thought. The return of Bernie Kelly had aged her. She felt like someone had turned her bones to sawdust. How was she going to tell Lottie?

'Gran, I know you wouldn't tell me earlier, but did Mam ask you to come over today?'

Rose hung the shirt on a hanger and picked up a creased T-shirt belonging to Lottie. How could she wear clothes unironed? 'Why do you think that?'

'It's just … Well, she was acting really weird this morning.'

'Isn't your mother always a bit weird?'

Katie laughed. 'You're right there. But she's been so much calmer and in better form since we moved. It's great to see her something close to happy again. But she got spooked this morning and I don't want her to go back to the way she used to be.'

'Spooked by what?' Rose held her breath, hoping that Bernie hadn't already made her move.

'I'm not sure. We were talking and then some sort of coin fell out of Louis' jacket pocket and she kind of freaked.'

'Don't worry your head about it. I'll have a chat with her when she gets home.' Rose wondered just how that chat would turn out.

*

Tony nursed his pint. Sniffed at a cold that he felt was surely trying to take hold and found his thoughts returning to Conor. Mrs D was putting on an act. He was sure of it. He'd seen her a few weeks before Conor had been released, and no way was she that bad. Was she making him pay a second time for the disgrace he'd brought to their door? Conor had served his time, but Vera Dowling was a proud woman, and now that Tony thought about it, she could be a dangerous one also.

The creamy head of the Guinness was seeping down into the black liquid.

'Here, Darren, put a head on this for me.' He handed the pint to the barman.

If Tony hadn't dirtied his bib, he'd still be married. He'd still have the house and not be living back in his old place. Just as well he hadn't sold it. He missed his parents. One after the other they'd died, two years ago. A month between them. And only in their sixties.

'Life's a bitch.'

'What's that, Tony?'

'Oh, nothing, Darren, just drowning my sorrows.' He took the pint and swallowed half of it in one go.

'Sad about those young women.'

'The murders?'

'Yes. The first two were in here Saturday night. Happy as anything. And now they're gone.'

Tony felt his breath lodge in his throat. 'It is sad.'

'Wasn't one of those found this morning the daughter of the builder fellow?'

'Cyril Gill.'

'That's the man. He's your boss, isn't he?'

'You know everything that goes on in this town, Darren.'

'I know a good bit, to tell you the truth.'

Tony lowered his head. Too many people knew too much.

'Saw your ex in here a while ago,' Darren said.

'I don't care.' But Tony felt the alcohol flip in his stomach.

'With a detective. That Kirby fella. Lost his girlfriend a few months ago.'

'Darren, I don't want to know about her or anyone she cares to go out with.' But he did care. Jesus Christ. A detective. That was all he needed.

He finished his pint and left the pub with more confusion than resolution.

*

When he had emptied the last basin of filthy water down the sink, Conor dressed his mother in clean clothes. He cringed every time his hand touched her skin. It wasn't right. Sons were not supposed to have to do this. If he didn't know it was impossible, he'd say she had developed her disability as a way of punishing him.

He shoved the dirty clothes into the washing machine and thought about that for a moment. She did have rheumatoid arthritis, didn't she? He'd seen the knobbly bones protruding every which way on her hands and knees. When had it got so bad? Was it just before he returned home, or had she been like that for years? He didn't want to bother the neighbours by asking them questions to which he, her son, should know the answers. They probably wouldn't tell him anything anyway. He'd have to speak to Tony.

He switched on the washing machine and dried the dishes. When the tiny kitchen was reasonably tidy, he peeped into the sitting room. She was snoring loudly. The odour was a little milder now. He'd sprayed Febreze on every surface, including the floor and curtains.

Sneaking out the door, he felt like a fifteen-year-old escaping for an illicit cigarette. The thought gave him the urge for nicotine. He had Tony's pack, but no lighter. Maybe he'd walk up to Tesco. The air was cold but fresh. The sky was dark. He didn't mind. After years of artificial light in his cell, he welcomed the black sky above his head.

At the end of his road, a car approached with full headlights on. It swerved up onto the footpath. Conor tried to jump out of the way and fell into a neatly trimmed evergreen hedge. Thorns tore through his jeans and scratched his hands as he pulled himself upright.

'What the …?' he yelled. 'What do you think you're playing—'

The words drowned in his throat as a fist smashed into his face. He felt one of his teeth crack, and blood poured from his mouth. As he attempted to stand, the second thump caught him on the side of the head, and he fell back into the hedge once again. He tried to see his assailant, but the car lights were blinding him. A kick to his stomach and a jab to his balls and he curled up with a scream. The black sky appeared to be full of twinkling stars where only a moment ago it had been boot-polish black. Then they began to disappear one by one. His eyelids drooped. He tried to focus, to see who had attacked him.

The last stars blinked out and the blackness melded into one long sheet of coal.

His eyes closed and his pain disappeared into unconsciousness.

CHAPTER 39

Lottie could sense that something was wrong with the first step inside her front door.

'Katie? Chloe? Sean? Where are you all?'

She burst into the kitchen. Her mother stood with her back to the counter, arms folded like a sergeant major. But the spark of mutiny that so often glinted in Rose's eyes was missing.

'What's wrong? Where are the kids?' Lottie threw her bag and jacket over the back of a chair and noticed the stack of clothes all ironed and neatly folded.

'They're upstairs.'

'Why? What's going on?'

'They've eaten. There's a plate of dinner in the microwave for you. Chloe and Sean are doing their homework, under protest, I may add, and Katie is putting Louis to bed.'

Lottie sighed with relief. 'Oh. Thank God.'

She heard Rose move towards her. She eased past her and switched on the microwave, suddenly overcome with the need to eat.

'We have to talk,' Rose said, sitting down.

'I have to eat.'

'Don't be so belligerent.'

'I'm not. I'm hungry.'

She waited impatiently while the plate twirled around inside her sparkling new microwave. Hearing the ping, she took out the plate, got a knife and fork and sat down at the table opposite Rose. The steak looked appetising, and she knew the mashed potato would be full of butter and milk.

'This is lovely. Thanks. I really appreciate it.'

'Tell me about the coin you found in Louis' clothes.'

'Katie told you?'

'Yes.'

'It's nothing.'

'It's a sign.'

'Don't go all superstitious.' At least Rose didn't know about the seeds, Lottie thought.

'I have something to tell you,' Rose said.

Lottie was starving and wanted nothing more than to dig into the food, but she laid down her fork. 'Go on. Tell me.' She looked at her mother, really looked, and saw that the lines were more deeply ingrained into her forehead and the crow's feet seemed to have multiplied in the last year. So much had happened. So much had eaten its way into both of their hearts, and most of it had not been good. The only shining light in their lives was the birth of baby Louis just over a year ago. Her heart contracted tightly with a love tinged with fear.

Rose took a deep breath and exhaled. 'Bernie Kelly called to my home last night.'

'What?' Lottie stared at her, her mouth hanging open. 'Are you okay? Did she harm you?' She could feel her blood beginning to bubble towards a hysterical boiling point.

'I was just a little shaken. She didn't threaten me, but she did frighten me.'

Trying to control her breathing, Lottie gasped, 'What did she do?'

'Nothing. It was her words.'

'Go on. Tell me. I have to know what she's up to. She's a very dangerous individual.'

'I know that,' Rose snapped. 'You knew she'd escaped?'

'Yes. There's a nationwide appeal out for sightings of her.'

'And you didn't warn me personally, or your children for that matter?'

'I put plans in place to protect you all, but I've four murders to investigate.' That was no excuse, and Lottie knew it. She waited for the onslaught.

'Once again you've put your job before your family. When will you learn? We could've been killed by that woman while you were out there working.'

'I didn't put my job first. I never do.' At least she didn't think she did. Not intentionally. 'I told Katie to stay in the house and I organised a taxi to bring Chloe and Sean to and from school. Anyway, Bernie has had ample opportunity to do something, but she hasn't. I just need to find her.'

Rose wrung her hands together. 'I saw the news report this morning.'

Oh shit, Lottie thought. 'Cynthia Rhodes will be hearing from me just as soon as I get my head together.'

'You never told your boss back then?'

'About what?'

'That Bernie is related to you.'

'He wasn't my boss then.' She sighed loudly. 'But he knows now, doesn't he?'

'Don't be such a smart-mouth, Lottie. It doesn't suit you.'

'Sorry.' As usual her mother had reduced her to her inner child. And that was never a good thing.

'Everyone will think I was a baby-snatcher.'

The fuse blew. Lottie jumped up.

'You! It's always about you. What about me and my family? What my father did was inexcusable, but the fact that you never told me is even worse. You kept the secret from me all my life and I had to find out at the end of a knife held by the woman who claimed to be my sister. She might as well have stuck it into my heart, the hurt was so hard to bear. I've been through worse and come out the other side, but now my children will have to know. How do you propose I tell them?'

Rose shook her head wearily. 'It's a mess, and I have no idea how to fix my wrongs.' She looked at Lottie, her eyes watery and older than their seventy-odd years. 'Bernie gave me a message for you.'

'She left a message for me last night too. A handful of seeds on my front step.'

'How do you know it was her?'

'Who else was obsessed with that kind of thing? Who else had a book on herbs and requested it for her cell? What did she want me to know?'

'I didn't want to tell you. I wasn't going to, but then I saw the news this morning and I knew I had to.'

'Go on.' Lottie wasn't at all sure she wanted to hear anything Bernie Kelly might have told her mother. She knew those words might be lethal.

'She babbled a lot. Talked incoherently for a while. Then she said I had to tell you that she would not go back to being incarcerated. She's going to disappear.' Rose's voice faltered. She coughed and continued. 'But before she does, she's going to kill each one of your children, and your grandson.'

Lottie felt bile rise from her stomach. 'Over my dead body.'

'What are you going to do?' Rose's voice quivered.

'I'm going to kill her first.'

CHAPTER 40

At first the young man wasn't very accommodating. Neither was his mangy dog. But she needed somewhere to sleep where no one would ask questions. She peeled off a fifty from the bundle of notes she'd stolen from Leo Belfield and waved it in the air.

'What's your name?' she asked the dirty-faced man.

'Everyone calls me Mick.'

'Well, Mick, here's some money. I want to rent your sleeping bag and this corner for the night. Deal?'

He swiped the money, unfurled himself from the boxes and newspapers and tumbled out of the sleeping bag. Wrapping the leash around his hand, he walked off with his dog.

She cast an eye around warily, wondering if anyone had seen the transaction. The supermarket across the road was closing for the night, shutters coming down. The car park was virtually empty. The corner was secluded enough. No one noticed the homeless people any more. They had become part of the infrastructure.

She could blend in. She was a master of impersonation. And a lot of other things. The smell didn't faze her. The young man had sweaty feet, but the bag was clean enough. Pulling it up over her head, Bernie Kelly settled down for the night, to plot and plan for tomorrow.

CHAPTER 41

Conor was late for work on Thursday morning. He hadn't slept well. When he'd eventually been prodded from unconsciousness by a passing dog walker, he'd stumbled home, his head throbbing. He'd entered the house as quietly as possible, slunk up the stairs and fallen on top of his bed.

Now, sneaking on to the site, the collar of his coat turned up, he tightened the Velcro on the cuffs of his gloves and picked up the wheelbarrow.

'Where do you think you're going with that?'

Bob Cleary was panting his way towards him, splashing sludge everywhere. If Conor was in charge, he'd have the site hosed down every day. It didn't cost much to be clean.

'I'm bringing this around the back. Gerry said he needed it for shifting sand.'

'I'll shift Gerry out the gate if he doesn't do what he's told. Put it down and come with me. The boss wants a word with you.'

'I didn't think he'd be in today.' Conor felt a snake of worry crawl through his blood.

'And why wouldn't he be?'

'His daughter. She was murdered, you know.'

'Of course I bloody know. The man is inconsolable. Doesn't stop him working. I reckon he needed to get out of the house and do something constructive. Come on.'

Constructive, Conor thought. Like firing me. He chewed the inside of his cheek. He didn't want to see the boss. He was sure it'd been Gill who'd beaten five shades of shite out of him last night.

'I have to bring this round or Gerry will fire me.'

'I do the hiring and firing and I say put the fucking thing down and come with me.'

Should he run or stay? Conor decided to take his chances.

*

Lottie had hardly shut an eye all night. The old anguish had taken root deep in the pit of her stomach, and she felt she could crouch over the toilet all day puking up her fear.

She'd spent the hours of darkness checking in on her children: stroking their hair while they slept; standing over Louis' cot listening to him breathing. If anything happened to any of them, she would never survive the pain and the guilt. She had to protect them.

With a mug of coffee turning cold on the table, she sat looking at her phone. Who could help? Leo Belfield? No. He'd already lost Bernie; he'd be useless despite the fact that he was a NYPD captain. She couldn't spare any of her diminished team. They were too busy. A squad car outside the house could only do so much. Could she justify putting her family under unofficial house arrest? A direct threat had been made, but she knew McMahon wouldn't sympathise like her old superintendent, Corrigan, would have done. He was too focused on his own performance and that of the district. Freeing up dwindling resources to house-sit his inspector's children was not on his agenda. Could she keep Chloe and Sean at home without telling them why? She didn't want to worry them, but at the same time they needed to be alert. What was she to do?

The doorbell shrieked through her musings and she knocked over her mug. She almost freaked out as she slowly headed to the door. Cynthia Rhodes stood on the step.

'Not you!' Lottie said with a groan.

'I come in peace.'

'Yeah, tell me another one.'

'Can I come in?'

'Cynthia, I'm about to leave for work. I haven't time.'

'A minute. That's all. I think I can help you.'

Lottie relented and led the reporter into the kitchen. Wiping up the spilled coffee she said, 'Tea or coffee?'

'No thanks.'

When they were seated, Cynthia fixed her black-rimmed spectacles on her nose and stared at Lottie. 'You look like you could do with a good night's sleep.'

'What do you want, Cynthia?'

'I want your story.'

'You can feck off. You're wasting my time. I'm going to work.' Lottie stood.

'Give me two minutes.'

Lottie remained standing, looking down at Cynthia's short dark curls. 'Go on.'

'I want the full Bernie Kelly story, and in return I might be able to help with the murders of the girls.'

'I don't buy into blackmail.'

'It's not blackmail.'

'Sounds like it to me.' Lottie picked up her jacket from the back of the chair and began to pull it on.

'I know something about Louise Gill.'

'Our investigation is just starting, so anything you can tell us will have to be recorded by a member of the team. You need to make an official statement.'

'Do you want to hear what I have to say or not?' Cynthia tapped a fingernail on the table.

They didn't have anything to go on with the girls' murders, so Lottie felt she was being taken hostage. But she wanted to know. 'Yes, I do, but I'm not promising anything in return.'

'That might make it more difficult for me unless I get something from you.'

'Tell me what you know and I'll consider it.' She had no intention of divulging anything to the reporter.

'Don't double-cross me.'

'Oh for Christ's sake, Cynthia, what do you know?' Lottie sat back down, her jacket half on, half off.

'Louise was pursuing a course in criminal behaviour.'

'I know that.'

'As part of that course, she interviewed prisoners.'

'I have her paperwork.' She had yet to read it.

'She spoke with Conor Dowling.'

'I'm sure she did.' Lottie could feel her cheeks burning. Cynthia was ahead of her.

'In the course of those interviews she revealed something to Conor Dowling that casts doubt on his conviction ten years ago.'

'You've been watching *Making a Murderer* on Netflix.' Lottie tried to keep the exasperation out of her voice, but failed. 'The evidence was tight. Conor Dowling terrorised an old man in his own home with a sawn-off shotgun, and once he'd beaten him, he ransacked the house. Louise Gill and Amy Whyte gave conclusive eyewitness testimony. They both saw Conor Dowling in the area that night.'

'Louise spoke to me after her conversation with Dowling in prison.'

'And why would she do that?'

'I was working on a story to coincide with his release. As it turns out, it never got aired. But I can tell you, she was racked with guilt.'

'For putting away a criminal?'

'She lied.'

'Come again.'

'You had no physical or forensic evidence on Conor Dowling. You never found the gun or the money. He never offered a defence. He was convicted on witness statements.'

'Correct so far.'

'Louise and Amy lied.'

'What?' Lottie had not been expecting that. She felt her jaw drop and hurriedly closed her mouth.

'The two girls were not sure it was Dowling they saw that night.'

'They gave sworn statements.'

'Two impressionable teenagers,' Cynthia said.

'They had details. He never denied the charge. He was guilty as hell.'

'I don't think he was.'

'Cynthia, this is bullshit and you know it.' Lottie felt a twitch of unease. What if the girls *had* lied? Had she sent an innocent man to prison? She didn't believe that, but still …

'Louise was contrite. Troubled. I got the feeling she was ready to unburden herself.'

'And did she?'

'No. When the programme was shelved by the powers that be, I arranged to meet her again. I couldn't let it go.'

'When was this?'

'That's the thing. I was due to meet her early next week. And now she's dead. As is Amy Whyte.'

'And two other young women.' Lottie churned Cynthia's words around in her head. No matter which way they fell, she couldn't make sense of them. 'What exactly did Louise tell you?'

'If I'm to divulge it, I need your story. How you fit in with Bernie Kelly's tale.'

'A tale. That's all it is. Bernie is a liar and a serial killer, in case you'd forgotten.'

'I hadn't forgotten, but I do believe you and your family are in danger.'

Lottie gulped loudly, looking around for her bag, anywhere but at Cynthia, who she knew was staring at her.

The reporter tapped the table again triumphantly. 'You know that already! I take it then that you've been threatened. By Bernie?'

'This is not up for discussion. I want to know about Louise and what she said. Do you have recordings of the conversation? I'd like them, please.'

Cynthia stood. 'When you decide to cooperate, Inspector, then I will consider handing them over.'

'I can have you arrested for impeding a murder investigation,' Lottie snapped.

'That would make a great headline. And I'm sure Superintendent McMahon would love that featuring on the nine o'clock news. Think about it.'

Before she could retort, Lottie was left standing alone in the middle of her bright new kitchen with her brain in turmoil.

If Cynthia wasn't going to tell her what Louise had divulged, she'd have to find out another way. First, though, she phoned the station to requisition a squad car with a couple of uniforms to watch over the house. She'd deal with McMahon when the need arose. She left a note for Chloe and Sean telling them she'd booked a taxi to take them to and from school, and to remain indoors after school until she returned home.

She hoped that was enough to keep her family safe.

CHAPTER 42

The heating was on full blast in the incident room. Lottie stripped off her jacket and dropped it on the floor beside the desk at the head of the room. Boyd sauntered up to her.

'You look awful,' he said. 'What's wrong?'

'I'll tell you later. We need to get these investigations motoring.'

She turned to study the sparse boards, and then set about recapping their progress over the last few days.

'Anything on CCTV?' she asked Kirby.

'It's painstaking work, but the relevant security cameras in the vicinity of Petit Lane and the car park are number one priority. Nothing to report so far. We're casting the net wider now, but we're so short-staffed, the job is almost impossible.'

'I don't want to hear what we don't have. I want answers.'

'I can't give you what I haven't got, boss. There's two lads working twenty-four seven, going blind squinting at blurry tapes. Myself and McKeown take over for a few hours at a time, but so far we've detected nothing suspicious.'

'The cameras from Cristina Lee's apartment block. Have you got that footage?'

'We prioritised the tapes from the first two murders, so I don't know when we'll get to that.'

'Can someone do a quick scan? See if anyone enters or leaves the apartment?'

'I'll do it,' McKeown said. Lottie thought he was being eager to please. She didn't care, as long as the job got done.

Kirby sighed loudly. 'Boss, we really need more bodies.' He blushed. 'I mean live ones.'

'I know what you mean.' She flicked through the report on the desk. 'Post-mortems have been completed on the first two victims. Both had their throats cut. I won't go into the technical details, but neither girl was sexually assaulted. No foreign DNA on their bodies so far as Jane could determine. No fingerprints recovered, which suggests the assailant wore gloves. A couple of hairs were found on both girls' clothing and these have been sent for analysis. Given that the crime scene was used as a doss house, we can't count on getting anything worthwhile from those hairs unless we have a suspect to compare them to. But Jane discovered a small pinprick at the base of each girl's neck and suspects they were injected. She's awaiting toxicology reports. What's the update on interviews with the people who were at the nightclub?'

Boyd tapped a keyboard. 'The doorman claims Amy left first, followed about half an hour later by Penny. The CCTV at the door confirms this. Both turned left as they exited, which suggests they headed towards Petit Lane. Penny's flat is in that direction and it's possible that Amy was taking a shortcut via the underpass.'

'Someone was watching and waiting. Does everyone at the club check out?'

'Those we were able to contact. We spoke to all the staff. Tracking down the patrons is a different story. Ducky Reilly was with both girls at one stage, but he remained at the club with a group of lads and they all verify this along with the CCTV. So that puts him in the clear.'

'I'm not discounting the fact that more than one person could be complicit in this crime.'

'Why?' Boyd enquired.

'I just think there was a lot of planning involved. After the first girl, Amy, was dealt with, the killer went back for the second. We need to establish which of them was the prime target, or was it both? The deaths of Louise Gill and Cristina Lee throw the cat among the pigeons, so to speak.' Lottie paused to catch her breath. Talking about the victims broke her heart a little each time she had to do it, but she had to distance herself slightly or she knew she wouldn't be able to do her job.

'The post-mortems on Louise and Cristina will be completed today, and I should have preliminary reports by late evening. Besides the fact that all four victims had their throats cut, the common denominator at both scenes is the coins. Anyone find out anything about them yet?'

Blank faces stared back at her.

'Nothing?'

'Not so far.' Boyd shook his head. 'McGlynn thinks they're home-made. Definitely not monetary. No symbols. He's trying to find out what type of machine might've made them.'

'Keep on to him about it.' She scanned the list in front of her. 'The phone we recovered from Richard Whyte's house. Please tell me we got something from that.'

More blank stares. 'Jesus, lads, will you wake up. There has to be someone working on it.'

'It's with the technical department,' Kirby said. 'It's an old Nokia. SIM card is missing. Nothing saved to the phone itself. No photos or numbers. Unless we find the SIM, it's useless.'

'Fingerprints?'

'Some have been extracted and are being compared to both Amy and Cristina. I'll know more later.'

'Step on it, Kirby. That phone belonged to either Richard Whyte or one of the girls. Why the need to hide it? Who were they in contact with? And where the hell is the SIM card? We'll go back and do a thorough search of the house. Boyd, you check with Richard Whyte to see if that's okay.'

'Will do.'

'And if he doesn't agree, we'll get a warrant.' She paused for a moment. 'The girls' own phones were all found with the bodies, with the exception of Louise's, which was in her room. Anything of interest found on them?'

'The usual social media,' Kirby said. 'Nothing jumping out to point to them being stalked by a serial killer.'

'Except for the coins found in Louise and Amy's rooms and the note in Amy's house. I've had a quick glance through Louise's notebooks and at first glance they all relate to her coursework. I could do with Lynch to go through them meticulously.' They were too stretched.

'Louise's laptop is similar,' Boyd said. 'Criminal behaviour assignments, and her search history is all to do with her research for those.'

Lottie recalled Cynthia Rhodes' revelation. 'Anything about visits to prisons?'

'Not yet,' he said. 'Why?'

'Read through everything. See if you can find any reference to Conor Dowling. I'm led to believe Louise went to see him in Mountjoy.'

Boyd raised a quizzical eyebrow. 'Who led you to believe that?'

'Doesn't matter who, just see if you can find any reference to him in her work.' She rolled up the sleeves of her faded-to-grey-in-the-wash white T-shirt, feeling light-headed from the stifling heat in the room.

'What about the murder weapon?' Boyd said.

'What about it? We haven't found it.'

'Exactly. Shouldn't we step up our efforts?'

'Uniforms have scoured all around Petit Lane and the car park. Bins and recycling bins. Gardens, the railway tracks. They've looked everywhere, plus the canal. If the killer used the same weapon on Louise and Cristina, we can assume he kept it. Once we get the post-mortem results we will know if he used the same one.'

'Right,' Boyd said. Lottie thought she detected a distinct grumpiness from him. She could do without that.

'Have the two lads who were knocked out at the house in Petit Lane been interviewed since I spoke to them in hospital?'

Kirby put up his hand. 'I've got the transcripts here. Nealon and McGrath were more than a bit hazy. They'd been drinking on the canal line and needed somewhere to kip. They think they were previously in that house about two weeks ago. They have no recollection of seeing anyone before they were attacked. Their tox levels were off the page. Alcohol and cannabis.'

'How were they knocked out?' Lottie asked.

'Both had contusions to the back of the head. Blunt object. Since nothing that could be the weapon was found at the scene, it's safe to say their assailant took it.'

'And they can't give any description?'

Kirby shook his head.

'Anyone got anything to add? We could do with a lead.' She sat on the chair and felt the tiredness of her sleepless night sink into her muscles.

'The note found in Amy's room,' Boyd said. 'It's been sent for fingerprint analysis. We still have no idea how she came to have it. Should we send it for further forensic tests?'

'Like what?'

'The ink. The paper type. Where it might have been purchased. Is it rare or mass-produced? All that kind of thing.'

'All that kind of thing costs money. Wait for the fingerprint analysis. The words are written in capital letters, so no point doing handwriting analysis. Keep it in mind, but no further action at the moment.'

'It was a direct threat to Amy. It's a major clue. We need to follow it up,' Boyd protested.

'How do you envisage we do that?'

'TV appeal?'

'You'll have the crazies crawling out of the woodwork. The coins are a different matter. We need to see if anyone recognises them. Maybe your friend Cynthia could help there.'

'She's no friend of mine,' Boyd said.

She let it go. 'We need house-to-house stepped up around Cristina's apartment. We need to establish her last-known movements, and the same for Louise. Her father says she left the house sometime after eight on Tuesday night. Her body was found yesterday morning. So I want a timeline for her movements during that interval.' She turned to look at the photos of the four victims on the board. 'What links these four young women to lead them to be the targets of a killer?'

'Amy and Louise gave evidence against Conor Dowling. Maybe he's exacting his revenge,' Boyd said.

'But why kill Penny and Cristina?' Kirby asked. 'That doesn't make sense.'

'To muddy the waters?' Boyd offered.

'Penny worked with Amy at one stage,' Lottie said. 'Did you find out anything worthwhile at the pharmacy, Kirby?'

'Just that she was let go for petty pilfering. Amy had secured her the job originally.'

'Penny's list of clients for her nail bar,' Lottie said, remembering the black appointment book. 'Anyone turn up there that might be suspicious?'

'I'll check it,' Kirby said, tapping his shirt pocket for his elusive cigar that he couldn't smoke inside anyway.

Lottie thought he looked a little brighter this morning. That makes one of us, she thought.

'Priorities for today. One, find out if Louise visited Conor Dowling in prison. There might be something in her coursework; if not, contact Mountjoy. Boyd, you do that. Two, the coins need to be identified. Kirby, you stick McGlynn on that one. And the phones. Especially the Nokia. I want the SIM card found. Once Richard Whyte gives the go-ahead, I want a full search of his house. McKeown, you also need to keep on top of the CCTV.'

'Will do,' Sam McKeown said.

'What are we going to do about Conor Dowling?' Boyd said.

'Request a twenty-four-hour surveillance detail to tail him,' Lottie said. 'I want to know what he eats and where he shits until this investigation is closed.'

'We better run that by the superintendent first.'

'I intend to do it straight away.'

'Wish you luck with that.'

'Then you and I are going to talk to Dowling's mother.'

'What for?'

'To shake up his weak alibi.'

CHAPTER 43

Tony lounged against the wall at the side of the courthouse. He saw Bob Cleary haul Conor into the office and reckoned he was going to be fired. In a way, he was glad. Conor was putting the shits up him and he didn't like it. Waiting for Cleary to return before continuing with his work, he wondered if a decision had been made about the body in the tunnel. If it was up to him, he'd go along with Conor's suggestion to ignore it so that they could get on with the job.

He doused his cigarette in a puddle and looked up, surprised to see Conor walking towards him.

'What did the boss want?' he said.

'Nothing to do with you.'

'We better get to work so, or the two of us will get the sack.' Tony marched off towards the site, where bricks were waiting to be hauled as the crane creaked overhead. He was glad it wasn't windy. 'Don't trust those bastards.'

'What bastards?'

'The cranes. Too high up, and only one man operating it. What would happen if he suddenly lost his rag and decided to drop a ton of concrete slabs down on top of us?'

'We'd be dead so we wouldn't give a shit.'

Tony laughed.

'What you laughing at?' Conor said.

'Just thought that was funny.'

'You're as weird as fuck. One minute you think the sky is going to fall in on top of you, and the next you're laughing to yourself. You going mad or what, Chicken Licken?'

They reached the area where they were due to work today and Tony turned to reply, but Conor was gone. He looked all around, but there was no sign of him. He glanced at the crane again as it swung around in the morning breeze, its cargo of wooden slats sliding precariously. It looked anything but safe.

*

Without speaking to McMahon to request additional resources, because she knew he'd say he'd already given her Sam McKeown, Lottie grabbed her keys and headed for the yard. Boyd came down the stairs behind her.

'What's wrong with you this morning?' he said.

'I'm tired, that's all.' She unlocked her car and slid into the driver's seat.

'Want me to drive?'

'Does it look like it?'

He jumped in beside her. 'It's Bernie Kelly, isn't it?'

Lottie nodded. 'She's around somewhere and it's eating me up that I don't know where.'

'Any word from Leo Belfield?'

'Nope. And I don't want him anywhere near me or I'll throttle him.' She shifted gears and sped out of the yard and down Main Street.

'Where are we headed?'

'Thought I'd have that word with Conor Dowling's mother.' She slowed at the traffic lights and swung into the lane to turn right for Gaol Street.

'Don't think he lives down this way.'

'Want to make sure he's at work first.'

'Before you harass his mother?'

'Yeah, something like that.'

The lights turned green and she turned right and drove to the building site. Ducky Reilly saluted her and waved her through the gate. She parked behind Cyril Gill's Mercedes.

'Looks like Mr Gill hasn't taken compassionate leave.'

'Not a crime,' Boyd said.

'Did I say it was?'

'You implied it.'

'Boyd, would you ever lighten up?' She stepped out of the car. The Portakabin door opened. She recognised the foreman from yesterday. Carey? Cleary?

'Good morning, Mr …'

'Bob Cleary,' he said. 'Can I help you, Inspector?'

'I was wondering if Conor Dowling is at work today.'

'It was a close thing with Mr Gill, but he's keeping him on. To keep an eye on him, he says.'

'Without interfering with my investigation, I hope.' Lottie tried to keep the preaching tone to a minimum.

'Of course.'

'Where is Dowling at the moment?'

Cleary looked around as if he hadn't a clue. 'He's here somewhere.'

'Isn't it your job to know where your employees are?'

'We have six gangs working. I think I put him on the tunnels. We have to pile them before the lift shaft goes in. Do you want me to fetch him for you?'

As he uttered the last word and turned away, an almighty bang reverberated around the site. Lottie instinctively ducked as timber, slates and bricks rained down. She felt Boyd's body fall on top of hers as he shoved her to the ground. Her face hit the mud and she swallowed dirt. Attempting to turn, she found she was unable to move, such was the dead weight on top of her. Darkness clouded everything.

'Boyd?' Her voice was hoarse. A swirl of dust caught in her nostrils and she gagged. She could not see a thing through the smog. Then voices rang out. Shouts. A scuffle of footsteps.

She yelled, 'Here!'

Still no movement from Boyd. His weight kept her flattened to the ground. She stilled herself. Listening for a heartbeat. Trying to feel any movement from him. But he was silent and motionless.

She tried to force air into her lungs. Mud caught between her lips, and then she tasted it. Blood. She didn't know if it was hers or Boyd's. She had to move. With an effort, she turned her head sideways and saw that they were both pinned beneath slabs of timber. Dust and mud and dirt rose into her face and a shard of light appeared as someone pulled debris free.

Dear God in heaven, she prayed, I know I don't always trust you and hardly believe in you, but I'm asking you, let Boyd be okay.

The voices grew louder.

'I have them. Two of them,' came the shout from above.

'Work carefully. Where's Ducky? Has anyone seen Ducky?'

'Do the job you're at. I'll search for him.'

'And the boss. He was inside.'

'If he was, he's mincemeat now.'

Hands worked fiercely to free them. Lottie let her head sink back to the ground. A dark swell of cloud ensnared her mind, and she drifted away.

*

Conor had slid down into the tunnel, lowered his head and entered the darkness. The lamp on his hard hat flickered on and off. He had to work fast. He felt his way along, his fingers brushing over fungus and dank water, and reached the wall that Cleary had found. He needed more light. Remembering the cigarette lighter, he flashed it in through the makeshift gap. The body was still there. He had to be sure.

He eased himself through the hole and fell with a thud on the ground. Careful not to disturb the body, he edged around it. He had a job to do.

'Ouch!' He dropped the lighter as it burned his finger.

Scrabbling around on the ground, he found it. Lit it again. Leaned in towards the bones and scrutinised the skeleton from the top of the cranium down over the eyeless skull. His gaze lingered on the scraps of clothing. A gulp of saliva lodged in his throat and he fought the urge to throw up.

A loud noise somewhere above his head caused him to pause. What if someone closed up the opening? What if he was trapped down here for ever? For once, he didn't really care. Then the walls of the tunnel shuddered. Damp earth fell on top of his head. He swiped it away, but still more pelted down on top of him. A moment of claustrophobia squeezed his chest tightly. He couldn't breathe. As the dirt hit the ground and rose in a cloud, he felt his throat close over and he began to choke. Stepping backwards, he came up against the wall. He was going to die here. He coughed. Tried to get a glob of mucus up and out, but the mustiness was clogging his airways.

Threading his hands along the brickwork, he found the hole and squeezed his body through, with no care for anything that he might have left behind. He had to save himself.

*

Kirby was pissed off. Watching CCTV was the most boring thing on earth. He'd been scrunched into a tiny cubicle with Sam McKeown for the last hour and he was getting double vision. The Petit Lane tapes had thrown up nothing. The nightclub footage had been scrutinised and verified. That left the discs and tapes they'd been able to secure from various businesses, and of course their own traffic cams. He'd discovered that the apartment complex where Cristina Lee lived had no working cameras.

He stood. 'I'm going for a smoke.'

'Don't be long,' Sam said. 'There are hours of this stuff to get through yet.'

Kirby could have pointed out that he was in charge and would do what he liked, but he couldn't be bothered. Then he realised that he and McKeown were on the same grade. He left before his mouth got him into trouble.

As he passed his desk, he tapped his keyboard and checked for new reports. Nothing. He put the computer into sleep mode and headed outside.

He lit up a cigar and took a long, deep drag. What else had he to do? Oh yes. Contact McGlynn about the coins. He tried ringing him on his mobile, but got no answer. He left a message. Urgent, he said. Of course McGlynn knew everything was urgent.

The Nokia bothered him. All the victims had fancy iPhones or Samsungs. Why the need for an old-fashioned brick? Why take out the SIM card if you were hiding the phone? It didn't make sense, and the more he thought about it, the more he came to the conclusion that the phone actually belonged to Richard Whyte. Why then did he keep it hidden?

As he made up his mind to find out, Garda Tom Thornton stuck his head out the door.

'Get your skates on, Kirby. We have an emergency at the courthouse.'

*

You know you're right when everyone is looking for you. You've done something that makes them sit up and take notice. But you still have to remain hidden from view. Unseen and unheard. I have ways of making myself seen and heard. The steel is cold beneath my fingers as I slide it into the machine. It's a bit antiquated but it was all I could get my hands on. It will do. I have one more to deliver. Because I'm not sure the first one was found. It was a risk sliding it into the kid's pocket while his mother was dressing, but I saw the chance and I took it.

I will do this last one and then I'm finished. I don't care if they find me once I make my mark.

I listen to the soft whirr of the machine and let the lever drop. And another perfect disc drops onto my lap.

This is for your family, Lottie Parker.

CHAPTER 44

When she was eventually dragged free, Lottie found herself sitting in a scene of chaos. Her head thumped agonisingly and blood streamed from a cut somewhere on her skull. She felt shaken but didn't think she was too badly hurt.

She looked around for Boyd. Where was he? A bolt of panic shot through her chest and she thought she was going to throw up. She tried to stand. Wobbled. Put out her hand to her rescuer for support. She had no idea who she was holding onto. She didn't care. She had to find Boyd.

'My partner. Where is he?'

The man pointed to the right. Boyd was lying on a makeshift stretcher of laths of timber while an ambulance driver desperately tried to get his vehicle onto the site.

'What's your name?' She thought she vaguely recalled the man from her earlier visits.

'Tony.'

'Help me over to Detective Boyd, please.' She leaned on his arm and carefully put one foot in front of the other. She noticed that the legs of her jeans were shredded.

'Take it slowly,' Tony said. 'This place is like a bomb went off.'

'Is that what happened?'

'No. The crane collapsed. It's as bad as a bomb, though.'

She looked around, pain shooting up her neck. She couldn't see the security hut or the Portakabin. Both structures had been flattened. Buried beneath mangled steel, concrete and timber. Sirens screamed down the street. As she reached Boyd, she noticed three bodies lined up with yellow work jackets placed over their heads.

'How many dead do you think, Tony?'

'I don't know. I'll leave you here now and go help the others.'

'Thanks.'

She knelt on the ground beside Boyd just as a paramedic arrived, having abandoned his vehicle outside the shattered hoarding. Crowds were beginning to gather. She should be coordinating the rescue. She should be doing something.

'You're hurt,' the paramedic said. His name badge read *Nigel*.

'Don't mind me, Nigel. Treat Boyd. Is he going to be okay?' She thought her voice sounded hoarse and weak.

'Give me room,' he said.

She rose unsteadily to her feet and watched as Nigel got to work. Boyd was deathly pale, his eyes tight shut, and she couldn't see his chest moving. Nigel fixed an oxygen mask to his mouth and tore open his shirt. She noticed a trail of blood from the back of Boyd's head, staining his collar deep red. The paramedic was setting up wires and intravenous lines; she had to turn away when he inserted a needle into Boyd's wrist.

Numb. That was how she felt. Her best friend and long-time colleague could be lying dead in the noise and dirt, and she felt bereft.

Eventually some of the debris was removed from the entrance and the ambulance made its way in. A fire truck screeched to a halt on the street and men ran onto the site, followed by her own colleagues. People were scrambling everywhere. Someone had to take control of this emergency, she thought. But she hadn't the energy to voice a command.

Smoke rose in pockets as men began to dig through the rubble, and she wondered how many had lost their lives in that tragic instant of carnage. Returning her gaze to Boyd, she caught Nigel's eye and cocked her head in question. He nodded. Boyd was going to be okay.

*

Kirby arrived with McKeown and Garda Thornton at the same time as Cynthia Rhodes. How the hell did journalists do that? The street was blocked and he could only get halfway down. He left the blue lights flashing on the car and parked up on the footpath, then got a roll of crime-scene tape from the boot and shouldered his way through the crowd.

At the entrance to the courthouse, the devastation was laid bare. Kirby grabbed hold of McKeown and told him to roll out the tape while he held onto the other end. He'd had the sense to throw on his work jacket, and people followed his commands and moved back. With the tape secured, he directed the uniforms not to let anyone pass through. McKeown got on the radio for more reinforcements.

The tall green crane that had held sway over the town's landscape for the last year was a tangled mass of steel. Part of it appeared to be sunk into a hole in the ground. It was impossible to get much further on to the site. Kirby felt a surge of panic as he saw the bodies lined up inside the gate, and he thought of Gilly and how she had died in a moment of violence. He knew he shouldn't be walking on and over the mangled mess, but he had to help. Two men were trying to pull someone out from beneath a shattered wall, and he started towards them. But then he saw Lottie standing in a daze, bloodied and lost.

'Boss? What the hell? What are you doing here?'

She stared at him, her eyes glazed over, her cheek cut and blood seeping from a wound somewhere on her head.

'Boyd,' she said, pointing.

He barely heard her above the din of machinery where work was continuing feverishly to free those interred.

'Come with me,' he said, taking her by the elbow. She fell against him, and he wrapped an arm around her and half carried, half dragged her off the site. As they climbed over a slab of concrete, he saw a stretcher being wheeled into an ambulance. He steered Lottie towards it.

'You need to be seen by a doctor,' he said. 'You're pumping blood.'

The paramedic strapped the stretcher inside and glanced at Lottie. 'Help her up. We'll take her too.'

Kirby guided Lottie up the steps. As he turned to climb out of the vehicle, he realised that it was Boyd on the stretcher.

The ambulance did a U-turn because it couldn't get back up the narrow clogged street. As it sped away, Kirby saw Cynthia Rhodes standing behind the barrier speaking rapidly into her phone. He reckoned she had more than enough material for her next bulletin.

Superintendent McMahon approached him.

'Thanks, Detective Kirby, but I'm in charge now.'

Kirby shook his head and walked away. He knew McMahon would make a bollocks of himself. He was tired and he missed Gilly. As he pushed his way through the crowd to his car, he felt his eyes stinging. Probably from all the dust, he thought.

*

Shielded by the swell of curious onlookers, Bernie stood at the window of the shop across the road from the courthouse. The mayhem filled her with a certain type of glee. A feeling she used to get when she stabbed or smothered one of her victims. This was an opportunity to strike. Lottie was in the back of an ambulance. Hopefully she'd be kept in overnight. But if not, Bernie still had time to make her half-sister pay. And she knew the best way to hurt someone was to target those they loved most.

*

Tony pulled off his gloves and lit a cigarette. A fireman growled at him to put it out. There could be leaking gas. There could be an explosion. Anything could happen. As if he didn't know all that. He grunted and doused the cigarette and chewed the end of a dirty thumbnail. He'd searched everywhere. Pulled up concrete with his bare hands. Moved bricks and blocks and timber. Dragged the injured to safety. Ferried the dead with as much dignity as was possible in the face of extreme pandemonium. But there was no sign of Conor. Where the hell was he?

He eyed the mangled remains of the crane, crushing the Portakabin and the security hut. They were waiting for another crane to arrive to lift the one that had collapsed like Lego. He scratched his head. His hair felt like it was crawling. He could murder a pint. Or three.

He reckoned Bob Cleary and Ducky Reilly were buried along with the boss beneath the rubble, because they had not been found yet.

Ten dead so far. Plus those three. Unlucky thirteen.

He took his gloves out of his pocket and, dismissing the idea of a creamy pint of Guinness, moved around the side of the courthouse, where a temporary mortuary had been set up. He'd have one final look at the bodies then he was calling it a day. Maybe Conor would be there. And if he was, Tony would be free of him for ever.

*

Conor eventually reached where he knew the entrance to the tunnel must be, but it was not there. The entire opening was now closed over with concrete and debris. His way out was blocked. And he was in total darkness.

He leaned against the wall, saving his breath because of the dust and debris clogging his airways. There was not much oxygen. He listened.

He could hear muffled noise above his head, but he knew what it was. Heavy machinery. Cutting and grinding. As work continued up there, masonry kept falling downwards. He moved away from the wall, and heard the drip, drip of water. He couldn't see, but he knew it was seeping from some unknown source and rising around his feet. Another step. Water splashed over the ankles of the steel-capped boots he was wearing. Pipes must have burst overhead. He knew a water main snaked along above some of the tunnels. He tried to remember if there was a tunnel adjacent to the one he was in. And still the water was rising.

The tunnel was going to be flooded. If he didn't manage to get out in time, he was going to drown.

He had no fear of being underground, but he sensed the terror of never getting out. Like the body encased behind him. And that thought gave him an idea.

He turned around and made his way back towards the body. It might be his only chance of escape.

CHAPTER 45

The wound in her head had been seen to. The cut on her cheek had been treated with antiseptic and four stitches. Lottie eased herself off the trolley in the packed A&E, and as she put her feet to the floor, her entire body jarred. Pain shot through her lower back and up her spine and nestled in an ache around her shoulders. She felt like shit. But she had too many other things to worry about to be concerned about herself.

She threaded through the crowd of staff and walking wounded. She needed information. But she couldn't see any of her team. Or Boyd.

Grabbing the arm of a passing medic, she said, 'Mark Boyd. He was brought in with me. Do you know where I can find him?'

'Check at reception.' He hurried away.

No way was she going out to reception. She'd never get back in. At each cubicle she peeked in through the drawn curtains. No sign of Boyd.

'Dear God, don't let him be dead,' she whispered. The emotion that had been numbed by the shock of the accident was back like an explosion.

She cornered a nurse and asked the same question.

'Treatment room,' the nurse said and pointed out directions.

Outside the door, Lottie rested her hand on the handle and peered in through the small rectangle of glass at eye level. He was in there. He looked alive. There was no one else present. She opened the door and rushed to his bedside.

'Boyd, you fecking idiot. Are you okay?'

He opened his eyes and smiled crookedly. A line of stitches ran from the corner of his bottom lip diagonally to his chin. 'You look a little worse for wear yourself,' he said, his voice a coarse whisper.

'Do I sound as weird as you?' The smoke and dust had torn shreds from her throat.

'Yeah.' He patted the edge of the bed. 'Sit.'

Perched on the bed, she took his hand in hers. 'I thought you were dead.'

'Hard to kill a bad thing.'

'Suppose so.' She glanced at the machinery surrounding the bed. 'What's all the monitors for?'

'Monitoring?'

'Smart-arse. What did the doctor say?'

'I can go home in an hour.'

'Liar.'

'No, honestly. Got the back of my head stitched up. Might have concussion, but that doesn't worry me. Bruising on my spine, but no broken bones.'

'Did you have an X-ray?'

'Yes. I'm grand. I'm all right.'

'An MRI? Surely they have to do an MRI? I'm creased with pain but you took the full weight of the rubble. You're not leaving here until you're fully checked out. Got it?' She knew there was no MRI equipment in Ragmullin Hospital, so Boyd would have to be transported to Tullamore. She would insist on it.

He tried to lean up on the pillows, but winced and sank back down. 'I feel at a disadvantage not being able to look you in the eye.'

'That's the way it should be.' She smiled softly.

'What happened, Lottie?'

'The crane collapsed. We were lucky. I don't think Cyril Gill or his foreman Bob Cleary were as fortunate. The Portakabin was flattened. Their bodies haven't been located yet as far as I know. If we'd been standing a few feet to our left, we wouldn't be here.'

'Mmm. We do seem to spend a lot of time in hospitals, don't we?'

'You know what I mean.' She tried to be angry with his flippancy, but she only felt concern as she patted his hand.

He said, 'First the daughter and now the father. Do you think he was a target?'

'What? You mean the Gills? Are you saying it might not have been an accident?' The thought hadn't crossed her mind.

'It's possible, isn't it?'

'A bit extreme. All that collateral damage.' But maybe Boyd had a point. 'There'll be a full-scale inquiry into the incident. The security cabin is gone too. I hope that young lad Ducky Reilly wasn't in there, but ...'

'It's likely he was.'

'Yes.'

'Lottie, I need to get out. We're stretched for resources as it is. Talk to a doctor. Tell him I'll come back for the tests tomorrow.'

'So you do have to have more tests. You really are a liar.'

'Please?' Boyd's fingers tightened around hers.

She knew she couldn't put him at risk. If he could lie, so could she.

'Sit tight. I'll see what I can do.' She leaned over, flinching with the pain in her neck, and let her lips rest softly on his good cheek. He moved his head and their lips touched.

'Thanks.' He smiled crookedly again. 'All it took was a ton of mangled steel on my back to soften your heart.'

'Who said it's softened?' She ran a finger along his forehead and picked grains of sand from his hair. 'Boyd?'

'What?'

'Don't ever die on me. I don't think I could live without you. You know, without you having my back.'

'Talk to a doctor. Get me out of here.'

'I'll see what they say. Get some rest.'

'You too.'

She smiled and walked to the door.

'Lottie?'

She turned to him.

'I love you.'

She bit her lip. She wanted to say the words, wanted to reassure him that her heart was bursting, but she couldn't. She opened the door and left.

*

When he reached the wall, Conor knew he had to crawl back in with the skeleton to get out the other side. He was leaving pieces of himself everywhere. Evidence that could be used against him. But he had a legitimate reason for being here. He'd been underground when something had happened up on the site, trapping him below. This was his only way out. He concocted answers in his head to possible questions that might be posed at a later date, but all that was dependent on him escaping and someone asking where he had been. Or maybe no one was left to ask the questions.

Keeping his eyes away from the body, he crept through the opening behind it and entered the darkness of a tunnel he prayed would lead up and out, otherwise he was doomed. Don't go there, he warned his inner self. No use thinking about what ifs.

There was less water here. That was a positive. He kept walking, head bent, the thin, flickering light from his hard hat guiding him. He rounded a winding corner and came to a junction. Two tunnels.

One right, one left. He tried to envisage where he was in relation to the lie of the land above him. But his sense of direction had deserted him. He remembered someone once telling him, 'When in doubt, go right.' When he had walked twenty paces, he wondered if the saying was actually 'go left'.

His path began to slope upwards. He clambered up on hands and knees. And then the light went out on his hat, plunging him into darkness, and he fell.

*

The sky was filled with ominous blackness, the horizon washy and watery. Birds nestled tightly on bare branches shielded by the odd remaining leaf. It wasn't cold. Small mercies and all that, Kirby thought as he pressed his finger on Megan's doorbell.

'I'm sorry. I didn't know it was your day off,' he said, standing awkwardly on the doorstep. Suddenly it didn't seem like the good idea it had done an hour ago. Superintendent McMahon had told him to get some rest and come back to the courthouse site in two hours. He'd sat in the station for half an hour going over logistics with McKeown before he realised he needed to talk to someone not involved in the disaster.

'They told me in the pharmacy. When I called in there to see you. But you weren't there. Oh shit, I don't know what I'm saying.' He ran his hand through his hair.

She smiled then, a weak one, but he caught it before her face slipped back into serious mode. 'I was just going to have a lie-down. The house is a mess. I can't ask you in.'

'Oh God, no. I didn't mean that … I wasn't asking to come in or anything. Just dropped round. I'll leave. Sorry to disturb you.' He walked away. Down the footpath, under the trees. Had his hand on the car door when she called out.

'Give me half an hour. I can meet you in town for a drink if you want?'

'Honestly, Megan, it's okay. I have work to do. I'm just on a break and felt like a chat and a coffee.'

'Half an hour. Cafferty's?'

'The street's cordoned off because of the crane collapsing. The whole town is blocked off. Maybe the Parkland Hotel?'

'Order an Irish coffee for me. I'll try to be there in twenty minutes.'

As Kirby drove to the hotel, he felt like smiling, but he was too tired and his heart was broken. Even though he wanted nothing further from Megan – didn't want to lead her on or anything – he really had no one else to talk to.

*

Lottie discharged herself with a quick flourish on a flimsy form and told the doctor to make sure Boyd got all the tests required to ensure he had no broken bones or internal injuries. She wanted him back at work, but she needed him healthy. In the main reception area she looked around hoping to find Kirby, McKeown or McMahon. Any garda would do. She needed information and a lift. But the only person who caught her eye was Cynthia Rhodes.

'Good God, Inspector, you look a fright.'

'Thanks, Cynthia. That makes me feel a whole lot better.' She looked out over the smaller woman's head. Not a single garda around. 'Got a cigarette?'

'Didn't know you smoked,' Cynthia said.

'I don't. Not really. But I feel like having one now.'

'Well I don't have any, but I'm sure you could bum one off someone outside. Come on. I'll link you.'

'I'm not that bad. I can walk.'

'All the same, you look like a ghost beneath that sheen of sand or cement or whatever it is glued to your face.'

Lottie put up a hand and it came away grey with dust.

Outside, she waited while Cynthia smooth-talked a woman in a dressing gown who was smoking behind a pillar. The entire campus was no smoking. But everyone knew rules were made to be broken. Cynthia returned with a lit cigarette and handed it over.

'Make sure you don't faint on me,' she said.

'Thanks.'

'Want to provide a comment?'

'Want to give me a lift back to the station?'

'No. But I will give you a lift home.'

'I have to see what needs to be done at the station first.' The nicotine was making her nauseous. She rested her back against the pillar and watched as a third ambulance joined two others already outside the entrance to A&E. Two trolley stretchers were rolled out and swiftly wheeled inside.

'There's at least ten dead, I heard,' Cynthia said. 'Many more injured. Some still buried beneath the rubble. So the death toll could be higher. This is a major news story, Inspector.'

'Why aren't you down at the courthouse then? That's where the story is.'

'I've done all I can there. I got a quote from your superintendent and the chief fire officer. One from you would be great, seeing as you were caught up in the middle of it all.'

'No comment.'

'I'm sick of that line.'

Lottie ground the cigarette out under her boot and realised how torn and bloody her clothes were. 'Maybe I will take that lift home if the offer still stands.'

Cynthia straightened her spectacles. 'Okay. But I still want a quote.'

'How about this – I feel like shit and I need a shower?'

*

This hotel was not one of his usual haunts. Kirby liked to be surrounded by familiar things and people. Familiarity suited him. Most of the time. He supposed he was a little old-fashioned like that. The ambience here was too modern, too clean, too comfortable. And too noisy. Give me Cafferty's any day, he thought as he ordered a pint of Guinness and added a shot of whiskey.

When he had downed the whiskey and paid for the drinks, he headed to a corner booth with a direct line of sight to the door. Then he realised there were two entrances. By the time Megan arrived, he'd have a crick in his neck.

She walked in twenty minutes later on the dot. He rose clumsily to take her coat.

'I'll keep it on, if you don't mind. It's a bit chilly.' She kept a hand on the buttoned-up tweed.

Kirby noticed that she had no handbag. She looked like she was about to run out on him. He felt nervous, though he had no reason to be.

'What will you have to drink?' he said.

'I told you to order me an Irish coffee.'

He'd forgotten. He felt the heat rise up his cheeks and he almost stumbled down the two steps from the booth. Her tone had been sharp, and suddenly he wished he hadn't sought her out. It was calmness he needed after the madness of the day's events. He was certain Megan was not going to provide it, but he ordered the drink anyway.

Sitting on the chair opposite her, he felt overweight and ugly. His hair needed cutting and his clothes needed changing, but on the other hand, she looked as haggard as he did.

'What was your day off like?' Small talk didn't come easy any more. He'd have to learn to socialise again.

'Pretty shit, to tell you the truth,' she said. 'I heard about the accident. Terrible altogether.'

'My boss and a colleague were caught up in it. They're both in hospital.'

'Oh God. That's awful. Will they be okay?'

'I don't know. I have to check.' Kirby felt as if he was all over the place. Maybe now wasn't the time to take out his phone to call his boss.

'Who are they?' Megan said.

'My inspector, Lottie Parker, and Sergeant Mark Boyd. They're two of the good guys.'

'Are you one of the bad ones?'

Her voice was hard, and Kirby wondered why he'd ever thought her company would be good for him. As her drink arrived, he was deciding how he could escape.

'I'm whatever people want me to be,' he said. 'I don't really care. I do my job to the best of my ability.'

'I didn't mean to imply you were not one of the best. Sorry. I'm just a little down since Amy's death, and not great company at the moment. Maybe I should leave.'

'Not at all. I think I'm a bit shook up myself after seeing the carnage at the courthouse.' His pint tasted sour, or maybe it was just the bile in his stomach. She had gulped down half of her drink already.

'On the news, they said there may be more bodies buried beneath the rubble. Something about tunnels under the courthouse that might have caused the crane to collapse. Is that true?'

'About the bodies or the tunnels?'

'Both, I suppose.'

'There are a number of dead,' he said. 'A long time ago I heard that there's a network of tunnels under the whole town. Goes back to medieval days. This is a garrison town, and in the 1800s it housed a jail for the midlands. It's possible the tunnels were used to transport prisoners from the jail to the courthouse.'

'Maybe some people escaped the accident that way. You know, if they got trapped beneath the rubble they might have found their way out through the tunnels.'

'Once the rescue operation is complete, we'll know the full toll of casualties.'

'There's a rumour that Cyril Gill might be one of the dead. Such a tragedy for that family, what with his daughter's murder also.'

'How is Richard Whyte holding up?' Kirby remembered he had to approach the man to see if he could search for the phone's SIM card.

'I haven't seen him. He hasn't been into the pharmacy since …' She took another mouthful of her Irish coffee. 'Since Amy was found murdered.'

'Who's standing in for you today then?'

'I'm entitled to my day off,' she said haughtily.

'Sorry, Megan, I was only asking.'

'We have a locum pharmacist. He's in today.' She drained her mug and stood. 'I'd better go. I've things to do. Hope your colleagues will be all right.'

He got up to let her pass, and she was gone before he sat back down again.

Richard Whyte opened the door and led Kirby inside.

'Would you like a coffee? Or a drink? I've the best Irish whiskey.'

'Whiskey sounds good.' Kirby slid onto a high stool at the breakfast bar as Whyte opened a cupboard and returned with two glasses. The bottle was already open on the counter.

'Forgive me, I'm a little drunk,' Whyte said, and sat beside Kirby.

'Sorry about your daughter.'

'Life's a bitch.'

'Isn't it just.'

Both men drained their whiskey and Whyte poured two more.

'Do you have any update on who killed Amy?'

'Not yet. But we're working flat out. That is, we were, until the accident at the courthouse.'

'Saw that on the news. I've been trying to call Cyril. No answer. I doubt he was on site, though, what with Louise and all ...'

'He's not among the dead so far. But we believe there are some people still buried under the rubble.' Kirby twisted around on the stool so that he could get a look at Whyte. The man was staring into the molten gold swimming in the bottom of his crystal glass. 'There's something I have to ask you.'

'Go ahead.'

'What's with the spare mobile phone, the one we found hidden here? It's not Cristina's or Amy's, is it?'

'I don't know whose it is.'

'It's not a model favoured by young people. All touch screens nowadays. Are you sure it's not yours?'

Kirby watched Richard's face intently as he struggled with what he should say.

'My girl is dead. Cyril's girl is dead. Doesn't matter now, I suppose.'

'The phone was yours?'

'Cyril's idea.'

Blinking hard, Kirby let that sink in. The boss had been sure it was something to do with Amy and Louise or even Cristina.

'Tell me about it.'

CHAPTER 46

In the end, Lottie persuaded Cynthia to drop her off at the station before sending her packing with a quote about sympathy for the victims of the accident and their families. She assumed Cynthia had already received that line from McMahon, but much to her relief, the reporter didn't press for anything further.

After passing through a relatively calm reception area, she made her way gingerly up the stairs to her office. It was so quiet it was almost silent. Everyone must be at the scene of the accident.

Without having to sniff under her arms, she knew she smelled rotten and should have gone home first, but she was too wound up on adrenaline to slow down. She knocked on McMahon's office door and stuck her head around it without waiting for an answer. Empty. She headed into the incident room, which was also empty, and walked up to the boards.

Four young women. All dead. And now at least ten others dead as the result of an accident. Boyd's words stuck in her brain. Was it really an accident, or could it have been an orchestrated plan to take out Cyril Gill? Surely there were other means.

Her eyes rested on the photograph of Conor Dowling from the old case file. He looked young and vulnerable. An image of what he looked like now sprung to her mind. He'd hardened in prison, but she thought he'd retained his youthful vulnerability beneath his hostile exterior. Could he have murdered the four young women in revenge? She traced a finger over his fathomless eyes. Where was he when the crane collapsed? Could he be among the dead? She'd ask Kirby to find out. She walked to the general office. No sign of him or anyone else.

She needed to check in at home to ensure that with all the traffic disruptions Chloe and Sean had been picked up safely by the taxi. Then she realised that her phone was in her bag, and her bag was buried somewhere under the rubble at the courthouse.

Her face ached and her head thumped. Every limb in her body felt like it had been hit with a concrete block. Which wasn't far from the truth. She decided a quick shower in the locker room would suffice.

She headed down the stairs to the basement, stripped off her filthy clothes and stood under the cold water. She realised she should have checked first to make sure she had a clean set of clothes in her locker. As the water drummed up goose bumps on her skin, she hoped with all her heart that Boyd was going to be okay. She needed him.

*

Tony escaped to the pub as soon as he could. The guards and emergency personnel had done everything possible in the circumstances. They now had to wait for lifting equipment to come from Dublin to raise the crushed remains of the crane. The fire service were using cutting equipment, but it was too dangerous as the ground underfoot kept giving way.

He'd just got inside when the clouds burst open. The site was going to be some mess now. He half expected Conor to be sitting nursing a pint, but there was no sign of him. The place seemed to be full of journalists and reporters. He quickly took off his jacket with *Gill Construction* emblazoned on the back. Better to be just another rubbernecker, he thought. He didn't want to have to answer any awkward questions.

Elbowing his way to the counter, he heard snippets of conversation, though nothing to concern himself with. He ordered his drink and waited. For the first time in ten years, he felt as if a weight had lifted from his shoulders. Now he just had to hope that Conor Dowling was one of the bodies beneath the rubble.

*

The T-shirt was too long and the jeans too tight, but Lottie had no choice but to squeeze into them. Deciding that her jacket was a lost cause, she found a lightweight garda one. Before she went home, she'd call to Conor Dowling's house, because that was where she'd been heading when she'd taken the detour to the building site, and because, after making enquiries, no one on the site had been able to contact him.

Nabbing a car from the pool in the yard, she sped around via the bypass, pulling up at Dowling's house fifteen minutes after she'd stepped out of the freezing-cold shower. She was so numb she couldn't feel any pain, and she wasn't sure if that was a good thing or not.

The house looked slightly more decrepit than its neighbours. She had never been house-proud herself, but she had to still an urge to find a cloth and clean the dirt off the windows.

She hammered with her fist on the cracked timber and cringed with the pain reverberating through the bones in her hand. The grass was long and trampled in places. Plenty of weeds, too, and a buckled bicycle wheel leaning against the inside of the wall. About to walk away, she heard a shuffling behind the door just before it was opened.

'Mrs Dowling?'

'What's with all the banging? Have you no patience? I'm not supposed to be up. What do you want?'

'I'm Detective Inspector Parker. I'd like a word with Conor, please.'

The woman's face appeared to shrink in on itself. Looking down on the balding head, Lottie thought Mrs Vera Dowling was about to take a bite out of her arm, so she shoved her hands into her flimsy jacket pockets.

'Conor? What do you want with him? Aren't you the one who locked him up?' Now the face had definitely taken on an evil quality. 'Bitch of a guard, you are. My boy did nothing wrong. But you believed those two young hussies over him.'

'Can I come in, please?' Lottie glanced back over her shoulder to where curtains were twitching across the road. 'You don't want the neighbours knowing your business, do you?'

Mrs Dowling twisted round on her walking sticks and beckoned. 'Come in so.'

Lottie had to wait for her to slowly shuffle along the narrow hall before she could enter and close the door behind her. She followed her into what she could only describe as the woman's living quarters.

From what she could see, it seemed Vera Dowling ate, slept and carried out her bathroom functions in the one room. A television stood in a corner with the sound blasting out a game show. The air was foul with the odour of unwashed flesh and clothes. She felt like opening a window to allow freshness in. There was nowhere to sit, so she stood, careful not to lean up against the wall, where condensation dripped down faded wallpaper and a wooden crucifix hung with black rosary beads fixed around Jesus' drooped head. A yellowed stock image of a house in a forest hung in a cracked wooden frame over an unlit fireplace.

At last Mrs Dowling was seated on a fetid pile of cushions. Dust motes rose in unison as if eager to escape being flattened by her bottom. Lottie felt like she had walked into a sepia-hazed nightmare.

'So why do you want to talk to Conor?'

'Can you lower the television sound, please?' Lottie couldn't hear a word the woman was saying.

After trying each of the four remote controls lined up on the arm of the chair, the woman eventually got the sound turned down. Lottie noticed how crooked and swollen the older woman's fingers were.

'Mrs Dowling, have you heard that there was an accident at the courthouse today?'

'Accident? Is Conor okay? I hope he isn't injured. I need him to look after me.'

'I don't know if he is or not,' Lottie said truthfully. 'I'm trying to locate him. Was he at work today?'

'Of course he was at work. He goes every day. He's a good lad, not that you believe that. He'll be home soon.'

'My office has been unable to contact him.'

Mrs Dowling blessed herself. 'Holy Mary, Mother of God, he better be all right. I spent ten years waiting for the day he'd be free to look after me, and now this happens.'

'Don't worry unduly. I'm sure he'll turn up.' Lottie wasn't at all certain of that, but she didn't want Mrs Dowling getting hysterical. Now that she was here, she itched to get home and check on her family, then return to the hospital to make sure Boyd hadn't discharged himself.

'Would you like me to make you a cup of tea?' Why on earth had she said that?

'Oh, that'd be great. The kitchen is that way.' Mrs Dowling pointed with her walking stick. 'I'm eaten alive with rheumatoid arthritis. Painful in the legs and hands. I depend on Conor for everything.'

'How did you manage when he was ... inside?'

'His friend Tony was good to me. He works with him on the site. A loyal friend, Tony is.'

'I'll make that tea then.'

In the scullery-like kitchen, Lottie filled the kettle and switched it on. 'Do you take milk?'

'Course I do. Otherwise it'd be like dishwater.'

Lottie found a carton in the fridge. 'Sugar?'

'There's a bowl in the cupboard. Two spoonfuls. Tea bags are in the caddy.'

'Does Conor stay in every night?' Lottie searched through the grimy cupboard.

'He does.'

She made the tea and brought a mug in to Mrs Dowling. 'Hope that's okay.'

'A bit weak,' the woman sniffed.

'And he goes shopping for you?'

'You hardly think I'm able to go around pushing a trolley, do you?'

'Tuesday night, was he in all evening? All night?'

Her legs were weak from the trauma of the accident, and the look Vera Dowling threw her made her feel like sinking to the floor.

'Are you accusing him of something? Like you did the last time?' Tea spilled from the mug and down the side of the chair, but the old woman didn't seem to notice. 'He was here. Every night. So you can piss off with whatever you think you're going to pin on him.'

'I wasn't—'

'Conor never did those things you accused him of. He never beat that old man to a pulp and he never stole his money.'

'He didn't deny it.'

'He didn't do it.'

'He offered no alibi.'

'How could he? I was working back then. Nights in the hospital. I used to be a nurse's aide. He was home. Alone.'

'Was he, though? He never said he was.' It had niggled Lottie at the time that Conor had offered no explanation for his whereabouts the night of the assault on Bill Thompson. In the end, with lack of forensic evidence and no denial from the accused, it was the two eyewitnesses who had swung the case.

Mrs Dowling set her mouth in a thin straight line and eyed her. 'He didn't do it. He had no access to a gun. Did you ever find the weapon? Did you ever find the money? Look around you, Inspector. Do you see any sign of wealth here?'

Lottie shook her head and shrugged. It didn't mean anything. He could have the money buried, awaiting an appropriate time to dig it up. They never did find out how much had been stolen, but bar staff estimated it could have been ten thousand euros. Bill Thompson hadn't brought home the takings every night. Usually only on a Sunday. And it had been a busy weekend. Conor Dowling had regularly frequented the pub. He knew Thompson's routine. Louise Gill and Amy Whyte had sworn they'd seen him rushing from the direction of Thompson's house that night. He never denied it. Never said a word. But Lottie was confident the right man had been jailed.

'Here, take this piss away. Trying to poison me, are you?'

Taking the mug, Lottie went back to the scullery. She looked out at the back garden as she swilled the tea down the sink. The outside area was neater than the front, but the overhanging trees could do with being cut back, not that she knew anything about gardening. The wooden shed appeared out of place, like it had been dropped from the sky. One side was slightly lower than the other, as if it had sunk into the ground. A large padlock hung on the bolt. Why? What was in there that needed protection from theft? Not an expensive lawnmower, she thought, seeing as the grass was so long. Hiding something? More than likely.

An ache drummed behind her eyes as she decided on the best approach to get Mrs Dowling to allow her access to the shed. She could just open the back door and go out to have a look, couldn't she?

'What are you doing in there?' The voice sounded closer and Lottie jumped when she turned round. Vera was standing in the doorway, leaning on her two walking sticks.

'You're snooping, you sneaky bitch.'

She straightened her shoulders, ignoring the pain shooting down her spine. 'I was wondering what you keep in your shed?'

'Conor's stuff is in there. And it's none of your business.'

'What stuff?'

'You'd like to know, wouldn't you? If you want to look, get a search warrant. Now before I kick you out, tell me why you're asking all these questions.' Mrs Dowling leaned against the door jamb and pointed a walking stick at Lottie's chest. But she wasn't letting herself be intimidated by a fetid crone.

'Four young women were murdered this week. I need to validate Conor's alibi.'

'Get out, scum pig.' Mrs Dowling raised the other stick and Lottie ducked as it swung through the air. 'Get the hell out of my house with your insane accusations.'

'I didn't accuse him of anything. I just need to know—'

'Go, and don't come back. You can rot in hell and take your accusations with you.'

Mrs Dowling's eyes blazed and Lottie felt her cheeks burn from the angry heat. She'd made a mess of this. Her head throbbed and her bones felt like jelly. She was leaving, but not without a last attempt.

'I want to know where Conor is now, where he was two nights ago, where he was Saturday night, and I want to know what's in that shed.'

'You're a nosy bitch. Piss off and don't come back unless you have a search warrant.'

Leaving the front door open so the older woman would have to walk along her hall to close it, Lottie moved slowly to the car. She looked across the road and saw a shape behind the curtains. Tomorrow she'd have the neighbours canvassed to see whether Conor had been at home when he said he'd been, though past experience told her she'd get nothing from them. But the little shit with his crazy mother wasn't going to best her. That's if he wasn't already buried beneath the courthouse rubble.

CHAPTER 47

Lottie was desperate to get home, but first she needed a phone. There would be a spare one at the station. Her mind was in such disarray that she hadn't thought of it before. She drove around by the ring road and snaked along with the traffic at the railway bridge. She wondered how Penny Brogan's family were faring. She really needed to call to them; it was going on tomorrow's to-do list.

Parking haphazardly, she jumped out of the unmarked Mondeo and ran through the spills of rain. Inside the station she headed to the storeroom and checked out a Samsung. She had no contact numbers but at least she had a phone. Before heading off again, she made her way to the office. It was still empty, Boyd's desk the neatest of the lot. Hopefully he'd be sitting there before too long. She gulped down her emotion and went into her own office to try and figure out how the phone worked.

She should make a report on her visit to Dowling's home. She was interested in finding out what Conor Dowling had in his garden shed. But how would she get a warrant? A gut feeling wasn't enough. She'd have to sleep on it.

There was a stack of pages on her desk with a Post-it on top signed by Sam McKeown. The new guy. She hadn't yet had a chance to get to know him. Once this was over, she'd have more time for introductions and familiarity, she thought with a grimace that made her stitches hurt.

As she flicked through the photocopies, she recognised pages from Louise Gill's notebooks.

'McKeown!' she yelled. But there was no one there. She began to read, her eyes still stinging.

'What?'

She jumped. 'Don't creep up on me like that.'

'You shouted for me. I'm sure you were heard across the road in the cathedral.'

Sam McKeown stood in front of her desk, sleeves rolled up to the elbows. No tie. Beads of perspiration glistened on his shaved head under the fluorescent light.

'Where've you been?' she said.

'Stuck in a cupboard-like office going through CCTV. It's a sauna in there.'

'I know. And in here. The superintendent is always going on about budgets, and here we are wasting gallons of heating oil.'

'Why don't you complain?'

'Because if we get it turned down now, when the really bad weather comes it will be a running battle to get it switched on again.'

'Can I make an observation?'

'Sit down first. I'm dizzy looking up at you.'

He sat. 'That's part of my observation.'

'What are you talking about?' She wanted to discuss the notes, but she had to hear him out otherwise she might alienate him when she needed him enthusiastic for the investigation.

He coughed, cleared his throat. 'It's just that you don't look great. You've been through a traumatic experience. Do you think you should be working?'

The cheek of him. He was hardly a day in the place and here he was voicing crap opinions.

'Detective McKeown, I'm your boss. Never, ever question my ability to do my job.'

'I wasn't—'

'You were.'

'I'm sorry. But have you looked in a mirror? You're bruised, cut and bleeding. I'm genuinely concerned. Nothing more.'

'Bleeding?'

'Yes. You seem to have burst one of the stitches on your cheek.'

'Oh feck. Sorry. I didn't mean to snap. You're right, it's been an awful experience, but both Boyd and myself are fine. Or will be. My main concern is the four dead girls. When I find out who killed them, then I'll take a break. Not before. Okay?'

'Okay.' He shuffled in the chair and placed his hands flat on his knees.

'Tell me what I'm looking at here.' She pointed to the pages, with lines of Louise's handwriting marked in pink highlighter.

'It was the only one I could find.'

'What?'

'The pink highlighter. No yellow anywhere. Believe me, I looked.'

Lottie hoped she hadn't inherited another OCD detective. One Boyd was enough, thank you very much. 'I mean the text!'

'Oh, right. Sorry.'

'Please don't say sorry again.'

'Okay. This notebook seems to be a diary of prison visits that Louise Gill made over the last year. May I?' He took the pages from Lottie and scanned them, then handed one back to her. 'This one here. Three months ago. Mountjoy Prison. See the name of the prisoner she visited?'

'I might have bloodshot eyes, but I can still read.' Lottie squinted at the neat spidery handwriting. 'Louise visited Dowling in prison a month before his release?'

McKeown nodded. 'Her notes read like a confession. In a nutshell, she told him that she was sorry. That she'd been sure he was the man she saw that night, but that maybe she'd made a mistake. That she was finding it hard to live with herself.'

Lottie swallowed hard.

'Are you okay?' Sam asked.

'Fine, thanks.'

'Do you need a drink of water? I can fetch a bottle for you. Or a coffee?'

'You're trying too hard. You don't have to impress me. Back to Louise and Dowling.'

'It seems to have been an angry meeting. He said he wouldn't forgive her. She told him that she intended to do something to uncover the truth.'

'The truth?' Lottie said. 'What was she going to do?' She hastily flipped through the remaining pages.

'She doesn't say. I'm still waiting for the transcripts from her computer. There might be something on those.'

'You need to find out if she met with Dowling after his release.'

'How will we do that?'

'*You* will do it. Talk to her mother. Her friends. Anyone you can find who knew her. Her course tutor. Use that detective's brain you have.'

He smiled then, a broad, toothy smile, and Lottie was amazed at his dental work. If only Rose had paid attention to her teeth when she was growing up, she wouldn't forever be smiling with closed lips.

'And I'll talk to Dowling when I find him.'

He stood. 'That reminds me of another thing.'

'Yes?'

'The list of casualties from the accident is in. Ten deceased so far. A crane is arriving at daylight to assist in recovery. There may be more bodies. But Conor Dowling is not on the list.'

'He might still be buried.'

'Possibly. I recognised one name from the Amy Whyte investigation reports, though.'

'Who's that?' She wondered if Cyril Gill had escaped without injury.

'Dermot Reilly.'

Lottie blew out a gasp of air. 'Poor Ducky.'

'He was only twenty-four.'

'So sad.'

'I'd better get back to work.' McKeown moved to the door.

'What about the CCTV you've been working on? The car park at Petit Lane.'

'I don't think we'll find anything. Whoever it was seems to have been able to disappear into thin air.'

Lottie glanced at her phone. Shit, she hadn't even succeeded in turning it on. 'Do you know how this works?'

'Of course I do.' He pressed a button on the side of the phone and it lit up.

'Thanks,' Lottie said. 'It's been a long day. Head home and be back in at six in the morning. You can get to work on Louise's friends then.'

'I'm grand. I'll punch in another few hours on the CCTV.'

'Up to you.'

As McKeown left, Kirby walked in.

Lottie beckoned him to sit. 'What's up with you? You look worse than I feel.'

He slumped into the chair and tried to flatten his hair with his stumpy fingers.

'I smell alcohol,' she said. 'My senses are heightened since I gave it up. Whiskey, if I'm not mistaken.'

'That's why you're the inspector and I'm not.' He grinned.

'You can wipe that smirk off your face. You can't go waltzing off to drink in the middle of an investigation.' She felt herself blush. She'd done it often enough. But those days were behind her. She hoped.

'Sorry, boss. Won't happen again.'

'Right so. Tell me you have news.'

'I had a drink with Councillor Whyte. I asked him about the phone you found hidden at his house.'

'And?' Lottie rubbed her hand over her furrowed brow, trying to smooth away the pain that was buzzing in her temple. Kirby was slipping in and out of focus. She needed to lie down. McKeown was right. She wasn't well at all.

'He told me the phone was his. He used it to communicate with Cyril Gill. He said Gill is convinced that smartphones aren't safe, that everything gets recorded and could be used against him.'

'Why? What has he to hide?'

'We've been here before, boss. Councillors and developers. Dodgy deals. Backhanders. Whyte wasn't too forthcoming when I pressed him.'

'Planning corruption again.' Lottie slapped her desk. 'He could be filling you with bullshit.'

'His daughter's dead. He's a man with nothing left to lose. Said he'd send in the SIM card when he finds it.'

Lottie leaned back in her chair and winced. Her back was in bits. 'I reckon he has enough time to either flush it down the toilet or wipe it clean.'

'He was fairly drunk. I think he told me the truth.'

'As soon as you get it, inform me. Anything else?'

'The CCTV seems to be a dead end.'

'You and McKeown need to keep on it.'

'Yes, boss.' Kirby stood and made for the door, his body slow and bulky.

'Will you do me a favour?'

'Sure.'

'Pull the Bill Thompson file again.'

'The assault and robbery case that Conor Dowling served ten years for?'

'Yes. Go through it with a fresh eye. I want to know if I missed something back in the original investigation.'

'Wasn't Superintendent Corrigan SIO on that?'

'Yes, but I did the legwork.'

'I'll check it out first thing in the morning.'

'And if you find something,' Lottie said, 'I want to be the only one that knows.'

*

Conor nursed his sore ankle and decided that rather than feel sorry for himself, he had to plough on. The darkness was filling his lungs as if it was a fog. He felt his way up the steep incline, fitting his feet into grooves in the brickwork. He'd discarded his hard hat, gloves and heavy jacket. It made climbing easier, or as easy as it could be in the circumstances. His nails were broken and bleeding, and it was painful to get a grip on anything. But he struggled on. He knew there had to be an exit at the end.

His fingers reached an obstruction that didn't feel like stone. He raised his head and it hit something hard. He edged his hand around what he thought must be a steel hatch, hoping to find a handle or latch. Something to get the damn thing open. But it was smooth and solid. It wouldn't budge. He wasn't giving up that easily, though. He leaned against the wall, took a couple of deep breaths of fusty air and willed strength into his body.

At last he felt a slight motion. The hatch was circular, so maybe he had to try to swivel it. He attempted it again and heard a hiss.

Yes! he thought. Now he was getting somewhere. Hopefully that somewhere was out.

And then he slipped and fell back down into the abyss.

CHAPTER 48

Arriving home, Lottie cursed the awkwardness of the Mondeo. Maybe it was just her and not the car. She'd have to go back to the hospital to check on Boyd. First, though, she had to ensure her children were home safe and had eaten.

Once inside, she inhaled the newness, trying to dislodge the musty, sick smell of Dowling's home that was still clogged at the back of her throat. Then she opened the front door again and looked outside. No sign of the squad car she'd assigned to watch her family now that Bernie Kelly was on the loose. McMahon must have sent everyone to the courthouse incident.

She glanced into the sitting room. Louis was propped up on a pillow, sipping from a beaker of juice, his feet on Sean's knee.

'*Fireman Sam*?' Lottie said.

'He likes it. Keeps him quiet.' Sean massaged Louis' feet.

'Did you eat?' She was amazed at how Louis could temper Sean's mood. Her son looked totally relaxed, with none of the teenage angst that had been plaguing him recently.

'Gran dropped over a casserole. I ate a little bit of it.' He made a face and stared at Lottie. 'What happened to you? That cut looks nasty.'

'I know. I'll bathe it in a minute.'

Sean sat up a little straighter. 'We were worried about you. Why didn't you answer your phone?'

She mussed his hair and sat on the arm of the couch. 'I got caught up in the incident. Lost my bag with my phone in it. Got a spare from the station, though I haven't any numbers. I'm here now.'

'Good.'

'I'm going to have a proper shower and change my clothes. Where are the girls?'

'They were worried when we couldn't contact you or Boyd. They went into town to have a look.'

'They could have rung the station.'

He shrugged his shoulders. 'I don't think they thought of that.'

'Will you text them to say I'm home now?'

'Sure. But Katie already texted to say they heard you were in the hospital and they were getting a lift there with some woman.'

'What woman?' The hairs on the back of Lottie's neck tingled and goose bumps stood to attention on her arms. She couldn't breathe for a moment.

'I don't know,' Sean said. 'Probably someone they met in town. Her first text said they were going to walk to the hospital then there was another that said they'd gone in a car with a woman. Bit weird.'

'When was this? When did they leave?' Lottie counted the number of shrugs Sean gave. She tried to keep her voice calm. Louis was staring at her, his big eyes like saucers. She couldn't distress him. She whispered with urgency, 'Sean, try to think.'

'They left not long after we got home from school. Mam, do we have to get the taxi all the time? It's so embarrassing in front of the lads. It's like I'm afraid to walk home.'

'Did Katie tell you her name?'

'Who?'

'Sean, listen to me, please. The woman they met in town. The woman the girls went with. Who is she?'

'I don't know. Katie asked me to watch Louis. Said they wouldn't be long. And then about twenty minutes later, she texted me. Here.' He held out his phone.

Lottie checked Katie's words. There was no hysteria in them. No fear or warning. Just that a woman had agreed to bring them to the hospital.

'Can I use this for a few minutes?'

'Sure. As long as you don't snoop around my Instagram or Snapchat. Oh, I think I need to charge it. Hold Louis. I'll be down in a minute.'

Lottie eagerly drank in the fragrance from the little boy's hair, his baby smell, his smile. She smothered his cheeks with kisses and tried not to worry. But that was impossible.

Where was Rose when she needed her? Where were the girls? She had to make sure they were okay. Otherwise the day from hell would be a freaking nightmare.

Her heart beat with loud palpitations and she wondered if she was getting a panic attack. The girls are okay, she willed into her head. Louis cooed softly and she carefully straightened his clothes, then sat him on the floor when Sean returned.

'Find Granny's number for me, please.'

He did as she asked and handed her the phone. She made her way to the kitchen and sighed at the mess of plates with half-eaten casserole hardened to the edges. But the dishes were the least of her worries.

When Rose answered, Lottie asked her to come over to stay with Sean and Louis. She reckoned Rose heard the fear in her voice, because she was at the front door within seven minutes. If her daughters were with Bernie Kelly, Lottie feared what could happen if she didn't act immediately.

'Keep me informed,' Rose said as Lottie sped down the path to the car.

'I will, and don't tell Sean about this.'

*

'Stay quiet and you won't come to any harm.'

That was what the woman had said when she brought them here. They were in a house. A room. But other than that, Katie had no idea where they were being held. She was extremely worried. The door was locked. And she knew they'd been conned.

She and Chloe had gone to the scene of the courthouse accident looking for their mother. They couldn't make contact with Boyd either, and Katie was sure something had happened to Lottie. When the woman emerged from the crowd and approached them, Katie thought she recognised her, though she wasn't sure.

'I know where your mum is. Will I take you to her?'

'Where is she?'

'She was brought to the hospital.'

'Oh, it's okay. We'll walk, thanks.' Katie had sent a quick text to Sean to tell him where they were going.

'She's not there now,' the woman had said. 'I'll take you to her.'

'Just tell us where she is and we'll make our own way.'

And then the woman's face had morphed from calm to an expression of intense evil. 'Come with me without making a sound. That's if you don't want something to happen to that beautiful little boy of yours.'

Katie's mouth had dried up and the cry died in her throat. She felt Chloe tugging her coat sleeve, urging her to run. But her feet were stuck to the wet ground. This woman had threatened harm to her son. Dear God! She had started another text and just as the phone was snapped out of her hand, she hit send.

'Did you find the coin I left for you?'

'Coin? What coin?' Katie said, finding her voice and racking her brain. Then she remembered the colour fading from her mother's face when the flat round disc had fallen from Louis' jacket pocket. Was this the person who'd been following her? Who had given her the feeling of being watched?

'This is a load of shit,' Chloe had said, and made to walk away.

'Shut up, Chloe.' This was surreal. They were in a crowd of people. Who the hell was this woman? 'Is our mother okay?'

'Come and see for yourselves. Don't make a fuss. Just keep thinking of that defenceless little boy of yours.'

What could they do? They had followed her through the crowds with no one to help them. Now here they were, locked into a room with no sign of their mother. Chloe had been banging incessantly on the door until her knuckles bled.

'You're wasting your time,' Katie said. 'I'm sure this place is either soundproofed or out in the middle of nowhere. Let's put our heads together and think of a way out of this mess.'

'What if she's gone to take Louis and Sean? Did you think of that, Miss Super-Cool?'

Katie had thought of it but tried not to. 'You're always the drama queen. I'll figure this out if you shut up for a minute.'

'Yeah, sure.'

'Chloe! Please. Let me think.'

But all she could think of was her little boy and her brother, and she prayed that they wouldn't be harmed.

CHAPTER 49

The Mondeo was dragging on one side and Lottie swore that if she had a flat tyre she was going to abandon it and run. Wind buffeted the vehicle, while the wet leaves on the road caused it to skid. With no time for a shower or change of clothes or even a bite of food, she'd tried the girls' phones from Sean's as she drove. Both were off. She swung round by the hospital and gave a description of her daughters to the security team there. But she knew it was unlikely Chloe and Katie had even been there.

She eventually pulled up at the station. Charging inside and up the stairs with adrenaline-filled energy, she reached the incident room. The night shift team were working the phones and writing up house-to-house reports from both murder incidents. No sign of Kirby or McKeown. She raced to the CCTV room. McKeown had been right. It was an airless cupboard. Struggling for the breath to speak, she motioned them both outside to the corridor.

'What's up now?' Kirby said.

'I need you to put a trace on these two phones.' She handed over Katie and Chloe's phone numbers. 'I want to know their locations. ASAP.'

'You need paperwork for that?' McKeown said.

Lottie dug her nails into the palms of her hands. There was no point in ranting at him. 'These are my daughters' phone numbers. They were together in town a couple of hours ago. And I can tell you, they never switch off their phones. So I want to know where they are.'

'Overprotective?' McKeown said, raising an eyebrow.

'Shut it,' Kirby said.

'No, I'm not being overprotective.' She didn't know if she should tell them about Bernie's threat. 'We've had four young women murdered in pairs this week. Some woman met my daughters and said she would take them to me, and now I can't locate them. That sounds fairly suspicious to me, don't you think?'

She eyed McKeown. She read the doubt written in his eyes.

'Not really,' he said.

She'd have to explain. 'I've been a target before. Bernie Kelly, who claims to be my half-sister, has escaped from a secure unit, as you already know. She called to my mother's house the other night and threatened my family.'

'I saw the news report about Kelly being your half-sister,' Kirby said.

'Not now, Kirby,' Lottie wheezed. Fear was catching in her breath. 'What is important is that I think this is her work. Every district in the country is looking for her, with no results so far. I believe she took my girls to get back at me for incarcerating her a year ago.'

McKeown whistled. 'Gee, sorry. I have a contact who will work on these numbers straight away.' He hurried down the hall.

'McKeown?' Lottie called.

'Yeah?'

'This is higher than urgent.'

'Got it.'

When he'd disappeared, Lottie felt Kirby taking her by the elbow and steering her towards their office. 'Do you think we need to notify the super?'

'No. I'll only get a lecture, and I've had one of those from him already. I want you to go to the Joyce Hotel. Talk to Leo Belfield.

We need to discover if he knew what Bernie was planning. I don't trust him. For all I know, he could be in on this with her.'

'I'll do that straight away. And boss, I've yet to source that Thompson file. Will it wait?'

'Yes. Finding my girls is top priority.' She marched around the desks. 'I could do with Boyd's expertise.'

'Am I not enough for you?'

She glanced at Kirby, but he was smiling. 'Talk to Belfield.'

'I'm already gone.'

*

Leo Belfield was a wreck. Kirby found him sitting at the bar in the Joyce nursing a brandy.

'And you haven't seen Bernie since?'

'No. I woke up and she was gone. I told all this to Lottie. I've scoured the town. Drove to the old family place. Walked the lake shores. She's vanished.'

'People don't vanish.'

'They do where I come from. Into the East River, most of them.'

'This is Ragmullin, not New York.' Kirby could feel the colour rising up his face. He felt like shaking Belfield into action. 'And Lottie's two daughters have apparently gone missing. So I could do with your help.'

'I told you, I've looked everywhere.'

'Did she say anything to you when you got her out on day release? Any clue about what she was planning to do?'

Belfield shook his head. 'She never said anything.'

Kirby didn't believe that line for a second. He hustled Belfield off the stool. 'You're coming with me. Grab your coat.'

'Where?'

'To face Lottie Parker. And I'm warning you, you'd better tell her what you know.'

*

Lottie walked to the incident room and, ignoring the bowed heads of the detectives and uniformed officers working hard on the murder investigations, studied the board.

Before and after photographs of the four victims. Killed in twos. She felt her heart sink deep down in her chest, and blood pounded a sinister beat behind her eyes. The photos blurred. Had the person who'd ended the lives of these young women so violently now got their hands on her daughters? That thought made her sway, and she leaned back against the desk. Surely not. No, she was certain that Bernie Kelly had taken them, and that she wasn't the killer they were looking for.

Kelly could not be responsible for those murders because she had been behind locked doors when the first two girls were killed. So which was worse? The idea that the unknown murderer could have her girls or that Bernie Kelly had them? She knew what Kelly was capable of. Hadn't she murdered indiscriminately to a point where she'd drowned her daughter's best friend in a barrel of water? A girl who'd turned out to be Bernie's own niece.

Lottie sighed deeply and tried to figure out which way to turn next while she waited for McKeown to trace their phones.

Boyd. She needed his wisdom and clear thinking. She turned to leave the room.

'Lottie, I came as soon as I heard.' Boyd grabbed her by the arm and steered her out to the corridor.

'You're a sight for sore eyes,' she tried to joke, but sobs lodged in her throat and she gulped them down. She leaned against the wall while he tipped up her chin. 'How did you hear?'

'Kirby swung by the hospital and brought me here. I tried to call you,' he said. 'Why have you got your phone switched off?'

'Don't talk to me about phones. Mine is lost and I got one from the stores that I can't figure out how to work.' She paused. 'You shouldn't be out of hospital.'

'Don't, Lottie.' He held up a bandaged hand. 'I'm a little bruised, and very sore, but nothing life-threatening. Tell me about Katie and Chloe.'

She bit her lip. Emotion welled up and she was afraid that if she spoke she would break down. And she had no time for that.

'Go on,' he said gently.

She shook her head and squeezed her eyes shut, unable to utter a word. She felt his arms go around her shoulders and he pulled her into his chest.

'Oh Boyd.'

'Shh. It's delayed shock. You've been through a traumatic experience. Your girls are missing. Cry if you need to.'

'I think Bernie Kelly might have taken them.'

'How can you be sure?'

'I'm not sure. Both their phones are off. McKeown is trying to get a trace on them.' She told Boyd what she knew so far.

'Perhaps they're still down at the courthouse?'

'Kirby said it's all sealed off and onlookers have been moved on. Bernie Kelly visited my mother the other night and made a threat to harm my children. That's why I've had a squad car parked outside and a taxi taking Sean and Chloe to school.'

'But you said a coin fell out of Louis' pocket. That's not Kelly's calling card. That's … you know … from our current murder sites.'

'I don't know what to think.'

'We'll put our heads together and come up with a plan.'

'You need to rest.'

'Like hell I do. We have to find your girls.'

She linked his arm and went back into the incident room. She felt that if anyone could find her daughters, it was Boyd.

Moments later, Acting Superintendent McMahon burst through the door.

'I thought you two were under medical observation,' he said. 'What are you doing here?'

He looked more dishevelled than Lottie had ever seen him, and stress lines inked their way around his eyes like dinosaurs' feet.

'We are perfectly able to work,' she said, though her voice was a low whisper.

'Right then. This major emergency just got worse. Apparently there are gas lines at risk, though it should be sorted in the next few hours, and we still haven't recovered all the bodies. I have a list of the dead identified on site, and their families need to be informed. I also want to know who is still missing and presumed dead at this stage. The chief fire officer is in charge of an incident centre at the council offices and I'm his second in command, along with the county manager. We're still awaiting the lifting equipment from Dublin so we can see what's beneath the crane and discover why and how this accident happened.'

Lottie stared at her boss. She could do with a quarter of his adrenaline at this moment.

'Sir,' she said, 'we have another situation.'

'I know.'

'You do?'

'There's still a murderer on the loose. Four young women and we haven't a single clue.'

Boyd said, 'We've been working flat out on it. Conor Dowling is our number one suspect, but he may have been killed in the accident.'

'His name is not on the list of dead,' McMahon said.

'That's not the situation I'm referring to,' Lottie said. Exhaustion seeped into her bones, exacerbating the aches, but she remained standing. She had to fight to find her daughters.

'What then? Spit it out.'

She knew he was going to give her short shrift. 'I have reason to believe that my daughters, Katie and Chloe, have been abducted.' Her heart began to palpitate at an alarming rate and she took a couple of slow, deep breaths.

'Explain,' he said, but he'd already turned his back.

'Sir, they went into town to look for me. They suspected I was caught up in the incident but they didn't know I was all right because my phone was buried. They met someone there who said she would bring them to me.'

'Parker, I am dealing with at least ten dead people, an unknown number missing, and a possible gas leak with potential to blow this town to kingdom come, and you come in here telling me you can't find your daughters. Get real. They've gone shopping. Went for a drink. Probably smoking dope somewhere. They have been known to do that, am I right?'

You're a prick, Lottie thought, but she said, 'I need to find them. I can't concentrate on anything else at the moment.'

'Inspector, I am ordering you to get your act together. First, get some sleep. You look like something a cat would find in a bin. Be back here tomorrow morning, and I want the killer of those four young women in a cell.'

You're just like a broken record, she thought.

'You're like a broken record,' Boyd said. Despite her pain, Lottie smiled. Their synchronicity was astounding at times. 'We need to take Inspector Parker seriously when she says her girls are missing. We have reason to believe that Bernie Kelly may have abducted them.'

'The same Kelly woman who is related to you, Parker. This is family stuff. I don't intend to waste garda resources on it. There's a country-wide alert for Kelly. She will be found. And, may I add, you still have a lot of explaining to do on that score.'

'That rest you mentioned,' Lottie said. 'I'm going to take it now.'

McMahon stared at her with his jaw hanging open. She turned and left. Boyd followed.

In her office, she bumped into McKeown.

'Any news on the phones?'

'Nothing. The last triangulation I can get – off the record, only because I know someone working with the network provider – puts them in the vicinity of Gaol Street, where the accident happened.'

'And nothing further?'

'Nothing.'

'Okay. What do we do next?'

Boyd said, 'From what we've learned about Bernie Kelly, she will want you to know she has the girls. She will make contact.'

'So you think we should sit and wait?'

'Yes, I do.'

'But if she tries to ring me, I've no phone. Unless …'

'What?' Boyd and McKeown spoke together.

'My mother. She visited her already. She may try to do so again.'

Kirby walked into the office. 'You're forgetting one thing.'

'What's that?'

'It may not be Kelly who has the girls.'

Behind him, Leo Belfield trailed in, his head low, his demeanour that of a condemned man.

'What do you mean?' Lottie said.

Leo shrugged his arms out of his coat. 'Gee, but it's hot in here.' He slumped into the nearest chair. 'If it is Bernie, I think she's just trying to get your attention.'

'She certainly has it now, so where is she?'

Boyd said, 'You need to find your phone.'

'Or you can have your number directed to the new phone,' Kirby said. 'McKeown can do that.'

'Thanks,' Lottie said. Why hadn't she thought of that? Why hadn't she thought of a lot of things.

She turned her attention to Belfield. 'Has she made contact with you?'

'No.'

'And you've seen no sign of her anywhere?'

'No.'

Lottie paced up and down the office, the motion making her head feel worse. 'She's out there with no mode of transport, no money and—'

'She might have money.'

Stopping in front of Belfield, Lottie stared down at the top of his head. 'What do you mean?'

'My wallet. All my cash was taken. The cards are still in it, but no—'

'And you never thought to tell me that nugget of information before now?'

'You never asked.'

'Jesus.' Lottie pulled on the ends of her hair. 'And you're an NYPD captain? God give me strength.'

Belfield just shrugged and kept his head down.

'Your number has been redirected to the new phone,' McKeown said.

Lottie pulled the phone from her pocket to make sure it had battery charge. It seemed okay. What to do now? Wait? She couldn't do that.

'Boyd, do you still have your phone?'

He tapped his trouser pocket. 'Yes, though the screen is smashed.'

'You have Cynthia Rhodes' mobile number?'

He squinted between the cracks and brought up his contacts. 'Yeah. Why?'

'Phone her. See if she knows anything.'

'What would she know?'

'She's a journalist.'

Boyd hit a number and moved to his desk. Lottie didn't listen in. She concentrated on Belfield.

'Leo, she must have said something to you.'

'She only wanted to see the old family house. I'm sorry, Lottie. I can't help you.'

Boyd held up a hand as he ended his call. 'Cynthia says she'll try to put something on the nine o'clock news bulletin, but she can't guarantee it.'

'McMahon will blow a gasket,' Kirby said.

'Fuck him,' Lottie said.

I took them. I was minding my own business watching the mayhem from the street across the road from the courthouse accident and saw an opportunity. The garda detail outside the Parker residence had been reassigned. The girls were more than anxious to come and see if their mother was okay. Telling them not to make a fuss and to think of their brother and the baby was a master stroke. Maybe Lottie has died in the accident. I hope not. I want her to suffer the loss of her two girls. I want to see her pain when she finds her dear daughters with their throats slit. That will teach her.

At least the banging has stopped. I hope they're asleep. There is no way out of that room and no one to hear them. I have to leave them for a little while. But I will be back, and then I can put the rest of my plan into motion. Then everyone will see why they should have noticed me. I am not invisible.

CHAPTER 50

Lottie sat up all night waiting. But no news came through on the whereabouts of Katie and Chloe, or Bernie Kelly. Louis was restless, missing his mother. Sean locked himself in his room and she hadn't the energy to argue with him. Rose eventually dozed on Katie's bed, keeping one eye on the baby.

In the kitchen, Boyd made fresh coffee. They said nothing. There was nothing to say. Cynthia had succeeded in getting a thirty-second segment aired on the news last night. It played on a loop on the national news app.

Lottie had rung every one of the girls' friends from Sean's phone until it ran out of credit and she had to buy more online. It was as if her daughters had vanished into the proverbial thin air. Her heart was breaking into tiny pieces and she had no idea how to stop it disintegrating. Before Adam died she'd made him a promise that she would safeguard their children. And what had she done since? Constantly put them in harm's way. All because of her damn job and her complex heritage. She tightened her hands into fists and scrunched them into her eyes.

Boyd placed two steaming mugs of coffee on the table and spooned in a copious amount of sugar. 'Drink up. You need to sustain your energy. At least until Katie and Chloe are home.'

'And when will that be, Boyd?' She ran her fingers over the coarse wool of Chloe's school sweater. Lifted it to her nose and inhaled her daughter's scent.

He didn't answer. Just sat there in silence, his bruised and cut face mirroring her own. When he put his arms around her, she rested her head on his shoulder, letting him soothe her with soft words. The beat of his heart was the only comfort she could endure.

The first rays of light broke through the dawn and the magpies fluttered their wings in the trees and cawed louder than the crows. Lottie stood, folded away Chloe's sweater, poured the cold coffee down the sink and went to wake her mother.

*

Kirby arrived at work early on Friday morning. Since Gilly's death, his sleep pattern was just one long night of wakefulness. He'd found his last clean shirt and bagged everything from the floor, with the intention of dropping it into the launderette later in the day.

He and Sam McKeown walked from the station to the accident area to witness the rescue work. Once there, it was clear that it was now a recovery mission. The lifting equipment had arrived on site and already the main stem of the fallen crane had been lifted onto the back of a trailer.

'Tragic,' McKeown said, stuffing his hands into his pockets.

Kirby turned up the collar of his jacket and zipped it to his neck. The air was cold and sharp. Inky clouds masked the sky. The site was already a mud bath; they could do without more rain.

Dipping awkwardly under the cordon tape, he grunted when McKeown easily swung his leg over it. Gilly had been telling him to lose weight, but he'd ignored her and she'd never seriously pressed him. But now he thought maybe he should take her ghost whispers to heart and do something about it.

Approaching Chief Fire Officer Cox, Kirby said, 'Any more bodies recovered?'

The man tipped his hard hat. 'Two. ID'd informally as Cyril Gill and Bob Cleary. We're just about ready to remove that section of crane and see if anyone else was caught under it.'

'Anything we can do?' McKeown said.

'Stay out of my way, if you don't mind,' Cox said. 'And you're not allowed on site without the correct safety gear.'

Kirby had spied a man in a hi-vis jacket working feverishly to one side of the courthouse, lifting and hauling bricks. He donned the hard hat handed to him by a fire officer and walked towards him.

'How's it going?'

The man lifted his head. He was panting with the exertion of his work. 'Slowly. There's a network of tunnels below here and I think someone might be buried.'

'Why don't you get some help?'

Standing upright, the man glared at Kirby. His face was framed by a swathe of black curls peeking out from the confines of his hard hat. 'My workmates are dead, or haven't you noticed that a big fucking crane collapsed on top of the site?'

'Why don't you wait until the recovery moves to this side?' Kirby offered.

'Would you ever piss off?' The man shook his head and bent down to continue his labour.

'What's your name?' Kirby said.

'Who wants to know?' The man kept working, his gloved hands tugging and pulling pieces of timber from the pile.

'Detective Larry Kirby.'

He stalled his work, poised like a statue. Hands outstretched, back humped. Then slowly he stood upright and turned. His face was smeared with dirt, his eyes like dark bullets that could pierce metal.

'So you're the guy who's been sniffing around my ex.'

Kirby leaned his head to one side, studying the man. 'What are you talking about?'

'Now you're going to tell me you don't know her.'

Looking around for support, he saw McKeown still chatting with the chief fire officer. 'Know who?'

The man sneered. 'She's a bit of all right, isn't she?'

Kirby stuffed his hands in his pockets. 'Who are you?'

'Tony Keegan. Megan Price is my ex-wife.'

Kirby took a step backwards. He felt the need to get away from Keegan. Something about his eyes.

'There's nothing going on, if you must know.' Why was he trying to explain?

'You're welcome to her,' Keegan said. 'Keeps her off my back. Can I carry on doing what I was at before you interrupted me?'

'Sure.' Kirby watched the man return to his work. 'Who do you think might be buried down there?'

'My friend.'

'Who might that be?'

Keegan kept working. 'Does the name Conor Dowling ring any bells?'

It sure did. 'Why do you think he's under there?'

'Because I can't find him anywhere else. His mother was on to me this morning. Frantic. No one to make her breakfast. Stupid wagon. How did she manage for the last ten years?'

How indeed? Kirby made his way back over the rubble towards McKeown.

As they walked up the street, McKeown said, 'If Dowling is buried under that lot, what will it mean for the murder investigations?'

'At least we'll be able to get his DNA and see if it matches any of the forensic material found on the bodies or at the crime scenes.'

CHAPTER 51

Megan Price entered the pharmacy feeling the dullness permeate the walls. It was odd without Richard there being his usual bustling self. He'd given her the keys and told her she was in charge until such time as he could get his head together and Amy's funeral organised.

She let in the first two assistants and asked Trisha to make tea. She hung up her coat and pulled on her white work coat. It was old-fashioned, but she liked it because it gave her a feeling of importance and differentiated her from the underlings who struggled to put in a day's work. At least Amy wasn't around any longer with her smart comments and pungent perfume. She hoped the assistants were on top form today, because she needed to take a few hours off.

The door opened and she looked out from behind her counter to see Detective Kirby marching towards her.

'Hi,' she said.

He glanced around furtively, then leaned over to her and whispered, 'You never told me about Tony Keegan.'

'What about him?'

'You were married to him.'

'That's no one's business but my own.'

'He's friends with Conor Dowling.'

Megan's expression was neutral. 'So?'

'Dowling is a person of interest in the recent murders. I'd have thought you'd tell me about your association with him.'

Sparks of red flashed behind her eyes. 'How dare you. I have no association with Dowling, nor with Tony. What are you insinuating?'

Kirby seemed to physically step back. 'Nothing. I don't know. I would've liked to know.'

'A sandwich and an Irish coffee doesn't mean there's anything between us. I thought you needed a companion, someone to share your grief with, but I was mistaken.' She paused to take a breath. 'I'd like you to leave.'

'Don't worry, I'm going.'

He turned and exited. She half expected him to bang the door, but it slid softly closed. Only then did she release her hands from the counter and see that they were white with the effort of clinging on.

*

Sam McKeown had a grin from ear to ear when Kirby stepped out of the pharmacy.

'What are you laughing at?' Kirby shuffled by him.

'You. What were you accusing her of?'

'Never you mind. Come on.'

Back at the station, there was still no word from Lottie or Boyd on the status of her daughters' whereabouts.

McMahon shoved his head around the door. 'Where is she?'

'Who?' Kirby asked in mock innocence.

'Inspector Parker, of course.'

'Not sure.' Play it neutral, he thought.

'Soon as she appears, I want her in my office.' McMahon walked away muttering audibly. 'When I get my hands on her … Using prime-time news slots for her delinquent kids …'

'He's narky this morning,' McKeown said.

'That's mild. Finish up that CCTV today, will you?'

'I will.'

Kirby pulled the Thompson file across his desk and opened it up.

*

'Lottie, we've been down this road twice already this morning.'

'I know, but they have to be somewhere. Pull in over there.'

Boyd parked the car and left the engine running. 'What do you want to do?'

'They're around here. I can feel it in my bones.'

'I can feel my bones and I can tell you they are fairly sore.'

'Thanks for saving me.'

'That's not what I meant.' He opened the door, stepped outside and lit a cigarette.

She joined him and took a pull, but it made her light-headed so she handed it back to him. Their breath hung in the cold air and she scanned the car park. The Petit Lane houses were to her right, and she wondered if Mrs Loughlin had remembered anything further from the weekend. But her mind wasn't on the murder investigations.

'Bernie's grandmother, Kitty Belfield, lived at Farranstown House. It's locked up. No one has been there since Kitty passed away. It might be worth checking out. Send someone to take a look.'

'Will do. Is the probate sorted yet?'

'I have no idea.' Lottie didn't want to talk about a family inheritance she had no desire to claim. She said, 'I'm sure Leo knows something. What was he thinking of, taking her out of a secure facility?'

'Being impulsive must run in your genes.' Boyd took a long drag on his cigarette and watched the smoke hang in the air.

'Don't you dare, Boyd. I want nothing to do with that family. Come on. We need to check in with the station.'

As they drove away, her eye caught the shadow of the lifting equipment over at the courthouse. Smoke billowed into the air. She had yet to discover if Cyril Gill was dead or alive. And then there was Conor Dowling to think of.

*

Detective Sam McKeown wasn't sure he was going to stick it much longer in Ragmullin. Everyone seemed to have an issue with someone or other. He pulled up the next disc of CCTV footage, forwarded it to the relevant time and leaned back in the chair to watch. He'd been through it all once and found nothing. The worst job in the world.

As he clicked the mouse, the time slid by on the screen. 01:00. 01:30. He yawned. 01:35. He sat up straight. Clicked the mouse again. Zoomed in. He could see the grainy image of a parked car. He'd seen it on the first run-through. But now a shadow caught his eye. Two shadows. Out of shot, at the rear of the car. He zoomed in again, trying to get a look at the number plate. It was covered in mud. Intentional or unintentional, he did not know.

He clicked the images forward, slowly this time. The shadows moved out of shot. At 03:02, one shadow reappeared and the car disappeared. It had been parked in such a position that the doors were not visible and he could not see the driver. Whoever it was knew exactly where the cameras were. He pulled up the traffic cams for the same time, but the car seemed to have disappeared. There were no cameras outside the houses where the first two bodies had been found. He brought up the council office cameras and scanned for the relevant times. Again, nothing.

He moved on to Monday night. Saw the two young men stumble across the car park towards the disused dwellings. Backed up the tape. Kept rewinding it. A shadow moved along the perimeter wall of the car park towards the council offices. And then it was gone. What the hell? It was too large for an animal, so it had to be human.

He pulled up the incident report from Monday night. Someone had been in the house when the two lads arrived. They had been attacked and one person had run out, according to Mrs Loughlin. He twisted the heels of his hands into his eyes, then opened them wide. Concentrate, he told himself. Think.

Forwarding the tape slowly, he kept his eyes glued to the wall. Waiting. Watching. Then he saw it again. The shadow moved in the opposite direction and disappeared.

It might be nothing, and then again it might be something. He printed off screen shots and went to tell Kirby.

*

Kirby's eyes felt like they were about to fall out of his head. The lines of print on the pages morphed into each other. He'd let himself down with Megan. It had been a silly move on his part. What difference did it make that she had been married to Tony Keegan? She was right. It had absolutely nothing to do with him. They'd only had a couple of coffees. You're a total arse, he told himself.

He blinked and turned a page. Garda reports were so boring.

Bill Thompson. Sixty-four years old. Publican and councillor. Interesting. Kirby hadn't heard any mention over the last few days that Thompson had been a councillor. He made a note. Continued to read. Turned the page. And then he saw a name that made the breath catch at the back of his throat. Surely that couldn't be right. It had to be a mistake. Or was it? He looked around, wishing Lottie was here. But neither she nor Boyd had appeared yet.

Why hadn't someone made the connection before now? He picked up the file to bring to McKeown.

McKeown was already standing behind him with a sheaf of pages in his hand.

'You have to see this,' they both said in unison.

CHAPTER 52

Lottie found Kirby and McKeown sitting side by side at Kirby's desk, their heads down, reading.

'Any news on my girls?'

The two men looked up.

Kirby spoke. 'No, boss. Nothing at all.'

'I've phoned all their friends and they haven't been seen. Have you coordinated searches?'

'Superintendent McMahon wouldn't okay them. Spouting about budgets and KPIs. Said the cost of running the murder investigations had sent his neatly balanced spreadsheets off the page. And he wants to see you.'

Lottie turned and bumped into Boyd. 'I'm going to have a word with McMahon.'

Boyd caught her by the elbow. 'Wait up. Don't go storming the castle just yet. Let's see what we have first.'

'I don't have my daughters.'

'I mean you'd better be armed with up-to-date information on the murders. That's his priority and you know it.'

'Not mine and you know it.'

'Be sensible. We need to get up to speed.'

She slumped against a desk and sensed the eyes of her three detectives on her. The heat was oppressive, and with the palpitations in her chest and the strain of worry in her brain, she felt weak-kneed. Boyd wheeled out a chair and she sat.

'I take it there's been no sighting of Bernie Kelly?' she said.

'None,' Kirby replied.

'Anything at Farranstown House?'

'Uniforms had a drive by. Nothing.'

'And no other searches organised?'

'Nope,' McKeown said. 'But I've got traffic and uniforms on the watch. Just to warn you, the superintendent is on the warpath over Cynthia Rhodes' news clip from last night.'

'Feck him. Any calls come in after that report?' She couldn't stop the sinking feeling in the pit of her stomach. Fear trawled through her brain, squeezing it tight in a blasting headache.

'A few cranks, but nothing concrete.'

'Okay. Bring me up to speed on the murders then, before I see the super.'

Kirby stood and paced the cluttered office. 'I was reviewing the Thompson file this morning, like you asked me to.'

'And?'

'I discovered that Bill Thompson was a councillor in his day.'

'True. But as far as I recall, that had no bearing on what happened. He was a noted publican in Ragmullin. His business made a lot of money. Money that was stolen from him on the night in question and never recovered.' She stood and went to the window. The crispness of the morning had given way to misty rain. 'So, you discovered he was a councillor. What else?'

'That made me wonder if there was another reason why he was targeted, apart from robbery.'

'What other reason?' Lottie frowned; she was finding it hard to follow where Kirby was leading her.

'I cross-referenced with the local newspapers to see what was going on in Ragmullin at that time.'

'And?' She listened to Kirby's feet pad around the office.

'Cyril Gill had drawn up fairly sophisticated and progressive plans for an urban renewal project in the town. Most of the area was in the vicinity of the council buildings and the courthouse. In other words, Gaol Street and Petit Lane. And we know Thompson's pub was situated on Gaol Street. A public meeting about rezoning of the development plan was held in the Joyce Hotel, recorded at the time by the local newspaper, *The Tribune*. One of the loudest objectors was Bill Thompson. He's quoted in the article.'

Lottie continued to stare out the window. Had she missed something ten years ago?

'In relation to the date of the attack on Thompson, when was that meeting held?'

'Three weeks prior.'

'It was unrelated,' she said, trying to instil certainty into her voice. Superintendent Corrigan had been the SIO and she'd been the investigating detective. She couldn't remember if they'd made the connection at the time. She'd have to read the file. When she got time. When she had her daughters home.

She turned to face the room. 'Let me get this straight. Cyril Gill was behind an urban renewal planning application ...'

'Worth millions in EU grants,' Kirby said.

'... and Bill Thompson, who was on the council at the time, objected to the rezoning. Am I right so far?' Jesus, her brain was in reverse this morning.

'Correct,' Kirby said.

'Okay. Then Thompson was attacked and robbed. We had two witnesses who placed Conor Dowling near the scene.'

'Cyril Gill's daughter, Louise,' Kirby said, 'and Councillor Richard Whyte's daughter, Amy.'

'Shit. Was Whyte a supporter of Gill's plans?'

'Very much so.'

'Double shit.' Lottie rubbed her bitten fingernails around her bruised chin. 'It sounds like a conspiracy theory. Are you trying to tell me that Conor Dowling was innocent and someone else beat up Thompson to silence his protests?'

'I don't know,' Kirby admitted.

'But how would Gill and Whyte get their daughters to tell such believable lies?'

'I don't know that either. The other question is, was Conor Dowling framed for something he didn't do, or did he do it at the behest of Cyril Gill, who then hung him out to dry?'

'Dowling never offered an alibi or any sort of defence,' Boyd said.

'But,' McKeown said, 'in Louise Gill's notebooks, she mentions a meeting she had with Dowling in prison. She writes that she's sorry and that she's going to find out the truth.'

'The truth about what, though?' Lottie said. 'Louise is dead, so we can't ask her. Amy is dead too. Do their deaths actually relate back to the attack on Bill Thompson? But then we have the murders of their friends, Penny Brogan and Cristina Lee. None of this makes sense.'

'And Cyril Gill is missing, presumed dead, after the incident at the courthouse,' Boyd said.

'Any update on that?'

'We went down there this morning,' Kirby said. 'Gill is listed among the dead.'

'And Conor Dowling?' Lottie asked. 'Any sign of him?'

'Mrs Dowling rang Conor's friend Tony Keegan, saying her son wasn't home.' Kirby paused, puffing out his chest as he took a deep breath, and Lottie thought his shirt buttons were about to pop. 'I found another anomaly in the Thompson file.'

'Dear God,' Lottie said. 'Next I'll have the commissioner breathing down my neck for making a balls-up of that case.'

'Hold your horses,' Boyd said. 'It's all conjecture at this stage. Isn't that right, Kirby?'

'Not really, to be truthful.' Kirby stood at his desk and turned back a few pages in the file. 'Tony Keegan was Conor Dowling's best friend. He was interviewed after Conor's arrest.'

The hairs stood to attention on Lottie's neck. 'You have the file. What does it say?'

'There's half a page. A brief interview. Just to confirm that he was not with Conor at the time.'

'Okay. What are you getting at?'

'I found out this morning that Tony Keegan was once married to Megan Price.'

'Who?'

'Megan Price is the pharmacist at Richard Whyte's shop, where Amy worked.'

'I'm not following you, Kirby,' Lottie said. She really wanted to get on to her daughters' disappearance. The fear for their safety was all-consuming.

'Megan Price is mentioned briefly in the file.'

'In what respect?'

'She was Bill Thompson's stepdaughter. Her mother died five years before the attack on Bill.'

Lottie paced a little, then walked into her own office and sat.

'You okay?' Boyd said.

'I'm thinking.' She didn't move.

'You don't look okay.'

'Speak for yourself. Close the door. Give me a couple of minutes.'

She heard the door close with a soft thud. Feeling faint, she rested her head on her folded arms and allowed the coolness to seep into the bones of her cheek.

*

Boyd turned to Kirby and McKeown. Kirby tried to turn down the heat on one of the radiators. Rattles rang out through the office as the water cooled inside the steel.

'Is the boss all right?' McKeown said.

'Give her a few minutes,' Boyd said. 'She's dealing with a lot.'

'You don't look the best yourself,' Kirby said.

'What's your thinking about these Tony and Megan characters?' Boyd sat and went to put his feet on the desk, but a pain shot up through his hip so he rested them on a stack of box files instead.

'I don't know what to think.'

'Could they have any connection to the current murders?' McKeown asked. Neither Kirby nor Boyd answered, so he added, 'I suppose anything is possible. But my money's on Conor Dowling.'

'We need to bring in Keegan and Price, and find Dowling,' Boyd said.

Kirby shrugged. 'He's probably buried in one of those tunnels.'

'What tunnels?'

Kirby explained the conversation he'd had with Tony Keegan.

'That's interesting.' McKeown waved the sheets of paper he had in his hand. 'I have CCTV stills here from the night the two drunk lads broke into the house at Petit Lane.' He laid them out on Boyd's desk.

'What am I looking at?'

'Shadows.'

'Jesus, what have shadows got to do with anything?'

'Give the man a minute,' Kirby said, and traced his finger along the edge of the wall.

'I see it.' Boyd spread the pages out in a line.

'And once it reaches this point, it disappears.' McKeown sounded triumphant.

'Probably a fox,' Kirby said.

'What's down there?' Boyd asked.

'I don't know yet. But when you mentioned tunnels, it got me thinking.'

'Dangerous,' Kirby said.

McKeown ignored the jibe. 'I'm going to the car park to walk the line where this shadow was and see what I come up with.'

'Do that,' Boyd said.

'Now?'

'Yes, now.'

'Will I tag along?' Kirby asked.

'No, I want to discuss this Tony Keegan character with you.'

The office door clattered against the wall. McMahon stood there, hair askew and cheeks billowed out with rage.

'Is she here yet?'

'Who?' Boyd said.

'Don't be smart with me.' He thumped across the floor, narrowly missing the stack of box files, and burst into Lottie's office.

*

Lottie lifted her head so quickly the blood didn't react in time, and the dizziness blinded her. She could see two McMahons bearing down on her. She blinked and shook her head.

'Sorry, sir. Did you want me?'

'Why else would I be standing here? What are you up to, getting national television to run a segment on your daughters? You know the protocol. Those girls are over eighteen.'

'Chloe's only seventeen!'

'They've only been gone a few hours, if they're missing at all. Good God Almighty, what were you thinking of? Don't answer that, because I really don't want to know. But I do know this: you are in shit right up to your bloodshot eyes, Inspector Parker. Deepest of shit.'

His speech didn't warrant a response, so Lottie clamped her lips tight. Just in case.

As if he couldn't bear her silence, he said, 'Say something.'

She shrugged.

'Not going to give me any excuse?'

Eyeballing him, she said, 'Do you have children, sir?'

'None that I know of.'

She drew herself up straight and said quietly, 'If you had, you'd understand that my daughters are the most important people in my life right now. Nothing else matters.' She took a breath. 'I know I have responsibilities to the families of the murder victims and to the team, but right now I need to find Katie and Chloe.'

'But you don't have to abuse your rank in the process. It makes a laughing stock of the station. You've damaged your reputation, not that that was hard, but you also made a mockery of mine.'

'I'll worry about reputations when I have my girls home safely.'

He sniffed. She thought it was in derision but she couldn't be sure. He said, 'Did you leak the Kelly woman's photo to the media? To Cynthia Rhodes?'

'I'm sure Cynthia had it on file.' No point in walking herself in deeper.

'Even so, you have no evidence to put Kelly out there as a person of interest in this supposed abduction you've concocted.'

'Her photo is already in the public domain following her escape.' Lottie suspected she should have kept her mouth shut; she wasn't going to win this battle with McMahon.

'There's nothing else you can do but wait. Remember your training. That's what we tell parents of missing children. Stay at home and wait. I'm not telling you to stay at home, but while you're waiting, get to work on the murders.'

'Yes, sir.'

'The courthouse incident has diverted media attention for the time being, but they will return, baying for blood and answers.'

'Yes, sir.' Feck off, sir, she added silently.

'Your team needs direction. Leadership. Can you give them that?'

Not at the moment, she thought, but she said, 'Yes, I can.'

'Get to work then. And you're to stay away from the Kelly case or I'll take you off the murder investigations too. Am I clear?'

She nodded.

'I've been up all night coordinating the rescue operation at the courthouse. I need to be able to depend on you.'

'You can.' Damn him.

When McMahon had left, Boyd entered the office. 'You okay?'

'Any word on Bernie Kelly?'

'Nothing yet. Belfield called to say he'll be out looking for her today, trawling the streets.'

'He's of the opinion that she didn't take Katie and Chloe. I don't know which is the worse scenario.'

'What do you mean?' Boyd's face was pale and his hair looked greyer; it was as if the weight of the rubble was still on his back.

'That Kelly took them, or that our murderer did.' She tried to recall if she'd mentioned to McMahon about the coin she'd found in Louis' jacket. If she hadn't, maybe now was the time to do it. It would impress on him the urgency of finding her daughters, if they were in the hands of the killer.

'Calm down, Lottie.'

'Don't, Boyd. Do not tell me to calm down.' She tried to keep her tone even, but it kept rising. 'The one anomaly in all this is the coin

I found in Louis' pocket.' She went to put on her jacket and realised she'd never taken it off. 'I'm going to drive around town again.'

'Leave it to traffic. What do we tell parents of missing children? Stay put.'

'I've heard that not two minutes ago. Were you earwigging?' She sighed. She felt so helpless. She had to work the case as if she was an outsider. Leave her emotions at the door. She had to look at all the angles as a detective, not a hysterical mother.

Boyd said, 'Listen to this. We might have something on the murderer.'

'What?'

'Come on, I'll show you.'

Anything to be doing something, she thought as she followed him out to the main office.

CHAPTER 53

A pall of smoke hung over the town as they walked to the Petit Lane car park. Traffic was being diverted from the centre to allow the recovery and rescue to continue at the courthouse. Lottie glanced over at the terrace where the first two bodies had been discovered. Mrs Loughlin stood at her gate. She returned Lottie's wave and made her way into her house.

Kirby and McKeown were up ahead, walking along the perimeter wall of the car park. Lottie and Boyd had parked there earlier. She'd seen the CCTV images and hadn't thought they meant anything. Still, she had approved this venture.

'Chasing shadows,' she muttered. 'I don't think McMahon will be too happy with us.'

Boyd said, 'The only thing he's ever happy about is a balanced budget.'

She had to agree with that statement. Walking behind him, she noticed how he winced as he moved. Her own bones ached, but neither of them was complaining. There was no time or sympathy for that. Walking wounded just about summed them up.

'It's about here that the shadow disappeared.' McKeown had stopped a few paces ahead of them. He held the image up, then surveyed the area.

'There's a manhole cover here.' Kirby bent down. 'It's been opened recently.'

'The council were probably clearing the drains,' Lottie said.

'But this isn't a drain, or a sewer. It hasn't got the correct markings.' He looked up hopefully. 'Anyone got a screwdriver or a knife?'

Lottie leaned against the wall and stared as McKeown took a knife from an ankle strap.

'That's not allowed,' she said, trying to keep her jaw from dropping.

'I didn't see anything,' Kirby said, taking the offered blade.

Lottie turned away as she heard Kirby sliding the knife around the edge of the manhole cover. It screeched as it moved.

'Got it!' he said.

As she turned back, a gust of wind blew litter into her face and the sky decided to take that moment to spill its load down on top of them. She pulled up her hood as the rain pounded on her head. 'It's just a sewer.'

'No, it's not.' McKeown hunched down beside Kirby. 'It's definitely an entrance to a tunnel.'

'It's still a sewer,' Lottie insisted. She leaned over Kirby's shoulder. An insane thought flew into her brain. Could her girls be hidden there? 'What are you waiting for?' she said with renewed urgency. 'You found it. Down you go.'

Kirby gave McKeown a nudge with his elbow. 'You discovered the shadow on the CCTV footage. I think you should go. Have you got a flashlight strapped to your other ankle?'

Boyd pulled a pencil torch from his inside pocket and handed it over. McKeown took the light and pointed it down into the darkness.

A voice echoed back up at the four detectives.

Lottie tottered against Boyd, and McKeown looked at Kirby.

Then they heard it again.

'Get me out of here.'

*

McKeown radioed for assistance while Kirby trotted across the car park to the cordoned-off scene at the courthouse. He came back with a couple of fire personnel and a ladder.

Lottie was on her knees, torch in hand, directing it into the tunnel. The muddy face of Conor Dowling stared back at her from possibly five to ten metres below ground.

'Are you okay?' she shouted.

'No. I need to get out of here.' His voice was hoarse. From shouting, she thought.

'Any injuries?'

'I'm thirsty and starving.'

The rain thundered down and water flowed into the hole.

'Hurry up,' Lottie told the assembled crew.

After the ladder was shunted downwards, a fire officer climbed down to make sure Dowling was strong enough to come up under his own steam.

'Is there anyone else with you?' Lottie asked.

'No,' echoed the reply. Closer now. He was climbing the ladder.

Lottie offered her hand as he reached ground level. He ignored it and hauled himself up and out. He lay on his back, inhaling fresh air. A squad car with uniformed officers arrived. Boyd took a heavy jacket from one of them and, after lifting Dowling to a sitting position, threw it over his shoulders.

'You're coming with us,' he said. 'You'll be checked over at the station.'

Lottie kept her focus on Dowling. He was shivering and dirty. But his eyes were alive and piercing. He returned her stare before turning to glance at the courthouse.

'What happened over there?'

'I thought you could tell us that,' Boyd said.

'Nothing to do with me. I was working below ground. Tried to get back out, but the entrance was blocked. I've spent all night in that dark hole, imagining that I would never be found.'

'Maybe you should have stayed in prison,' Lottie offered. 'Go with McKeown. I'll talk to you in a while.'

While Dowling was escorted to the car, Lottie remained standing at the opening to the tunnel. The fire officer made to remove the ladder.

'Leave it,' she said. 'I want to have a look.'

Boyd put a hand on her arm. 'I think Amy and Penny's killer used this tunnel.'

'Because of the shadow on the CCTV footage?'

'I doubt it was used as a means of escape, but it would be an ideal place to stash a murder weapon.'

Kirby piped up. 'We need to get our hands on maps or drawings first. There's probably a maze of tunnels down there. No point in any of us ending up lost.'

'And none of you geniuses thought of getting one before we left the station?' Lottie said.

They shook their heads.

'I'm going down,' she said. 'Katie and Chloe might be in there.'

'Boss,' Kirby said. 'Dowling has been down there since the incident, so there's no way he could have taken your daughters.'

'I don't care. I need to see for myself. Hold that flashlight, Boyd, and when I'm safely down, follow me.'

Without waiting to hear any further argument, Lottie gripped the ends of the ladder, eased herself over the opening and carefully made her way downwards.

*

The dark was all-encompassing. The walls were close and the roof closer still. She hunched her back and felt around her with her hands. Damp and cold.

The light returned as Boyd's feet thumped down beside her and slime splashed up over her boots and legs. She grabbed the torch and turned.

'I really think we should get a map first,' he protested.

'Follow me or go back.' Adrenalin fused her resolve. Could her girls be down here? Logic told her no, but all reason had deserted her. 'I hope there's fresh batteries in this fiddly yoke.'

'Of course.'

She came across Dowling's work jacket and hard hat.

'Maybe you should put that on,' Boyd said.

She kept walking. A junction in the tunnel stalled her progress. 'Which way do you think we should go?'

'I'd chance right.'

'Let's go this way and see where it leads us.' She hoped she wouldn't come across a rat, or she'd be jumping into Boyd's arms, and she wasn't in any humour for that.

There was less air now, and what little there was, was dank. She could feel it sticking to her as if it had a form of its own. She felt as if they'd been walking for ever, but she estimated it'd only been about five minutes, slowed by the low roof and narrow passage, when she stopped.

'Wait,' she said. She bit her bottom lip, the torch flickering up and down in her hand as she attempted to focus it on something that had caught the thin shaft of light. 'Boyd, what's that?'

She stepped into a curved cavern. The way ahead was blocked by a brick wall, though a hole seemed to have been bored in it. Bricks and cement lay in a pile. But that wasn't what had caught her attention. Illogically, she thought she'd found either Chloe or Katie, and her heart seemed to suspend its motion before kicking off again, racing like a sprinter. Dropping to her knees, she felt Boyd's breath on the back of her neck.

'It's a body,' he said. 'Here a while by the looks of it.'

'Is it male or female?' She stared at the skeletonised remains.

'Remnants of a shirt and denim jeans. It could be either sex. I'd say the rats had a good feast on this one.'

'Shut up, Boyd.' She glanced around, moving the light up and down the walls and along the floor. 'No footwear, and no bag or anything that could give us an identity.'

'We'll need to get SOCOs on site.'

'Either this person was murdered or they were left down here to die. That wall looks more recent than the rest of the tunnel.' She pointed to the brickwork with the gaping hole smashed through the middle. 'But why? Who? Jesus, I don't know what's going on.'

'We'd better make our way back and call it in.'

'What was Dowling doing down here when the crane collapsed? And why was he alone?'

'We will ask him those questions.'

She cast the light once more over the body leaning against the wall. 'Should I move it? There might be some evidence behind or under it.'

'Leave it be. We need to have it forensically examined *in situ*. You don't want to damage something that might give us an identity or perhaps provide us with a reason why this poor soul was abandoned here.'

'You're right. My head hurts anyway. Come on.' Her girls were not here. She should be relieved, but it was no consolation. She had no idea where they were.

As she turned to leave, her eye caught the glint of something silver on the ground, just beside the bones of the left hand.

'Fuck,' Boyd said.

'Double fuck,' Lottie agreed.

CHAPTER 54

Lottie's knees hurt and her ankles screamed for rest as she reached up her hand and allowed Kirby to haul her out of the tunnel. She was glad to be out in the little daylight allowed by the thunderous skies overhead. But there was no relief. Her daughters were still missing.

'Call in SOCOs,' she instructed the detective.

'What did you find?' he asked.

Boyd hauled himself out beside Lottie. 'A body. Skeleton really.'

Kirby scratched his drenched head. 'Left over from the time of the old gaol?'

'More recent than the nineteenth century, unless they wore Levi's and checked shirts back then,' Lottie said. While Kirby got on the phone, she checked her own. Nothing. 'You sure my number is linked to this device?'

'Didn't McKeown fix it up?' Boyd said.

'Yeah.' She shoved the phone back in her pocket and looked around for a car to take her back to the station. She didn't think her legs could carry her much further.

She spied a squad car at the perimeter and made her way to it as Kirby began the process of erecting a cordon around the tunnel entrance. She twisted the plastic bag containing the two coins in her hand, and wondered what secrets the network of tunnels beneath Ragmullin had yet to yield.

*

Lottie's throat felt dry and as sore as the rest of her body, and as she walked towards the interview room, her jeans began to steam.

'I always knew you were hot, but you are positively steaming,' Boyd said with a wink.

'Now is not the time or the place, Boyd. Is Dowling in here?'

'Ready and waiting. Doc says he's fine. Not a scratch on him. Unlike the two of us.'

She took off her jacket and rolled it into a ball as McKeown came out of the interview room.

'Has he said anything?'

'Other than not to tell his mother, nothing.'

'Not to tell her what?'

'I presumed he meant that he was out, though he doesn't strike me as the type of person to be afraid of his mother.'

'I've met her. I don't blame him.'

'That bad, huh?'

'Bad enough.' She turned to Boyd. 'Let's get cracking. I want to hear what he knows about Katie and Chloe.'

Lottie opened the door and entered the small, suffocating room. The smell of the underground tunnel seemed to trail in with her, or maybe, she thought, it was emanating from Dowling. His elbows were on the table, with one hand propping up his head. His face was washed clean and his hands looked scrubbed. The same filthy clothes hung from his thin frame. He appeared to be asleep, but as she shoved her jacket into a corner, he sat upright.

'Took your time,' he said.

Boyd switched on the recording equipment and gave the time, date and names of those present.

'Hey, hold on a minute,' Dowling said. 'Is this a formal interview? I've done nothing wrong. This is harassment.'

'Shut the fuck up,' Lottie said.

'Inspector.' Boyd leaned his head to one side, indicating that they were being recorded.

Lottie stretched over the table. Eyeballed Dowling. 'I don't give a fiddler's about you or your harassment. I want to know what you did with my daughters.'

'I'd give them a good ride if I knew them.'

Lottie had to dig her nails into the palms of her hands so as not to reach out and slap the insolence off his face.

'Why were you in the tunnel?'

'Working, like I told you.'

'On your own.'

'Yes.'

'Is that allowed by Health and Safety?'

'Must be, because that's what I was at.'

'What type of work were you doing?'

'Assessing the tunnel to make sure it wouldn't collapse when the lift shaft was constructed.'

'Are you qualified to do that?'

'Yeah. Ask Tony Keegan. Or Bob Cleary. He's the foreman, as you know.'

'Cleary's dead,' she said. 'As is Cyril Gill and a host of your work colleagues.'

'Bad luck for them and good luck for me so.'

'I think you ventured into that tunnel because you knew there was a body there.'

He opened his eyes wide. 'A body? Where?'

Lottie slapped the desk so hard, even Boyd shuddered. 'Don't play silly buggers with me, Conor.'

He sniffed and shrugged. As he folded his arms, the smell of must and dampness grew stronger.

'Answer me,' she said.

'Ask a question so.'

'Who is it?'

'Who?'

'The body.'

'I don't know.'

'Why were you in the tunnel?'

'Working. I told you that already.'

'I don't buy it. Let me tell you what I think.'

'Do I have a choice?'

'I think you took advantage of the mayhem surrounding the crane accident to go down there and move the body that you put there in the first place.'

'I didn't know there'd been an accident until I tried to get out of the fucking place.'

'What was the sequence of events?'

He let out a long, exhausted sigh. 'I had a meeting with the foreman and the boss. Mr Gill was angry. He wanted to make sure I had nothing to do with his daughter's murder. Which I hadn't, for your information. After that, I left the office and started work. That's it. Oh, I had a fag with Tony first. Ask him. He'll tell you, if he's still alive. Is he?'

'Yes.'

Conor's face sank into itself. Lottie couldn't determine if he was pleased or not.

He continued. 'Then I got stuck underground and had to find my way through the tunnels to try to get out. Lucky you guys turned up.' He raised an eyebrow quizzically. 'Why were you there? Did you know I was trapped?'

Ignoring his question, Lottie said, 'What about the body?'

Conor leaned back into his chair. 'Are you trying to charge me with that as well as everything else?'

'Just answer the bloody question,' Boyd said.

Conor blew out a breath of sour air. 'The body was there when I crawled through the hole in the bricks. I couldn't get out the way I'd gone into the tunnel, so I had to keep going. But then I realised I was stuck. Only time I've been glad to see the guards.'

Lottie wished she had a notebook or file in front of her as a prop. With exhaustion eating its way into her bones, she needed all her energy to concentrate. Had he really just stumbled on the body like she had, or was something more sinister at play? Her gut told her he knew more than he was letting on. How to get him to admit it, though?

She said, 'I found something interesting in that tomb, for want of a better word.'

'Tomb?'

Was he really as dumb as he appeared? She was getting weary and getting nowhere. 'Two silver coins.'

Studying his face intently, she thought his skin had paled, but she couldn't be sure. A few ginger freckles dotted his nose; otherwise he was a deathly white.

'Know nothing about them,' he said, and chewed the inside of his cheek.

Time to change tactics. 'I visited your mother yesterday.'

His cheeks turned red. Instantly. 'My mother! What the fuck you going near her for?'

'I called to your home because I actually wanted to talk to you.'

'You leave my mother out of this.'

'I had to check your alibi.'

'What alibi?'

He was riled now. Good, she thought.

'Your alibi for the murders of Amy Whyte and Penny Brogan. Also those of Louise Gill and Cristina Lee. Didn't you say you were home with your mother last Saturday and Tuesday nights?'

'I'm home every night. Not last night, of course, because I was stuck in a fucking dark hole.'

'True.'

'You stay away from my mother, you hear me?' He thumped the table.

'Are you threatening me, Mr Dowling?'

'Don't you mister me.'

Now that she had irritated him, Lottie changed direction. 'Katie and Chloe. Do you know them?'

'Who the hell are they?'

'My daughters.'

'God help them then.'

Boyd nudged Lottie's ankle. She paid no attention to him. She was not going to rise to Dowling's provocation. 'My daughters have been abducted. I know you couldn't have personally taken them, but maybe you know who might have.'

'I don't know a fucking thing about your daughters. You going to pin every crime that happens in this town on me now? You know what? I want my solicitor. Now. Right this fucking minute. I know my rights.'

'I'm sure you do, having spent ten years in prison.'

'For a crime I didn't commit.'

'You were tried and convicted.'

'Doesn't mean anything in this crooked country. You fitted me up then like you're trying to do now. I don't know where your poxy daughters are, but if you were my mother, I'd make sure I was never found.'

She warned herself not to let him spike her temper again. 'You never offered an alibi for the Thompson assault and robbery. Why was that?'

'No comment.'

'You're not going to start that, are you?'

'No comment.'

A white lie never hurt anyone, so she decided to go for it. 'I had a snoop around the shed in your mother's back garden.'

The change in his demeanour was instantaneous. He leaped out of his chair, lunged across the table and grabbed Lottie's hair. She screamed, more from shock than pain. Boyd jumped up and seized Dowling's wrist, and together he and Lottie subdued the younger man.

'You're a sneaky bitch,' Dowling spat. 'I did ten years because of your incompetence, and I can guarantee you, I won't do another second behind bars. The justice system in this country sucks. Sucks, do you hear me?'

'Assault of a garda officer is a serious offence,' Boyd said. 'Sit down.'

Lottie was speechless. Her head throbbed and she noticed strands of her hair stuck between Dowling's fingers.

After a few deep breaths, he seemed to realise the enormity of what he'd done, because he said, 'Sorry. I didn't mean to do that.'

Lottie swallowed what she really wanted to say. 'I'll consider your apology when you give us some information.'

He nodded, his shaven head gleaming with beads of perspiration.

She leaned over and whispered to Boyd to get the file on Amy Whyte. While they awaited his return, she continued to stare at Dowling's bowed head. She recalled the young man in court, eyes wide with disbelief when he was convicted. Back then she'd felt a moment of panic. Had she got the right man? And now she felt the exact same thing. Forensics ten years ago were not what they were today. They had no physical evidence to link him to the assault and robbery, only two eyewitnesses who'd said they'd seen him rushing from the area. Corrigan had been an inspector then, and SIO. Had he led Lottie in a direction he wanted her to go? For an early resolution of the case? To detract from something more ominous? Maybe she needed to review that case. Once she had her daughters home.

The thought of Katie and Chloe being held against their will, or even worse, catapulted her back to reality. Boyd returned with the file. Opening it, Lottie slid a piece of paper across the table.

'Look at this, Conor. I showed it to you before and you denied all knowledge of having sent it to Amy Whyte. Do you want to change that story?'

He read aloud. '"I am watching you."'

'And?'

His shoulders slumped as he shoved the page back at her. 'Okay. Right. Yes. I did write the note. Happy now?'

She glanced sideways at Boyd. He gave her a discreet thumbs-up.

'When did you send it?'

'A week after I was released from prison. Just wanted to scare her. I know she lied about seeing me that night.'

'Why did she lie?'

'I don't know.'

'And the coin?'

'What coin?'

'The one that was in the envelope with the note.'

His eyes told her he hadn't a clue what she was talking about.

'I don't know anything about a coin.' He stared at the note before lifting his eyes to hers. 'There wasn't an envelope either.'

'So how did you get the note to her?'

'Dropped it into the pharmacy where she worked. Have you a copy of the back of it?'

Where was he going with this? Lottie took a second page from the file. *AMY* was scrawled on one half, as if the note had been folded in two and her name written on the outside. She had noticed this before but hadn't paid it much heed. After all, the note had been in an envelope when she found it.

'There you are,' he said. 'I went into the pharmacy thinking Amy would be there. I wanted to look her in the eye when I handed the note to her, but there was no one behind the counter. I heard a door open somewhere, and before I knew what I was doing, I'd left it on the counter and fled. That's the truth. No envelope. No coin.'

'Who did you give it to?'

'Told you, I just left it there. Didn't see anyone. I dropped it and got out as quick as I could. Can I go now?'

'No, you cannot.'

'Look, Inspector, I had no reason to kill any of those girls.'

'Louise and Amy's eyewitness accounts got you convicted.'

'Louise visited me in prison. She told me she was sorry. She didn't give me any details, but she did say that she would do her best to make it right. I did not assault or rob Bill Thompson, and if Louise had come clean, I would have been exonerated. Why would I kill her?'

Why indeed? Lottie thought. 'You never offered a defence at the time. Why?'

He shrugged and bowed his head.

'Why did you leave that note for Amy?'

'I was in a foul mood. Feeling sorry for myself. Wanted her to experience a little of what it was like for me in prison. In there, eyes are on you twenty-four seven. That's all. I swear to God.'

Could she believe him? If she did, then she'd made an unforgivable cock-up ten years ago. Or rather her boss, Corrigan, had. And if Dowling hadn't carried out the assault on Thompson, then who had?

CHAPTER 55

Kirby returned from the canteen with croissants and coffee. Lottie grabbed a cup and felt the warm liquid hit the bottom of her empty stomach.

'You need to eat,' Boyd said. 'I can hear the rumbling over here.'

'Still no word?' she asked Kirby.

He knew she was referring to her daughters and shook his head slowly.

McKeown hung up the call he was on. 'This is interesting. Might be something or may be nothing.'

Lottie grabbed a croissant and perched on the edge of his desk. Lynch's desk. In a funny sort of way, she missed Lynch. At least the detective was getting to spend time with her family, while Lottie continued to put her own in harm's way.

'That was Miranda from Flame, a hair and beauty salon. At least I think it's Miranda.' McKeown squinted at the illegible scrawl in his notebook.

'Go on,' Lottie said impatiently.

'She recognised Bernie Kelly's photo on the news last night. Says a woman fitting her description came into the salon yesterday morning. Got a tight haircut and a spray tan. Paid in cash. This Miranda is one hundred per cent sure it was Kelly.'

'No wonder no one can find her,' Kirby said. 'She'll look totally different.'

'She also said that the woman had two Primark shopping bags with her. After her tan was done, she changed into new clothes and left her old ones behind in the bags.'

'Description of the clothes she's now wearing?' Lottie said.

'Black leggings. Long black T-shirt. Boots and a green parka jacket with black fur on the hood.'

'Describes half the population of Ragmullin in this weather.' Lottie tried to imagine Bernie Kelly without her long red tresses. 'Call down to this Miranda with Kelly's photograph and ask her to describe the new hairstyle. We can then issue a photofit image. Might jog someone into calling us.'

Boyd said, 'You'll have to okay that with the super.'

'I need to find Kelly. I want my girls back.'

'But in the interview with Dowling, you were just about accusing him of having something to do with their disappearance. I don't get it.'

'I'm covering all bases.'

She put down the cup and stood. She didn't know what she was thinking. The coin in Louis' jacket pointed to their serial killer, but the seeds left on her doorstep implicated Bernie Kelly.

Shoving her hands deep into her jeans pockets, she said, 'The longer this goes on, the more likely it is that I'll never see my girls alive again.' She stifled the sob that threatened to explode. An arm went around her shoulder as Kirby pulled her into a hug.

'We'll find them,' he said. 'No one else belonging to any of us is going to end up in Jane Dore's mortuary. You hear me?'

She managed a weak smile, but Kirby's words instilled more fear in her heart than hope.

'Anything else?' She needed to refocus her brain.

Kirby ambled over to his desk. 'I sent uniforms to bring in Tony Keegan, like you asked. He's in interview room two.'

'Good.' She looked at McKeown. 'After you've visited Miranda, read over the transcripts from Louise Gill's computer, and Kirby, phone everyone in Penny's appointment book for a second time.' She paused, trying to get her thoughts in a line. 'McKeown. That CCTV footage. Is there anything to *prove* our killer went down through the tunnel? I didn't see any evidence.'

'I told Jim McGlynn to get some of his SOCO team to navigate their way through as much of the network as they can, looking for evidence that someone had been down there recently. It's possible that that's where the murder weapon was dumped. I think the coins tell us someone was there.'

'Unless they were left there at the time that poor soul was abandoned to rot.' She thought for a moment. 'The damaged brick wall. It seemed newer than the tunnel walls. See if you can find out if there's a record of when it was built, and by whom. That might lead us to who the body is and why it was down there.'

'I'll see what plans I can find,' McKeown said. 'I'm sure this town has a local historian who can help.'

Lottie nodded and turned to Kirby, 'I want you to check with the staff at Whyte's Pharmacy. Dowling says he left the note for Amy there, without an envelope. When I found it at her house, it was in an envelope with a coin.'

'Will do.'

With another glance at her silent phone, Lottie said, 'Give me five minutes, Boyd, before we see what Mr Keegan has to say for himself. I want to scan through this Thompson burglary and assault file.'

She opened the file and began to read. She needed to find out for herself whether she had been misdirected or misled during the original investigation. She hoped to God she hadn't put the wrong man away.

But her gut was twisting inside her, telling her that the assault on Bill Thompson was linked to her current murders.

She took up the crime-scene photos. Held them close to her nose, trying to see if there were coins anywhere. Something they might have missed. Once Dowling had been identified by the eyewitnesses, they had swooped on him. With no alibi offered, he was charged, tried and convicted. Case closed.

She put down the photos and read another page.

Bill Thompson had never recovered after suffering a stroke following the assault. He was unable to speak. He couldn't describe his assailant. House-to-house had yielded nothing. The safe had been left open and the money taken.

The safe.

She picked up the photos again. A floor safe. Opened by a key in a lock. The lid was on the floor beside the gaping hole.

She closed her eyes. Tried to remember the scene. But it had been ten years ago. A thought struck her. How had the burglar got the key?

She looked for a photo of Bill Thompson. They had none of him at the crime scene. Medics had arrived before the guards and whisked him straight to hospital. From there he'd been airlifted to Dublin, where he'd undergone five hours of brain surgery.

The photo she found at the back of the file was of a sprightly sixty-four-year-old. Greying hair, and a large nose. But he'd been handsome, she noted. And fit. Had he had the key on his person? Had he been interrupted while he was putting the takings in the safe? If not, how did the burglar know about the safe?

She put down the photo and scoured the report for evidence of what had happened to the key. There was no mention of it.

Closing her eyes, she tried to remember. Flicked through the file until she found Conor Dowling's arrest sheet. No mention of a key on his person. Nor the money, for that matter.

She shuffled through the photographs again. Found another one of the open safe. Coins were scattered around the floor as if they'd fallen from a bank money bag.

Shit.

CHAPTER 56

Lottie couldn't believe she was about to conduct another interview while her daughters were still missing. Before entering the room, she phoned her mother to make sure all was okay with Sean and Louis and to confirm her house was still monitored with a squad car outside it. She had to keep working otherwise she'd go insane.

Tony Keegan's stomach was pressed up against the table and his greasy hair fell to his shoulders, with wayward curls around his forehead. His eyes travelled from Lottie to Boyd, then, as he tried to focus on a point above their heads, he gave up and studied his thick hands resting on the table. If Lottie had to describe him, she would have said he was rough but shifty. She would need to delve deep beneath his exterior. She knew murderers came in all guises, and so far the killer of four young women was like a feather in the wind.

'Can I take off my jacket?' he asked.

'Sure.' Lottie had a file with her this time to give the impression that she was reading before addressing him.

Boyd concluded the introductions for the recording.

Lottie began. 'Mr Keegan, what can you tell me about Conor Dowling?'

'Ah, well, you know all about Conor, don't you? He's not long out of jail.'

'Tell us something we don't already know.'

'How would I know what you do or don't know?'

'Humour me,' she said, fighting down rising irritation. She was sure Boyd and Keegan could hear the beating of her heart, such was her anxiety. She had to find her daughters before it was too late. She wanted to breathe in their youthful scent, not this sweaty idiot's. But she had to follow this route in order to discover any information that might lead her to them. Concentrate. Focus.

The shifty eyes landed on her. 'He says you're harassing him.'

'I'm talking about the murders, smart-arse.'

'Oh. I know nothing about them.'

Her exasperation boiled over. 'Do you read the newspapers? You can read, can't you? Or watch television, or follow Twitter and Facebook? I'm sure you've heard about Amy Whyte, Penny Brogan, Cristina Lee and Louise Gill.'

'Course I heard about them. Doesn't mean I knew them.'

'Your boss is Cyril Gill. You'd have seen Louise around, I'm sure.'

'I know all the girls to see.'

Lottie stared at him. 'Tell me how you know them.'

He made to fold his arms, but his girth restricted him in the confined space. A waft of stale cigarettes accompanied his movement, and Lottie regretted having just eaten the croissant. Her stomach churned. The lack of fresh air in their interview rooms was a constant bugbear.

Keegan chewed loudly on a piece of gum, squelching it between his teeth. 'I saw Amy whenever I went in the pharmacy, which wasn't often, because I try to avoid my ex-wife. She works there.' He paused as if he had sucked something rotten into his mouth. 'Then Penny, I only ever saw her if I was out at the clubs, which wasn't often either.'

'And Louise Gill?'

'Never saw much of her. She never hung around the site. Don't think there was much love lost between her and her daddy. I knew her lesbian lover to see. Though I doubt Mr Gill was aware of that relationship.'

'So you think Cyril Gill would have objected to Louise's choice of partner?'

'Shit, yeah. He hated all that rainbow stuff. Out-and-out bigot he was. And not afraid to let you know either.'

'You ever have any disagreements with him?'

'Not really. No.' The chewing continued.

'How long have you worked for Cyril Gill?'

'Since I finished school.'

'Which was when?'

'I didn't hang around to do my Leaving Cert. I must've been about sixteen. That'd be nearly twenty years ago, give or take.'

'It's a wonder you never rose to the rank of foreman.' On second thoughts, she doubted Keegan had the mentality for that sort of job. Without waiting for his reply, she said, 'Marrying Megan Price must have been a step up the ladder for you. How did you meet her?'

Tony shifted uneasily on the chair. 'My marriage has nothing to do with anything.'

'I will decide that.'

The more he shifted, the more she wanted to get up and run. Search for Katie and Chloe. But she had to go through the motions in case Keegan knew something about them because of his connection to Dowling.

'Go on,' she said. 'You were telling me about Ms Price.'

'I wasn't. You're not even listening to me.' He took a deep breath and sighed it outwards. She could see the gum stuck to his teeth. 'Me and Megan, we were complicated.'

Aren't we all, she thought. 'Did you know her before her stepfather, Bill Thompson, was attacked?'

'We hung out a bit. A gang of us. Including Conor. Megan was wild back then, even though she was in college. She always looked down on us, but I thought she was a goddess.'

'You'd do anything for her?'

'I fell in love with her. Doesn't mean I'd do anything for her. Couldn't believe she said yes when I asked her to marry me. When I look back on it, it wasn't long after Bill Thompson died, so maybe I got her on the rebound.'

'Rebound?'

'You know. She loved the old man and then he was gone, so I was next in her line of fire.'

'Strange choice of words.'

He whittled away at a piece of skin at the edge of a nail until he drew blood. 'That's what it turned out like in the end. I was always in her line of fire.' He coughed, chewed and looked at Lottie. 'I can't see what this has to do with the murder of those girls.'

Lottie couldn't see it either. Yet. But she couldn't let Keegan know that. 'So you would have done anything for Megan?'

'Sure. Back then. Not now.'

'You'd even help stitch up your friend Conor. Back then,' she emphasised.

His eyes nearly bulged out of their sockets. 'Hold on a minute. What are you trying to make me say?'

Scenarios were forming in her brain. What if it was all about the money and Megan wanted her stepfather's cash? No, that didn't make sense. 'Maybe it was Cyril Gill who got you to stitch up your friend, then?'

Keegan shook his head, dots of dandruff drifting like fireflies through the air. 'I don't follow you at all.'

Good, Lottie thought. Confuse the enemy at all times. 'Ten years ago, it's possible that Cyril Gill wanted Bill Thompson out of the way so that he could proceed with a planning application.'

'I have absolutely no idea what you're talking about.'

'The urban development project. You would have known. You told me yourself you've been working for Gill for nearly twenty years.'

He clamped his mouth shut.

Lottie continued. 'Either you or Conor Dowling did Gill's dirty work by taking Thompson out of the picture. Whichever of you it was, Dowling got the blame and paid with ten years of his life.

Keegan's already puce cheeks turned purple. Snot poured out of his nose and he tried to sniff it back down his throat. 'I had nothing to do with that.'

Lottie turned to Boyd. 'I think he protests too much, don't you?'

Boyd nodded, and she reckoned he thought he knew where she was headed with this. But he'd be wrong. She didn't even know herself. She wished for the hundredth time that day that she wasn't so distracted.

From the file she extracted a photograph. Sliding it across the table, she kept her eyes screwed onto Keegan's face. His tongue ran the length of his teeth behind his lips, pushing out his jaw. Concocting a story? She knew he recognised the image in the photograph.

He shook his head. Too vehemently. 'Don't know what that is.'

'It's a coin. One of a number found in the vicinity of the young women's bodies.'

'So?' He kept his eyes on the photo.

'Explain it to me. Tell me what it means.'

'Don't know.'

'You do know.'

He shrugged his bulky shoulders. 'Looks like some sort of medal.'

She glanced at Boyd. A medal? They'd been so convinced the discs were coins that they'd become blind to the fact that they could in fact be something else. There were no inscriptions on any of them.

Boyd said, 'What kind of medal?'

Another shrug. 'It's just a suggestion. I've never seen it before.'

She filed away his suggestion for later. 'Tell me about the body in the tunnel.'

Now the puce faded to white. 'You know about that?'

Bingo!

'Yes. I do.'

He looked around the sparse room frantically. 'Shit. If Gill was still alive, he'd go apeshit.'

'Cyril Gill knew about it too?'

Clamped lips told Lottie that Keegan had gone too far. Said something he shouldn't have.

'Go on, Tony. You started so you can finish.'

'I'm going to get in a whole load of trouble for this.'

'I'm dealing with four murders and now this body. You're already in a whole load of trouble.'

'Goddam it,' he said, and leaned across the table, his expression earnest. 'Earlier this week, it might have been Wednesday, Bob Cleary, our foreman, came across this brick wall in the tunnel. He'd gone down to assess it to see what we had to do to support the lift shaft, you know.' Lottie nodded like she understood. 'He came back up, gathered a crew and brought us down to break through the wall. That's when I first saw the bones. Cleary was fit to be tied. Made us swear not to say a word until he figured out how to tell the boss.'

'And did you say a word of this to anyone?'

'I told Conor. I don't know if Bob told the boss or not. That's all I know about the body. I swear to God.'

Lottie wasn't sure whether to believe him or not. But if he had told his friend, then Dowling had lied when he said he hadn't known about the body before. Or had she asked him that specific question? She'd have to check with Boyd later and read the interview transcript. She ran her hand through her hair. This was going round in circles. And she was still no closer to finding her daughters.

'Where are Katie and Chloe Parker?'

'Who?'

'You heard me.'

'Don't know them.'

'They're my daughters. And they're missing.'

'What're you doing in here then? If they were my daughters, I'd be out looking for them.'

'Smart-mouth,' Boyd said.

Lottie felt her heart miss a beat. Keegan was right. 'One final question. What does Dowling do in the shed in his garden?'

'The shed? I don't know.'

But his facial expression told Lottie he did. 'What's in the shed? And don't tell me to go and look.'

'Tools mainly. He used to do woodcraft and stuff.'

'Stuff?'

Keegan blew out a fetid breath. 'You know, little wooden toys, and then he started making jewellery.'

'What kind of jewellery?'

'Just stuff. Ask him about it.'

'I will.'

She turned to Boyd, asking him with her eyes if he had any further questions.

He said, 'The coin we showed you earlier. Could Conor have made it?'

Keegan bit his lip. 'It's possible, I suppose. Yeah.'

CHAPTER 57

Lottie sat at her desk and checked in with Rose again. Still no news. Sean and Louis were fine. She knew she had to keep busy, while all the time her heart was shredding itself into tiny fragments.

She tried to assess everything she had learned from the two interviews. Both men would have to be released. She had no hard evidence of any wrongdoing on their part. They couldn't be held on her instinct alone. Was it possible that Dowling had made the coins? How could she obtain a search warrant for his shed? Not a shred of evidence placed him at any of the murder scenes, and gut feeling wouldn't convince a judge. Unless she returned to soft-soap Vera Dowling. Boyd was good at that kind of thing.

'Boyd!'

He limped in.

'You need to come with me to Dowling's house. I want you to talk nice to Vera. Make her tea or whatever while I have a snoop in the garden shed.'

'Are you crazy?' He leaned wearily against the door jamb. 'I think you took a harder bang to the head than I did.'

'You'll have to work your charm and get her to give us permission.'

'Lottie, you're not thinking straight. We have so much other stuff to be doing.'

She stood. 'Are you coming with me, or are you just going to stand there feeling sorry for yourself?'

Harsh words, because he really did look awful.

'I've no choice, I suppose.'

*

Kirby popped in to Whyte's Pharmacy. The assistant, Trisha, said Megan had left to get something to eat before the late shift.

'When will she be back?'

'We're open until nine, so she should be back soon.' She checked the clock hanging above the door. 'Maybe fifteen minutes. Do you want to wait?'

'No, I'm busy.' He thought quickly. 'Don't tell her I called.'

'Sure.'

At the door he said, 'Do you think she went home for her break?'

Trisha shrugged her shoulders.

He had to talk to Megan. 'I'll be back,' he said.

Outside, he felt the dark of the afternoon sitting heavily on his shoulders. He missed Gilly at times like this. Her comforting words or silly remarks. He wondered how his boss was able to function not knowing where her daughters were. God, he didn't want to think the worst. They'd be fine. But in his heart, he felt they were not.

'Damn it,' he said. Jumping into the car he'd parked on double yellow lines, he headed for Megan's house.

*

This time Mrs Dowling was more accommodating. Boyd turned on his magic smile and made tea. He arranged a blanket around her knees. She told him he could call her Vera.

Once he'd succeeded in getting the television sound turned down, he said, 'Vera, is it okay for my inspector to take a look around?'

'I don't like her,' Vera whispered conspiratorially. 'But I've nothing to hide.' She looked up at Lottie. 'You're not to take anything.'

'I won't.'

Lottie grabbed a shiny new key from a hook in the kitchen. Opening the lock on the shed door, she entered the cold, damp space. Finding a string for the light, she pulled it and surveyed the equipment in front of her. With gloved hands she lifted a square of sheet metal. It was similar in weight and colour to the coins they'd found with the bodies, including the body in the tunnel.

Scanning the workbench, she noticed woodturning equipment but nothing that resembled what she thought might be used to pound medals or coins out of the sheet metal. As she looked around, her eyes were drawn to a gap on the bench. A hole had been bored into the wood, and as she ran her hand carefully around the bottom of it, tiny shards of metal came away on her fingertips. She held them up to the light, where they glinted.

Where was the machine that had fitted in here? She'd have to call SOCOs to take samples to compare with the coins found at the crime scenes. There was nothing further of interest, so she made her way through the wet grass and went back inside.

She smiled at Boyd's strained face. Torture, she thought. He didn't deserve that. Time to rescue him. 'Mrs Dowling, does anyone else have access to Conor's shed?'

'His workshop, you mean. That lad was always hammering or cutting something out there. All hours of the night. He had dreams of becoming an architect once upon a time. Before you lot framed him.' Her eyes slid into slits.

Lottie was undeterred. 'An architect?'

'He worked part-time as an apprentice for that Cyril Gill before he ended up in prison.'

Now that Vera said it, Lottie vaguely remembered it from the Thompson case.

'There seems to be a piece of equipment missing. Do you know who might have taken it?' If Conor hadn't dumped it himself, she thought.

'He was giving out loads when he came home from prison. Saying I'd let someone into the shed. He never said anything was missing, though.'

'So who did have access to it?'

'I never let anyone take nothing. Are you saying I did? Are you accusing me?'

'No, I'm not.' Lottie dug her fingers into the palms of her hands. 'Who comes in and out of your house?'

'The Meals on Wheels crowd. The community nurse, though she hasn't called in ages.'

'Anyone else?'

'Conor's friend Tony. He helped me out a bit. With shopping and the like. That nice wife of his called once. Lovely girl.'

'Megan Price?'

'Oh, is she not called Keegan? They were married, you know.'

'I think they're separated, or else she never changed her name,' Lottie said. Maybe she needed to check that out, but she had more pressing matters at the moment. 'Were they ever here together? Megan and Tony.'

'Not that I can think of straight off.'

'When was the last time either of them called?'

'I can't remember that.'

This was going nowhere. 'Did Conor ever say something was missing from his workshop?'

'All that lad does is moan since he came home.' Vera slapped her walking stick on the floor.

'Mrs Dowling,' Lottie said, 'I have to get someone from our forensic team to examine the workshop. There may be evidence there linked to a crime.'

'I knew it. You!' Vera pointed the stick at Boyd. 'With your smiles and your tea, chatting me up so I'd let that woman snoop around my house. Trying to catch me off guard. Do you know what? I may have let you look once, but if you want men in white suits to come in here, they better have a warrant. Now leave, both of you. And don't come back. Stitching my boy up again. Corrupt. That's what you are. You guards are all the same.'

Lottie and Boyd escaped before Vera Dowling could slam her stick into either or both of them.

'For a woman with chronic arthritis,' Boyd said, 'she sure has strength.'

CHAPTER 58

Lottie asked Boyd to draw up a request for a search warrant for the Dowling premises, and as she tapped her phone screen to check with her mother once again, Sam McKeown appeared at the door.

She cancelled the call. 'Did you find something?'

'Your daughters' phones.' He held up two evidence bags. Through the plastic she could see what she knew for certain were Katie and Chloe's mobile phones.

Her heart lurched and bile rose into her throat. 'Where were they found? Where are my girls?'

'They were in a rubbish bin outside the Clerk lounge bar, across the street from the courthouse. I've asked uniforms to access all the security footage from businesses, but with the area still sealed off following the accident, it will take time. Obviously we're trawling council CCTV for yesterday's relevant timeline.'

'How can two girls disappear just like that?'

'You know how, boss, without me spelling it out for you.'

She knew. She said, 'The network of tunnels may have been used. I want the drawings and maps on my desk.'

'I've been trying to find someone to get me that information. But it's hard.'

'My daughters' lives are at stake. Don't tell me something is hard.'

He opened his mouth and shut it again.

'Why are you still standing there?' She clenched her hands so tightly the knuckles turned white. The urge to thump them into a wall was overwhelming. 'Did you speak with that Miranda girl at the salon?'

'There's an officer with her at the moment taking her statement. But can I say something?' He pulled at his awkwardly rolled-up shirtsleeves. 'I've made some connections, and I wanted to run them by you. It's nothing to do with Bernie Kelly or your girls, but … Anyway, will I leave it until later?'

She needed something to focus on. 'Tell me, McKeown.'

'In Penny Brogan's appointment book, Kirby found that Belinda Gill, Cyril's wife, was a regular customer. Do you think I should speak with her?'

'I'll do it. But wish me luck trying to extract a coherent word out of her.' Lottie recalled how Belinda had downed glasses of gin when she'd called following Louise's death.

'Also, the transcript from Louise's laptop makes interesting reading. This course she was doing, it seems to have screwed with her brain.'

'How so?'

'Her work appears to be all about miscarriages of justice, with a large concentration of words devoted to the Conor Dowling case.'

'Did you read over the Thompson file?'

'I did. Yes. Kirby gave it to me.' He shifted uneasily from foot to foot. Shit, Lottie thought.

'You discovered something I missed ten years ago?'

'Maybe not you. But I think Superintendent Corrigan directed the investigation the way he wanted it to go.'

'What do you mean?' But she had thought this herself earlier.

'He was a strong supporter of Cyril Gill's project.'

'Doesn't mean diddly.'

'Just saying.'

'What else?'

'We've received official confirmation that the body of Cyril Gill has been recovered from the accident site.'

'A dead man can't answer any questions.'

'He sure can't.'

'Is that all?'

'Jim McGlynn is ready to extract the body from the tunnel. Says it will be an arduous business.' McKeown took a deep breath. 'He reckons it could've been there for up to ten years.'

'How can he know until it's been examined by a forensic anthropologist?'

'Apparently there was a dated receipt in the shirt pocket.'

'The body was decomposed. Only bones and rags left. Surely a receipt from ten years ago would have disintegrated?'

McKeown's eyes widened; he was eager to relay his information. 'McGlynn tried to explain to me the way the human body decomposes. Something about how bodily fluids follow gravity, seeping downwards. The receipt was in the remnants of the front shirt pocket. Therefore it was preserved.

'Jesus.' Lottie scratched her head, trying to digest what McKeown said. 'A receipt for what?'

'He said he'd get someone to drop it off. I just took the call.'

'Okay.' She studied him. He looked like he wanted to say something else, and she ran her fingers over the evidence bag containing her daughters' phones. 'What is it, McKeown?'

'Just trying to read my handwriting here. Oh, yes. McGlynn thinks from the bone structure that the body might be of Asian origin. And it's female. Just in his opinion, he said.'

Lottie tried to make sense of this. 'I know you're up to your proverbial, but could you do a quick search on the missing persons database? An Asian woman, missing for ten years.'

*

Leo Belfield checked the email when it pinged on his phone. Detective McKeown had sent him a new description of Bernie. He studied the image. He thought he had seen someone like that in the distance a few hours earlier. He leaned against the shopfront and scanned the street. It was busy. But he missed the noise and rush of New York. Once he had righted his wrong over losing his half-sister, he decided he no longer wanted anything to do with his heritage or Farranstown House. Lottie Parker was welcome to their fractured family history. But maybe he should take one more look out there.

Pushing himself away from the wall, he went to fetch his rental car. A drive into the countryside might just activate his detective's brain into motion.

*

Kirby had been at Megan's house yesterday, but now he remembered it from the Bill Thompson file. Megan still lived in her stepfather's home. He'd had no reason to make the connection before.

As he stepped from the car, he lit a cigar and took a deep drag. Coughed out the smoke and looked around. Trees surrounded the old two-storey building. The lights from the canal walkway cast yellow shadows on the bare branches. He wondered how Louise and Amy had seen Conor Dowling in this area. And what were they doing out this way late at night? They'd only been fourteen years old at the time. He'd have to read their witness statements again.

The ground floor had a bay window, and a garage attached to the house. He noticed that the blue paint on the front door was cracked and peeling. Megan wasn't keeping the place very well, he remarked to himself. Not that he could talk.

He rang the bell. Listened. Waited. Rang it again. He walked around to the back of the house and hammered on the door there. He heard a sound. Like a muffled yelp. Did Megan have a dog? He had no idea. Maybe he'd have been better off checking her Facebook page.

He put his ear to the door.

Silence.

Lighting his cigar again, he walked back round to his car. He took a pull, puffed out the smoke and stopped. Could something have happened to Megan on her break from work? Shit. He moved over to the garage. It was timber, double-doored. On one door there was a small silver handle with a Yale-type slit. He tried it. Not a budge. Nothing was that easy.

As he turned to leave, he heard the muffled sound once more. The front door opened and Megan stepped out.

'What the hell are you doing here?'

*

Lottie wanted to be anywhere but in this house, oozing money and coldness.

She eyed Boyd, willing him to take the lead, but he was staring at the marble floor. Glassy-eyed, Belinda Gill poured herself a cup of water from a dispenser on her massive black fridge.

'I know this is an awful shock. If there's anything we can do, just let us know.'

'I think you've done enough already. First you come to search my murdered daughter's room, and then you arrive to tell me my husband is dead.' She looked wildly around the mausoleum of a kitchen. 'I need a proper drink.'

'Sit down, Belinda. We need to talk to you.'

'You'd better come through to the living room.'

Lottie and Boyd followed the woman and stood waiting as she poured herself a large brandy. They weren't offered anything, though Lottie felt she could do with a drink to still the racing in her chest. So far she had resisted the urge to drown her anxiety in alcohol. She wasn't sure how long that would last.

'At least Cyril died doing something he loved.'

'Pardon?'

'His job. Louise first, work second. I didn't even register.'

'It was an accident, Mrs Gill,' Boyd said.

'Oh, for God's sake, call me Belinda. I ceased being Mrs Gill a long time ago. Cyril was an entrepreneur in more things than building projects.'

'I don't follow,' Boyd said, and Lottie caught his confused glance. She felt the same way.

'Women,' Belinda said. 'He liked them all, except me.'

Lottie tried to get the conversation on track. 'Do you recall any trouble he may have experienced with the project he was pioneering a decade ago?'

'That pie-in-the-sky development that almost bankrupted him?' She snorted. 'Yes, I remember. Cost him a fortune buying up property before he even had a deal. Then Bill Thompson stuck his oar in and scuppered the whole thing.'

'Really?' Lottie hadn't heard anything about that. She'd been aware that Thompson opposed the project, but that was all.

'He stood up at a public meeting and denounced Cyril in front of half the town. It was enough to damage Cyril's reputation. The council pulled the project. That was the end of all the work he'd put into it. He'd been planning it for three years. And it just took one mouthpiece to shatter everything.'

'That mouthpiece being Bill Thompson?' Boyd said.

'Yes. He got his come-uppance, though, didn't he?' Belinda laughed but it turned into a sob, so she poured another drink.

'Do you think Cyril might have had anything to do with the attack on Mr Thompson?'

Belinda looked at Lottie like she had three heads. 'Cyril was devastated, but not enough to beat up an old man and rob him of a few measly grand. Didn't that Dowling lad do it?'

'He was convicted, but new information casts some doubt on it. Unless Cyril got him to—'

'Don't you dare sully my husband's name.'

The irony was clearly lost on Belinda, Lottie thought. 'Conor Dowling worked for your husband back then. Did you know him?'

'Cyril wouldn't let me have anything to do with his business.'

Lottie detected a note of derision in the woman's voice. 'So he sidelined you in all his business dealings?'

'Correct.' Belinda slumped into the nearest plush armchair. Lottie and Boyd remained standing awkwardly in the centre of the large room. 'But I knew young Dowling.'

Lottie's phone vibrated with a text. 'Sorry, I have to check this.' Her head pounded and she felt ill when she saw Sam McKeown's name. Could there be word on Katie and Chloe?

She opened it and read it. Nothing to do with the girls, but interesting all the same. She returned her attention to Belinda.

'How did you know Conor Dowling?'

'He was always hanging around here. Going over drawings and plans with Cyril. He was working as an apprentice draughtsman or something. Cyril took more of an interest in the lad than in his own daughter then. Always wanted a son, he said, but after I had Louise, he wasn't interested in me enough to try for another.'

Lottie decided to change direction. 'Do you employ a housekeeper?'

Patricia Gibney

'No.' Belinda's eyes slid into two dark lines. 'Why?'

'But you used to, isn't that right?'

Belinda got up and filled her glass, then wandered around the room running one finger along surfaces as if checking for dust. 'You wouldn't be asking if you didn't already know.'

'What happened to her?'

'I've had many housekeepers over the years. To whom are you referring?'

'I don't have a name yet, but it was ten years ago. Thought you might remember.'

'We did have a young lady working here. She went out one night and never returned. We had no home address for her, or contacts. No one ever came looking for her.'

'Did you report her missing?'

'We didn't know she *was* missing. She just went out and never came back. We assumed she'd got a job elsewhere.'

'Without taking her belongings?'

Belinda shrugged. 'Cyril sent whatever she'd left behind to a charity shop.'

'Oh, and how long did he wait before getting rid of it?'

'I've no idea.'

'Can you remember anything about the night she went missing?'

'My memory is not what it used to be. Let me think.' She pressed the glass to her forehead. 'No. Nothing unusual really. Oh, was that the night Louise and her friend saw young Dowling after he'd assaulted and robbed Bill Thompson? It might have been, come to think of it.'

Lottie could feel Boyd's eyes boring into her. He hadn't seen McKeown's text, so he had no idea what she was at.

'Was your housekeeper an Asian woman?'

'How did you know?'

'We've found a body,' Lottie said. 'In a tunnel under the court-house.'

The glass shattered on the wooden floor and Boyd rushed to catch Belinda before she hit the ground.

CHAPTER 59

The old house looked like something out of a Dickens novel. Leo's mother – well, the woman he thought of as his mother – used to read him the classics, and he thought Farranstown House could have comfortably housed Miss Havisham.

He walked around the outside, checking the gravel for any signs of recent footprints. The ground was mucky and wet, and the deep footprints of the uniformed officers who had checked it out when looking for Bernie made distinguishing anything of interest next to impossible. He stood on the doorstep surveying the landscape. The inky sky touched the lake in the distance, and a thin, pale stream sheeted the horizon in expectation of night.

No point in hammering on the door, he thought, and made his way around the side, checking through the darkened windows as he walked. All he could make out was sheeted furniture standing like ghosted sentries. He recalled Alexis telling him about a basement. In New York, most of these had an external door. He couldn't see one here. He'd have to search inside, but he had no key. He lifted the latch in hope. No such luck. He put his eye to the keyhole. There was a key on the inside of the lock.

On the ground, he found a piece of wire and jiggled it around in the lock. After a couple of minutes he heard the key drop to the floor. Now he could get somewhere. He worked the piece of wire until he heard a click, and the door opened.

He pushed it inwards and stepped inside the house that he knew should rightfully be his. Flicking a switch, he was amazed to see the hallway slowly fill with muted light. That, at least, was a bonus. Closing the door behind him, he made his way into the spacious farmhouse-type kitchen.

Tendrils of icy cold swathed the stillness. His detective's antennae were on their highest alert level. He knew he was not alone in the old house.

*

'Are you in a hurry to get back to work?' Kirby said.

'I am, actually,' Megan replied. 'What are you doing here?'

He wanted to talk to her in a civilised setting, not out on her dark driveway.

'It will only take a few minutes. You don't have to make tea; I just want you to answer a couple of questions.'

He studied her face, her hair knotted at the nape of her neck, her camel coat and blue scarf. She wore flat-soled knee-length black boots. He thought she looked pretty.

'I'm sorry. I have to go,' she said. 'I'm already late.'

'Aren't you going to close your front door?'

She fumbled in her bag for her keys as she pulled the door closed. She turned the key in the lock.

'Look, Detective Kirby. You're a nice man, but you're going through a grieving process. I don't think I'm the right person to help you. Maybe you should visit a therapist.' Her voice was sharp and professional.

'Do you have a pet?'

'No.'

'Is this where your father lived?'

'Stepfather.'

'And your mother?'

'She died, must be fifteen years ago.'

'And did you inherit this house when your stepfather died?'

She stalled beside her car. 'Why are you asking me these questions?'

'Did you receive a note from Conor Dowling to deliver to Amy Whyte?'

'You're talking utter rubbish. I can give you the number of a therapist if you'd like.'

She opened the car and sat in.

Kirby leaned on the open door. 'Can I have a look around your house?'

'No you cannot. Just leave.'

'Oh, don't worry. I'm going.'

'Good. I'm heading back to work.'

She slammed the door and Kirby had to jump out of the way as she reversed out onto the road and drove off with water splashing from the potholes.

He watched her go before making his way to his own car. He threw his phone on the seat, then sat in and returned his attention to Megan's house.

*

She emerged up the stairs from the basement like a shadow creeping out of a coffin. All in black, her hair shorn and her skin an unusual pallor.

'I thought *she* would find me before you,' she said.

Leo leaned against the kitchen table, wondering how he was going to handle this.

'Where are Lottie's girls?'

'You'd like to know, wouldn't you?'

As she took a step onto the flagstones, he noticed she was twisting a rope round and round her hand. The end of it was shaped like a noose. He prayed she hadn't already killed them.

'It doesn't have to be this way, Bernie.' Edging along the length of the table, he knocked against a chair, the sound screeching in the fusty air.

'Stop!' She raised her other hand. In the moonlight streaming through the window, he saw the steel of a knife glinting in her hand.

*

Back at the station, after they'd settled Belinda Gill with a blanket and a cup of tea with plenty of sugar, Lottie and Boyd entered the incident room. Dowling and Keegan had been released. There was nothing she could have done to prevent it, so she would just have to follow the evidence. McKeown surfaced from the midst of a group of detectives and hurried over to them. His tie was sticking out of his pocket and his shirt was undone at the neck. He looked like she felt. Exhausted.

'Boss,' he said. 'We rushed through the DNA from Dowling and Keegan. The forensics lab have outdone themselves this time. Probably because we now have five bodies.'

Lottie perched on the edge of a desk, tapping a text to her mother. 'Go on.'

'Do you remember the hairs found on the bodies at the first murder scene?'

'Yes.' She glanced at the incident board, where a photograph of said hairs was pinned. 'But we didn't think we'd get much success seeing as they came from a doss house.'

'Anyway, we already had Dowling's DNA on file from the original case. Though I don't think any comparative analysis was ever carried out, once you had the witnesses.'

'Things were different then,' Lottie said. 'Samples had to be sent to the UK. It cost a lot of money, and budgets were as tight as they are now.'

'Well, just to let you know, it isn't a match for the hair.'

'Doesn't prove anything.'

'I know. But I thought it was important. I've fast-tracked Keegan's DNA sample to the lab. My contact there said he should have something within four hours.'

'That must be a record,' Boyd said.

'It's all about who you know,' McKeown said, and tapped the side of his nose.

Lottie read the reply from her mother. No word on the girls. She pocketed her phone.

McKeown was still talking. 'But this is the good bit. They got a hit on the hairs from an unrelated case.'

'What?' Lottie and Boyd said.

'It may be nothing, but a couple of years ago, Whyte's Pharmacy was broken into. Samples were taken from all the employees to rule them out of the incident. I don't know if the culprit was ever found. You might remember it, boss.'

'McKeown, will you get to the point.' Lottie slid off the desk and paced up and down in front of the boards.

'The hair found on the bodies is a match for Megan Price.'

'What? The hair from the crime scene at Petit Lane?' Lottie digested the new information.

Boyd said, 'Megan worked with Amy Whyte. It could have trans-ferred from her clothing if their coats were hanging close together.'

'No, Boyd,' Lottie said. 'Amy was out clubbing. Her clothing was nothing like what she would wear to work. And hairs were also found on Penny Brogan. We need to bring Megan in for questioning.' She glanced around the room. 'Where's Kirby?'

They all looked round.

'Didn't you send him to Whyte's Pharmacy to ask about the note Dowling sent to Amy?' Boyd said.

Lottie had her phone in her hand calling Kirby as she ran out of the incident room.

There was no answer from Kirby, but as she went to tap his number for a third time, the phone vibrated with a text.

'Leo,' Lottie said.

'What does it say?' Boyd asked.

She read it out. '"Farranstown. Injured."'

'Does he say anything about Katie and Chloe?'

'No.' She sprang into action. 'McKeown, you try to reach Kirby. Head down to the pharmacy and see if he's still there. Take uniforms and bring in Megan Price. Boyd and I have to go to Farranstown.'

In the yard, she told Boyd to drive. He was a faster and safer driver. The sky was dark, with the yellow hue of street lights giving it a gothic air.

'Will I put on the flashers?'

'Yeah, do.'

'We should radio for backup.'

'Let's see what Leo's found first.'

Boyd switched on the flashing blue lights and headed out on the road towards Farranstown House.

'Do you think Bernie's there?'

'I've no idea.'

'If she is, she's liable to do anything. We should radio for backup just in case.'

'Shut up, Boyd.'

'You're being irrational, Lottie, though that's nothing new.'

She refused to answer him.

'It could be a trap,' he said eventually.

'I thought of that.' And she had. Every scenario was tripping over itself in her brain. 'Okay. Radio for an armed unit to follow us.'

'We should wait for them.'

'Just drive the fucking car, Boyd.'

*

As far as Kirby knew, Megan didn't have a pet. But the noise had sounded like an animal. Or something. Or someone.

Curiosity got the better of him, so he got out of his car and walked around the side of the house again. Ears pricked. Listening. Nothing. He stood at the back door, pressed his ear up against it. Definitely nothing. Back around to the front again, and to the garage. Silence. But he had to go in. He wished he had McKeown's knife.

He jiggled his car key in the garage lock. Pulled it, twisted it. No go. Looking around on the ground, he found a sharp piece of slate, but it broke the second he tried to jimmy the lock. He stood back and surveyed the doors. Hinges. He set to work on the screws with his key.

One hinge was on the ground, with three more to go, when he heard a car screech into the gravelled drive.

CHAPTER 60

There were no lights on in the house up ahead as Boyd turned off the main road and made his way up the unlit avenue.

'It's as dark and forbidding as the first time we were here.'

'That was a year ago, Boyd.'

'I know, but some things imprint themselves on your brain and you can never erase them.'

'I'm not listening to that shite.' Lottie jumped out of the car almost before he had the brake on.

He followed her with two torches he'd taken from the boot. 'Are you going to ring the bell?'

'I've a key. Somewhere.' She twiddled her key ring around in her hand, trying to find the right one.

'How come you have that?'

'It's my biological grandmother's home. The solicitor gave me the key and asked me to keep an eye on it while probate is being conducted.'

'You never told me that.'

'Jesus Christ, Boyd. I don't tell you everything.' She found the correct key, and after a couple of nervous tries, it slid it into the new lock that had been fitted after Kitty Belfield had died.

'Have you been out here at all since ... you know?'

'No. Shush.'

Stepping onto the cold stone floor, Lottie listened to the door creak open and felt Boyd's soft breath on her neck. In different circumstances she would have welcomed his closeness, the safety of having him by her side. But her daughters' lives were at stake, and all she could think about was that they might be here. With Leo and Bernie. Whether Leo was in cahoots with Bernie was something she would soon find out.

'This way. I see a faint light,' she whispered.

'What's down there?'

'The kitchen.'

She edged along the wall towards the room at the end, where a thin shaft of light seeped from beneath the door. She wondered what awaited her.

With one hand on the handle, she took a deep breath and opened the door.

'Sweet Mother of Jesus,' Boyd exclaimed.

'Holy shit,' Lottie said once she could form the words.

The ambulance rushed with sirens and flashing lights down the avenue while Lottie and Boyd waited for SOCOs. Bernie Kelly was no longer on the run. No longer in the wind. No longer a threat to Lottie's family. She lay curled on the floor, hardened froth on her lips and her eyes hysterically open in death.

Leo had knife wounds to his upper chest, but he was conscious, his phone in his hand. There was no sign of Katie or Chloe, and no evidence that they had been in the house.

Lottie's phone rang.

'What's up, McKeown?'

'I can't locate Kirby anywhere. He's not answering his phone.'

'Did you try the pubs?' Boyd said into Lottie's ear, for McKeown's benefit.

'We're on our way back into town,' Lottie said. 'Be there in five minutes.'

She hung up and walked quickly out of the house to the car.

'Give me the keys,' she said to Boyd. 'I need to concentrate on something before I go out of my mind trying to figure out what Bernie was doing.'

'I think it's obvious. She wanted to wipe out all of her siblings.'

'Okay, but I'm still alive, and so is Leo.' She started the car as Boyd hauled his long legs into the passenger footwell.

'But she might have thought Leo was dead. And you …'

'She's done something to Chloe and Katie. That's how she wants me to suffer.'

She gunned the engine, and with gravel flying into the damp night air, she left Farranstown House with the body of her half-sister lying dead on a cold stone floor.

The office was abuzz with noise, heat and anxiety. No one had any idea where Kirby had got to. Lottie sat at his desk and flicked though the open documents on his computer, trying to find an answer.

'What did the pharmacy staff say?' she asked.

McKeown said, 'Just that he called in looking to speak to Megan Price, and when he was told she was on her break, he left.'

'Where does she go for her break?'

'Sometimes she eats in town, other times she goes home.'

'Did you get her number?'

'Yes. Goes straight to voice message.'

'Why haven't you brought her in? Where does she live? Did you call to her home?'

McKeown sighed. 'I haven't called out there yet. This was on Kirby's desk.'

Lottie took the photocopied page. It was from Penny Brogan's appointment book. One name was highlighted in a yellow circle. Megan Price.

'When I was in the pharmacy,' McKeown said, 'I had a look around too. I asked if Amy had a locker. An assistant, Trisha I think her name was, said Detective Kirby had asked about it early in the week, but he hadn't looked in it.'

'And you did?' Lottie balled her hands into fists. She hoped Kirby hadn't fucked up.

McKeown dropped an evidence bag of clothing on the desk. And then another, with a pink-covered notebook.

'What's that?' Lottie pulled protective gloves from a drawer and dragged them over her sweaty hands. She took out the notebook and opened it to a page that had a corner turned down. 'This is about the night Louise and Amy saw Conor Dowling. Amy says they came out of the teenage disco in Jomo's and were waiting to be picked up when someone ran by them wearing a baseball cap. Louise said she recognised it as belonging to Conor Dowling, who worked as an apprentice for her father.'

'Bill Thompson's house is only a stone's throw away from the nightclub, if you take the railway underpass by the canal,' Boyd said.

'But why was Dowling coming that way?' That had always bothered Lottie. 'If he had committed the crime, wouldn't he have been running a million miles from town?'

'I suppose so,' Boyd agreed. 'But in the heat of the moment, maybe he became disorientated and ran towards town instead of away.'

'I don't think the girls made a mistake that night. I think they did see Conor Dowling.'

'That was agreed at trial.'

'Yes. But what if he had committed a different crime, and that's why he never gave an alibi for the Thompson assault and robbery?'

'What are you getting at?'

'I think Dowling had something to do with the body in the tunnel. That's where he was running from. Not from Thompson's. He came up through a tunnel. Either the one we were at earlier, or one nearby.'

'So did he kill our victims or not?'

'Whoever killed Amy and Penny had knowledge of the tunnels. From McKeown's work on the CCTV, we can deduce that the murderer used a tunnel to either hide, make a getaway or stash the murder weapon.'

'So who would know about it?'

'Tony Keegan. He's worked for Gill for twenty years. He had to know. He's friends with Dowling, who may have told him.'

'So you think Keegan beat up and robbed his future wife's stepfather?' McKeown said.

Lottie threw down the notebook and wrenched the heels of her hands into her eyes. None of this was bringing her any closer to her daughters' whereabouts, but she was convinced the original Thompson case held the key. She just had to find it.

'First things first. Give me Megan Price's address. I'm going to see if Kirby is there. Then we'll bring Dowling and Keegan back in. Boyd, you're with me.'

CHAPTER 61

Kirby's car was in the drive. Lottie stood with Boyd and listened. A train chugged in the distance, traffic buzzed on the bypass a few kilometres away, a swing in someone's garden squealed in the rising night wind. Normality in the midst of confusion, she thought.

Rain fell steadily as she approached the house. No lights blazed and no one opened the door.

'The garage door is open,' Boyd said.

Lottie pushed past him and stared. The door was indeed slightly ajar.

'Should we wait for backup?'

'I'm waiting for no one.'

The door scraped on the bare concrete floor as she pushed it inwards. The interior was lit dimly by the red glow from a light on a fridge freezer. A bench with tools lined one wall. She shone her torch around searching for a light switch, but couldn't see one, though a fluorescent tube hung from the ceiling on a chain. Returning her attention to the bench, she caught sight of the glint of metal shards.

'Boyd, look.'

'It's a workbench.'

'I know, but those shavings are similar to what I saw in Conor Dowling's shed.' She continued shining the light up and down the area in front of her until the beam illuminated an unusual circular piece of equipment. 'What do you think that's for?'

Boyd just shrugged and turned up his mouth.

Even in her anxiety to find Kirby and her daughters, Lottie remembered her training and tugged on gloves. Running her finger along the inside edge of the circle, she said, 'This is what was used to make the coins found at the murder scenes. And it came from Conor Dowling's house.'

A groan alerted her senses.

'What's that?' she whispered.

Boyd had heard it too. He rushed to the internal door and pushed it. He found a switch and light fell into the garage. 'In here.'

Lottie followed him. On the floor of what looked like a utility room lay Kirby.

'Shit, are you okay?' Boyd knelt down beside the prone figure.

'How could someone have overpowered him? Surely not Megan?' She paused as Boyd administered to Kirby. 'Unless Tony Keegan is here. He might have Megan captive.' She looked down at her two detectives. 'Is he okay?'

'I can't see any blood. Maybe he was drugged.'

Kirby groaned again and opened his eyes. He quickly closed them again as if the light had blinded him. 'Neck,' he groaned.

Boyd ran his fingers around Kirby's neck, turned the detective's head to one side. But he still couldn't see a wound.

'Needle,' whispered Kirby.

'He's been drugged.' Boyd whipped out his phone and called for medical backup.

Lottie was about to reply when she heard a sound overhead. She patted Boyd on the shoulder to tell him that he was to stay with Kirby, then made her way from the utility room into a darkened kitchen. She had no idea what she was facing, so she decided not to turn on a light. The hair on the back of her neck stood to attention and her heart picked up pace. She was certain that if there was anyone in the room they would surely hear it. But it was empty. The torch beam caught the outline of a table and chairs and wall cupboards, and that was it. Scanning the light over the walls she found they were bare. She made her way to the next door and opened it.

A low moaning, like the keening of a banshee, whispered from above. At the end of the short hallway she came to a staircase. A few coats hung on the banister, the only sign that someone lived here. Hoping it wouldn't creak, she put her foot on the first step, then made her way slowly upwards. On each step she could see a coin similar to those at the murder scenes. Her heart picked up speed in her chest and she held her breath, trying to subdue the rising surge of panic.

All the doors were open. Dim light seeped out from one. She made her way quickly, the beat of her heart almost deafening her. With no idea of what horror might await her, with no fear for her own safety, she stepped into the room.

Her mouth opened automatically to issue a scream, but all that came out was a choked gurgle. She tried to call out to Boyd, but the words would not form. She was rooted to the spot as if superglue was attached to her boots. Frozen in a time frame of terror.

Megan Price was nowhere to be seen.

But her two daughters lay side by side on the floor.

Their hands were bound in front of them. Legs outstretched. Their heads, one dark and the other dyed blonde, were both a straggling mess of blood. No movement. No breath that she could see. The scene of horror simultaneously iced her brain and her body.

She had no idea how long she stood transfixed, her heart shattering into a million fragments, her eyes pouring forth tears of pain. Her hands trembling, her knees weak as she fell to the floor. Her babies. Her girls. Her life. Entrusted to her to care for. To look after.

To love. After Adam had died, her sole responsibility was to their children. To love them and protect them. And she'd fucked it all up.

It must have been only a few moments that she stood like that, and then she screamed.

CHAPTER 62

Boyd found her on her knees. Screaming inconsolably. He quickly assessed the scene and got to work, checking for vital signs. Backup and ambulances were on the way, and he prayed they wouldn't be too late.

He turned back to Lottie. 'They're alive. Come on. Help me.'

She was frozen. Face white with fear and shock.

He yelled, 'Lottie! Now. I need help. Ambulance is on the way.'

She awoke as if from a sudden stupor and, hardly daring to breathe, crawled on hands and knees across the coin-littered floor to reach her girls.

'Katie. Chloe. Dear God.'

She put a trembling hand under her younger daughter's chin and lifted her head. Chloe's eyes were closed and her mouth drooped on one side. Lottie put her face close. Skin to skin. She felt the soft breath ease from Chloe's mouth. At last she could exhale herself. She did the same to Katie. Her daughters were alive.

But where had the blood come from? She ran quivering fingers through the girls' hair until they connected with the wounds. Both had been bludgeoned. A strip of bloody timber lay in the corner of the room. Then she noticed a cut on Chloe's throat, just beneath her ear.

Sirens screeched in the near distance as she held her girls close to her breast and shed tears of relief. Though she had no idea how badly injured they were, she was just thankful in that moment that they were alive.

'Chloe was cut,' she whispered.

'She'll be fine once the paramedics get here,' Boyd said. 'And Kirby will be fine too when whatever he was injected with wears off.'

She felt Boyd's hand on her shoulder, and then the room filled with noise and people, and reluctantly she released her girls into the hands of the experts.

As she cried uncontrollable sobs. She felt as if her body was expunging the fear she'd been keeping under wraps since last night. And she didn't know if she would ever be able to stop.

CHAPTER 63

Conor opened the door to Tony and led him past the living room, where his mother was asleep, and into the kitchen. He took two cans of Foster's from a plastic bag on the floor. They sat at the narrow table, flipped the tabs and drank. Neither man could look the other in the eye.

'Bob Cleary and Cyril Gill are dead,' Tony said. 'It's been confirmed.'

'I heard. Good riddance.' Conor slurped his drink and burped loudly. 'There's blood on your hands,' he said, noticing Tony's knuckles.

Tony appeared nonplussed. 'Scraped them shifting rubble this morning. Haven't had a chance to wash. I'm sure I smell.'

'You do. But I'm accustomed to bad odours around here.' Conor nodded towards the door behind which his mother snored.

They sat in silence and drank.

'Got another one?' Tony said.

'You seem nervous. Anything you want to tell me?' Conor extracted two more cans from the bag.

'I'll get straight to the point so.' Tony cradled his can between his burly fingers. 'Why did you take the blame for the Thompson assault and robbery?'

'How do you know I didn't do it?'

'Because I know who did.'

'Yeah,' Conor said, running his hand over his freshly shaved head. He stared pointedly at Tony. 'So do I.'

'You needn't look at me like that.'

'Like what? You know what you did.'

'And I think I know what you did too.' Tony played with the tab on the can, pressing it so hard it cut the edge of his thumb.

'What would that be?'

'You know right well, Conor. Those girls, Amy and Louise. They saw you that night, and you never denied it. Never offered an alibi or a defence.'

'So?'

'So,' Tony repeated. 'I think you were running from something else. I think you'd done something much worse than assault and rob Bill Thompson.'

'Something? Like what?'

'Like hiding a body in the tunnel.'

'And why would I do that?' Conor eyed Tony and wondered just how much his friend really knew.

Tony stood suddenly. 'Stop playing games. Come on. Tell me.'

'Thought you knew it all.' Conor was fed up. He'd carried his secret for ten years; he wasn't about to spout it out now. Tony could feck off.

'You had your eye on that housekeeper up at Gill's. What was her name? Hannah something or other? Cute little Chinese chick. You were always asking her out but she wouldn't date you. After that night, I never remember seeing her again. That's odd, don't you think?'

'Maybe she went back to China.'

'Maybe she did, but I don't think so.'

Conor felt a slight relief in his chest. He sipped his beer, slowly this time, and studied Tony's plump red face. Did he know or did he just suspect? Probably the latter.

'Okay, the truth is, I had a thing with her. We didn't tell the Gills because Cyril couldn't keep his eyes or his hands off her. She threatened to leave them. And I think she did.'

Tony's lips curled into a sneer. 'She was dumped in a tunnel with no escape. You left her there.'

'We both have secrets from that night, Tony, so don't go making accusations, especially without proof.'

Tony dug his hand in his pocket and put a silver coin on the table.

Conor glanced at it, then looked up. 'Where did you get that?'

'Found it in the tunnel. The day we went down with Bob. When did you go back to build the wall? You must have dropped it then.'

Conor knew he could deny it, but then who was Tony going to tell without implicating himself in another crime? He put the can to his lips and drained his beer, then opened another.

He was about to tell Tony the truth when there was a knock at the door.

*

Lottie felt herself being half carried out to the car. Boyd sat into the seat beside her.

'The blood?' she sobbed.

'Paramedics don't think either girl was stabbed. Chloe has a slight cut to her neck as if a knife was held there. Maybe it slipped. No visible stab wounds on Katie. They both took a bang to the head and were most likely drugged.'

'Who did it?' She furiously rubbed the tears from her eyes. 'Megan Price?'

'Or Tony Keegan.' Boyd reversed the car onto the road. 'Will I drop you home?'

'Just a minute. Think, Boyd. We'll get plenty of forensic evidence from their clothes, and from Kirby. We need to bring in Price, Keegan and Dowling. We have no idea where Megan is, but let's send a team to Keegan's house, and we'll get Dowling.'

Boyd grabbed the radio and asked for McKeown. Gave him the instructions and also told him to send a team to Dowling's house. He eyed Lottie. 'Can I drop you off first?'

'I'll see this through and then I'm taking time out for my family.'

'I've heard that before.'

'Just drive the car, Boyd.'

*

The kitchen was too small. Not like when they were younger and his mother was at work and they could all hang out and laugh and smoke and drink vodka from mugs. Megan told Conor to drive her car.

'Where are we going?'

'I want to show you something. Go down past Petit Lane car park.'

'That place is crawling with guards,' Tony protested.

'Not that exact area. I think Conor knows an entrance to the tunnel that no one else is aware of,' Megan laughed. She saw his shoulders hunch and knew she was right.

'Why do you want to bring us there?' Conor said. 'Back to the scene of the bloody crime.'

'What crime would that be?' Tony scoffed. 'I think you're the one that has blood on your hands.'

'Shut your mouth, Keegan.'

The three one-time friends got out of the car at the north side of the council buildings. Hoarding covered the area where once Gill had outlined his visionary plans for regeneration and renewal. Megan could see the house where Amy and Penny had met their deaths. In the distance, if it wasn't dark, she'd be able to see her own house, and further beyond that lay the scene where Louise and Cristina had died. Full circle, she thought.

'Open it,' she said, pointing to the door cut into the hoarding.

'Come on, Megs,' Tony said. 'This is mad.'

'Don't you ever call me that. My name is Megan. I want to hear the truth from both of you and then I'll be gone.'

'You need to see a doctor,' Conor offered. 'You're losing a lot of blood.'

Megan eyed the two men. She knew her arm was covered in blood, but she didn't care. That aggressive blonde bitch had lunged at her and the knife had slipped as she was about to cut her throat. She'd stuck a needle in their necks to subdue them and decided to leave them for later. First she'd deal with the two rats in her life, then she'd take her time with the girls and Detective Kirby.

She held the knife down by her leg and stood waiting. One or both of them could easily overpower her, but somehow they were transfixed by what she was about to say.

She pushed past Conor and opened the door. 'Where is the entrance?'

'To what?'

'The tunnel where you brought Hannah Lee.'

Conor shifted from foot to foot, his face a ghostly mask in the yellow hue of the street lights. 'Hannah?'

'I know you killed her.'

'And how would you know that?' The wind carried his voice across to her.

'Because if you hadn't been killing her and disposing of her body that night, Tony would never have escaped justice for murdering my stepfather.'

Tony stood up straight. 'Hey, just a minute. I never killed anyone.'

Megan laughed. 'You stole my key to the safe and you broke in to rob my stepfather. Then you proceeded to beat him to a pulp. He never regained consciousness.'

'He died from a stroke.'

'Brought on by your violence. How could you do that to me?'

'Shit, he was only your stepfather, not your real dad.'

She lashed out then, striking him on the cheek with the knife. The cut wasn't deep but the blood ran freely down his face, and he dropped to his knees in the mud, whimpering.

Conor reacted though, and made to grab the knife from her hand, but she whipped it around in his direction and drew it along his arm, tearing through the stiff material of his jacket. He clutched the wound and yelled, 'Fuck you, you're a mad bitch.'

'Open up the tunnel,' she said.

*

Outside Conor Dowling's house, with his mother ranting from the doorstep, Lottie walked around in circles.

'Where did they go?' she said.

'Vera says she was asleep but woke up when Megan Price near knocked the door down with her hammering. She heard Keegan and Conor talking in the hall and then they were gone.'

'We missed them by a few minutes. Shit.'

McKeown arrived with a wad of papers in his hand. 'I think I might know where they are.'

'Let's get into the car,' Boyd said as the rain began to beat down harder.

'What have you got?' Lottie asked.

'I eventually got hold of some old maps from a local historian. She arrived with them earlier when she heard on the news about the body we found in the tunnel.'

They sat into the car. Boyd switched on the engine to get the heat going.

'And?' Lottie said.

'There's a network of tunnels all right, and one of them has an entrance on this patch of waste ground.' He pointed to the folded map in his hand.

'Where's that?'

'Cyril Gill bought up the land when he came up with his big project ten years ago. It was laid waste when his plans were scuppered. It's on the other side of the council buildings, not a million miles away from the house where we found Amy and Penny.'

'But why do you think we'll find Dowling and the others there?' Boyd asked.

'Have you got a brighter idea?' Lottie said.

*

Conor knew he could easily take the knife from Megan, but he wanted to hear what she had to say. He walked slowly across the ground, holding his damaged arm, wishing there was more light. But maybe he could use the dull hue from the distant street lights to his advantage.

'Why did you kill the girls?' he asked.

'I killed no one,' Tony said.

'Not you, you moron. Her.' Conor had had enough of the pussyfooting. He stopped and turned to face Megan.

'Why do you think I had anything to do with that?' Her voice was weaker now. That was a good thing, Conor thought. But he had to get the truth out of her first.

'I know it wasn't me,' he said, 'and I don't think Tony had the wit to carry it out.'

'You always were smarter than him.' Her sarcastic laugh was carried away on the edge of a breeze as rain poured down.

'But I don't understand how you knew about this place.'

'Bill, my stepdad, had all the maps. One reason he was such a vehement objector to Cyril Gill's project was because he knew the medieval history of Ragmullin would be lost if Gill got his way. He showed me ancient maps of the underground network. I couldn't care less about them at the time. But I remembered them.'

'What sparked that memory?' Conor had to keep her talking.

'Penny Brogan couldn't keep her mouth shut.'

'Penny?' Keegan said. 'What did she know?'

'She was my manicurist. Always gabbing about everybody's business. She told me about Cristina Lee coming over to Ireland, following in the footsteps of her aunt who used to work for the Gills. The family hadn't heard from Hannah in years, according to Penny, but she'd been in Ireland illegally so no formal report had ever been made to the authorities. As it turned out, Cristina was here illegally too. You know, I'd forgotten all about Hannah Lee until that very moment. With the attack on Bill and the court case and all that followed, I never gave her a thought.' She pointed the knife at Keegan. 'And then I married you. You let me lead a lie for my entire adult life. Whatever became of the money you stole?'

'I stole nothing.'

'Oh for Christ's sake, Tony. The time for lies is well past. It had to be you.'

Conor edged to one side. While Megan was getting angrier by the second, waving the knife erratically with each word, he was figuring out a way to escape. It meant going back down the tunnel, but he could suffer that if it got him out of here alive.

CHAPTER 64

Boyd silenced the siren as they approached the area McKeown had marked on the map.

'No point in alerting them,' Lottie said. 'Look.' A car was parked with all the doors open outside the hoarding.

He glided the car up behind a Ford Fiesta. 'What's the plan?'

Lottie wanted this over and done with. She wanted to be at her daughters' bedsides. She knew she should be there already, but she also knew they were in safe hands. Once she had this wrapped up, they would get her undivided attention. Her heart lurched with guilt, but she couldn't deal with that right now.

'Let's see if they're in there,' she said.

They left the car, closing the doors quietly, and made their way to the open door in the hoarding.

Lottie put her finger to her lips and eased up against the timber. Voices carried towards her as she peered inside.

*

Tony said, 'The money was well spent on that lavish wedding you had. You should have known I couldn't have earned enough as a labourer to afford that, but you never questioned it.'

'Biggest mistake of my life,' Megan said. She put one hand in her pocket and extracted a handful of coins. She threw them on the ground, where they sank into the grey water of muck and dirt.

Conor took a step backwards.

She spun her head around, pointing the knife at him. 'If you had come clean, I would have been spared a lifetime of misery.'

'But now you know why I didn't. You made your own decisions. Nothing to do with me.'

'I loved you, you know.'

'You what?' Conor ran his hand over his head, streaking it with blood.

'Yes, but you only had eyes for that housekeeper.' She took a step towards him. 'What did you do to her?'

'It was an accident.' Conor recalled the night when at last he'd got Hannah alone, down by the railway tracks about a hundred metres from where he now stood. And then she'd changed her mind. Didn't want him near her and had tried to fight him off. But he was young and hormone-fuelled, and when he forced himself on her, she crashed her head against a rock he hadn't known was sticking up in the overgrown bank. He hadn't murdered her, but she'd died and he had panicked. He told Megan this.

'If it was an accident, why did you hide her body?'

'Let's just say I'm not a methodical killer like you. I panicked. I ran. Afterwards, I went back and hid the body.' He stared into her hard eyes. 'Why did you have to murder Amy and Louise and the others?'

'Because I found out the truth,' she sobbed. 'Don't you see, Conor? I've had to live my life without you because they gave sworn statements that they saw you that night, and because of that you ended up in prison. You should have spoken up. I left coins at the scenes in memory of what you'd done to me. You betrayed me with your lies. Just like a Judas. Just like those silly girls.'

'But they *did* see me.'

'You didn't assault or rob my stepfather.'

'Why does it matter now?' Conor said wearily.

'When you got out of prison, you never even called to see me.'

'I was in the pharmacy one day and—'

'Yeah, you were. With a note for Amy. Never even asked about me. So I reckoned it was time to make you notice me.'

It was then that Conor sensed the silence around them. The wind had dipped and the rain had eased slightly, and the three of them, standing in the middle of the piece of waste ground, were like a tripod abandoned by some weary photographer. And he knew they were not alone. He scanned his eyes around and behind Megan. Over at the door in the hoarding, he saw movement.

'Run!' he shouted.

As Tony and Megan swirled around in confusion, three people rushed towards them. Conor turned and fled.

He used to know where the entrance to the tunnel was. But now, ten years later, in the dark, he couldn't find it. As a hand gripped his shoulder and hauled him down, he was aware only of the wet ground rising up to meet him, and he closed his eyes.

CHAPTER 65

One week later

Leo Belfield was propped up with pillows, but all the monitors had been removed.

'Are you ready to give a statement?' Lottie asked.

'It all happened so fast.'

'I'm sure you can recall some of it.' She sat on a chair beside his bed.

'She went for me with the knife. Shouting that she wanted to take your daughters but someone had got them first. Apparently she'd seen Megan talking to them at the accident site. She said she knew you'd come to Farranstown at some stage and she'd get you then.'

'What did you do?'

'Defended myself. She had the knife in one hand and a noose in the other. She lashed out. Kept stabbing while I tried to wrench the knife from her hand. One wound was fairly deep and I knew I was losing a lot of blood, but eventually I was able to twist her arm enough so that she dropped the knife.'

'Mmm. So how come she ended up with a rope around her neck and the life choked out of her?' Lottie returned Leo's stare.

'Do you want me to go to prison?'

'No.'

'Let's say she got entangled in it as we fought. And leave it at that.'

Lottie wasn't one for leaving things. But Bernie Kelly would no longer be able to stalk her family, and that was good enough for her. As long as the forensic evidence didn't say otherwise, Leo should be in the clear.

'I'll see,' she said. 'Rose is outside. You up to listening to her?'

'Sure.'

His hand reached for hers. She shared the same biological mother with this man, but still she saw him as a stranger. She stood and put her hands in her pockets. 'I'll send her in.'

CHAPTER 66

They didn't say much. Katie or Chloe. That worried Lottie. It was as if they had bonded in the hours they'd been held captive and were keeping her outside that experience. They seemed determined to ensure she remained outside.

Katie was sitting on the couch with Louis asleep in her arms, and Chloe was lying with her head on Katie's lap. They'd been injected with a concoction of drugs by Megan Price, none of which had lasting medical effects. Lottie wondered when, if ever, the psychological effects would evaporate. Easing the door closed, she stood in the hall listening. Boyd was upstairs with Sean. Playing a computer game, no doubt.

Making her way to the kitchen, she felt the unease of failure settling like a wet blanket on her shoulders. Failure at being a good mother.

As she filled the kettle to make tea, she knew what she really wanted was an alcoholic drink, but she had lasted so far without falling back into that bad habit, so tea was all she would drink.

Kirby had recovered quickly and had been back in the office the next day, even more morose than in the weeks following Gilly's death. Lottie had yet to deal with his error in not searching Amy's locker. In one of the tunnels, McGlynn had discovered Amy and Louise's handbags, and bloodstained clothing most likely used by Megan.

She was glad that McKeown had settled in well with the team, and was looking forward to having him working with Maria Lynch when she was back from maternity leave. That was if McMahon allowed her to remain as detective inspector. She'd asked Cynthia Rhodes to have a word with him, to make him think it was Cynthia's idea to run the missing persons news report on Katie and Chloe. She now owed Cynthia big-time. There was also the question of a review being conducted into Conor Dowling's conviction and Superintendent Corrigan's role. But judging by past experience, Lottie knew that could take years.

Leo Belfield was recovering, and Rose had said he could stay with her until he was able to return to America. Lottie was acutely aware that Leo was her last remaining biological relative. Something she needed to address, but not right now.

She thought of Megan Price, who was in Mountjoy women's prison awaiting trial. The loss of four young lives just because Megan felt betrayed by Conor Dowling and the whole damn world. So many families shattered, and for what? It surely wasn't love, Lottie thought. Conor had been arrested for the death of Hannah Lee and Tony Keegan had been arrested in connection with the assault and robbery of Bill Thompson. Both were out on bail.

Lottie sighed wearily as Boyd came into the kitchen.

'All okay?' he asked.

'Things can only get better.' She smiled at him and took mugs down from the cupboard. 'I have two IKEA cabinets upstairs, still flat-packed, if you're at a loose end.'

He was looking shifty, rubbing his hands into each other. 'Lottie, I've something to ask you.'

'I'm busy. Can't it wait?'

'Busy? You're just making tea. And no, it can't wait.'

'Go ahead so.' She put tea bags into the mugs.

He came to stand in front of her, turned her to face him. She felt the touch of his skin on her hand. 'It's kind of awkward. I've only ever said this once before, and that didn't work out the way it was supposed to.'

'Boyd, get a move on. I want a cup of tea and I need to get into the office for a few hours. I've so much paperwork to do, the rainforests are in mortal danger of extinction.'

'I think they are anyway, with or without you.'

Lottie stared at his bruised and battered face. She hoped he wasn't looking for a transfer. No, it definitely was not the time to ask for a transfer.

'I'm listening,' she said, and silently prepared her speech as she folded her arms and leaned back against the counter.

He grabbed her hand again and held it to his lips.

'Lottie, will you marry me?'

'What did you say?' She felt his hand tighten on hers.

'Will you marry me?'

Nervous laughter crept up her throat. 'Boyd, I think that knock on your head was more serious than you thought. You should have had the MRI like the doctors wanted. I don't want you passing out on the job and—'

'Will you stop talking for a minute?'

She clamped her lips tightly shut and felt her eyes widening in disbelief. Had he really said what she thought he'd said?

'I'm serious,' he told her.

'I don't know what to say, Boyd. This is so sudden …'

His voice sounded more determined. 'I've been thinking about asking you for the last year. I wanted to ask you many times, but I never had the courage.'

'So what changed?'

'When that crane came down, I stared death in the face and woke up.'

'Is that from Shakespeare or someone?'

He rolled his eyes and put an arm either side of her, his hands on the counter. She could feel the heat from his body and it charged through her own. She didn't know where to look.

'I know this isn't the most romantic setting, but it's so difficult to get you on your own without an audience, and to get you in a good mood.'

'This is my good mood?' She tried to still the racing in her heart. 'Christ, Boyd, you don't know me at all.'

'I think I know you better than you know yourself. So, is it to be or not to be? And that *is* Shakespeare.'

'You crack me up.' Should she run or should she stay? Oh God, she didn't know what to do.

'I'm serious.' He didn't take his eyes off hers.

'Jesus, Boyd.' Emotions churned so quickly, she felt them tumbling around in her stomach. An ache spread across her chest and she didn't know if it was physical or emotional. What did she want? She had no idea.

'Say something,' he said, tugging at his clean-shaven scarred chin.

'I … I don't know what I want. Thank you. Oh God, Mark, thank you for asking me, but I need to think about it.'

'What do you need to think about? We're not getting any younger. Life is dangerous and unpredictable.'

'*I'm* dangerous and unpredictable.'

'You're right there.' He smiled and her heart thumped a little faster.

Yes, she wanted Boyd. But did she want him all the time? Every day. Every minute of the day? She needed time.

'Okay. Take time to think about it,' he said.

She took his hands in hers and squeezed. 'Thank you.'

'I love you, Lottie.'

She didn't answer. Just stared at him. He took a deep breath, feathered a kiss on her lips, then turned and picked up his jacket from the back of the chair. She heard the soft thud of the door closing.

She stared at the empty space he'd left in his wake. Alone, she sat down and thought of all she had wanted to say to him and hadn't.

She hoped it wasn't too late.

A LETTER FROM PATRICIA

Hello, dear reader,

Sincere thanks to you for reading my sixth novel, *Final Betrayal*. If you enjoyed the book and would like to join my mailing list to be kept informed of my new releases, please click here:

www.bookouture.com/patricia-gibney

I'm so grateful to you for sharing your precious time with Lottie Parker, her family and her team. If you enjoyed the read, you might like to follow Lottie throughout the series of novels. To those of you who have already read the first five Lottie Parker books, *The Missing Ones, The Stolen Girls, The Lost Child, No Safe Place* and *Tell Nobody*, I thank you for your support and reviews.

It would be fantastic if you could post a review on Amazon or Goodreads, or indeed on the site where you purchased the book. It would mean so much to me. And thank you for the reviews received so far. You can also connect with me on my Facebook author page or Twitter, and I have a blog (which I try to keep up to date).

Thanks again, and I hope you will join me for book seven in the series.

Love,
Patricia

www.patriciagibney.com

 trisha460

@trisha460

ACKNOWLEDGEMENTS

This is the sixth book in the Lottie Parker series, and I am hugely indebted to so many people for supporting me on this writing journey.

First, and most importantly, to you, my reader, thank you for reading *Final Betrayal* and for your continued support.

A few years ago, I sent my first manuscript to an agent and she totally believed in me and my writing, surprising the life out of me. Ger Nichol of The Book Bureau has worked tirelessly on my behalf, negotiating contracts and looking out for me and my writing welfare. Thank you, Ger. I would never have got this far without you. Thanks also to Hannah at The Rights People.

I'm grateful to have a great team working with me at Bookouture. I wish to thank Lydia Vassar Smith for her professional editorial input on *Final Betrayal*. Special thanks to Kim Nash and Noelle Holten for their media work, for organising blog tours and publicity. Thank you also to those who work directly on my books: Alexandra Holmes (publishing), Leodora Darlington, Alex Crow and Jules McAdam (marketing). Jane Selley for her excellent copyediting skills.

Michele Moran brings my books to life in audio format, so thanks to Michele and the team at The Audiobook Producers.

The writing community is very supportive of me and my work. Thank you to all who have listened to me, chatted and advised me, especially my fellow Bookouture authors. Special thanks to Carol Wyer and Angela Marsons, who give advice when I look for it. Also thank you to Caroline Mitchell, fellow Irish writer, and Robert Bryndza.

Thank you to Vanessa Fox O'Loughlin, who is a strong supporter of my writing and who organised Ireland's first Murder One crime festival in 2018, along with Writing.ie and Dublin UNESCO City of Literature. I hope there will be many more. Thanks also to the Town of Books Festival, Red Line Festival and Harrogate Crime Festival for having me on panels in 2018. It was a massive honour to have *The Stolen Girls* shortlisted for the Irish Book Awards 2018 Ryan Tubridy Listeners' Choice Award. Thank you Ryan and your listeners for your support.

Thanks to Ger Holland for the enjoyable photo shoot in Dublin, and also Barry Cronin for such a fun day photographing me in the eerie forest near Ballinafid Lake.

To all the bloggers who give freely of their time to read and review and take part in blog tours, thank you. And to each reader who has posted reviews, I am so grateful. You all make a difference.

I wish to acknowledge the tireless work of libraries and their staff. Thanks also to local and national media, and bookstores. I have spoken at many book club events over the course of the last year and I wish to thank everyone for your warmth and kindness.

Special thanks to Brian Gibson for advice on one aspect of this book, and John Quinn. I write crime fiction and seek advice where necessary, but inaccuracies are all my own. I fictionalise police procedure in places, to help with the pace and the storyline. It is fiction after all!

I started writing when Aidan my husband, died after a short illness, to keep me from sinking into a black hole of despair. I love my writing; it keeps me focused and alive. But I would not be able to continue without a supportive network around me. My circle of friends has grown since I started writing. Special thanks to Jackie

Walsh for the writing trips away, Grainne Daly for the words of wisdom and the good vibes when I need them, and Niamh Brennan for advice. Jo and Antoinette have always been there to pick me up, so thank you too.

Thanks to my mother and father, William and Kathleen Ward, and to Lily Gibney and family, my sister Cathy Thornton and my brother Gerard Ward. Special thanks to my sister Marie Brennan for reading early drafts of this book (all my books, actually). I appreciate your time and input. I don't always listen, but at least we no longer pull each other's hair like we did as kids!

My children, Aisling, Orla and Cathal, are three of the strongest, most polite and respectful young people I know. As teenagers, they lost their dad to cancer, but they met life head on and have grown into fine young adults. I am so proud of you and thankful to have you in my life. A mention to Gary, Darren and Dawn who keep them grounded.

I have dedicated *Final Betrayal* to my grandchildren. I hope by continuing to focus on my writing I can show them that with hard work, perseverance and commitment you really can get 'stuff' done. Daisy, Shay, Caitlyn and Lola give me a new outlook on life and fill me with love.

All characters in my books are fictional, as is the town of Ragmullin, but real life has influenced my life and my writing. Thank you to the people of Mullingar, my home town, for supporting me and my work.

Made in the USA
Las Vegas, NV
11 June 2021

24587977R10236